IN A
COUNTRY
OF MOTHERS

IN A
COUNTRY
OF MOTHERS

A. M. HOMES

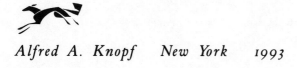

Alfred A. Knopf New York 1993

THIS IS A BORZOI BOOK
PUBLISHED BY ALFRED A. KNOPF, INC.

Grateful acknowledgment is made to TRO–Devon Music, Inc.,
for permission to reprint from "Substitute," words and music by
Peter Townshend. Copyright © 1966 by Fabulous Music Ltd., Lon-
don, England. TRO–Devon Music, Inc., New York, controls all
publication rights for the U.S.A. and Canada. Used by permission.

Library of Congress Cataloging-in-Publication Data
Homes, A. M.
In a country of mothers / A. M. Homes. — 1st ed.
p. cm.
ISBN 0-679-41568-8
I. Title.
PS3558.O44815   1993
813'.54—dc20   92-31860
                                                  CIP

Manufactured in the United States of America

First Edition

For my mother, Phyllis Homes

Substitute me for him,
Substitute my coke for gin.
Substitute you for my mum,
At least I'll get my washing done.
—PETE TOWNSHEND

BOOK ONE

1

*J*ody was already dialing when Harry came up from behind and put his fat thumb down on the hook, disconnecting her.

"No spy reports," he said.

"I was making a shrink appointment. You're driving me crazy."

"I'm flattered," Harry said, plucking the quarter from the coin return, dropping it into her open palm. "Try again."

Once more Jody put the quarter in and dialed. She turned to face Harry. The short metal phone cord pulled close against her throat. Later, she would notice it had left a thick red mark like a scar across her neck, as though someone had tried to strangle her. But then, waiting for the call to go through, she ignored the pressure at her throat and fixed on Harry. Fat, swollen up like a dead whale, Harry's stomach started at his collar and went down to his knees, jutting out in front of him in one solid lump. His thick, pink lips were pulled down by age and too many years of pretending to pout. She imagined his skin was cold and clammy to the touch.

When Claire Roth's answering machine finally beeped, Jody smiled at Harry and left the following message:

"Hi, this is Jody Goodman, you don't know me. I'm having some trouble making career decisions."

Harry's face curled into a scowl.

"Barbara Schwartz gave me your number. I think I should make an appointment. I can't be reached at work, but my number at home is 555-2102. Thanks."

"Taking to the couch over me?" Harry asked when Jody hung up. "How wonderful."

"You're an asshole," Jody answered, loud enough for the crew hovering around her to hear.

"And you, good girl," Harry said, blushing, "are an angel." He kissed her forehead and drifted back onto the set.

Jody dropped another quarter into the phone and called the office.

"Michael Miller Productions, can you hold?"

"It's me," Jody said. "Is he there?"

"Hold, please."

There was a buzz, then the clattering of Michael Miller picking up his prized Lego phone.

"What?" Michael said.

" 'What?'? No 'Hi, hello?' " Jody asked.

There was silence. After spending two years as Michael's assistant, Jody was often spoken to in a kind of small talk that was sometimes no talk.

"Fine," Jody said. "I guess when you're losing millions of dollars, the little niceties are the first thing to go. Well, he knows I'm checking in. He just kissed the top of my forehead. A saliva ball remains in my hair. I think I can feel it."

"Aside from your personal injury?"

"He's taking his time. Going over everything again and again. There's no way he'll finish on schedule."

"Let me know more as soon as you can. I may have to try and bring in some new money. Speaking of which, where did you put that European check?"

"In the production account. By the way, I think I'm on to something. I just called Harry an asshole and he blushed." She hung up quickly before Michael could respond.

"Lock it up," the production assistants screamed down the street. Within minutes traffic was stopped, pedestrians held behind barricades, and a rented police car, sirens wailing, raced up a side street past the first camera position, turned wide onto Broadway, spinning a little in front of a bank of lights and a second camera, then came to a screeching halt in front of Zabar's, third position. An actor dressed as a cop jumped out of the front seat, opened the back door, and a woman in a thick wool coat, played by the legendary Carol Heberton, stepped out.

"Do you want anything?" Jody said, mouthing Heberton's lines in synch with the action. "I won't be more than a minute."

"Cut," someone shouted into a megaphone. "Once more, positions."

Jody pushed her way through the crowd, mentally calculating the cost of another take. Film was money; cost was associated with everything.

As she started to duck under one of the barricades, a real cop stopped her. "You'll have to cross on the other side."

"I don't think so," Jody said, and went forward.

The cop caught her by the shoulder and held her until a production assistant came to the rescue. "She's okay," he said. "She's okay, she's one of us."

Jody dusted herself off.

"Harry's been asking for you," the PA said, "barking 'Good girl, good girl,' into someone's walkie-talkie."

"Great," Jody said, turning to look at the crowd of hangers-on, thinking the whole thing was ridiculous. Michael Miller Productions—a.k.a. Forgettable Films. She'd taken the job with the idea that if she wanted to be a filmmaker she ought to learn something about the business. For the entire two years she'd been there, Michael had been scraping money together so that old Harry Birenbaum, creator of hybrid, sweeping, pseudo-European romantic epics, could try his hand at a new kind of movie, one that had commercial potential, and ideally would earn back all the money Michael had begged, borrowed, and worse. If the film failed, Michael Miller Productions would probably become Michael Miller Lawn Service: WE CLEAN GUTTERS.

A homeless man appeared out of nowhere and scurried up to the food table. Jody watched him pile bananas, oranges, and apples into the crook of his free arm. He was almost at a dozen when a technician startled him—"And don't come back!" The last orange fell, bounced on the sidewalk, and rolled into the street.

Michael had talked Jody into loaning herself out to Harry during the New York location work by describing it as a unique opportunity to see one of the masters in action. So far, all she'd learned from watching the great one was that maybe she should have applied to UCLA's law school instead of the film department.

Jody knocked on Harry's trailer door, marked COSTUME to deter celebrity maniacs.

"Please," Harry called.

The door opened and Karl, Harry's assistant, came flying out as if he'd been fired from a cannon.

Harry himself was sitting sideways at the table, too fat to fit in facing front. "Come and have lunch with me," he said.

Jody didn't answer.

"Well, come on. Can't leave the door open like that. Someone might see."

Jody climbed in and sat across from Harry at the dinette.

"What do you think—A or B?" He aimed a remote control at a television set built into the wall and played two video versions of a scene they'd shot the day before. The A sequence was neither here nor there, acceptable but boring, definitely not the stuff of Academy Award nominations. The B shot was classic Harry, so tight that the images overflowed the frame. Instead of Carol Heberton from fifteen feet, it was Heberton's left eye, a subtle shift in the pupil, a dilation that registered her having seen something, consciously or unconsciously. Playing the known against the unknown, that was Harry's strength.

"A or B?" Harry asked again.

She didn't want to answer. Harry really was one of the great filmmakers, but he was slumming. His last three films had lost fortunes, his shooting style of rehearsal, take, and retake was so expensive that producers wouldn't go near him. Regardless, he wasn't someone you pictured behind the wheel of a cop-and-robber flick.

"Sweetheart," he said. "You want to be a director? Directors make decisions."

"B," Jody said.

"And why?"

"It builds tension, reveals more without giving anything away. The other one is too diffuse, there's too much in the background, it's distracting."

"A-plus, little one, A-plus. Do you know what that boy who was in here said?"

Jody shook her head. Karl had to be at least forty years old.

"He said A, because Carol looks old in the B shot. But she *is* old. For weeks I've been trying to make her look exactly like this, and suddenly he's complaining. Old is nice, isn't it?"

"Lovely," Jody said, standing to leave.

"This isn't a beauty contest," Harry said.

There was a knock on the trailer door. Karl slipped in and deposited a huge tray of food in the middle of the table.

"That's all for now," Harry said.

After Karl turned and left, Jody also started for the door.

"You don't expect me to eat alone?" Harry asked.

Jody shrugged and lied. "I'm not a food person."

"But I am."

And so Jody sat and watched Harry suck up his lunch like a vacuum cleaner, thinking about her own life, past, present, and future. She envisioned a high crane shot beginning inside the trailer: Harry chewing on the small bones of a roasted baby something—chicken, lamb, child; the crane pulling up through the skylight to reveal the set outside—technicians scurrying for lights, gaffer's tape, the cinematographer riding his camera back and forth on dolly tracks, Heberton repetitiously rehearsing her lines, the pedestrians tripping over one another to get a closer look; and then the camera pulling away even more, sweeping past Michael in his office crunching numbers, and moving still farther away to an aerial view of Manhattan—New York from a distance, earth as seen from space.

By the time Harry was finished, Jody was nauseated as hell, partly from the sight of the great man with carroty flecks of cole slaw at the corners of his corpulent mouth, a wide yellow slap of mustard across his cheek, and partly from the anxiety of her own thoughts. Who did she think she was that she could make it in this business, where the recipe for success seemed to be equal amounts of arrogance, assholism, and unbridled brilliance? All she had for sure was curiosity and a peculiar little vision. When Karl returned with a huge pot of coffee and a tray of cookies, Jody immediately drank four cups, ate a dozen cookies, and spent the rest of the afternoon wishing there was a convenient building tall enough to jump off of.

2

*B*etween patients, Claire napped on the sofa in her office. Something—perhaps a dream, the sound of the phone ringing, or the young woman's voice on the answering machine—woke her. Whatever it was came like a flash, a fleeting electrocution that left her with the sensation of having been ripped back and forth through time.

She sat up, convinced something horrible had happened. If she hadn't been expecting a patient, Claire would've gone home and examined her children for signs of damage. She would've told them to open their mouths and say aah while she shined a flashlight in. She'd press her ear to their chests, her hand to their backs, and ask them to breathe deeply. Instead she went to her desk, and called the apartment.

"Everything all right?" Claire asked Frecia.

"Adam and I are making cookies, Jake's watching TV," the housekeeper answered, her voice a comforting singsong.

"Don't let him get too close to the oven. He likes to look in."

"His head won't catch fire," Frecia said firmly. She'd been with Claire for years. She was used to this.

The buzzer in Claire's office went off.

"Sam called and said he won't be home until after eleven," Frecia said.

The buzzer sounded again. It reminded Claire of the air-raid test sirens in elementary school: the first Wednesday of every month, from 11:00 a.m. until 11:03—every month of every year, and always it came as a surprise. She looked out the window. A woman was crossing the street with a stroller. The light was changing, and a bus was about to force its way through the intersection. Claire held her breath until the woman and the stroller were safely on the other side.

"My four o'clock's waiting," Claire told Frecia. "See you later." She buzzed the patient in and turned the volume on her answering machine all the way down.

It wasn't until she was saying hello to her six o'clock that she remembered the phone ringing during her nap. She tried to focus on what the client was saying, but her mind kept circling back to the phone call. Somehow she thought it was from someone she knew.

"It's really wonderful that you just sit and listen to me blabber," the patient was saying. "You never judge me. I like that. Thank you."

Patients were always thanking Claire, telling her how wonderful she was, how much she'd helped them. And while she appreciated these thoughts, they didn't really count. They weren't thanking her; they were thanking a little piece of her that, in terms of the whole, wasn't much. They thanked their fantasy of Claire. If her patients really knew her, Claire figured, they'd never come back.

She smiled, nodded. "See you Thursday," she said fifty minutes later, leading the patient to the door.

Alone at her desk, she pressed "play" on the answering machine and listened.

"Hi, how are you?" It was her friend Naomi. "Do we have theater tickets for Saturday? If you've got a sitter maybe we should leave our kids at your place—two for the price of one."

Claire fast-forwarded.

"This is Jody Goodman, you don't know me. I'm having some trouble making career decisions. Barbara Schwartz gave me your number. I think I should make an appointment. I can't be reached at work, but my number at home is 555-2102. Thanks."

Claire rewound the message and played it again, writing down word for word what the girl said. Years ago, when she got her first answering machine, Claire had started transcribing phone messages from patients or would-be patients. The way she saw it, the calls were filled with clues: what the callers did or didn't say, their tone of voice, the way they dealt with the machine. She'd never told anyone. The transcriptions would have seemed like a peculiar habit, the kind of tic only a shrink would have.

In session, listening as intently as she could, Claire often felt as though she heard nothing. Writing it down gave her the sensation of studying something, making it tangible. If she'd thought her patients would stand for it, she would have taped their sessions. But then the tapes would just be there, piled up in a closet she would have to keep locked. When the therapy was terminated, what would she do—give the tapes back to the patient? Or would she be expected to erase them, as if the person had never existed?

She dialed Jody Goodman's number. A machine answered, and as Claire started to leave a message, someone picked up. "Hello? Hello?"

"I'm trying to reach Jody Goodman," Claire said.

"It's me."

"This is Claire Roth, returning your call."

"Oh, hi," Jody said. "Sorry if my message sounded a little strange, my boss was standing over my shoulder. Literally."

Claire didn't say anything.

"I think I should make an appointment with you," Jody said.

"Could you tell me why?"

"Graduate school," Jody said.

A simple answer. She didn't say she'd been seeing spotted elephants walking down Broadway. She didn't say her boyfriend had threatened to kill her and had just gone out for pizza but would be back any minute. In other words, it wasn't an emergency. Claire relaxed. She hated talking to strangers.

"How do you know Barbara Schwartz?" Claire asked.

"She used to be my shrink."

"How long ago?"

"Two years. I stopped when I moved to New York."

"Would you like to come in tomorrow? I could see you at twelve-thirty."

"Yeah, sure. I think that'll work."

"See you then," Claire said, and hung up.

She flipped through her Rolodex, found Barbara Schwartz's number, and started to dial, but then stopped herself. She didn't want anyone's impressions to interfere with her own. If she needed to talk to Barbara, she'd do it later.

Barbara Schwartz. Whenever the past crossed into the present, Claire got nervous. All day she saw what memory was for people: a stomping ground for bad feelings, frozen worst moments, gone over again and again until they were smooth and hard like calluses or beach glass. When things got bad for Claire, Sam tried to make her feel better by saying, "What happened, happened. Look at it this way: if you had to do it over again, you'd do it differently—who wouldn't?" Claire accepted it. She accepted what had happened with the kind of resignation that was in some way expected of her. There was no reason to discuss it. What happened, happened. Past is past.

Barbara Schwartz, an immigrant from Tucson, Arizona. "The onliest Jew in the West" was what she'd called herself. Nineteen sixty-seven. Little Barbie in Baltimore, with her frizzy brown hair dyed blond. A row house subdivided into apartments; Barbara, the young social worker with her first grown-up job, downstairs, and Claire, depressed, upstairs. Barbarella Schwartz, who borrowed Claire's cashmere sweaters for dates. Claire lent them, not caring that they came back with stains or cigarette burns. Somehow, if her sweaters went out on dates, it counted for Claire too. She'd sit up watching television, waiting for her sweater to come home. And when it got back, Claire would carry the contents of her refrigerator into her bed, and she and Barbara would lie there watching the late movie and saying nasty things about men. It was on one of those nights that Claire almost told Barbara her secret—the truly worst thing about a man, the reason she was in Baltimore. But she chickened out, afraid the story would ruin their friendship.

Baltimore was more than twenty years ago. Claire had arrived almost a year before Barbara, and stayed two years after she left. The whole time, the whole four years, she'd waited there in that same apartment, secretly hoping that what had been done would somehow, of its own volition, become undone. If only she waited long enough.

It was 1966 when Claire's father had stormed out of their suburban Virginia split-level house shouting, "Something has to be done! This has to be put to rest!," while Claire lay on her twin bed, staring at the white lacquered furniture set, a child for the last time. She imagined her father going off to the local veterinarian and arranging to have her put to sleep. She imagined she wouldn't live to get old. Her mother came in and silently started packing Claire's things, putting in a few odd pieces of her own clothing as gifts. When her father returned, Claire followed her suitcase out to the car, and in silence they drove away. It was dark when he pulled up in front of the house in Baltimore, a place that might as well have been on the moon considering that Claire had never been there either. He carried the bag up the steps, unlocked the apartment, and dropped the suitcase inside. "Here," he said, handing her the keys and an envelope from the bank. "Make it last. We can't afford this kind of thing."

Her father drove off, and Claire stood in the front window, dumb-founded.

As far as she knew, neither of her parents had ever told anyone. Her mother once said that if anyone asked, she'd say, "She's gone off to Goucher College to study English literature"—something Claire would have gladly done, if only Goucher had accepted pregnant students.

The phone rang just as Claire was putting on her jacket, getting ready to leave the office.

"I know we're getting together on Saturday, but how about meeting me for dinner tonight?" her friend Naomi asked. "I called your house and Sam isn't coming home until late."

"I haven't been home all day," Claire said.

"What's another hour?"

The golden hour, the difference between life and death for trauma patients. "Sure," Claire said. "Ten minutes."

They didn't have to discuss where to go. They always met at the same Italian cafe on Thompson Street.

"My family," Naomi said, "is driving me nuts."

Although Claire had never told her so, Naomi was her alter ego. She did and said all the things Claire only imagined.

"I feel like running away," Naomi said. "I just want to say goodbye, close the door, and be gone. Sometimes I look at Roger and I want to know why. Why did I do this? Why did I get married? It's like having a fourth child. If I'd stayed by myself and adopted a baby, at least I'd be alone when I got into bed at night. There's no escaping. It's either his children or him."

Claire nodded. She twirled pasta on her fork and slipped it into her mouth. She smiled.

"There's nowhere I can go for a minute of silence. I've started hiding in the kitchen. I stay in there all night purposely burning things that smell terrible so they'll leave me alone."

"Not a good sign," Claire said, blotting marinara sauce from her lips. "Why don't you go away for a weekend?"

"By myself?"

"Why not?"

"What would I do? Who would I talk to? I'd end up staying in the hotel room the whole time."

"Go to a bed and breakfast upstate, or out to the beach. There's a spa in Montauk, get a massage, an herbal mud wrap."

The couple at the table behind them were arguing about something unbelievably stupid, destroying their relationship because both of them were determined to win. Eating her pasta, Claire realized that if she were really doing her job, if she turned around and explained it to them, her work would never end.

"Not to change the subject, but can I ask you a completely unrelated question?"

Claire nodded.

"How do you get your hair to do that?" Naomi asked. "Is it like a goy thing?"

Claire put her hand to her hair, which was up in a bun. "Hidden pins," she said. "I'll show you sometime."

"Anybody home?" Claire called as she opened the front door. The television was blaring. "Hello . . . *hello?*" She made a mental note to talk to Frecia again about the television. She hung up her coat, flipped through the mail, and went into the living room. Adam was curled up on the sofa with his stuffed rabbit. His hair was still damp from his bath. He looked tired, as though recovering from something. Jake sat next to him, eyes fixed on the TV. Frecia was at the far end of the sofa, folding laundry, stacking clean clothing on the coffee table. Claire went to Adam and kissed him on the forehead, leaving her lips against his skin a little longer than necessary, trying to decide whether or not to take his temperature.

"How was your day?" she asked.

No one answered.

"Anyone call?"

Frecia shook her head. Claire picked up the remote and turned the TV off.

"Mom, it's the middle," Jake said, still staring at the screen.

"Sorry," she said. "Did you finish your homework?"

As much as she wanted to leave her children alone, to let them run their own lives, she couldn't. They sprawled like inert objects, deflated balloons. Neither of them could focus on anything for more than a minute without becoming distracted. She was sure it was a birth defect that would become increasingly pronounced, so that by the time they were eighteen, when all the other kids were going off to college, hers would have to be institutionalized. She and Sam would begin new lives, adopting children from some far-off, war-torn country, raising them fully, lovingly. On Sundays she and Sam and the new children would go on long car rides to the distant institution where her old children lounged on plastic-covered, drool-protected sofas.

"Did you do your homework?"

Jake shrugged. He was in the sixth grade, at the beginning of real homework. He absolutely failed to understand that the amount and difficulty of the assignments would increase for the next fifteen years, until finally he would be expected to write a thesis. Without that he would be abandoned by his school, parents, and friends, and left to fend for himself in a world where people actually worked for a living.

"Get your book and bring it here, right now."

Jake just looked at her, eyes thick as if covered by a strange film. She imagined that the news would arrive in tomorrow's paper: TELEVISION FOUND TO CAUSE BLINDNESS AND RETARDATION. LONG-TERM EFFECTS SIMILAR TO PROGRESSIVE LEAD POISONING.

"You," she said to Adam, "are going to sleep."

"No I'm not."

"Yes you are."

Jake pulled his textbook out of the sofa cushions. "Here," he said, handing it to Claire.

"It's not for me, sweetie. Open it and get to work."

Claire lifted Adam off the sofa and carried him to the boys' room. Just inside their door, toys crunched under her feet. She flipped the light switch. Every goddamned piece of molded plastic her sons owned was spread out across the floor.

"What happened in here?" Claire demanded.

"Playing," Adam said innocently. His sweetness saved him.

She kicked a clear path to the bed, laid Adam down, read him a quick story, and turned out the light. Tomorrow she would remind Frecia to remind the children to put their toys away.

"I feel sick," Adam said, as she reached the door.

"Go to sleep," Claire whispered.

"But I feel sick."

"Close your eyes and think about what a wonderful day tomorrow will be."

She gently pulled the door closed. Adam began to cry. What would happen if she opened the door? Adam would be forty years old and still living at home. If she left it shut, he'd become a mass murderer.

She stood at the door listening. The crying stopped and there was a horrible sound, the rumble and roar of a child throwing up. She opened the door and flicked on the light. Adam was sitting up in bed—his blanket, pajamas, and stuffed rabbit covered in vomit.

"Oh, sweetie," she said, running to get a cold washcloth from the bathroom. She lifted his pajama top off and carefully took it and the blanket into the bathroom and put them in a plastic trash bag. She put the stuffed rabbit into the sink and turned on the water. "Frecia?" Claire called.

Frecia came into the room, already in her coat.

"Can you do me a favor on your way out? Put these clothes in the machine downstairs—there're some quarters on my dresser."

"We used them today for the bus."

"Then check my purse."

Frecia took the bag from Claire. "See you tomorrow," she said.

"What happened?" Jake asked, rushing to the scene five minutes after the fact, reinforcing Claire's idea that he was growing slower and stupider as he got older. "Oh, stinko," he said. "I'm not sleeping in here." Adam started crying.

"Is your homework finished?" Claire asked.

Jake nodded.

"Then go take a bath."

"Shit," Jake said.

"What?"

It wasn't like Jake to swear. The beginning of the end: in the morning he'd come to breakfast with an unfiltered Camel hanging out the corner of his eleven-year-old mouth.

"I'm pretending I didn't hear that," she said. "Why did you throw up?" she asked Adam, as if he'd be able to explain.

"Cookie dough," Jake said. "He ate cookie dough before Frecia baked it. I had some too. Oh my God," he said, clutching his stomach, scaring Claire for a second, "I'm going to be sick too." Jake imitated throwing up all over Adam, who loved it.

"I want my rabbit," Adam said.

"I have to clean him first," Claire said, and Adam started crying again.

She changed Adam's sheets, then went into the bathroom to wash Woozy Rabbit. She heard Sam's key in the lock and then him in the hall taking off his shoes so his step would be light and the children wouldn't be awakened.

"We're in here," Claire yelled.

Sam stomped flat-footed down the hall and into the room. "What's going on?"

"I threw up," Adam said.

"You did? What a wonderful boy. God, I wish I could throw up," Sam said. He sat down on Adam's bed and took off his shirt and tie, which Adam immediately put on.

"God, I'm happy," Sam said, running his fingers through the thick hair on his chest. He unbuckled his belt, pulled it out through the loops, and dropped it on the floor. Adam stood up on the bed, posing in his father's shirt. Sam reached up for him.

"Don't start or he'll throw up again," Claire said. She hated it when Sam came home excessively cheerful after a long day. The worse things got, the more Sam glowed. Originally, it was something she'd liked about him, and she still did on occasion, but on a regular basis all the smiling, the jokes, could bring a person down.

"You mean, if I play with you, you'll throw up again?" Sam asked Adam. "If I touch you even just for a second, to give you a hug, you'll throw up?"

Adam nodded, grinned, laughed.

Claire was sure that if she hadn't been standing there, Sam would have started tickling him. She gave Sam the evil eye and went back into the bathroom, washed the rabbit, and hung it from its ears, where Adam could see it from his bed. "Tomorrow he'll be ready for you. Now, let's put on some fresh p.j.'s."

Adam shook his head and pulled at his father's shirt, which came down to his ankles. "This is my nightgown," he said.

"Not the tie," Sam said, slipping it over Adam's head.

Claire kissed Adam goodnight. "I'm sorry I didn't pay attention when you said you felt sick."

"I told you," he said, looking at his father for confirmation.

"Yeah, he told you," Sam said, crossing his arms in front of his chest.

She knew Sam was kidding, but it made her feel like they were ganging up on her. After all, there were three of them and just one of her. Besides, she was their mother, Sam's wife, she took care of them. They should be nicer to her.

"I know you did, sweetie," Claire said. "And I'm sorry. Sleep well."
She went out of the room and left Sam to tuck them in.

In the master bedroom, even though she wanted to collapse onto the
bed, she first flipped through the closet and thought about her schedule
for the next day. A new patient. The former patient of an old friend, a
colleague. She'd better look good in case the girl reported back.

Claire used to believe that looking good inspired trust, gave the impression that the shrink could actually do something for her patients—if
not rid them of their angst, at least upgrade their sense of style. All the
same, she'd given up on it, deciding that a flawless costume caused patients
to feel competitive with the therapist. Her current theory was that a well-
dressed shrink seemed superior and therefore served as a depressant. These
days, Claire dressed as though she were going to lunch with a girlfriend:
nice, but relaxed—approachable, was how she liked to think of it. She
picked out a very short black skirt and a silk blouse, hung them on the
doorknob, and went looking for pantyhose. She knew the outfit might be
considered unacceptable, sexually provocative; but her legs were long—
why not show off?—and besides, it was late, she was exhausted, and,
more importantly, nothing else was clean.

3

At noon the next day, while Harry was immersed in a debate with the special-effects guy about the fine art of splattering fake blood, Jody sneaked off the set.

"I have an, uh, appointment," she whispered to Karl. "Be back in ninety minutes." She figured fifty for the shrinking, forty there and back.

"Gotcha," Karl said, winking.

She walked straight down Broadway, passing the bookstore where they were shooting, the production trailers and trucks, smiling, nodding hello and good morning. Once she was in the clear, with everything and everyone behind her, she flagged a cab. Within seconds she was stuck in traffic.

It was as if all of Manhattan had poured out onto the streets, the city itself doing a snakish shuffle-and-stop, shuffle-and-stop, like the "Soul Train" dance line. She checked her watch. She could've taken the subway, but the last time she was on it, something horrible had happened: the train ran over a man and they'd kept the subway doors closed until the police came. Jody was forced to sit there while the man moaned somewhere beneath her on the tracks.

The shrink's office was on Sixth Avenue near Houston, seventy-some blocks from the location and about fifteen from Jody's apartment. She was late. Timing the two-minute-forty-second wait for the elevator, she figured how much standing in the lobby was costing her. On the way up she entertained herself with questions like: Do all the offices in the building belong to shrinks? Is everyone in this elevator crazy?

On the third floor, she found Claire's office and pushed the buzzer marked "Roth."

"Hello," a muffled voice called through a small speaker in the wall.

Jody considered not going in, not meeting Claire Roth face-to-face but having the session out there in the hall, chatting it up with a hidden voice, as if talking to the Wizard of Oz. "It's Jody Goodman."

The door unlocked with a thick sound like a joy buzzer. Jody grabbed the knob and pushed.

The waiting room was long and thin, three doors with chairs in the spaces between the doors. Jody sat on the chair closest to the door going out, unsure whether you were supposed to sit in an assigned chair—the chair next to the door that belonged to your shrink? The whole thing felt like a puzzle, a test designed to reveal something significant about Jody's psyche. She had the urge to get up, take the subway back uptown, and call later to say she'd realized that she'd left the toaster oven on and had to hurry home. Reschedule? Well, right now I'm kind of busy. Oh, there's my other line. Gotta go.

There were two noise machines on the floor, filling the room with the rushing sound of mechanically driven air. She was proud of herself for knowing what they were: shrink technology, white noise. They sounded like a constantly droning vacuum cleaner. Jody closed her eyes and imagined holding one to her ear like a shell. More than once, when she and Barbara reached sensitive points in what Jody called their "negotiations," she'd wanted to lean forward and say, "Your sound machines don't do shit."

The door at the end of the hall opened. "See you Thursday," a soft voice said. Because she couldn't decide who to look at, the patient or the shrink, Jody saw nothing.

"Hi, I'm Claire," the shrink said, extending her hand.

"Hi," Jody said, shaking hands, worried that the shrink could feel her trembling, her sweat.

"Would you like to come in?"

I must be crazy, Jody thought as she walked over the threshold into the office. There were floor-to-ceiling bookshelves, an old wooden desk, a leather sofa, a small table for the requisite box of Kleenex, and one chair. Claire sat in the chair, Jody on the sofa. It was easy, obvious.

"So," Claire said, picking up a big yellow legal pad and resting it on her lap. "What's going on?"

"I really shouldn't be doing this," Jody said, laughing a little. "I just escaped from the set of a movie, and coming here, sitting here, I feel like I'm in a movie." Jody paused.

Two seconds had passed. Jody couldn't imagine lasting an hour. There was silence. Jody looked at Claire and noticed she was wearing a short skirt. She'd never seen a shrink in a short skirt before. She hoped it was a good sign.

"You made the appointment," Claire said. "There must be something on your mind."

Jody had the sensation of auditioning to be Claire's patient. At the end of the hour, just like a casting director or a theatrical agent, Claire would stand up and say, Look, this is all very interesting, but I really don't work with people like you.

"On the phone you said you were having some difficulty making career decisions. Would you like to talk about that?"

Again Jody laughed, but it came out more like a snort. "For as long as I can remember I wanted to go to UCLA film school, so this year I applied, got in. And now, all of a sudden, I'm not sure."

Jody wanted Claire to like her, to choose her. She didn't want to say anything about herself that would seem too terrible, too complicated. She wanted Claire to think she was easy.

"So you're afraid? Is that the problem?"

Of course that was the problem, or at least part of it. But she wasn't ready to talk about it, so she started telling jokes. "I'm not so sure it's the school I'm afraid of. I think it's getting there, flying. I used to love it. Up in the air, Junior Birdman. Up in the air, Victory." It was the first session and Jody was singing at the top of her lungs, making her fingers into goggles and pressing them up to her eyes, making faces.

Claire was smiling at Jody. "You're very funny. That's great."

Not only did Claire understand; she appreciated, she approved. Jody felt incredible. She felt as though she could relax, could confess all the things she'd never been able to tell Barbara, all the things she'd never told anyone; anything and everything.

She closed her eyes and saw herself as a World War I flying ace. She was flying to Los Angeles in a leather jacket and goggles, a white silk scarf flapping back into her mother's face. Her mother wore a leather hood and big glasses and kept shouting directions into Jody's ear. The directions were based on a trip she'd made to California by bus thirty years before.

"Is there any other reason you might not want to go away?" Claire asked. "Do you have a boyfriend?"

"No," Jody said.

"Do you want one?"

It seemed like a strange question. "Are you giving them away?" Jody asked.

Claire laughed. At the rate this was going, by the end of the session Jody could have the "HBO Comedy Hour" all to herself.

"What about your family?" Claire asked.

Jody raised her eyebrows.

"Who's in your family?"

Oddly phrased, as though Claire wanted names, famous names, like Clark Gable and Rock Hudson. "I have a mother, a father, and a grandfather," she said uncertainly.

"What are they like?"

"Well," she said, teasing, "my aunt was Lucille Ball—you know, 'I Love Lucy.' It was really hard on my mom, not being the funny one." Jody noticed Claire writing something down on her legal pad and got nervous. "Don't write that down."

"I didn't," Claire said, looking up.

"Why not?" Jody asked.

"You don't look anything like Lucy."

"I'm adopted," Jody said, and Claire's expression changed. "My aunt and I were very close."

"What I'd like to do," Claire said, "is see you three times—then I'll have a better sense of things and we can talk about where to go from there. Does that sound okay to you?"

Jody nodded. She hated this part. Business before pleasure.

"What kind of a job do you have?"

"I work for a film production company."

"Are your parents helping you?"

"A little."

"Can you afford ninety-five dollars an hour?"

Jody nodded.

"Are you sure?"

Jody nodded again. There was something about Claire that made Jody think that even if she couldn't afford it, she wouldn't say no. She'd find a way.

Claire picked up her appointment book. "Could you come the day after tomorrow at one?"

"Do you have anything later?"

"Three?"

Jody nodded.

"I'll see you then," Claire said, standing.

Jody couldn't believe the session was over. Okay, so she'd been a few minutes late, but this had to be the fastest fifty minutes in history.

"Have you got the time?" Jody asked, getting up, noticing that Claire was quite tall, at least five nine or ten—model material.

"It's one-thirty-five, we ran a few minutes over."

"Wow."

"See you Thursday," Claire said, closing the door behind her.

Instead of waiting for the elevator, Jody ran down the stairs, hailed a cab, and raced back uptown.

Some strange and primal magic had been exchanged. Jody went back to work with more energy than she could ever remember having, so much energy that it was a little frightening.

"Ahh," Harry said, turning from a quick conference with one of the lighting guys. "I missed you at lunch."

Jody was at the food table, slapping cream cheese onto a bagel. She blushed, took a bite, and looked up.

Harry reached out, wiped a blob of cream cheese off her face, and popped his finger into his mouth. "We should have dinner sometime," he said.

Jody didn't answer. She chewed. One of the other lighting guys called Harry over to check something, and Jody ducked around the corner into a phone booth.

"What's the word?" Michael said.

"Not much. They're on the bookstore scene," Jody said, staring at the Shakespeare & Co. marquee.

"Is everything going right?"

"Well, they're splattering fake blood all over stacks of books and then trying to clean them off and do it again."

"I hope they're not real books," Michael muttered. "Check and make sure we're not buying the whole inventory—and if we are, at least get them to use paperbacks."

Jody took another bite of her bagel. "Am I getting overtime? I should definitely be getting more money."

"Are you eating something?"

"No," she said, spitting the bread into her hand and dropping it, as nonchalantly as possible, into the gutter.

"It's disgusting. You're eating while I'm talking."

"I'm not eating. Look, Michael, I'm not exactly clear about what you expect me to do here."

"Kiss Harry's ass and then tell me how hairy it is. That's your job."

"I never knew you were such a romantic," Jody said. Michael hung up and Jody felt cheated out of one of her favorite moments, slamming the phone down. She dialed Ellen's number at work.

"Third National," Ellen said in a smooth voice.

"Hi," Jody said.

"Are you eating something?" Ellen asked.

"A bagel," Jody said with her mouth full.

"Can I have a bite?"

"Yeah, sure," Jody said, swallowing. "So listen, I went to this shrink, you know, and it was kind of weird."

"Is she good?"

"She's either very good or very dangerous. I go back in two days."

"Can we not talk about your problems?" Ellen said. "Can we just talk about me? I'm so depressed."

"Sorry."

"Well, you don't really have any problems. You got into UCLA, you like your shrink. On the other hand, what am I doing with my life? I can't keep going out with Robert. He's an insurance salesman. I don't care about insurance. I don't even have any. He wants me to marry him. Meanwhile, in this restaurant this afternoon, I met this actor-waiter type and went in the back and kind of . . . I really like him."

"Kind of *what*? Isn't this the fourth person in three weeks that you kind-of'ed? Are you being careful?"

"The other ones don't count. They're from before. And this was really fun. We went out of the restaurant, opened those metal cellar doors you see on the sidewalk, went down there, and did it with the door open. If someone was walking by and had looked in, they would have seen us. It was—"

"You're nuts," Jody said. "And when you're dying of AIDS, you'll expect me to visit you and bring you popcorn, play with your respirator and everything."

"Don't be mean."

"Don't be stupid," Jody said. "You can't keep doing this."

"It's just because I'm bored."

"Go bowling," Jody said. The pay phone beeped and a nasty woman's recorded voice cut in, demanding money for more time. "I'm out of change," Jody said, as she patted a huge lump of coins in her front pocket. "Gotta go, talk to you later."

"How come you didn't call me back last night?" Jody's mother asked when she called at eleven, when Jody was three-quarters asleep. "I called twice. Didn't you get the message?"

"I was busy," Jody said.

"Well, you could have called back and told me that you were too busy to talk. I would've understood."

"No you wouldn't."

"Anyway," her mother said, "I got tickets for us to fly out to UCLA and look around. Week after next. You'll have to come home the day before."

"I'm not sure I can take the time off work. We're in the middle of shooting."

"Of course you can. If I can take the time, you can take the time. Besides, you're quitting soon anyway."

"Mom, don't push me."

"Push you? You're the one who applied to school in California. The tickets are in my hand. They aren't returnable."

Jody felt confused. Everyone she knew said her mother was amazing. Supportive. That was the word, for all the people who were, or had ever been, in therapy. Supportive.

"I know these things are hard for you," her mother said. "I just want to help."

"I started therapy today," Jody said, as if it were something you signed up for, like a dance class.

"I thought you were through with that."

"It's kind of a refresher course. Look, I'm really tired, can we talk about this later? Like when I'm thirty or something?"

"Fine," her mother said. "You're tired. Go to sleep. I'll call back tomorrow."

As soon as Jody hung up, she was wide awake. She lay in bed for half an hour, thinking about how everyone thought her relationship with her mother was great. "You talk," Ellen said. "Do you know how many daughters don't *speak* to their mothers? It's special. Don't knock it." Special, yes, Jody thought, but not entirely marvelous.

At midnight, she got up, took out the ingredients for brownies, and started baking. At one-thirty, when the brownies were cool, she sprinkled them with powdered sugar, poured herself a huge glass of milk, and sat eating while she flipped through the phone book. There was only one listing for Claire Roth, the same number Jody had called before. The real question was, Where did she live? Knowing things about her shrinks that were supposed to be secrets made Jody feel more comfortable. It gave her something to think about—which, she realized, was theoretically the reason she wasn't supposed to know anything.

There was a listing for Samuel B. Roth at 2 Fifth Avenue. Too close, Jody thought. After all, who'd want to live up the street and around the corner from her office—especially a shrink? Plus, "Samuel" was an old man's name. Jody decided that Claire worked downtown but lived on the Upper West Side, and probably didn't even know that old Samuel B. was practically a neighbor.

Jody stayed on the floor eating brownies, getting smashed on the chocolate and sugar, questioning why she'd bothered calling a shrink in the first place. She was definitely going to graduate school. How could she even think about not going? Sure, California was hovering on the edge of the ocean, about to fall in. Sure, it was farther from home than she'd ever been for more than two weeks. But the fact that California was on the other side of everything didn't mean she had to go into therapy. The problem was geographical, not psychological.

After all, she'd graduated. Jody was the only person she knew who had actually graduated from therapy. She envisioned a little box surrounded by wedding announcements in the back of the Style section of the Sunday *Times*:

Mr. and Mrs. Stanley Goodman of Bethesda, Maryland, are pleased to announce that after seven years of grueling biweekly sessions their daughter, Jody Beth, has finished therapy, graduating with honors from the practice of Barbara Schwartz in Georgetown. Jody's degree is in human relations and self-actualization. She is in the process of finally leaving home and will be working for a film production company in New York City. The graduate will keep both her name and her sanity.

It wasn't as if Jody had been an inpatient, locked up behind doors that said FIRE EXIT ONLY. She was a perfectly normal twenty-four-year-old who'd been in therapy for more than half her life and therefore would never again be normal, not in the truest sense of the word.

She imagined her mother hovering over her crib, watching for the first signs of maladaptation.

"I'm not going," Jody had said. She was three years old and starting nursery school.

"Please go," her mother said.

They were sitting in the parking lot arguing while all the other mothers were unloading little children from their station wagons.

"Get out of the car," her mother said.

Jody shook her head.

"I'll pick you up at noon, sweetie, I promise—just go on."

There was something in her mother's voice that made it impossible for Jody to leave the car, even though secretly she liked the idea of nursery school.

The first time Jody went to "see someone," she was in the fourth grade. Her mother made the appointment with one of their pediatricians.

"This doctor does a special thing," her mother said. "Besides taking care of colds, he talks to children."

"About what?" Jody asked.

"Anything you like."

The doctor was running late, so Jody and her mother sat for an hour in the waiting room with all the sick children. Jody didn't want to play with anything. The toys, even the lava lamp, had lost their charm. She watched children and mothers come out of the bathroom with urine samples in clear plastic cups and thought about what this man was going to ask her. All that came to mind was sex. He would ask if she'd gotten her period yet, and Jody would have to tell him that she was only nine and wouldn't be expecting it for a good while yet. He'd ask all kinds of questions like that and then he might make her take her clothes off. After all, he was a doctor. Jody didn't want to go. When the nurse called her name, Jody stood up slowly and her mother pushed her forward. She started walking down the hall toward the doctor at the end, but then turned and saw the open door behind her and the sky and the parking lot outside. Jody ran. She ran outside and around and around in the parking lot until she found the car, then opened the door and locked herself in.

The doctor and her mother came out, pressed their faces to the window, and begged her to open the door. Her mother tapped the window with her car keys, as if to rub in the fact that if she wanted to, she could unlock the door herself. Jody held the door button down with such pressure that her fingers turned white, bloodless. The doctor shook his head at her mother and she put away the keys. "You don't want to force her," he said in a voice that sounded soft through the glass. He smiled at her. She'd never seen a doctor out of context before. The strangeness of his white coat against the sea of cars confused her. She bent her fingers around the button as if to pull it up, but then came to her senses. No matter how much she might have wanted to give in, to have the doctor ever so gently take her hand and lead her down to the hall to his office, there was something so incredibly strange about the idea of just sitting there talking to him that she couldn't go through with it.

"Maybe another time," the doctor said, and he and Jody's mother turned around and went back into the building.

A few minutes later Jody's mother came out again, alone. Watching her mother walk empty-faced toward the car, Jody hated her more than anything. Jody unlocked the door, crawled over the front seat and into the back. They didn't say anything the whole way home.

The next time, her mother took her to someone whose office was in an apartment building. The waiting room was just off the kitchen; the doctor's office was the bedroom. Jody thought the whole thing was a bad trick, a disgusting disguise. The psychiatrist tried to get her to play cards and checkers with him, hoping she'd slip and say something incredibly important if he let her jump his king.

"Why do you think you get so many sore throats?" he once asked when they were playing gin.

Jody put down her cards and opened her mouth. "Well," she said, pointing down her throat so far she nearly gagged, "the part back here gets a kind of a cold in it and turns red. I think it's red now." She opened her mouth again, but he didn't look. "And then it really starts to hurt and it goes up into my ear and I have to put my whole head on a heating pad."

"But *why* do you get so many sore throats?" he asked again.

In retrospect, Jody wondered what he had expected her to say: Well, I was never breast-fed, and considering the throat and mouth as an important area of contact between mother and child, I guess you could say that a soreness or pain in this area later in life might result from not having fulfilled the original bonding between mother and child.

Why do I get so many sore throats? I'm a hypochondriac, of course. Or maybe I'm a lazy fucking asshole. I'm in sixth grade and I'd rather stay home and eat ice cream all day, watch soap operas, and read the porno magazines I found down in the basement. That's my idea of the good life.

"Why don't you talk to my mother?" Jody said, then opened the door and pulled her mother into the room. There were only two chairs in the doctor's office, so Jody sat on the floor at her mother's feet and refused to talk. She was onto something, even if she couldn't tell anyone what it was: by bringing her mother in, and making her do the talking, Jody was telling the shrink that it was her mother who was the problem. But no one seemed to get it.

When she was in high school and her report card featured more absences than presences, her mother took her to see Barbara Schwartz. She dropped Jody off in front of the building in Georgetown, gave her the office number, and said she'd be waiting right there by the curb. For seven years—through high school and on college vacations, once a week, twice a week, sometimes three times a week—she'd gone to Barbara Schwartz. For seven years Jody sat in the same chair and looked out the big windows onto the parking lot while stories of her life escaped her like various gases, sometimes toxic, sometimes not. A lifetime in a chair.

In the end Barbara said, "We've been talking about your leaving for a while now—do you have any last thoughts about it?"

Jody was still sitting in the same exact chair. The chrome arms were losing their shine, they were starting to get wobbly, and sometimes she could feel little sharp things poking her ass through the cushion. She wanted to say, I was thinking that maybe if I could buy this chair from you, if I could take it with me wherever I go and sit on it for an hour or so a couple of times a week, everything will be all right. But instead she said, "I'm just a little nervous."

Jody had said "I'm just a little nervous" in the same way Dustin Hoffman said "I'm just a little worried about my future" in *The Graduate*.

"Do you know that when they made *The Graduate*," Jody said, "Dustin Hoffman was thirty and Anne Bancroft was only thirty-seven. Isn't that amazing?"

"You'll do very well," Barbara said. "You really don't need me anymore. You know who you are, what you need. You're grown up." She paused. "I have a friend in New York who's very nice. She's a therapist. I can give you her number if you feel you might need it. She's in the Village. Isn't that where you'll be living?"

"I thought I was graduating," Jody said.

"You'll be fine, but if you want a name?"

Jody shook her head. "I'd have to start all over again, and I'd never be able to convince a stranger that I'm not really crazy."

Barbara smiled. "I can just give you the number. You don't have to use it." She went to her desk, which was covered with things her children had made—they hadn't even been born when Jody started seeing Barbara, and now one was almost six years old.

Sometimes Jody thought she was special, not in the usual sense, but like the young women in television movies—girls whose tormented pasts keep them from living normal lives until they meet the good doctor who knows just how to fix them, schizophrenics who end up being only slightly learning-disabled, cripples who become concert pianists.

Barbara wrote the name and phone number on a piece of scratch paper and handed it to Jody, who immediately jammed it deep into her pocket. For more than a year she'd kept it in her wallet like a condom, in case of emergency.

"Thanks," Jody had said to Barbara, putting her coat on without even thinking if the hour was up or not. It didn't matter.

"Stay in touch," Barbara said.

"Thanks a lot," Jody said. "Really, thanks a lot."

Barbara smiled again and moved towards her, and for a second Jody thought Barbara might hug her. If Barbara hugged her, she'd die. Barbara put her hand out and quickly Jody did the same. They shook.

"Goodbye," Barbara said.

"Yeah, see you later," Jody said, thinking about what she'd do after this last session. McDonald's, she figured—for lunch, not a career.

And now, what seemed like a hundred years later, at two in the morning, Jody was sitting on the floor of her apartment—in Greenwich Village, in New York City, two hundred and fifty miles from Barbara, from her mother, from everyone—eating brownies. Why had she gone to see Claire—was she an idiot? Jody had graduated. She'd done it. She was proud of herself. Until she'd picked up the phone and called Claire Roth, she'd thought of herself as the strongest person alive.

4

*D*uring her afternoon break, Claire sat on Bob Rosenblatt's extra chair. She didn't lie on the couch because, as she saw it, she wasn't a patient. She'd paid her therapy dues long ago. No, she was coming to a respected colleague for advice. Rosenblatt was older, wiser, a professor at Columbia who had Oriental rugs and good art in his office, all qualities Claire admired in a psychiatrist.

The problem was her relationship with Jake. She was angry. She resented his sluggishness, which she was afraid might be the core of his personality. It had occurred to Claire that it might be best to ignore him and just assume that one day he'd become a highly motivated genius. At the same time she thought of sending him away to school—something regimented, perhaps agricultural in nature, where he'd be forced to work. Even if it didn't help, at least she wouldn't have to see him languishing on the sofa. The third possibility was that this period of absolute inertia was merely a resting place, the last quiet moment before his body was filled with the hormonal rush of adolescence.

"Describe yourself as a child," Rosenblatt said.

Claire closed her eyes and tried to give Bob what she thought he wanted. "My mother was very fussy, everything had its place. In the living room there was a bookcase filled with china figurines. Our house was a sanctuary, a place where my father came to relax after work. Maintaining calm was the focus. My younger sister was the good one. They used to say I was filled with the devil. I left home when I was eighteen and a half."

"So," Rosenblatt said, quickly, definitely, "you were a difficult child, a hell-raiser?"

Claire was shocked. Hadn't he heard what she said? God, what a lousy shrink. Why was he supposed to be so great? "Hardly," she said, trying not to overreact. "Just because they *thought* I was wild doesn't mean that I was."

Rosenblatt nodded. "You described how your parents saw you, but not what you were like."

"What was I like?" Claire said. "I tried hard." She was so annoyed it was hard to think. She thought she'd made it clear on the phone that she wanted to talk about Jake. Five more minutes, that's all he was getting.

"So, what were you like?"

"Frustrated, just like I am now," she said, figuring there wasn't much to lose. If she got into a huge fight with Rosenblatt, she'd go to fewer shrink parties, spend more time at home with Jake. Maybe that's what he needed, anyway: his mother to bust his ass and drive him nuts.

Rosenblatt laughed. "Just like you are now, exactly! Why?"

"Because you don't understand what I just told you five minutes ago."

"Good," he said.

Claire didn't get it. She felt like a child, a dog being patted on the head. She didn't have a clue where he was leading her. She looked around Rosenblatt's office, bigger than hers, with more windows and a better view. It marked the difference between psychiatrists and psychologists. Money.

"Do you think your son is frustrated?"

"No," Claire said. "I think he's brain dead."

"Let's get back to your family."

"I've made myself a life they can't imagine."

"What do you mean, 'they can't imagine'?"

"I live in New York City. I married a man who makes a living defending criminals and likes it. I have a career and two children and my parents still act as though I'm a failure, as though I'll come running home any minute now. They live in a split-level house in northern Virginia with a two-car garage, and every Sunday morning my sister, her husband, and their three daughters pick them up, take them to church, and then out to lunch."

"Church?" Rosenblatt asked.

Claire nodded. She knew what he was getting at but wasn't about to give it to him. It came up everywhere—Adam's preschool, whether to send Jake to Hebrew school—and affected the way people perceived her, how they acted. There was never a way around it.

"Are you Jewish?" Rosenblatt asked. He meant, *aren't you?* But this way, he thought he was being tactful.

"By marriage," Claire said.

"Aha," Rosenblatt said softly.

You bet. Claire wondered exactly what it meant to him. Was she a whole new person, the blond shiksa, simultaneously despised and worshiped? Did Rosenblatt look at her and think everything came easily, that she was as simple, clean, and easily digested as white bread and mayonnaise?

Rosenblatt flashed her a condescending smile: I'm the shrink, you're the shrinkee. I'm the Jew, you're the goy. I'm a medical doctor, you're a Ph.D. You're the girl, I'm the boy. I win. He shifted his weight around in the chair and crossed his legs.

"My sister, Laura, the good one, got married when she was nineteen. She works with 'special children' because it's the right thing to do. It doesn't threaten her family or her husband. She manages her life as if it was a retarded child. We speak twice a year."

"Is that a loss? Do you wish you were closer?"

"No," Claire said. "But I feel like I have no family; no one who knew me as a child. I have Sam and the kids, but Sam doesn't *belong* to me." She paused. "And my children are spoiled slugs."

Claire almost started crying, but stopped herself. There were huge holes in what she said, but she knew Rosenblatt didn't see them. She'd done a good job. All the same, as she sat in Rosenblatt's big leather chair, talking, she felt as though she was starting to fall through. She wouldn't tell him the whole story; she'd promised herself that.

The silence made her uncomfortable. She looked at Rosenblatt. He was someone she knew. She knew a million people who knew him. On the phone, she'd made it clear she was coming in for a bit of advice, not a whole big thing, just some clues from a seasoned expert who had one kid at Yale and another at Harvard. Rosenblatt was staring at her knees—bony and poking out from the edge of her skirt—hiding his discomfort behind his glasses and the pose of the elder, a professional, a man. He could do it to her and get away with it.

Claire told herself to keep it all a little more tightly wrapped. Talk to Sam, she told herself. Sam never seemed to think anything was all that strange.

More silence. Claire pulled herself back to the surface and got angry.

Her anger would save her. She tried to get really mad, but was exhausted from the effort of sorting her life into two piles, secrets and things that were all right to discuss. She'd done well. None of the really messy stuff had come out—not Baltimore, not anything about her life after she left home. The one saving grace was that it sounded normal enough to say you left home at eighteen. She never added that in her parents' home, the expectation was that she wouldn't leave until her wedding day.

"We're running out of time," he said. "Where should we go from here?"

Bob Rosenblatt had done her a disservice, opening everything up. One could argue that like certain types of surgery, it needed to be done; that it was necessary to release the pressure before it built into an explosion. All the same, the side effects included the loss of her good sense.

"Would you like to come in again—say, next Monday at nine?"

Claire took out her appointment book. That she also did this for a living seemed strange. She felt like a fraud.

"Fine," Claire said, getting up to leave, annoyed that she'd gone ahead and made another appointment instead of saying what she really thought.

She walked down Fifth Avenue toward Sixteenth Street, trying to shake off the Rosenblatt effect, stopping to look in windows along the way. She was meeting Sam for lunch, something they did once every couple of weeks, often enough that it didn't feel like a doomed occasion where one of them would confess to something horrible: I'm leaving, the test came back, I've done something you won't forgive me for. Claire got to the restaurant a little early and had a glass of wine at the bar.

"Whose fault is it?" Sam whispered in her ear, taking her arm and following the maitre d' to their table. "If it's genetic, it's your side. Jews are never like that."

The restaurant was filled with good-looking, well-dressed men and women gorging themselves on expense accounts. When the waiter handed them menus, Claire hid behind hers. Over four-tomato soup with floating goat cheese she began to cry. Sam's face wrinkled. He always cried when she cried. The people at the next table stared. Claire forced herself to stop, blotted her eyes, and then looked up.

"A joke?" Sam asked, pouring her a glass of wine.

Claire nodded.

"Two guys, Abe and Louie. A promise: first one dies calls the other, tells him what heaven's like. Twenty years later, Abe dies. Couple months go by, Louie's phone rings. 'Abe?' 'Louie?' 'Abe, is that you?' 'Louie?' 'So tell me, Abe, what's it like?' 'You wouldn't believe. Wake up in the morning, have sex, a little breakfast, a nap. Lunch, some sex, rest till dinner, a little nosh, more sex, then sleep all night like a baby.' 'Heaven sounds incredible, Abe.' 'Heaven, Schmeven—I'm a bear in Colorado.' "

Claire only smiled, having sunk too far into herself to laugh. She ate her soup looking at Sam. It was normal to go back, to reconsider, to move backwards before going forward. She remembered that when she first met Sam, his hair had been thick, cut like a thatched roof—a Jewish Robert Redford. In her mind, the closest she'd get to marrying him would be sleeping with him two, maybe three times, and then he'd move on to someone more challenging, more sophisticated. Sam was too good for her. Everything was too good.

They met at a demonstration at Columbia; she was getting her Ph.D. in psych and he had just finished law school. They were both watching friends get arrested. He grabbed her hand and pulled her away from the crowd. Together they went to the police station and waited for their friends to be released. Afterwards they all went out for Chinese food, and one of Sam's friends explained in minute detail how carefully a male cop had searched her. "I had some dope on me and he was getting close, so I stated telling him how much he was turning me on and gave him a blow job to keep him distracted. It worked," she said, pulling a baggie of pot out of her pocket and handing it to Sam. "I owe you this, for coming to get me."

Later, in Claire's apartment on 106th Street, Claire and Sam smoked the dope. Claire wasn't used to getting stoned, and freaked out, confessing everything. "I had a baby," she told him.

"You mean you had an abortion," Sam said.

"No, I had a baby. No one knows. Years ago, a little girl. My parents made me give her away. I never should have given her up." The words repeated themselves in her head, and then, as if something in her had broken, Claire started crying and repeating "I had a baby, I had a baby" again and again, wailing, bellowing like an animal. She was crying so hard and so strangely that she scared herself. She started thinking that the dope had been laced with something, that this feeling would last forever and she would never be herself again.

Sam got a cool washcloth and rubbed it over her face and arms. He found a Valium in the medicine cabinet and slipped it into her mouth. Sitting next to her on the bed, he held her hands until she fell asleep; and while she slept he cleaned the apartment, rearranged things so that the place seemed larger, took down the dark red curtains she'd made herself, and washed the windows. She woke up in a different world.

Claire picked at the swordfish she'd ordered and watched Sam spin the tricolored pasta onto his fork. The older Sam got, the better he looked, the more relaxed he seemed. If she weren't so miserable, she'd be happy.

"Are you okay?" he asked, cutting a piece of her fish for himself.

"I'll be fine." She reached under the table, pretending she'd dropped her napkin, and rubbed his crotch. "Do you want to come back to my office after lunch?"

"Can't," he said, chewing.

"I love you," Claire said, her hand still under the table. Sam leaned across the wineglasses and kissed her. Out of the corner of her eye, Claire saw the two women at the next table watching.

Back in the office, Claire told herself she had to focus on something. Work more. Being a shrink was lonely business; most of the people Claire knew were also shrinks who, between their practices and their real lives, were too busy for anything other than a quick breezy chat between sessions. And then there were her patients, but they weren't exactly available for afternoon cappuccino. A little high from the three glasses of wine, Claire sat looking out the window, waiting for her next victim, thinking she should put a sign up: TODAY ONLY, HALF-PRICE SPECIAL, SPACED-OUT SHRINK.

The buzzer went off. "Yes," Claire said in a distant voice.

"It's Jody Goodman."

Claire had completely forgotten that she'd switched Polly and her would-be husband—if only he'd make a commitment—to another time. Good, she thought, pressing the button that unlocked the front door. Jody will make me feel better.

5

"My mother wants me to fly to L.A. next week," Jody said.

"And?"

"I don't want to go."

"Because of the flying?"

"Flight 206. It sounds like a number you hear on the news when they talk about the worst aviation disaster in history. 'Flight 206, originating in Washington, D.C., bound for Los Angeles, crashed today, killing all aboard.' I can't do it."

"The plane isn't going to crash. You're rerouting your anxiety."

"That's really brilliant," Jody said, and when she saw Claire looked hurt, she apologized. She'd never worried about hurting a shrink's feelings before. She hadn't figured they were exactly human.

"What could you do to make this work?" Claire asked. "Could you take some Valium?"

Jody shook her head.

"Why not?"

"Don't you know that's why so many people die in these things? They're too stoned or drunk to get up and walk out."

Claire laughed. "If you're serious about going to school out there, you should definitely take a look. That way, if you decide to go, you'll be more comfortable in the fall. It'll seem familiar."

"I am going," Jody said. "I have to go. Nine million people apply to film school and only about two get in."

"You must be very talented."

Jody shrugged. She usually hated it when people complimented her, but Claire had a way of doing it that actually made her feel good. When Claire said something, Jody believed it.

"It's nice of your mother to go with you. Is she always like that? Is she especially nice?"

"Ellen says so," Jody said.

"Who's Ellen?"

"My friend. She lives in my building, grew up where I grew up. Like I was saying," Jody said, pausing for effect, "Ellen says I should be happy that my mother and I get along."

"And?"

"That's it. Mostly Ellen talks about herself."

"Oh. I was hoping you'd tell me a little bit about your mother, your family."

"The family's a push-and-pull thing," Jody said. "They want me to grow up and be independent, but they also want me to stay with them— not at home, just on their level. Then there's the idea that I should go off and do everything, fulfill all of everyone's undone dreams. But they're also afraid I'll go too far and I won't need them anymore."

"Is that possible?"

"I dunno, I haven't gone anywhere yet."

"You're here."

Jody laughed. "I have this vision that I'll be called home like a kid out late on a summer night. My mother will open the front door to New York City and yell, 'Jody, come home.' I'll be outside playing. I won't turn around. I won't answer. She'll call me at the office. 'Jody, come home.' I'll be waiting in a movie line. 'Jody, come home, it's eight-thirty, I'm running your bath.' At a restaurant. 'Jody, get in this house right now.' After a while, I won't have any friends left, they'll be repulsed by me and my family. No one will want to play with me. And I'll be torn between staying with my ex-friends, even though I'm unwanted, and going home to be plunked into a vat of Mr. Bubble and left there till I'm all shrively."

"What an imagination," Claire said, clearly enjoying herself. "Now, tell me something else about your family."

There was a shift between Claire's listening for pleasure and her determination to gather information for purposes that weren't entirely clear.

"I don't know what to say," Jody said, instinctively withdrawing, shrugging in apology. "Sometimes, with people I like or people who I want to like me, I get very quiet. With people I don't care about, I'm a regular Chatty Cathy." Jody was quiet.

"Does that mean you care about me?" Claire asked.

Jody glared at her. She didn't care about her, didn't know her well enough to have any particular feelings about her. Shrinks always did that—insisted that you care about them, that you secretly loved them—but Jody never had. Maybe that's why she was still the way she was.

"You don't have to worry about saying something that will scare me away."

"Yeah, right," Jody said.

Claire smiled. "It's true. I can take it."

Jody allowed herself to make eye contact for a fraction of a second. Claire's eyes were green and encouraging. She looked, and like an idiot let herself be seduced. Claire actually could take it, she thought. She felt like she'd never been in a room with a woman so strong. Jody had the urge to say "Here's my life" and dump it on her lap like a knotted necklace. Here, fix it for me, make it good again.

"When you tell someone something," she said, "what you tell them doesn't just belong to you, it also belongs to the person listening. People say certain things because they want something back from the listener, something in exchange." Jody stopped herself.

"If you're right, then you must want something from me," Claire said. "The question is what."

Jody shrugged and ignored her. "Most people give what comes easiest."

"You didn't answer my question. What do you want from me?"

"Nothing," Jody said. "I wasn't talking about you. It has nothing to do with you. You're the shrink, not a person. You can't want something from a shrink."

"Hostile," Claire said. "Very hostile."

"Maybe."

"People want things from their therapists all the time," Claire said. "Approval, love, attention."

They were silent. Jody stared at the tan wall. Like everything else in the office, it was the color of a desert—a person could get lost.

"We were talking about your family," Claire said.

"Yeah, I was about to tell you a secret. It's not really a secret," Jody said. "It's something everyone knows, everyone except you."

"I'm listening."

"I had a brother," Jody said. "He died six months before I was born. There was something wrong with his heart, a defect. He'd been sick since he was a baby."

"That's very sad."

"I was adopted," Jody said. "After my mother had him, she couldn't have any more children, so they brought me in to replace him."

Claire lifted her eyebrows as if to ask whether this was fact or fiction.

"It's true," Jody said, surprised that Claire was looking at her like she didn't already know. She'd imagined that as soon as she'd called for an appointment, Claire had called Barbara, who'd told her everything. What did shrinks say to each other? It sounded like a joke, but what was the punch line? Time's up for today.

"Tell me again," Claire said, picking up her legal pad. "How old was the child?"

"Nine," Jody said.

"And how old were you when you were adopted?"

"Brand-new."

"Months, weeks?"

"Days." Jody glanced at Claire, whose eyes were red, as if she'd been crying. Jody made the shrink cry. She'd hardly said anything. "It's nothing, I swear," she added, laughing nervously.

"I'd like to see you again tomorrow," Claire said.

Jody couldn't believe it. She'd thought she'd been torturing Claire, and now Claire wanted to do it again tomorrow. Why not? There was something about throwing all this emotional information around without having any idea where it would land that was invigorating and kind of scary. Cheap thrills, only it wasn't so cheap.

"Three o'clock?" Claire asked.

"Sure," Jody said, worried about sneaking off the set again. Most people who had jobs went to work and stayed there. That was the basic premise, or didn't Claire know that? Should she remind her?

Claire took a card off her desk, wrote something on it, and handed it to Jody. "It's my home number. I want you to call me if you need to."

"I can't," Jody said, handing the card back to Claire, who refused to take it.

"What do you mean you can't?"

"I just can't, okay? I can't call anyone, my friends always call me. Even my mother calls me every night at eleven," Jody said. "I have a special phone that doesn't even have a dial on it."

"If you don't want to call me at home, you can always leave a message on the machine here. I check in quite often."

Barbara hadn't given Jody her home phone number until she'd been seeing her for a year and a half. In the whole seven years Jody had used it once, and regretted it. She'd had a huge fight with her mother, and when she called, Barbara had spoken in little clipped sentences. Then one of her kids walked into the room, and Barbara put her hand over the receiver. Jody felt like a leper. She could hear the sound of a kid crying in the background, a reminder that the shrink had her own private life. No, Jody thought. No way, no thanks.

"You can call me," Claire said. "I want you to."

"Nope."

"Why not? You did it before. You called me to make an appointment."

"I was crazy then," Jody said. "I'm better now."

Claire laughed, and Jody headed for the door.

"By the way," Claire called after her, "you're going to California."

Jody had the cab drop her at Seventy-second Street and then walked along the park toward the Seventy-ninth Street location.

"You," Harry said, shaking a fat finger at Jody from halfway down the block.

Jody went white.

"You," Harry said, wagging the finger again as she got closer.

"I'm sorry," Jody blurted. She'd have to call Claire and cancel.

"*You* are a *fool.*" Harry took Jody's hand and guided her down the street, along the lines of cable leading toward the Museum of Natural History. "This morning Michael told me I'm losing you to UCLA. Do not go to school, good girl. You've done that already. That's finished. I know about these things."

"Why do you even care?" Jody asked, still thinking about the appointment with Claire.

"I like you, good girl. You're tough—you've got a little extra heart where most people keep their credit cards."

"On my ass?"

"No, here," Harry said, patting his breast pocket. "I've been to film school on many occasions." He then did an elaborate impression of an overzealous grad student. " 'Excuse me, Mr. Birenbaum, but in your work, like that of da Vinci or van Gogh, the shades of the palette seem to carry such significance—especially for me in *Shadows from Fall*, which was albeit a little heavy-handed; the house was white, her dress was red, and the car they drove away in was blue. But could you tell us something about that, about your relation to color as political statement?' Actually, I'm color-blind," Harry mocked, shrugging off the question.

He slid his arm under Jody's so it rubbed against her breast, the better to guide her. "You," he said, "should know better. If you want to make movies, make movies. Don't get a degree in it."

"But—"

"Dear one, nothing can convince me it's not injurious to the process. Film students are retards."

Jody didn't say anything.

"Now that I've depressed you, let me make you happy again. I'm invited to something tomorrow night, I don't remember what, but I have to go. I'm hoping you'll be my date?"

Jody still didn't say anything.

"You'd have to wear a dress," Harry said. "You do have at least one dress, don't you?"

Jody nodded.

"I'll pick you up at eight." Harry took a large book out of his pocket and had Jody write her address and phone number on a page already thick with names and numbers.

6

After Jody left, Claire had an attack of paranoia. She decided that Jody was afraid of nothing—a laser beam, a nuclear warhead. Her fear of flying, her anxieties were affectations to make her seem less powerful, less overwhelming, more normal. Claire conjured Jody's image: the smooth, open face needed no makeup, no correction; wavy brown hair, stylishly cut; cerulean blue eyes, quick to look and then to look away; shoulders back, neck extended, the posture of confidence—someone you'd notice. Despite what Jody said, how she hemmed and hawed, pretended to suffer crushing self-doubt, her appearance was that of someone who knew where she was going and exactly how she'd be getting there; the sort of young woman who caused people to ask "Who *is* that?" in sweaty, eager tones.

Jody was toying with Claire. She never had a brother. She wasn't adopted. She'd come to undo Claire, to dismantle her. She could see right through Claire and was playing with all the weak links, reducing her to nothingness.

Claire flipped through her Rolodex, found Barbara Schwartz's number, and left a message on her machine. The second she hung up, Claire regretted having called. She had nothing to say to Barbara. Past was past. Certainly Claire couldn't call out of the blue and discuss the idea of her patient as a demon, the devil incarnate.

She had two back-to-back cancellations and a free hour. Instead of lingering in the office, filling out insurance forms and writing up bills, she went shopping.

In Macy's, the salesclerk asked, "For your grandchild?" as Claire picked up a new stuffed animal for Adam.

"My son," Claire said.

When Adam was twenty-eight, Claire would be nearly seventy. She would wear her white hair in a bun, her pull-on pants too short, adult diapers bunched up underneath. Adam wouldn't allow himself to be seen with her, and Claire wouldn't blame him.

"Can I ring that for you, ma'am?" the clerk asked. In her daze Claire thought she'd called her "Mom." She glared at the girl, handed her the stuffed animal and her Macy's card, and dropped back into her dream. Claire had worked hard to make herself this life, this marriage, these children, and now she suspected that she'd done all this as a cover-up, so no one would notice she was a fraud. She lived in fear of being discovered.

In the children's department, surrounded by infant clothing, Claire thought about her missing baby. The baby that was old enough to have a baby of its own by now. There was something undeniably different about having sons rather than daughters. Living in a house that was strictly male felt like a never-ending frat party. Only Claire seemed to care if they left their underwear in the living room or wore any in the first place. If she weren't there, she was convinced, they'd pee in the sinks, out the windows, in dirty coffee cups, wherever it was convenient. There were times when all Claire did was play the maid, the referee, the police officer who kept them from having fun. If she left, if she ran away, they'd be pleased as long as they still had their take-out menus.

The boys were Sam's, his duplicates in every way. The day after Jake was born, she and Sam had a horrible fight. The nurse had come in and innocently asked "Are you circumcising?" and all hell broke loose. Somehow they'd never discussed it. Sam assumed they would; Claire assumed they wouldn't. "What's the point?" Claire said. "You're not religious."

"It's not about religion, it's tradition. I'm a Jew!" Sam bellowed. "This is what Jews do. Besides, it's healthier."

"It seems so unnecessary. He's a little baby. Why do you want to start cutting him up?"

"Because it's what you do!" Sam screamed. "They don't really feel it. It's not something you remember when you're older—'Oy, the day they cut my dick!' "

It went on and on, so loudly that at one point a nurse's aide stuck her head in and asked them to keep it down.

Sam ended it by saying, "This is my son. I want to be able to stand next to him in a locker room and not feel like we're at a conference of Christians and Jews. I want him to be like me."

Claire couldn't argue with that. She couldn't say, "And I want him to be like my father, like the first boy I ever slept with." And so it was done, without ceremony, before Jake went home from the hospital. The next time they were ready. When Adam was born, they did it the traditional way, a bris, with the baby's godfather holding the baby, Sam and Claire standing off to the side, hoping not to faint when the mohel did his thing.

Claire imagined having a daughter. She imagined taking the little girl to the hairdresser's with her. She thought it was a shame that women didn't have their hair done anymore. Every two months they just went and had it cut. She remembered when she was little, sitting on a stack of phone books under the dryer, imitating the ladies. She remembered her mother indulging her and letting the manicurist put clear polish on her nails.

Claire had held her baby girl only once. The nurse lowered the baby into Claire's arms as she sat in a wheelchair on her way out of the hospital. She'd never held a baby before. She wasn't one of those girls who was a mother's helper during summer vacations or baby-sat the neighbor's kids. Claire was afraid of children; she watched them from a distance and worried about what she'd do when she had her own. The closest she'd gotten to her sister, Laura, was sitting on the other side of the room while her mother changed diapers.

"Don't look," she remembered her mother saying.

In 1966, in Washington, D.C., when a nurse deposited Claire's daughter into her lap, Claire felt a rush as though she were going instantly insane. The blue-eyed thing that lay in her arms had come from her own body and yet was a stranger, a complete and total stranger. She gave it up before she ever knew who it was.

The lawyer, posing as Claire's father, followed the maternity nurse who wheeled Claire and the baby to the lobby. Claire accepted the hospital's baby-girl gift bag, signed out, and then the nurse said goodbye and left Claire in the lawyer's command. There was no reason for Claire to be sitting there in the wheelchair like a cripple except that it was hospital policy. She could have walked. She could have gotten up and run if only the baby hadn't been sleeping in her lap. The lawyer, in a black cashmere overcoat, went up to a woman in a tweed car coat who was standing alone.

"Is that the baby?" the woman asked, nodding in Claire's direction.

"Yes," the lawyer said.

As the two of them approached, Claire felt weak for the first time since the birth. The lawyer lifted the baby from her lap, and it was as if some vital organ had been ripped out. On the baby's wrist was a name bracelet made out of tiny square pink and white beads—all blank. Claire wanted to take the bracelet off so she'd have something to keep, but she was afraid the child would cry and attract attention.

The lawyer handed the baby to the woman. "If you ever see her again," he said, pointing at Claire, "do not acknowledge her."

The woman nodded and looked down at the baby in her arms. "Pretty baby," she said. "Your new mommy and daddy are going to be so glad to have you."

The lawyer rolled Claire out the door behind the woman and the baby. Claire stared at her back and tried to read her mind, wondering who she was under that big, thick coat. Outside, the lawyer slipped the gift bag over the woman's shoulder and she walked off, trailing the twin vapors of her breath and the baby's.

Claire closed her eyes, not wanting to see the child leave. If Claire had been a stronger person, she would have stopped them. She would have screamed, "My baby, my baby, they've stolen my baby!" and the hospital security guard would have chased after the woman. The lawyer, seeing the commotion, thinking it best not to be involved, would have simply gotten into his car and driven off. Instead, he pulled his Buick up to the hospital entrance and drove Claire to a nearby park, where her father was waiting. An envelope was exchanged and the lawyer took off, tires spinning in the gravel.

The whole way back to Baltimore, all her father said was "I had to take off work to do this."

As Claire climbed out of the car, her father added, "I hope things will be easier now," and tried to pat her on the back, but she was already most of the way out, and his hand landed on her rear end. He blushed and brusquely told her to close the door quickly—"Cold air's coming in."

Claire went back to Baltimore with nothing except the memory of a three-day-old monkey face, pink cheeks, thick brown hair that stood in a point, and blue eyes she was sure already saw through her and hated her. She went back to the apartment and found that nothing had changed except the milk in the refrigerator had turned.

"It's better this way," her mother said on the phone while her father was at work. "Believe me."

In Macy's, Claire bought Jake and Adam clothes and toys and tapes and books. She charged over four hundred dollars' worth and then had a hard time stuffing everything into a cab.

The phone was ringing when she stepped into her office. She grabbed it just before the machine picked up.

"Hi, it's Barbara Schwartz. Were you in session?"

"No, just coming in the door," Claire said. "Hang on." She pulled all of her packages in, closed the door, and brought the phone over to the sofa.

"So, how are you?" Claire asked.

"Good," Barbara said. "Tired, but good. I only have a minute between patients, but I wanted to call you back."

"I'm seeing Jody Goodman. She's been accepted into graduate school and can't decide whether or not to go."

"UCLA?"

"Yes."

"Great," Barbara said. "That's what she's always wanted. Jody's special—a great imagination, smart. A thinker. Sometimes she feels obligated to kid around, to compensate for the dark stuff. But basically she's all there. The main thing was getting her away from her family. They're pretty dependent, and she's always been too involved. She needs a lot of support, reassurance."

"Any secrets?" Claire asked. There was noise in the background. Barbara didn't seem to hear the question. Claire looked around her office; compared with Rosenblatt's, it was quiet, humble, a relief.

"Oh God, here's my patient. Anything else?" Barbara said.

"Is she a game player?"

"Game player?"

"You know," Claire said. "Tall tales. Manipulative?"

"Not at all," Barbara said, surprised. "Why?"

"Just curious. How're the kids?"

"Great. Yours?"

"Fine. Everything's fine."

"Stay in touch. I'm glad you're seeing her."

Claire hung up, thinking she liked Barbara even more than she remembered, if only because Barbara was too busy to talk about Jody or, more importantly, anything else.

7

"Your plane didn't crash," Claire said. She stood in the door to her office, smiling.

"Beginner's luck," Jody said.

"So, how'd it go?"

"I got into a fight with my mother on the way to the airport." Jody turned in her chair and prepared to pantomime. "Me: 'I don't want to go to Los Angeles. I never said I wanted to go. I don't even want to go to film school. I lied. I want to be a receptionist in a dentist's office.' My mother: 'The dentist? You hate the dentist. Why would you want to work there?' " Jody said it slowly and deadpan. "Had a nervous breakdown on the runway. The engines started and it was like my guilt weighed enough to bring the plane down. My mother doesn't want me to go away. It's true. She secretly wants me to live with her forever. As we're going down the runway, I start apologizing all over the place. The plane lifts up off the ground—we're at the angle where you feel like an astronaut—and my mother squeezes my hand and says, 'It would be good if you could learn to be nicer to me. After all, I won't last forever.' Up in the air, I'm chanting to myself: 'I will never be mean to my mother again. I will never be mean . . .' They served dinner. My mother kept trying to lower my tray table and I kept putting it back up. I didn't want anything. She says, 'You paid for it, at least let them give it to you.' And I'm like, 'Who's gonna eat it—the guy snoring across the aisle?' My mother ate her dinner and then all of mine."

Claire laughed.

"It's true," Jody said.

"Did anything good happen?"

"I guess you could call the plane not crashing good, depending on how you look at it."

"What happened once you were there?"

"We looked around, flew home, and I took the train back to New York."

"I don't believe you."

Jody looked at Claire. How could she not believe her. "Okay, we *didn't* look around and then we flew home." She paused. "I made my mother go to Forest Lawn and spend two hours looking around for graves of famous people. All she said was, 'Well, it's nice to be outside on such a beautiful day.' "

"I think you had a good time and don't want to admit it,"Claire said.

"Don't start thinking you're brilliant or anything," Jody said. "It's pretty basic."

"Some people's mothers wouldn't have gone at all."

"It's not a comparison study," Jody said. "It's just my life, okay?"

"Sorry," Claire said. "You're right. So what about UCLA—are you going?"

"Harry says I'm a fool if I go to graduate school. 'Film students are retards.' " She did a perfect imitation.

"Who's Harry?"

"Harry Birenbaum, the film director. He made *Trial of Love* and a bunch of other stuff."

"Really?" Claire said, excited. "That's my favorite movie."

"It's everyone's favorite movie."

"That's who you work for?"

"No. Technically I work for a film producer, who sent me to spy on Harry. Last week, before I left, Harry gave me a long lecture and then took me to some benefit dinner dance at the Plaza where everyone kept saying they didn't know he had a daughter so grown-up."

"What's he like?"

"He wanted to have a sleepover. I should probably introduce him to my friend Ellen. All they both talk about is fucking. Who they fuck, why they fuck, how much more they want to fuck. Every week or so Harry picks a female project and works on them until they either give in or quit."

"Are you one of his projects?"

"I'm not talking about myself. Every word out of my mouth is not about me," Jody said, and immediately wished she hadn't. She had the urge to apologize, to start the session over, walk in the door and go on about how sunny and warm California was. She was quiet.

"Is there something you'd like to talk about?"

"The weather," Jody said.

Claire smiled. They sat silently. The longer they were quiet, the more nervous Jody got. She played with the ends of her shoelaces, with a quarter from her pocket, with a piece of hangnail on her thumb. She crossed and recrossed her legs, trying not to look at Claire. She looked at Claire's shoes, brown suede slip-ons. Nice. Probably from Saks. She looked at the air conditioner. She wiggled around, trying to look like she wasn't wiggling. She fought the overwhelming desire to fall asleep. There was no air in the room. There *was* air in the room but it was treated with special tranquilizer dust. Claire had pushed a secret button on her chair and released an invisible cloud of the stuff and Jody was falling asleep. Her head was weaving around. Her neck felt too thin and weak to support her skull. Not only was it exhausting not to talk, but it made the hour seem incredibly long.

"Are you all right?" Claire asked.

"Fine," Jody said.

"Well, we're out of time for today," Claire said.

Jody had a hard time getting out of the chair. Her body was like lead.

"Would you like to come in on Wednesday, same time?" Claire asked.

I have to work, Jody thought. I have a job. I like having a job even if I don't fully understand what I'm supposed to be doing. But Claire was nice to her. She'd gone all the way to Los Angeles for Claire. She couldn't say no.

"So Wednesday's all right?" Claire asked. Jody nodded. "We'll talk more about things then."

Jody walked out. She might not want to talk about things Wednesday. She might not want to talk about them later in the week, later in the year, or ever.

She called Ellen from the phone in Harry's trailer while Harry went out to lunch with a reporter from *Premiere*.

"Third National," Ellen said.

"I screwed up at shrink," Jody said, glancing out the window at the Hell's Kitchen location—special security guards had been hired for the afternoon to keep panhandlers away.

"And how may I help you this afternoon, Ms. Goodman?"

"I didn't talk. I must be having a nervous breakdown."

"No, we don't give oral sex for opening new accounts anymore. It's toasters. One moment, please, I have to put you on hold." There was a long pause, and Jody started opening the cabinets in the trailer; one was filled with boxes of Jiffy Pop microwave popcorn, the other with packs of unused Polaroid film. Jody slipped some film into her knapsack.

"Sweetie," Ellen said, "you don't just walk into a shrink's office a few times and all of a sudden have a nervous breakdown. All day long people go to shrinks and don't say anything, it's no big deal."

"I kept looking at her shoes, her feet and stuff, and the more I didn't talk, the worse it got. Then she made an appointment for Wednesday. She used to want me to come in every day. I don't think she likes me anymore."

"You've only been going for two weeks? Why do you care what she thinks? Maybe she's busy tomorrow. Maybe there's a sale at Bergdorf's or something. Don't take it personally."

"I am taking it personally."

"Majorly. She sounds like a lousy shrink. How come she didn't do anything to make you start talking? You haven't known her long enough to be completely silent together. Look, I met this guy—maybe you want to come out with us tonight."

"Penis four thousand fifty-four."

"I like sex, okay?" Ellen said loudly. Jody could picture all the other people behind their desks at the bank whirling around and staring. "I like it a lot. Everyone always tries to make me feel bad about it, like I'm some kind of pervert. I like to fuck, to get fucked—what's wrong with that? If we weren't supposed to, we'd be built differently!"

"You're yelling," Jody said.

"No, I'm not!" Ellen yelled. "I'm just talking to you and you don't like it."

"I worry about you," Jody said. "It's selfish, but if something happened to you I wouldn't have anyone to talk to. Sex is dangerous. It's not like when we were growing up."

"I have to go," Ellen said. "Someone's waving at me. Talk to you later."

Later that afternoon, the assistant director barked "It's over" down the street, and Carol Heberton was led from her trailer to a waiting car. Two guys in suits climbed into another trailer behind Harry, and someone dumped the rest of the coffee from the huge insulated vat into the gutter. The PAs were checking their walkie-talkies in for a recharge, and one of them turned to Jody. "We're going for beers, wanna come?"

It was the first time they'd invited her anywhere. Every night she'd seen packs of production assistants walking off the set together, relaxed, laughing, never looking back.

"So, are you related to someone?" one of them asked as they walked down Eighth Avenue.

"No," Jody said, "Not related."

"Well, so, what's your job exactly? Me," he said, "every morning I buy flowers for Heberton's trailer, I buy her a fried-egg sandwich at a quality diner. I spend my days fetching whatever needs to be fetched. Before I check out, I turn in receipts and get paid back. But what do you do and who do you do it for?"

"I work for Michael Miller. I help raise money, but for now I'm on loan to Harry."

As they walked, weaving their way through the west side of Midtown, breathing in the thick fumes of tunnel traffic, they passed places Jody had always wanted to go, places she'd been and meant to come back to: the Film Center Cafe, the Cupcake Cafe, Restaurant Bellevues. She assumed they had something better in mind. She figured they knew where they were going. When they turned into the doorway of a place marked BAR/ PIZZA in neon, Jody's stomach sank. She wished she'd eaten that last bagel on the food table. Production assistants seemed to revel in their lack of taste, their psychotic roommates and below-poverty-level standard of living. Jody made it a point to sit as far way from the florist/fetcher as possible. They ordered pitchers of beer and a pitcher of Coke for the alcoholics, of which there seemed to be quite a few.

"When this one wraps, I'm getting a regular, boring job," one of the women said.

"If you want to stay in film," Jody said, "you should write Michael a letter. My job will be open soon."

"And where will you be going?" the florist/fetcher asked. "Off to direct your first feature, or to spend the summer in Paris?"

Jody didn't answer right away. There was no way she could tell them about film school, about Claire, about Ellen, Harry, or anything. "I'm going back to Montana," she finally said. "My father has a ranch there and they always need an extra hand."

They ordered five pizzas for seven people, bad pizza with cardboard crust, sauce like watered-down blood, and cheese like shoe rubber. In the end Jody was walking down Seventh Avenue with a huge pizza box in her hands.

"Really, you take it," one of the PAs had said. "After all, you put in the most money."

Out of guilt, Jody thought.

She passed a homeless man camped out in a small park. "Would you like a pizza?" Jody asked, holding out the box.

"Is it poison?"

"No, I ate some. It's just not very good, too chewy." Jody lifted the top so the man could see.

"Has it got tomato sauce on it? That looks like tomato."

"Yeah, well, it's a pizza."

"I can't take the tomato," the man said. "Doesn't agree with my stomach. I like that other kind, though. What do they call it—white pizza. You got any of that?"

Jody shrugged. "Sorry."

"Well, I guess you could go on and leave it on the bench. I'm expecting company later, maybe they'll want some."

Jody put down the pizza and walked away.

"Next time," he called after her, "get the other kind. It's healthier."

8

Sam sat on the edge of the bed in the glow of the television, an old set of heavily padded earphones circling his head. Ever since the playoffs, when night after night they'd found Jake asleep with his head pressed against the wall, the house rule was that Sam couldn't watch sports at night without the headset. He was also forbidden to carry on discussions with the commentators, although occasionally his feet pounded the floor and Jake would yell "What happened, what happened?" from the kids' bedroom.

Claire climbed over the bed and sat at the small desk jammed into the corner against the windows. When Adam was born, they'd converted the master bedroom into the boys' room and taken the little one for themselves. It was ridiculous—a queen-sized bed, a double dresser, a desk, a chair, and two adults crammed into an eleven-by-fourteen box. She looked out the window into the apartment across the street. It was bigger than theirs, nine windows across; there were flowers in some of the windows, and the walls were painted interesting colors, probably by a decorator.

"Remember Karen Armstrong?" Claire said to Sam. He didn't answer. "They just bought an apartment in the San Remo—they were asking eight-five, but Karen got it for seven-eighty. Her sister Susan's curating an exhibit at the Whitney that's traveling to four cities." Sam didn't respond. Claire stood in front of the TV, raised her shirt, and flashed her breasts at him. His feet stamped the floor in a brief tantrum, and Claire left the room.

She called her friend Naomi.

"Can't talk now," Naomi said. "I'm trying to get the kids to bed."

"It's ten o'clock," Claire said. "Maybe you should get one of those tranquilizer dart guns."

"Yeah, and send them to the zoo. I'll call you tomorrow."

Claire hung up. Her life was fine, according to some people perfect. There was a reassuring rhythm and routine to it. But now she wanted something else—something to hook her in, to take her to the next level, to keep her interested.

She made a microwave pizza, put it on a tray along with a bottle of seltzer and two glasses, and carried it into the bedroom. Sam took his half of the pizza, rolled it into a tube, and ate it in less than seven bites, letting crumbs fall all over the floor. Great, Claire thought; all we need is a mouse again—maybe a sewer rat this time.

She lay back on the bed and hooked the elastic band of Sam's underwear with her toes. She pulled it away from his body and then let it snap back against his skin, again and again, until Sam reached back and grabbed her foot. After five minutes, when nothing else happened, Claire folded her foot underneath her and picked up a book.

Their apartment was definitely too small. At night it shrank, as though someone upstairs held marionette strings attached to the walls and gave a firm yank at eight p.m., drawing the walls closer together. Until now, Claire had thought living in close quarters was good for a family. It taught them how to get along, how to find private space when there was none, and how not to need so much. It was impossible for Jake or any of them to have a secret life, no way to sneak anything in or out. And yet there was a major drawback in knowing everything your kid did. For example, when Jake did nothing, when he lay in his room staring at the ceiling, waiting for his life to begin, it annoyed her no end. And as much as setting them free scared her, she really didn't want to know so much about them anymore. They were beyond the stage where it was cute. She looked at Sam watching TV and wished the game would end so they could have a serious discussion.

Claire crawled under the covers and thought of how her parents would see things. Her father: Big deal he's a lawyer, they're all lawyers. That's how they get all the money. You should see how they live—not that I've ever been there, my other daughter told me. Children running around the house in their underwear. Slobs. Hippies, that's what they are. Never grew up. They live in that Greenwich Village, like animals. Bohemians. It's disgusting.

Her sister actually came to visit: "I love Fifth Avenue—are you sure this is really Fifth Avenue? Well, it must be the poor part. And what's going on in that park, Washington Square? All day today I watched them. People with radios the size of suitcases doing gymnastics, waiting for people to throw money at them. What is that? How can so many people be out there all day long, on a weekday no less? Doesn't anyone have a job?"

Her mother: "You shouldn't let the maid call you by your first name. I never did that. You have to keep people in their place. How can you take a month off work every summer? I would think you'd lose your job. Well, I realize you work for yourself, but no one takes August off unless they retire. I don't know why you always have to do things exactly the opposite of how everyone else does them."

She thought of her new patient Jody Goodman, who'd just flown out to Los Angeles with her mother, a woman who sounded perfectly wonderful, like a friend. Claire had never talked to anyone about the idea of adoption as replacement. She'd had adopted clients before, but somehow the concept of replacing a lost child had never come up. Maybe that was the best way to do it, mother a stranger. It worked for Claire—a hundred dollars an hour, sometimes a little more, sometimes a little less. It was a living.

At two in the morning, Claire stood at the kitchen counter, waiting for water to boil, going over notes for a lecture she was supposed to give next week on anxiety attacks and their attachment to loss.

It was Claire's opinion that anxiety attacks were like allergic reactions. They symbolized the body's insistence on preserving life and occurred in response to direct-conscious or indirect-unconscious experiences. Situations exposing the patient to death and/or loss—the primal-infantile equivalent of separation—resulted in the patient facing extinction, the feared death of the self, and caused an overwhelming flood of response, a chemical pinball racing through the body, bouncing off nerve receptors, the repetitious, ricocheting ding-dinging driving the score higher and higher. Pulse rises, palms sweat, pupils become hypersensitive to light, breathing becomes shallow and rapid. These signals attract the victim's attention, alerting him or, more likely, her to the state of the body and mind.

The primal fear of being abandoned was the trigger. Claire imagined apes in the jungle separated from their group having anxiety attacks and becoming ferocious. Unarticulated anxiety existed in everything, Claire wrote; and unfortunately, because it is not in keeping with our conception of what is normal, we are not trained to express our anxious urges. She figured that people were supposed to live in groups and were not programmed for extreme independent behavior. She thought back to an internship she had at Hopkins, when she was finally getting her B.S. She worked in a clinic, interviewing potential candidates for surgical sex reassignment. Often the men who had sex-change surgery became depressed and suicidal. Years after Claire left for New York, Hopkins stopped performing the surgery. All along, Claire had suspected that the depression was the result of severe anxiety stemming from a decision to reject the tribe of birth. And although many of the men saw their surgery as a welcoming of the true self, their core self could not be separated from its historical past, ultimately resulting in a rejection of the self. And so on . . . Claire stood at the kitchen counter writing for two and a half hours in the middle of the night, drinking cup after cup of instant coffee, thinking each one was the last.

At six Adam climbed into their bed and wedged himself between Claire and Sam. Claire refused to let on that she was awake. It was Sam's turn; that's what marriage and family life were supposed to be about, alternating, taking turns. Finally Sam got up, turned on the television, and went back to sleep, leaving Adam at the foot of their bed in a cartoon trance.

At seven Claire woke Jake and made the kids breakfast. By the time she got to her office she was exhausted. Her ten o'clock buzzed at nine-fifty-three. Claire heard her patient crying in the waiting room, but waited the full seven minutes before opening the door, hoping the girl would stop.

"Come in," Claire said, smiling.

Polly gathered up her purse, her own personal box of Kleenex, and her jacket. "I'm pregnant," she said before she even sat down. "I can't believe he did this to me."

"Are you sure?" Claire asked. It was her job to always remain calm. It was what was expected of her. The girl could get angry and scream right into Claire's face, but that was part of the job as well, acting like a giant sponge. The trick was not to let it really soak in.

"Positive," Polly said. "He came over Monday night and got the rest of his stuff and yesterday I realized I've been feeling kind of strange, so I bought one of those kits and it was positive, so I went back and bought a different kind and it was positive, and then I went to the doctor and he said definitely."

"What are you thinking of doing?"

Polly glared at her. "Obviously, I can't rely on Phil."

Claire was listening more to the subtext of what Polly was saying rather than focusing on the actual words.

"I can't rely on Phil," she said. (Or you, she meant.) "I'll have to deal with it on my own." (I don't need your help anyway.)

"I'll just go and take care of it. I'll get rid of it." (And myself too.)

"It's like poison in my body. I just want to scream." (Fear and truth.)

"I want to scream." (What would you do if I started screaming? If I sat here and howled? You'd do something, wouldn't you? You'd kick me out, I know it.)

"The doctor gave me the number of a place to call."

"How will you feel if you don't have this baby?" Claire asked.

"It's not a baby. It's nothing." Polly paused. (I can't deal with it, therefore I deny it.) "Are you telling me I shouldn't have an abortion?"

Claire imagined telling Polly the truth according to Claire. It never ends. It's a recurring nightmare where the baby you killed comes back and does all kinds of things to you. There's the constant remembering; the possibility of not being able to get pregnant later. Guilt. You didn't know that when you gave it up once, you gave it up forever. What if she had a baby later and there was something horribly wrong with it? What if it died? It might not be a baby now, but what about later?

"Sometimes," Claire finally said, "it's not as simple as getting it over with. People have feelings they may not recognize until later. There can be aftereffects, emotional and otherwise."

"You're scaring me," the girl said.

Claire looked at Polly and remembered when she'd first come in. There were patients Claire looked forward to seeing and others that seemed less important; Polly fell into the second group—the unloved. It wasn't that Claire hated her; but there were others she enjoyed far more. Claire thought she worked hardest with the ones she liked least and was probably less effective with clients she liked because she was too much like a friend, too easy.

"It's not my intention to frighten you."

"I cannot have this baby. I don't want a baby!" Polly screamed. "Change the subject."

"You're very angry." Part of Claire's job was to point out the obvious.

"That's right. I'm pissed off. You're making me feel like I'm doing something wrong, like I'm screwing up my whole life."

"How am I making you feel like you're doing something wrong?"

"You're asking a million questions. I don't know what to say to make you happy."

"You don't have to make me happy. You have to decide what you want."

"Do I look like I'm in a position to become someone's mother?"

"Is there someone who could go to the clinic with you?"

"You know I don't have any friends anymore. Phil made me get rid of them. We already talked about that."

"What about a relative? Don't you have a cousin in town?"

"I just told you, I don't want anyone to know." Polly started crying again. "I can't believe this is happening to me. A month ago I was talking about getting married—now I'm sitting here, I don't even have a boyfriend, and I'm pregnant."

Watching someone cry was one of Claire's least favorite moments. She often had the urge to comfort her patients—to squeeze their shoulders, pat them on the back, whatever was necessary—but she knew they had to cry alone. Giving the patient an opportunity to let go was more important than immediate pain relief, so she taught herself to sit like stone when the tears came. Sometimes she handed the patient a tissue, and it came across as a gesture of concern. With certain patients—like Polly—who cried all the time, Claire got frustrated, although she tried not to let on. They came into the office and the first thing they did was burst into tears, every session, for months on end, years. What did they get out of it—release? An excuse not to talk about something? As far as Claire was concerned, the prognosis for a constant crier was not good.

"Would it be helpful if I went with you?" Claire asked, once Polly stopped sniffling. She'd said it before she realized what she was saying. This was the part of Claire that her patients thought made her a great therapist: she was a real person. This was also the part of Claire that was dangerous. As much as she tried to act like Mount Rushmore, they could always see the living flesh in the background.

Polly looked surprised.

"If you need me to go with you, I will." Claire had done something like this only once before. She'd taken a completely petrified woman to the dentist and sat in the waiting room while the woman had her teeth cleaned and two fillings done.

How can I do this? Claire asked herself while Polly was talking. How can I not? Together they called the clinic, made a time, a date, and a plan.

Claire's next patient, Bea, was a fifty-five-year-old woman without a life. Unhappily married to someone who was perfectly nice, she'd raised two children, one married, the other at Brown. And now, with no orthodontist appointments, piano lessons, or family dinners to prepare, Bea had nothing to do. She felt as if she were dying. She'd been referred to Claire after spending three weeks in Payne Whitney being treated for depression. The psychiatrists had recommended antidepressants and reeducation via Claire, with the idea being that if Bea developed some interests of her own, her boring marriage would no longer be the focus of her life.

"My classes at Marymount started last night. Herbert was annoyed that I got home late, but I think I enjoyed myself. I'm not really sure. I haven't been to school in more than thirty years."

"Did you talk to anyone?" Claire asked.

Bea shook her head.

"Next time, you should try. Ask one of the other women to have coffee with you afterwards and you can talk about the class."

"Herbert wouldn't be happy."

"It's all right," Claire said. "Tell him ahead of time that you'll be out late. A new show opened at the Guggenheim; maybe you could take a walk over there."

"I still don't like going places by myself."

"It takes practice, but it's near your apartment and should be something you can manage. Have you made any arrangements about doing volunteer work?"

"I decided I don't want to be around sick people."

"Plenty of places use volunteers—Lincoln Center, the Metropolitan Museum, the Whitney."

"I don't want to make a commitment. What if Herbert wants to go away for a few days?"

"Then you tell them you'll be away. You're doing them a favor. It's not a problem if you have to leave."

Bea's life was not in crisis, it never was. Twenty years of absolute passivity had claimed this woman, and Claire was trying to wake her, gently. There were times when Claire felt she was expected to be the leader of all women. She was the one who had to nourish them with hidden supplies, goods brought in from the other side, behind enemy lines. She had to give them what they never got. She had to make them strong and teach them to kill.

It was almost noon when Bea left. They'd gone a few minutes over, planning Bea's activities for the next few days. Claire checked her book and realized that she had a parent/teacher conference at Jake's school that was supposed to start at eleven-forty-five. She threw her book into her bag and, not waiting for the elevator, ran down the steps and race-walked east across Houston to Lafayette.

The Lang School was the hippest school downtown. Its students were the sons and daughters of gallery owners, actors, name-brand heirs, and rock stars. The twin daughters of Jake's heavy-metal hero were in his class; every afternoon a cocaine-white limo carried them the seven blocks home to their soundproofed triplex apartment around the corner from Tower Records. Jake swore he was in love.

Claire gave the guard at the front door her name, flashed her Parents of Lang photo ID card, and hurried toward the sixth-grade classroom. The hallways were lined with floor-to-ceiling bulletin boards, plastered with thumbtacks and art that looked exactly like the stuff Claire used to see when she worked with inpatients at Bellevue.

"It really is very nice. You should go sometime," Sam was saying when Claire burst into the room, panting.

She squeezed herself into a kid-sized desk and tried to catch her breath. "I'm sorry," she said, "I was with someone. It couldn't be helped."

"Il Cantinori," Sam said. "Tenth, between University and Broadway." He picked up Claire's hand and squeezed it. "It's our favorite."

"I'll go this weekend."

Get a grant first, Claire thought, wondering why Sam had talked the teacher into trying a restaurant she obviously couldn't afford.

"Sally's getting married," he explained.

Sally was the teacher. According to Lang educational philosophy, students called everyone from the principal to the janitor by his or her first name. This was to inspire self-confidence. Claire could never remember Sally's last name, and it drove her crazy.

"Congratulations," Claire said.

It was recess. Claire could hear two hundred and fifty kids screaming as they ran up and down the barricaded street outside.

"About Jake . . ." Sally said.

Claire could feel the other shoe about to fall. Her stomach sank. She leaned forward, subtly tilting her head down, trying to keep from fainting.

"I get the feeling he needs more structure at home," Sally said. "He needs a clearer idea of what's expected of him and how he can achieve those goals."

Sam and Claire nodded vigorously. If Jake were bumped out of this school, they'd have big problems. It would be hard, if not impossible, to get him into another good school; even if they did, one of them would have to drag him uptown every morning and someone would have to pick him up every afternoon. And if he didn't get in, he'd end up in public school—something to be avoided at all costs.

"What do you suggest?" Sam asked.

"Are his afternoons planned? Does he have any specific activities?"

There was no way to present Frecia as a strong, stimulating role model, or to explain that her job was simply to keep the children alive until Claire or Sam got home. Structure and planned activities were out of the question.

"What I'm thinking of," Sally said, "is an after-school program. Sports and music—nothing specifically academic." She paused. "Jake could stand to run around a little. He's at that age. And he's not doing nearly as well as he should be or as we'd hoped."

She didn't continue. Claire knew "that age" was one where boys were either frenzied or like bumps on a log. Jake was a bump. Perhaps the damage was reversible.

"We do have a program here. I've checked and there is space. He could start right away."

Of course they had a program. And of course the program cost an extra thirty-five hundred dollars a year—on top of the nine thousand they were already paying—and of course Sam and Claire signed him up. Claire imagined that if they said no, the next time Sally would skip the friendly little chat and call the Department of Social Services. She's a shrink, he's a lawyer, and their kid's a little shit. The father's kind of cute, so obviously it's all her fault. Arrest her.

Claire and Sam went out the door arm in arm, smiling, whispering. As soon as they were on the sidewalk, Claire pulled away. "What a little bitch," she said. "It's hush money. Give us thirty-five hundred and we'll keep him."

"It might be good for him."

"That's not what I'm talking about."

Sam shrugged. "You want an ice cream?"

Claire didn't answer. They walked five blocks and couldn't find a place that made sundaes. Ice cream was too uncool, unhealthy, drippy. They ended up at Mondadori Cafe with the high-cheekboned crowd, cappuccinos and three-berry tart.

9

Wednesday at six-thirty in the morning Jody's phone rang.

"I had a horrible nightmare," Ellen said. "Can you have breakfast with me?"

Jody grunted.

"Come on, get up, I'll take you out. I have to take a fast shower and get rid of someone. It'll be about twenty minutes. Meet me in the lobby."

Jody stood up and pulled her nightgown off over her head. "There isn't a federal law that requires you to notify me every time you sleep with a stranger."

"He's not a stranger anymore."

"You're right. Bring him to breakfast."

"I'm not sure he speaks English," Ellen said.

"So," Jody said, when they were safely awake, around the corner in the coffee shop. "What did you dream?"

"The bank went under and I had to turn sex into a profession. All my customers were men I'd known all my life—friends of the family, old teachers, the president of the bank. All day I had to fuck and fuck." Ellen spoke loudly, but no one in the coffee shop seemed to notice. "I had to do all these strange things exactly the way they wanted or I wouldn't get paid. In the end, I stole a gun from this cop I'm blowing and shot myself in the crotch."

"It's been done before," Jody said, breaking an egg yolk with a corner of toast, mopping up the yellow.

"What do you mean, 'done before'?"

"Shot in the crotch. I can't remember the name—a French film with Gérard Depardieu, and that old Frenchwoman, maybe Jeanne Moreau.

In the end she puts the gun inside her and pulls the trigger, makes a huge mess, and takes a long time for her to die. Very symbolic. Almost heavy-handed."

"You're telling me my life's been *done* before? My nightmare?"

"Everything." Jody flagged the waiter for more coffee. "Can I ask you an intensely personal question?"

Ellen nodded.

"Do you always wear sunglasses indoors at seven a.m., or is it something you want to talk about?"

"I have a boo-boo."

"What, like the stranger's fist met your face?"

"Unfortunately, more embarrassing." Ellen took off the glasses for a second, flashing a semicircular black-and-blue mark at Jody.

"I'm listening."

"We were, shall I say, engaged, and I kind of reared up and came down hard on the edge of the headboard."

"That metal thing?"

Ellen nodded. "Completely knocked me out, only I don't think he noticed. When I came to we were still doing it."

"Well, you must not have been out very long."

"If I go to work like this, they'll think someone did it."

"Someone did. So say you were in a cab accident, they smashed into a truck, your face was slammed against the Plexiglas. Happens all the time."

Ellen laid her hand out on the table. On her right hand, fourth finger, was a shiny diamond ring. "Rob gave me this yesterday. What do you think?"

"He gave you an engagement ring and you brought a stranger home?"

"He didn't exactly say it was an engagement ring. He should know better than to try and marry me."

"You're nuts."

"You're just jealous. Here, try it on." Ellen took off the ring and tried to slip it onto Jody's finger. "With this ring, I thee wed."

Jody pulled her hand away. "You need professional help."

Ellen shook her head. "Every time I go to a shrink all they want to do is fuck me."

"Go to a woman."

"What makes you think she wouldn't want to fuck me?"

"Ellen, I know this will be hard for you to accept, but not everyone wants to sleep with you, and that's all right. It's supposed to be like that."

"I couldn't. I hate women. Disgusting. I can't imagine what I'd tell a woman."

The waiter brought the check and Ellen grabbed it. "Whoever does the most talking pays."

"Thanks," Jody said.

"You never said anything about L.A.—how was it?"

"Nice. Very nice. Sunny, warm."

"Is everyone really good-looking?"

"I didn't notice."

Ellen tapped her face. "Do you think I can cover this with makeup?"

"Take a piece of gauze, tape it over your face, and tell people how long you had to sit in the emergency room waiting to get your skull x-rayed."

"Do you think about your brother a lot?" Claire asked. Five minutes into the session, Jody was starting to space out. It was pouring rain outside. She looked past Claire and out the window. Somehow it was easier to look over Claire's shoulder than to deal with things inside.

"Would it be better if I closed the blind?" Claire asked.

"No. Sorry," Jody said.

"How would you describe your relationship to your brother?"

"My relationship? He died before I was born."

"Do you think of him as your friend? Your enemy?"

"My ghost," Jody said. "I am him, he is me."

"What does that mean?" Claire asked, eyebrows raised.

Jody shrugged. This was getting a little too close for comfort.

"Did your parents want a boy, or did they purposely adopt you because you were a girl?"

"They adopted me before I was born," Jody said, annoyed. "The deal was, whatever the baby was, it was theirs. The guy who was in on it called my parents when I was born and said, 'Your package is here and it's wrapped up in pink ribbons.' Isn't that incredibly queer? 'Your package.' What did they do, mail-order me?"

"People didn't talk about adoption very openly twenty-five years ago."

"Tell me about it," Jody said.

"Why don't you tell me," Claire said.

They were silent. Rain splattered down onto the air conditioner outside, and Jody forgot where she was for a minute, slipping back and forth in time and geography.

"The whole year I was nine," she said, "I thought I was going to die. Every day I waited. I didn't know how it would happen—if it would be a sudden, quick snapping thing or something that would creep across me for days or weeks. After that, regardless of what happened, I always felt like one of those miracle cancer patients who lives despite the odds."

"What made you think you were going to die?"

"He was nine when he died and somehow in my head I figured all children died. That was just the way it went."

"Depressing," Claire said.

"Very," Jody said.

"Did you ever have fun?"

"Yeah," Jody said, laughing. "I played funeral home with the kid who lived next door. I made her lie down flat and then I covered her face with baby powder." Jody paused. "You're looking at me funny."

"You say the most upsetting things and somehow they sound funny. I'm not sure whether you're kidding."

"The funnier it gets, the less I'm kidding," Jody said dryly. "Can we change the subject?"

"Do you find it difficult to talk about your family?"

"No, it's like eating a York Peppermint Patty, uplifting, refreshing, get the sensation."

"You're very angry."

"Annoyed, not angry. When I get angry, little flames start coming out of my ears, it's a whole different thing."

What do you want from me? Jody was tempted to ask.

"I'm curious why you're having such a hard time today," Claire said. "The trip to L.A. went well, so there should be some acknowledgment of success, but you don't seem willing to discuss that, either. Maybe you want me to know that despite your ability to succeed, there's still something you need me for."

Jody shrugged. She was nailed. She tried to play it cool.

"I'm here," Claire said. "You can tell me the most horrible thing in the world or the most wonderful thing. Either way I'm still here."

"My life, my brother, my family has made me into a very different person from the one I was born as," Jody said. "When I think about it, I have the sensation of being separated from myself. I'm not into this adoption thing, okay? I love my parents, I really do. But there's something, some strange something. Maybe it's from being adopted, maybe it's just me, but I don't get too attached to anyone. To anything. I don't want to. I'm convinced that if do, I'll get fucked over. Call it fear of rejection, whatever.

"When you're a baby you look at your mother's face and it's your face. She smiles at you and at that moment she *is* you. When you're a little older, you smile back at her and somehow the smile on your face is her smile, it's you becoming her."

Jody paused and looked at Claire, who was nodding intensely. Though she didn't usually wear makeup, Claire had lipstick on, and one side of it went up above the lip line, making her look a little demented. Jody forgot what she was thinking for a second.

"But when you're adopted, you look up at your mother and she's trying to look at you, to understand you, and in my case there was also this ghost of a child between us. What I saw was not a mirror; it was neither myself nor my mother, but something confusing and much less clear. The root it plants is a strange kind of detachment, an insecurity." Jody stopped and fixed on Claire.

"Do you still feel the insecurity?" Claire asked.

Jody sighed. She wondered if shrinks made their families stay up late at night and talk about everything in microscopic detail. So fucking obsessed, no surprise that they worked in offices by themselves. No one could stand to be around them.

"There is something, some lack of something."

"What?"

Jody flashed Claire a hard look. Even if she knew, she wouldn't tell anyone, ever.

Claire didn't react except to glance at the clock and then pick up her appointment book and start flipping through the pages. Were they out of time? Jody wondered. It was as if they'd been under water and suddenly had raced back to the surface for air.

"There's a lot to talk about," Claire said.

Jody nodded.

"Would you like to keep going?"

Jody didn't know exactly what Claire meant.

"We could have a double session," Claire said. "I'm not seeing anyone until five. What do you think?"

Jody shrugged. She still wasn't clear about what was going on. She'd never heard of anyone going overtime. Didn't Claire have better things to do? Didn't Jody have a job? A life?

"Do you want to stay?" Claire asked.

Of course Jody wanted to stay, didn't everyone? But at the same time, she'd had enough. She'd said the things she'd said knowing that within the hour Claire would throw her out. There were no major consequences. You didn't have to live with your words for more than fifty minutes. That was the beauty of therapy, you always ran out of time. You could always say something incredibly important in the last five minutes and there was nothing the shrink could do except say, We'll have to talk about that next week, or, It's so interesting how you save the very best things for last. No matter what, you left when the hour was up. That was one of the rules.

"Well?" Claire asked.

Jody shrugged.

"Are you leaving it up to me?"

She nodded.

"Then let's keep going—but first I have to go to the bathroom. I'll be right back."

Claire walked out, leaving the door open. Jody never had a shrink who went to the bathroom before. She'd always thought they were like teachers: they just didn't go.

Claire's purse was on her desk along with a huge stack of notes, a pile of yellow legal pads. Jody could have gone through everything. She could have stolen Claire's wallet and then played dumb. She could have flipped through her appointment book, making a list of the names and numbers of all her other patients. Later that night she'd be able to sit down with a bowl of popcorn and make crank calls.

Hi, I'm calling for Claire Roth. She asked me to let you know that you're so incredibly neurotic that it's driven her crazy and she had to be admitted to the hospital. Hi, this is Claire Roth's secretary. She asked me to leave you a message: get a new shrink.

The phone rang just as Claire was coming out of the bathroom. "Don't answer it," she yelled, running back into her office, picking up just as the tape clicked on. "Hello," she said, breathless.

From her side of the room, Jody could hear a woman's voice squeaking through the receiver.

"I'm with someone now," Claire said curtly. "Can I call you later?"

"So," Claire said, hanging up and sitting back down in her chair. "Tell me how your parents adopted you."

The mood had completely changed. They'd come back to the surface and now, with barely a breath of air, Claire wanted to go under again. Jody wasn't sure she could do it. If she'd been the person she wished she was, the great pillar of strength and wisdom, she would have explained that while she was grateful for the offer, she'd had enough for one day and really had to get back to work.

"Do you know the details about where you came from?" Claire asked.

"Yeah," Jody said. "The sperm bashed its head against the egg and here I am."

"How romantic," Claire said. "But did you come from an agency or an orphanage?"

"You really want to hear all this?"

Claire nodded.

"My parents told me I came from an agency."

"How old were you when they told you?"

"Just born," Jody said. "I came home from the hospital and they said, 'Hi, how are you? This is the house, this is the kitchen, this is the front hall, we'll take you to your room. Oh, and by the way, you're adopted, but don't think twice about it.'"

"Do you remember them telling you?"

"They always told me. They had this book, not something in general circulation, but like something an adoption company would sell you. A two-volume boxed set, *The Adopted Family*. One book was a picture book for the kid, and the other was the more serious stuff for the adoptive parents, things like what problems you might have, how to love the stranger's child, blah, blah, blah."

"Was finding out you were adopted traumatic? Do you wish they hadn't told you?"

"It's like learning your name. You don't remember learning it, it's just there, it belongs to you. I'm adopted. A-D-O-P-T-E-D. It's the first word I learned to spell."

Claire grimaced.

"Kidding," Jody said. Every time she said something, Claire's face flashed a reaction. At first Jody had really liked that—it was proof that a human being was sitting across from her—but sometimes she wished everything wasn't so damn interesting, didn't mean so much to Claire.

"Everything is not a natural disaster," Jody said. " 'Adopted' . . . I know the word, but what does it mean? I have no idea."

"Do you *feel* adopted? Earlier you were talking about your mother and not mirroring her."

"Yeah, but I don't know if that comes from being adopted or having a dead brother."

"How long before you were born did he die?"

"Six months."

"It is kind of close," Claire said.

"I know." Jody was tempted to tell Claire to take a tranquilizer or to point out that therapeutically speaking, all Claire's expressions might not be a good thing. If Jody were not Jody, if she were a seriously disturbed maniac, someone who couldn't take a little criticism, all Claire's heaving and hoing might throw her right over the edge. Fortunately, what Jody was saying was old hat. There were no shocking new revelations about her past. She was telling the story of her life, and the facts came easily.

"Barbara used to hound me about didn't I think it was strange that an agency would give an infant to a family whose child had just died. She kept pestering me, like maybe she knew something I didn't, but she never came out and said it. Anyway, I used to bug my mom for information, I always had the feeling that there were things nobody was telling me. I'd hit her up for a recount whenever I knew she'd be weak, like the kid's birthday or the anniversary of his death."

"How did you know when his birthday was, or when he died?"

Fucking detective, Jody thought. "My mother would say, 'Today's Blank's birthday. Today it's ten years since Blank died.' I never heard her tell anyone else, but she'd always tell me in a kind of conspiratorial whisper."

"That wasn't very fair, was it?" Claire said, then quickly added in a soft voice, "I wish you'd tell me his name."

Jody shrugged, her stomach turning in on itself; it was as if Claire was asking Jody to share her brother. Jody was aware of the betrayal, the obviousness of leaving her brother's name out, but she had to keep something for herself. Claire couldn't have everything.

"Anyway, I'd hit her for info, and then when I was about twenty, it came out that they didn't get me from some agency, but on the black market, and the lady who lived next door went to the hospital to pick me up because my mom was too chicken to meet my real mom. They traded me in the back of a cab for an envelope of money."

Jody glanced at Claire, who looked as if she were having an allergic reaction. Her nose and eyes were all red. "The thing that kills me—well, among the things that kill me—is no one will tell me how much they paid for me. I mean, I'd like to know. I asked and my mom said, 'Whatever it was, it wasn't worth it.' "

Claire looked surprised.

"She was kidding," Jody said. "The other thing that kills me is that it's still not clear to me if Barbara knew something or not, and if she did, how come she played along and didn't tell me?"

"I don't know," Claire said. "You'd have to ask Barbara."

"No one ever tells me shit."

"Do you feel like people are purposely deceiving you?"

A fucking obvious test question. Did Jody also think people were out to get her? That everyone was working together in a plot to ruin her life? She looked at Claire as if to say, Don't you think I see what you're getting at? Don't fucking condescend to me. Fuckwad.

"Is there some reason why people would keep the truth from you?" Claire asked.

Jody shrugged.

"What else do you know?"

"Why are we talking about this?" Jody asked.

"Why?" Claire said.

"Yeah, what does being adopted have to do with going to UCLA?"

"You tell me."

"No, you tell *me*."

Claire looked at the clock. "Well, neither of us can say much more today. Let's talk for a minute about your schedule. Do you work every day?"

Jody nodded.

"Are you going to keep working until you leave for California?"

"That's a big subject if we're out of time," Jody said.

"So let's talk about it more later," Claire said. "What's tomorrow like for you?"

"Fine," Jody said, wondering how the hell she'd pay for all this. All of a sudden she needed to see Claire all the time. Not once a week but every day. She had the urge to tell Claire everything, even the things she really didn't want her to know. It was as if Jody needed to unload herself, her whole self, to empty everything onto Claire and then, scrubbed clean, leave for California. And Jody also had the strangest gut feeling that Claire somehow needed her as well; she reprimanded herself for it. That was truly sick, a sure sign of major neurosis. Of course Claire didn't need her, she had a life of her own: a husband, probably kids, and a million other patients, including the one who'd just buzzed into the waiting room.

"We really have to stop," Claire said. "Is nine-thirty all right?"

"In the morning?"

Claire laughed. "Too early?"

"It's all right," Jody said. Didn't Claire know that America worked from nine to five, that structure was good for people? Nine-thirty in the goddamn morning was way too soon. Nothing was going to happen between now and then. Jody would eat dinner, watch TV, sleep, then be back here with Claire. Why was Jody throwing herself at Claire? Moreover, why was Claire letting her do it? Shouldn't Claire set some limits, say something like, I know you'd really like to see me again soon, but it's not healthy, not productive. You must learn to solve your own problems, be independent, otherwise how are you going to get to California and make a name for yourself?

The rain had stopped, and a veil of late-afternoon sun was poking through dark clouds. Somewhere—maybe in Vermont, where Claire probably had a weekend house—there was a beautiful rainbow. The air was warm from the rain. Jody crossed Houston and walked up to Washington Square, which was empty, the junkies temporarily chased out by the weather. A couple of street people pushing grocery carts were circling each other, staking out the best bench. She walked east toward Broadway, not at all sure where she was going. It was twenty past five. She'd been in the shrink's office for the whole fucking afternoon.

The phone rang at ten-thirty and Jody knew a stranger was calling. She'd already said goodnight to her mother, Michael was out of town and wouldn't have bothered to take her number, Ellen was on a date, and Harry was at an opening at the Museum of Modern Art.

"Hello," Jody said, prepared to hang up without saying another word. She held the phone in one hand and, with the other, pulled back the window shade enough so she could peek outside, as though the caller would be standing at the pay phone on the corner.

"I don't think you know me," a man's voice said.

Jody was tempted to slam the phone down, but there was something kind of nervous and pathetic about the voice. Jody let go of the shade.

"This is Peter Sears. Ann gave me your number."

Ann who? Jody wondered.

"She told me you were living in the city and suggested I call you."

Peter Sears had gone to Wesleyan along with Jody and about fifty people named Ann. His father was a famous record producer, and she'd considered trying to be friends with him, but she realized this impulse was based more on his father's success than on any qualities Peter himself might have had, so she ignored him. Plus, he was good-looking, really good-looking, so good-looking, in fact, that Jody couldn't figure why he was calling her in the first place.

"So, how is Ann?" she asked, still not sure who they were talking about.

"Fine," Peter said. "She said that since graduation you've been doing some film work."

"A little. I'm helping Harry Birenbaum on a project," Jody said, figuring that Peter would recognize Harry's name. Harry and Mr. Sears probably played whatever it was that men played together. "But in the fall I'll be going to UCLA."

"Wow, great."

Yeah, wow, great, Jody thought. Every time she said "UCLA" a wave of anxiety washed over her. At least it sounded good to other people.

"What have you been doing?" Jody asked.

"Some writing," Peter said.

He probably didn't have to work. Jody imagined Peter living a life of extreme luxury in the brownstone his father owned but never lived in for more than three days in a row. Peter probably woke up at ten a.m., watched cartoons until eleven, drank fresh-squeezed juice in bed, and finally got up around noon, giving the maid a chance to straighten up before doing the shopping.

"I have tickets to a screening of *Tin Beard* tomorrow night and was wondering if you might want to go."

"I saw it already, last week," Jody said. "It's not great."

"There's a party at the Ark afterwards—would you want to go to that?"

"All right," Jody said, as if she'd been talked into something.

"Pick you up at ten-thirty."

Jody hung up, curious how come Peter Sears had to dig up strangers from college in order to get a date. She tried to remember which Anns he'd been friends with. There were four of them—interchangeable as far as Jody was concerned—Ann Weinstein, Ann Salzman and Anns Bankowsky and Willers.

The phone rang again. It was either Peter Sears calling to say he'd come to his senses and there was no way he was going anywhere with Jody, or the guy at the phone booth on the corner had finally found her number. She peeled back the shade and looked outside again. The phone booth was empty.

"Hello," Jody snapped, turning on the answering machine even though it was after the fact.

"Is everything all right?"

Jody was silent, terrified.

"Jody, are you there? It's Claire Roth."

"Yeah, I'm here," Jody said.

"Sorry to call you at home. I was looking at my book and realized I made a mistake. I have to change our appointment time for tomorrow. Would four-forty-five be all right?"

"Yeah, sure, fine."

"Are you sure you're all right?"

"Positive," Jody said, banging her knee against the filing cabinet nervously, again and again. Tomorrow it would be black and blue and she'd look at it and wonder if it meant something, leukemia or hemophilia.

"Good. Then I'll see you tomorrow," Claire said. " 'Night."

Her voice was as soft as they pretended Kleenex was on television. It floated down over Jody and she breathed it in like a kiss.

10

Claire sat in her office, hoping Polly would cancel. When the buzzer went off, she let Polly into the waiting room and, feeling obligated to offer Polly a chance to talk herself out of it, opened the office door and asked, "Do you want to come in?"

"Could we just go?"

Claire locked the door and they stood silently in the hall, waiting for the elevator. Without the structure of the office, the two chairs, the fifty minutes, Polly didn't know what to do. Claire wasn't supposed to step out of context, much less out of the office. She was supposed to live within the walls, waiting for her patients, sitting near the phone twenty-four hours a day in case of emergency.

"Is it still raining?" Claire asked, casually, but making it clear that while this wasn't a session, it wasn't a social event, either.

"I don't know," Polly said.

Outside, Claire flagged a cab, and Polly gave the driver the address. Sitting in the backseat with Polly, Claire started thinking about what people she met at parties did when they found out she was a shrink. Men told every therapy joke they'd ever heard and eventually ran off to the bar for a refill and never returned. Women pretended to understand. They looked at Claire, smiled, and eventually they'd whisper something about their children and a problem. Claire inevitably said, "It's perfectly normal. It'll pass," and the women would seem relieved.

The reactions were always based on the person's feelings about therapy. The worst were those who had been "in" for a long time. Analysands refused to speak to her—as if Claire were responsible for all the shrinks throughout history. If Freud was wrong, it was her fault. Therefore it was mostly true that shrinks hung out with other shrinks or, more likely, didn't hang out at all.

Polly was mute, acting as if she'd regressed to a preverbal stage and was expecting Claire to take care of her. When Polly smiled at her, Claire felt she was waiting for her to do something, say something, that would indicate her willingness to be the mother.

"Do you feel all right?" Claire asked.

"Yeah. I took two Valiums this morning."

"Were you supposed to do that?" Claire asked, surprised.

Polly didn't answer.

"Make sure you tell them when we get there."

Claire could picture Polly not saying anything, and during the procedure the doctor would give her another drug that would cause a horrible reaction. They'd call an ambulance and take the comatose, brain-dead, half-aborted girl to the hospital. It would all be Claire's fault.

"I don't really need you to do this," the girl said after a while. "I can take care myself."

Claire simply nodded. They got out at the corner. Polly paid the driver and, without waiting, started off down the street towards the clinic.

"Let's stop for a second," Claire said, and Polly stopped. "Are you sure you want to do this?"

"Of course I'm sure."

"Well, I want you to know that if at any point you change your mind, it's okay. I won't feel as though you've wasted this time. It wouldn't bother me at all."

"Great," Polly said, and started walking toward the clinic again.

Inside, all of a sudden Polly got shy. She sat in the chair closest to the door and looked up at Claire, pleadingly, indicating her wish for Claire to handle everything.

"I think you're supposed to check in at the desk," Claire said calmly, and then tried not to watch as Polly fumbled with the forms, the questions, pretending not to be nervous. When she watched her, she started hating her. It wasn't productive. She focused on the nature posters taped on the walls. Someone had tried to make the clinic look like a pleasant place. Claire could picture the decorations being ripped down during an anti-abortion protest. She could see the receptionist ordering not one duck-pond poster but two or three, maybe half-dozen at a time. It was all very clean and neat. It could have been a podiatrist's office. Claire found it hard to believe anything happened there. The room offered no clues, no sounds, no signs, nothing.

She glanced at Polly. Claire hadn't heard her say anything about the two Valium.

"Did you tell them about the Valium?" Claire called across the office.

Polly turned around and flashed her an annoyed look.

"How many milligrams?" the nurse asked.

"Two blue ones," Polly said.

"Ten milligrams?"

"Yeah."

If Claire had taken two blue Valiums that morning, she'd be on the floor by now. The difference between what a body could take at twenty and at forty-three was amazing.

"Have a seat and we'll call you."

"Why did you tell them?" Polly asked.

"Because you didn't," Claire said.

Five minutes later, when the nurse stepped out from behind her desk, Claire wondered if she should talk to her, explain who she was. She felt like an undercover agent. "Polly?" the nurse said. "You can come in now."

Polly stood up.

"Your friend can come with you, if you like."

"She's not my friend," Polly said, "she's my shrink."

And she's a blabbermouth, Claire expected her to add.

"She can come with you, if you like," the nurse repeated as if she hadn't heard. Claire was the girl's shrink. Didn't that mean anything? Was it every day that a shrink brought someone in?

Polly turned around and looked at Claire, "It's okay. Just wish me luck."

"I do," Claire said.

For a second, she'd seen herself in the operating room—if that's what they called it—holding Polly's hand and seeing more of her, literally and figuratively, than she ever wanted to. She saw herself forced to watch the whole thing, the unborn sucked in bits and pieces into a glass jar.

The nurse took Polly away, and Claire was glad to be alone. Her thoughts had agitated her to the point where if she hadn't been with a patient, she would've tried to get a little Valium of her own somewhere. She took a couple of deep breaths and closed her eyes. She'd been there before. She could feel it in her shoulders, in the back of her neck. Déjà vu, sort of. It was much different then. In 1966 there were no pregnancy tests on sale at the drugstore. There were no abortion clinics listed in the yellow pages.

• • •

Eighteen and a half years old, finishing her first year at George Washington University, she was involved with Mark Ein, an English professor just out of Yale with a novel already published. Intense, with curly brown hair, sexy pursed lips, and blue eyes. He was like no one Claire had ever known. He said he avoided eye contact because he was afraid of burning holes into people, and described himself as a nonteacher. "We're in this together," he told the class. "This is an exploration, the beginning of what should become an unending process."

As part of the exploration, he took Claire out. He took her for meals she'd never eaten, to movies she'd never heard of, to hot spots where they danced to strange new music. And then she was pregnant. In 1966 that's how an eighteen-year-old knew; she figured it out. It didn't take a genius. No red tag sale, the curse that didn't come.

"I'm pregnant," Claire finally told him as they walked into an ice cream store.

Standing in line, Mark leaned over and whispered in her ear. "I should tell you something. I'm married. My wife's in graduate school at Berkeley." He ordered a mint chocolate chip cone for himself and turned to Claire, who was about to throw up. "Want anything?"

She shook her head and bit down hard, grinding her teeth together.

"You don't have to have it," he said. "I can find a place."

Claire wasn't sure what he was talking about. What kind of a place? A place where she and the baby could hide? Where he'd keep her as his extra wife?

On the warmest day of spring, Mark picked Claire up in his green MG and drove her into a part of Washington she'd never seen before: street after street of row houses, not brick townhouses like they had in Georgetown, elegant and expensive, but rundown wood and brick. Some had little front porches; some had faded striped awnings and half-rusted aluminum porch furniture. There were a few children, a few older men shuffling around, the occasional dog loping toward home. Claire felt exposed, in danger. She wondered if Mark was taking her to the nanny who'd raised him and was going to leave her there. She would live in the nanny's house, and sometimes Mark would sneak away and come visit her. By the time the nanny got old and died, the neighbors would be so used to Claire that she'd just go on living there for the rest of her life.

"Come in," a tall black woman said, holding open the screen door.

They stepped up onto her porch. "I'm Luanne," she said, leading them through the house, into the kitchen in the back. "Lie down." She pointed to the kitchen table covered with a neatly pressed white sheet. Claire lay back on the table—the same table, she supposed, they ate their dinner on every night. She didn't know what she was doing there. Mark hadn't said a word. Would he make her do something she might not want to do? Would this woman operate on her, just like that, without warning?

"Relax," Luanne said, smiling. Her smile was filled with dark tooth gaps and bright pink gums. Claire looked at her uneven grin and decided they'd come for some sort of special treatment that would make the baby dissolve and disappear. Luanne closed her kitchen door and came to Claire. She lifted Claire's shirt and put her hands on Claire's belly.

"How long?" she asked.

"Two months, maybe a little more," Claire said.

With dry, bony fingers Luanne kneaded Claire's stomach.

Mark stood in the corner gnawing his cuticles. Claire could see him out of the corner of her eye. He no longer seemed so wonderful, larger than life. He looked small, nervous, unpleasant.

"I can do it," the woman said. "You come back and I'll do it. You stay overnight. Think about it. I make no guarantee. There could always be a problem, and there'd be nothing I could do except try and get you to the hospital. I don't have a car, and it's hard to get a taxi. I'm telling you that."

Claire nodded. She finally understood what they'd been talking about all along, although she had no idea of how it would be done. Would the woman cut her belly open? Punch a hole with a knitting needle and stir things around?

"I'll think about it," Claire said, trying to be polite. There was no way she was coming back. The whole time she'd been lying on the table, all she could think about was the family eating dinner. She could see this woman taking her child, making stew out of it, and serving it up to a table full of people. Fresh, deep red, and tender.

"We'll be back," Mark said easily to the woman.

The woman nodded and smiled at him. Claire wondered if he'd been there before. She didn't ask. She didn't really want to know. For the next month she avoided Mark. The semester ended. For the first time in her life, Claire had straight A's.

"Guess you're having it," Mark said to her. They were in his office after the last class.

Until he said it, Claire had never really believed that if she did nothing, in six months she would be forced—if only by gravity and the infant's self-determination—to have a baby. She wondered how much it would hurt. Just having sex, having a man inside her, was enough. She couldn't imagine a baby coming out without killing her. She pictured herself trying to hold it in, for months, years, the rest of her life.

"Maybe you'll have a miscarriage or something," Mark said hopefully.

Claire shrugged and pretended not to be offended. She could already feel it rooted inside her, not about to give up.

"Sorry," he said simply, as if he'd accidentally stepped on her toe. "I'll walk you to the bus." They walked out into the clear May afternoon. Claire saw the bus coming down Pennsylvania Avenue and, without a word, took off running toward it and never saw Mark Ein again.

She waited until it was no longer possible not to tell her parents. She pulled her mother into her room and sat her down on the bed; but when Claire started to speak, no words came out.

"Is something wrong?" her mother asked, starting to get up. "Maybe you should suck on a lozenge." Claire pushed her back down on the bed, lifted her blouse, pushed down the elastic waistband of her skirt, and turned to the side, so her mother would see the bulge. In profile, it looked like what it was.

"Oh my lord," her mother said, covering her mouth with her hand, as if to push back a longer stream of words, the stream that turned into an overflowing river when her father found out.

Her mother ran out of the room and into the kitchen, where she made hushed phone call after hushed phone call. Then she ordered Claire into the car. She drove her to the doctor—not the family physician but a different one in downtown Washington—to make sure the protrusion wasn't something else. Claire imagined her mother wishing it was some complicated disease, something there would be no shame in dying from. Cancer would have been good.

"It's true," the doctor said, as though he too had first believed Claire was concealing a tumor under her skirt.

Her mother leaned far over the doctor's desk and whispered, so softly that later it would seem as though she'd never said it, "Is there anything that can be done about it?"

The doctor shook his head, leaned forward, and whispered back. "Too late for that."

Claire's father rented a truck and made a point of going up and down the street telling the neighbors he was taking a load of old furniture down to the "poor folks" and that if they had anything to add, he'd be glad to take it. Claire ended up alone in an apartment in Baltimore with all of Hillside Street's discarded furniture. It was depressing as hell. It was also the only time she'd been away from her family since spending two weeks at Christian Fellowship camp when she was thirteen. In 1966, maternity wear was basically huge cotton underpants and tent dresses in frightening prints, not the kind of thing that looked good on a nineteen-year-old, so Claire stayed indoors unless it was absolutely necessary to go out.

For no reason other than her determination to embrace everything and anything she was not, Claire decided that if the baby was going to be given up for adoption, it should go to a Jewish family. They'd make a better home for it. They understood sorrow, suffering, loss, what it meant to be an outsider. She thought of the holiday Mark had told her about, the one where they welcomed strangers; they would leave the door open and set a place for a mysterious prophet who'd come in and sit at their table, drink their wine.

"You're crazy," her father said. "Always have been. If the boy had been a decent Christian, you'd be married now."

Claire didn't bother telling him that Mark was already married. There was no point.

"They're like that," her father said. "Slimy sons of . . . Go ahead, give it to one of them. The further from us, the better."

It almost went wrong. A family was found, but three weeks later they backed out. The lawyer said it was because they knew, in a roundabout way, who the father was.

"Of course they knew," her father said. "What do you expect? They all know each other."

"The family wanted a child with no background at all," the lawyer said.

Claire tried to conjure a child arriving with no past, only a future.

A second family was found. Through the lawyers sanitized descriptions were exchanged. No one wanted to take chances; it was getting late. Only the most minimal information was passed along. "A lovely family. A mother, a father, a little boy. Because of complications they can't have more of their own, and yet," the lawyer said, winking, "they have a lot of love to give."

He meant money, Claire understood. She wondered how much it was costing them.

"Upper-middle-class. College-educated. Jews."

Claire was glad they weren't first-time parents. A baby wouldn't be a surprise. And it would have a big brother; Claire had always wanted a brother. When she thought of her baby, she imagined a girl named Rachel splashing in a wading pool with all her cousins and the neighbors' children. She saw her daughter going off to school in a brand-new dress, new shoes, carrying her brother's old lunch box. She pictured her sitting on a braided rug during story hour, playing with the curls of the girl in front of her, giggling. She figured there would be an extended family; grandparents coming up from Florida with sacks of oranges and grape-fruit, and stubby old fingers just right for pinching cheeks. She saw love and comfort. The child would never know she'd started off belonging to someone else.

Claire knew her daughter only as she grew inside her. She loved her by rubbing the child's kicking foot through the walls of her body.

A woman came charging into the clinic and stopped in front of Claire. "First time?" she bellowed.

"I'm waiting for someone," Claire said, startled.

"Oh," the woman said, as if she didn't believe her. "This is my third. It's nothing, really. I'm sure your daughter will be fine."

"Oh no," Claire said, shaking her head. "It's not my daughter." It came out sounding drastically different from how she meant it. The woman shrugged and didn't say anything else. Claire went up to the desk and asked the nurse how much longer it would be. The answer was hours, not minutes.

"I have to leave," Claire said. "I'll be back." She hurried out of the office, sure that if she didn't get out in less than thirty seconds, she'd lose consciousness, and masked men would haul her into the back room. They'd give her an abortion even though she didn't need one. They'd get her anyway, suck whatever they could out of her, just because.

• • •

That night, when Sam reached across the bed and pulled her toward him, Claire screamed.

"I know it's been a while," he said. "But has it really been that long?"

They started again. When it seemed certain that neither Jake nor Adam was going to stumble in, Claire reached into her night-table drawer, pulled out her old diaphragm, and filled it with jelly, thinking she probably should turn on the light and check it for holes.

"Are you off the pill?" Sam asked.

"No," Claire said, handing him the gooped-up disc.

He disappeared under the covers. She could feel him playing, pretending he didn't know what to do. He ran his mouth over her thighs, blew a stream of air inside her, teased her with his teeth, and finally the diaphragm popped into place.

"What's up?" he asked, reappearing, tickling and kissing her.

"I feel like I need to be very careful," Claire said.

It was a major regression. When Claire met Sam she was taking the pill, had an IUD, and a diaphragm in the drawer, and was also trying out this new kind of foam that was like shaving cream and gave some guys a rash. The joke among Claire's friends was that men needed special protection to keep from turning impotent around her.

"I just don't want to get pregnant. Is that asking too much?" Claire would demand. She'd stand naked at the foot of the bed ranting and raving about responsibility, starving, unwanted children in third-world countries, the war in Vietnam, anything and everything, until finally, exhausted, she'd collapse onto the water bed and allow herself to be taken.

"Do you not want to do this?" Sam asked twenty minutes later, when nothing was happening, when it still seemed like Claire was somewhere else, not even phoning it in. "I could just put on a videotape and do it myself," he said.

Claire didn't respond.

"Maybe I should take a shower." Sam moved to get out of the bed.

Claire reached down under the blanket and grabbed him by the balls. "I'll kill you," she said.

"Now we're talking."

"I've had a very long day," Claire said, squeezing Sam until he was on the verge of real pain. "Don't give me a bad time."

He pulled away and hurried out of the room, his half-hard dick leading the way. He came back with an old bottle of Jack Daniel's and something hidden behind his back. "I can do this to you or you can do it to me," he said, opening his hand, flashing the heavy-duty handcuffs Jake had brought home from school the day before with no explanation.

"Do you have the keys?"

Sam swung the little skeleton keys back and forth hypnotically. He opened the bottle and took a slug. "Who's it gonna be?"

Claire reached for the Jack Daniel's, took a long pull, another, and another, then lay back and let Sam handcuff her to the bed frame.

"Let me ask you something," Rosenblatt said, leaning forward in his chair, pressing his palms together. "Do you ever have fun?"

Claire looked confused. "I'm not sure what you mean," she said.

"It sounds like you don't have fun."

"I wasn't aware I said that."

"You didn't say it," Rosenblatt said. "But you never talk about enjoying yourself. Enjoying your family." He leaned back in his chair, his hands crossed behind his head. "What gives you pleasure?"

"My work," Claire said. "I work very hard, and it makes me feel good."

"Besides work. Tell me what you enjoy—the theater, eating out, sailing on weekends? There must be something."

Claire shrugged. He was pissing her off again. Every time he did this, she swore she wouldn't come back, and every time she made another appointment. It was humiliating to be constantly asked if she wanted another appointment; it was like being forced to get down on your knees and beg for more help. A normal therapist would suggest the next week at three, keeping the process going without constantly addressing the issue of needing help. Rosenblatt, she knew, did it to feed his ego.

"Why are you here?" he asked.

"You know why I'm here."

"Tell me again."

Claire was glad she didn't have to sleep with him. Fucking this guy would be hell. He'd do his thing, come, and then fall off snoring before his dick was even dry.

"I'm having a hard time with my children," Claire said.

"Could it be because you don't have any fun? You don't play?"

Now Claire was getting really angry.

"Do you ever laugh?" Rosenblatt asked.

"Of course," she said.

"When?"

"Whenever I see a new Woody Allen movie," Claire said.

"You're very defensive," Rosenblatt said. "I could tell you to relax more, to try and enjoy yourself. But the real issue is *why* you don't have fun. I suspect that you simply won't allow yourself. That's why you like your work so much. I know what you do for a living. It's constant torture."

"Then why don't you stop?" Claire said, shifting in her chair.

"Why don't *you* stop?" Rosenblatt asked. "Because you have to punish yourself. Because everything has to be taken so seriously. Because it would be wrong for you to enjoy anything."

Claire shrugged. So Rosenblatt was right, big deal. So what? Most people didn't have fun. She didn't need to have fun. She liked being miserable. That was her fun.

"I'm right," Rosenblatt said.

"Perhaps."

"The question is, What horrible thing did you do? What made you so guilty that you're not allowed to have any pleasure? What crime did you commit?"

Claire didn't answer.

"We're out of time. Would you like to come back again next week?"

"I'm afraid I'm pretty much tied up for the next few weeks," Claire said.

"You're afraid, that's right. How about on the twentieth?" Rosenblatt asked. And then, before Claire had a chance to answer, he added, "I was thinking it might be useful for you to bring your son in with you. I'd like to meet him. No big deal. One session."

Claire didn't say anything. As much as the problem was Jake, she didn't want to involve him in all this stuff, not yet.

"It would be helpful," Rosenblatt said.

"I'll think about it."

"I have some Saturday hours. Why don't we make an appointment for then. That way, he won't miss school and you won't be working."

Claire scribbled the time and date into her little black book and stood to leave.

"A homework assignment," Rosenblatt said. "Before you come in again, do something fun."

11

*T*he session wasn't going well. That happened sometimes. Jody wondered if there was a way to mathematically compute how often it went sour and why. Did men or women have more bad sessions? What were the demographics?

She was definitely coming down with something. When she swallowed, it felt like razor blades were shredding her throat—not a sensation that inspired her to be particularly chatty.

"You look tired," Claire said.

Jody nodded. She'd been up half the night deciding to tell Michael that she'd only work part-time from now until she left for California. That way it would be easier to spend time with Claire. But there was something dangerous in her thinking, something that worried her. She remembered in eighth-grade gym class, during sex education, the teacher stood in front of them and talked about masturbation. "It's not danger-ous," she said. "It's not a bad thing, unless you start avoiding social activities in order to do it." In other words, playing with yourself was a mini-perversion, a bad habit that, like having a drink before dinner, was basically all right as long as you kept it in check.

"Do you want to talk a little bit about your plans?"

"Not today," Jody said. "I have a sore throat."

She couldn't believe she'd said that. Claire would think she was a hy-pochondriac. Oh, so you're worried about going to L.A.? Well, have a sore throat, and if that's not enough to stop you, what about chest pains or shortness of breath? Hey, I even have a little dizziness left from the last nut case, you want it?

"Do you have a fever?" Claire got up out of her chair and pressed her palm to Jody's forehead. Jody tensed. Shrinks were not supposed to walk across the room and take their patients' temperatures; they weren't even supposed to believe in physical illness. According to almost any self-respecting shrinky-dink, even cancer was something you willed upon yourself.

"You look flushed," Claire said, moving her hand from Jody's forehead to her cheek.

Jody hated it when people touched her. She hated it when near-strangers kissed her goodbye or hello, when her friends insisted she hug them. Everyone read her discomfort as a marker of immaturity, but in fact it was something more—a refusal to partake in false intimacy. She wished Claire would just keep her hands off her.

But Claire stood there for a minute or more with her hand on Jody's face, looking worried.

"It's fine," Jody finally said.

"I think you're coming down with something. Do you have a headache?" Claire went to her desk, rummaged around, and found some aspirin. "Here, I want you to take these," she said, going out of the office into the bathroom and returning with a tiny cup of water. "Go on," she said, and Jody was obligated to swallow the pills even though she really wanted to say "no thanks" and hand them back.

"Finish the water," Claire said.

Jody swallowed the rest. "Do you believe in illness?" she asked.

"Do I believe in illness?" Claire asked. It was a standard shrink technique to repeat a question. Penny for your thoughts. Question for a question.

"Do you think people actually get sick as opposed to wanting to get sick or getting sick to avoid something?"

"Of course people get sick," Claire said. "In fact, most people don't admit they're sick. Everyone used to say things were psychological in origin; but now, especially here in the city, between TB, AIDS, cancer, and who knows what, it's pretty clear that we're not all that crazy and repressed. There's a lot of denial."

"I was sick when I was a little kid," Jody said. This was something she'd never discussed with anyone.

"What was wrong with you?" Claire asked.

Jody tapped the side of her head, "My ears," she said. "I had surgery, even x-ray treatments. Any moment now I could get a brain tumor from all the radiation." Jody smiled. "My earliest memories are medical."

"What was the problem?"

"Don't exactly know," Jody said. "According to my mother, I was losing my hearing and they decided to shrink the tissues by x-raying them. See my teeth?" Jody rolled back her lip and flashed a row of gray teeth. "They didn't know that if they give you tetracycline before your permanent teeth come in, they show up gray like this." She flashed her teeth again. "It probably wouldn't have been so bad if there hadn't been another kid before me. According to Barbara, my parents got me to make them feel better after the kid died, and then I got sick and they freaked. It was too much. Nine years with one sick kid and then the new one turns out defective too."

"Do you remember them being upset?"

"Not exactly. I remember other things; being taken to the hospital, lying on a metal table, a huge x-ray machine hanging over me. Through a little window in the door, I could see my parents' faces on the other side. And all anyone said to me was, 'Whatever you do, don't move.' "

"What else?" Claire said.

"My grandparents visited, brought me a tiny stuffed dog I still have. Then my mom drove me home in our new car, and right when we pulled into the driveway, I threw up. My mother took me inside, gave me some apple juice, and then went back out to clean the car. I felt really guilty."

"How old were you?"

"Three."

"And you remember all that?"

"More," Jody said.

"Go on."

"Isn't that enough?"

"It sounds incredibly frightening."

"I wasn't scared. When I think about it, I have the sensation of being frustrated, of people not listening. One time I had surgery on my ears, and my mother came into the operating room with me and held my feet while they gave me the gas. I was crying and saying I didn't want it, because I remembered how bad it smelled and tasted from the last time, and all these guys were standing around with green masks on, and the ear doctor said, 'It's a new flavor, you'll like it.' And so I breathed the stuff and it was the same as always, and I was really, really mad, but there was nothing I could do. I passed out hating everybody."

"Who were these people?" Claire asked, incredulous.

"My mother, the doctors. That's how they did it then. They figured you could lie to a kid because kids don't remember. Later I told my mother and she said no, that wasn't true, it wasn't like that. But it was. I'm not an idiot."

"Are you angry now?"

Jody shrugged. "My teeth are puke gray; I could have a brain tumor at any moment. I'm not exactly pleased. I'd rather die than go to a doctor, but no, I'm not angry."

"Why didn't your parents protect you?"

Jody made a face at Claire. "They were right there, believing whatever the idiot doctors said because they didn't know who else to believe. All they wanted was a healthy baby. They would've done anything if they thought it would make me better, bring back the other kid, or both."

"If I were you I'd be furious."

You're not me, Jody thought, and how come you're saying that? You're never supposed to say how you'd react. This isn't about you, this is about me. "What's the point of being angry?" Jody said.

They sat in silence for a few minutes.

"It's sad," Claire said.

"Do I seem incredibly affected?" Then Jody quickly said, "Don't answer. I don't want to know."

"I wonder about your parents."

"Don't," Jody said.

"Don't you think not only about the parents who adopted you but also the ones that gave you up?"

"The ones that gave me up weren't parents. They were two people who probably didn't know each other very well."

Jody spent the last quarter of the session in silence. She'd always questioned whether getting sick as a child was a kind of failure to thrive. Was it from the stress of being without her natural mother, the anxiety of having the ghost of a dead kid hanging over her? Or was it completely unrelated, a genetic glitch, an unaffiliated infection? Still, even now, there was a weakness in her, and she could feel it lying dormant, waiting.

• • •

Night shooting. It sounded romantic—falling stars, midnight riverboat cruises. The idea of staying awake while the rest of the world slept was filled with possibilities. The crew started arriving between four and five in the afternoon at the edge of Central Park. They set up lights, dolly tracks, miles of electric cable, and the ever-present food table. According to union rules every location was required to have one ton of food, half hot, half cold, delivered at specifically timed intervals for the sustenance of cast and crew. The day before, the table had been heaped high with Twinkies, Hostess cupcakes, and fruit pies. "Someone's birthday?" the cinematographer asked.

"Mine," Harry said, popping a whole Twinkie into his mouth. With white filling squirting out of the corners of his thick lips, he turned to Jody. "Do you taste better than this?"

She stood there, dumbfounded.

Harry offered her the second Twinkie. "Want some?"

She shook her head, locking her jaw shut.

"It's plump enough," Harry had said, "but don't you think it should be a little bigger?" He took a bite and threw the rest into the trash.

As the sky dropped down into darkness, Jody felt the rhythm of the city playing itself out around her; she also felt her throat hurting more and more. Early on, the passersby were people coming home from work. They stopped at the barricades for a few minutes but quickly grew tired of shifting from one aching foot to another. Kids on their way to nowhere hung out forever, always asking which movie this was. Guys who'd once done something on some other film stopped and wanted to know who was directing, who was on crew, and whether the production was hiring extra help. Later on, the after-dinner crowd, the theater crowd, the club crowd, ten thousand maniacs, prostitutes, two-bit muggers, and looney-toons paraded back and forth past the blue barricades marked POLICE LINE DO NOT CROSS.

The shot they were going for was a chase that ended at the fountain with the Plaza looming in the background. Carol Heberton was going to fire five shots into a bad guy, who'd spring a thousand leaks, fall backwards into the fountain, and turn the clear water pink. The fountain was so well lit that it was positively glowing. Carriages passed in front of it, and special assistants hired for the evening followed behind the horses with brooms and large dustpans. On film this would all look incredibly romantic. The best of New York suddenly intruded upon by the worst—compare and contrast, seduce and shock.

Even though it was summer, the night got chilly. Jody sipped endless cups of tea, and when Harry pulled her toward him some time after midnight, she let him hold her under his armpit. His body was warm, almost hot. Under the lights Harry looked sort of cute. His thin, silvery hair was slicked back, his bifocals resting on top of his head, his linen suit wrinkled, his custom-made shirt unbuttoned, his gray chest hair poking out. The rumpled look wore well after dark. Jody watched Harry deftly leading the actors and technicians through the scene, making changes on the spot. Strange things could happen in the middle of the night. But as soon as the sun crossed the horizon and the sour smell of the warming city wafted up from the sidewalks, everything good disappeared as quickly as a dream.

At six-thirty in the morning, when they couldn't hold the location anymore, when the cinematographer was so bleary-eyed he could barely guarantee focus, they called it quits.

"Share a cab with me," Carol Heberton said, not willing to wait for her car and driver. Jody was trying to flag down anything that moved.

"Two stops," she told the driver, sliding into the cab after the actress.

"The Carlyle," Heberton said. She was the old-fashioned kind of movie star—elegant, graceful, otherworldly—the Carlyle made perfect sense. Jody couldn't picture her with Harry at the Royalton—so hip that inside, instead of a front desk, there was just a telephone you had to pick up in order to find out anything, including your own room number.

Carol Heberton turned to her. "Who are you and what do you do?"

"I work for Michael Miller."

"Aah, you're the one."

The one *what?* Jody wanted to ask.

"Don't mind Harry. He's impressed by women who say no—it fascinates him." Heberton looked at Jody carefully. "You remind me of myself when I was young, but at my age I guess everyone does." Heberton took a long, sad movie-star breath. Jody noticed the driver staring into the rearview mirror.

"This movie gives me nightmares," Heberton said. "It's so frightening. I've never played a working-class person before. Maybe I should have my face done again. What do you think?" Again she looked at Jody. She put her bony-beyond-belief hand on Jody's knee and squeezed it hard. "I've been approached to do a commercial. Laundry detergent. I haven't done my own laundry since I was nineteen."

The cab pulled up in front of the Carlyle and a uniformed doorman hurried over. Heberton fumbled through her jacket pocket for money.

"I've got it," Jody said.

"You're a pal. Would you like to come in for breakfast?" And before Jody could answer, Heberton climbed out. "No, I guess not. You're young, you have a life." The doorman took her by the elbow and led her toward the hotel.

"Where to?" the driver asked.

Jody checked her pockets. All she had was a ten and some tokens. Two paychecks were waiting at the office, but she'd been too busy to put in a personal appearance. "Broadway and Forty-fourth," she said.

When she arrived, she flicked on the fluorescents, stuffed the checks into her back pocket, and sat at Michael's desk, looking out over New York. Then she picked up Michael's Lego phone and dialed home.

"Hi, Ma, it's me."

"Is something wrong?" her mother asked. "It's seven-forty-five in the morning."

"I know. I just had a minute and thought I'd say hi."

"I called you last night, you weren't home."

"We worked all night. I'm at the office now."

"You were out on the streets all night? I don't like that. That's not a good idea."

"It's fine. There were plenty of people around. I rode home with Carol Heberton."

"Oh, I like her. She used to make such nice films."

Jody heard the office door opening. "Hello?" a man's voice called. "Who's in here?"

"Got to go," Jody said. "Talk to you later."

"Call me tonight," her mother said.

Jody hung up and stepped out into the hall. Raymond—one of Michael's protégés—was standing there, brandishing a thick wooden coat hanger.

"It's all I could find," he said sheepishly, throwing the hanger into a closet. "Why are you here so early? You look terrible. Did something happen?"

Jody realized she hadn't seen herself in twenty-four hours, hadn't brushed her hair or washed her face or changed her clothing. She probably smelled. And now her ear was hurting too.

"Night shoot," Jody said, her voice cracking, the sore throat finally breaking into something real.

Raymond nodded.

"I rode back with Carol Heberton."

He nodded again. "Be careful," he said.

"Why?"

"She competes with Harry for all the sweet young things."

"Really?" Jody asked.

" 'Really?' " Raymond said, mocking her. "*Please.* Let's try and live in the real world, shall we?"

12

*T*he first time Claire thought Jody might be her daughter, she threw up. She had the thought and instantly her stomach rose to her throat and she ran for the bathroom.

"Are you all right?" Sam asked. "Do you need help?"

"No," Claire said, grateful to be alone. She sat on the edge of the tub, afraid to move.

Jody reminded her of herself, but that didn't necessarily mean they were related. They'd both grown up in and around Washington, which could explain certain sensibilities and ways of speaking. The resemblance was cultural, Claire told herself, not familial. Clearly, her own upbringing had been radically different from Jody's. The similarity was their shared determination to overcome a family, an accident, to somehow make a life even though the essential ingredients seemed to be missing. The problem Jody posed was a countertransference complicated by the mutual adoption experience and Claire's temptation to mother. It was not to be taken literally.

A couple of weeks later, after Jody had mentioned her curiosity about her biological father, Claire dreamt about Mark Ein. They were back in college, at the English department, Mark sitting at his desk and Claire, too frightened to sit, standing at the door. She was very pregnant.

"I want you to give me the child," Mark said. "You're completely incompetent. Give her to me and when she's grown I'll have her call you."

He looked the same as when Claire had first met him: intense, his hair and clothing thrown off balance by his energy. Seeing him again after twenty-four years, she found the familiarity of his features comforting, until she placed Jody beside him. They were identical; the same clear eyes, wavy hair, sweet lips, the same urgent nature that compelled Claire to offer herself up as if she could save them. And in the dream, when Jody appeared next to Mark, Claire could swear that his face changed to accommodate her, to become her. Hysterical, Claire began flailing at Mark, and Jody disappeared. Claire hit him again and again as hard as she could on his chest, his head, his face. His nose started to bleed but he did nothing, offered no resistance. Blood dripped down onto the desk. Finally, still screaming, still waving her fists, she ran out into the hall. Her mother and father were there, waiting to take her away.

The bedroom was dark. Next to her Sam snored steadily. Using the top sheet, she wiped sweat from her neck and chest. She curled against Sam and tried to put together what she remembered. Bits and pieces, fragments, not enough. It was never enough. She wanted to make sure Jody wasn't her daughter; simultaneously, she wanted Jody to be her daughter. Sam shifted in his sleep, rolling away from her, and Claire got up to make herself a cup of tea.

In the kitchen at three in the morning, she decided that Barbara knew Jody was her child. Barbara had conducted a search when Jody was her patient. She'd done it because she was curious, and because she had to stay home half-days, pregnant with her complicated first child. She had time on her hands and, on the verge of motherhood herself, was obsessed by the psychological and genetic nature of things. She did it because she thought it would help her help Jody. All the people who'd held back on Jody, who'd refused to give her information, offered it freely and willingly to Barbara. After all, she was a professional. She knew best. And ultimately, giving away the goods relieved the guilt associated with having kept a secret for so long—a secret that didn't belong to them in the first place. First thing in the morning, Claire would call Barbara. She watched her tea whirling around in the microwave. She looked out the kitchen window at the dark building across the way.

She wouldn't call Barbara in the morning, or ever. If she was wrong, if she was making this whole thing up, Barbara would think she'd gone over the edge. Not quite sure what to do, she'd call Sam at the office. Together they'd decide that Barbara should call Jody and tell her to get out while there was still time. She'd refer Jody to someone else. If Barbara found out, she'd take Jody away. She'd ruin everything.

J-O-D-Y. Claire wrote her name across a legal pad in the good script she used for important letters to her children's teachers, to patients who'd moved many miles away, to sign Chanukah and Easter cards. J-O-D-Y R-O-T-H. J-O-D-Y S-T-E-V-E-N-S—Claire's maiden name. J-O-D-Y E-I-N. What the hell *was* her name? Jody Goodman. She wrote it over and over a million times, in every possible combination.

"I'm so bored," Naomi said when she called Claire at seven-thirty. "You're sleeping? I've been up since six. I can't take it anymore. Can we do something today—just for us? Go to Soho for lunch, walk around, spend money?"

"Patients all day," Claire said. "Maybe next week I can juggle the schedule."

"So busy," Naomi said. "Are you sure you're not having an affair?"

"Just busy," she said.

Claire wished she could talk to Naomi about Jody. She wanted someone to know, but the one time she had tried to tell her, it hadn't gone over well. "You act like you're in love," Naomi said. "The way you talk about her, you get all jazzed up." Claire shrugged and said, "Well, she's interesting," and then dropped the subject permanently.

At nine-forty-five Claire buzzed Polly in. In the taxi as they left the clinic, Polly had told Claire she was going home for a while and wouldn't make the next few appointments. Claire wasn't sure she believed her. Maybe mixing Claire with the abortion experience had been too much. Maybe just the sight of a shrink out of context made the world too confusing; maybe that's why shrinks saw people in offices. But it had seemed like the right thing to do.

"How're you feeling?" Claire asked.

For once Polly wasn't crying. She wasn't carrying her own personal box of Kleenex. Some days she'd start up in the waiting room. Now there was nothing on her face except a vaguely blank look. Worried, Claire half-wished for tears and considered what their absence meant. Resignation, strange surrender, or perhaps even progress? "Was it good to go home for a while?" Claire asked.

Polly didn't answer, and they sat quietly for a few minutes. Claire decided that calling attention to the crying or lack thereof would be too aggressive. Sometimes you had to let things play out. If she mentioned noticing a difference, the temptation to regress would get stronger.

"Is there something special you'd like to talk about?"

Polly didn't speak. They sat in silence for the full session, something Claire found difficult but had trained herself to do. The real trick was figuring out what she should do with herself. She'd learned to relax in her chair, to look comfortable and communicative while daydreaming behind an expression of sincerity.

At the end of the hour, Claire said softly, "Should we make an appointment for next week?"

Polly nodded. At least she didn't say "No," or "I'll be dead by next week." Claire hated it when patients did that, especially at the end of the session. She'd have five minutes or less to sweet-talk them into living a week longer, all the time sweating the details: How serious were they, what was the likelihood, and would it be her fault?

"Tuesday at two," Claire said.

Polly nodded, then got up and left.

Jody was coming just as Polly walked out and had to turn sideways to avoid a collision.

"What'd you do, steal her Hershey bar?" Jody asked Claire once the door was closed.

Claire smiled but didn't answer. She wasn't allowed to.

Jody walked into the office and sat down. "What's up?"

Claire raised her eyebrows.

"Did you have a good weekend? Do you want to talk about it?" Jody asked.

Claire didn't say anything. The fastest way to get Jody to change the subject was to ignore her.

"Okay. Let's talk about the multitude of ways a person can get to California," Jody said. "There's two roads, it's your basic low-road, high-road deal. You can take the bus, like my father did forty years ago. It still takes a week. Or is it a month? There's a train that goes straight from New York to Chicago, but then you have to switch, and keep on switching the whole rest of the way across, even out in the desert, where they have poisonous train-switching desert snakes." She paused, as if waiting for a laugh track. "Or you can take my mother's car. She's getting a new one. We're driving out together. It's kind of a mother-daughter thing. She even wants my father to go, but I said no way. Not because I don't like him, but realistically, all three of us in the car for five days, it could get ugly. My dad offered to do it himself. To drop me off in L.A. But I really need my mom. Is that terrible? Okay, I'm admitting it. I need my mother.

If I get to a new place without her, I freak. I don't know what to do—how to unpack or arrange the closets. I have zero nesting instinct."

Claire still didn't say anything. Polly's silence had rubbed off on her.

"I'm leaving in about a month."

"I'll miss you," Claire said, staring at Jody, thinking about the dream, trying to remember what Mark really looked like, how he carried himself.

"Yeah, well . . ." Jody said. "Anyway, don't you think I should start getting ready, if only conceptually?"

"Soon," Claire said, and then was quiet for a minute. "I've been thinking about your being adopted."

"That's really nice of you," Jody said. "I've been slacking off myself."

Claire felt guilty. She was doing this for herself. It had nothing to do with Jody, and it was bad practice. "We don't have to talk about it if you don't want to," she said, giving Jody an out.

"I can talk about it," Jody said.

Claire pretended to be unaware of the fact that Jody would do whatever Claire wanted her to. "When is your birthday?"

"Why?" Jody asked. "Do you want to buy me a present? I don't have a CD player or a Cuisinart."

"Do you know what hospital you were born at?" Claire asked matter-of-factly, looking at the sky outside her windows.

"It went out of business."

"I'm trying to have a serious conversation," Claire said, annoyed, focusing in.

"Sorry, but it's true. It went bankrupt or corrupt or something and closed. A little depressing, isn't it? My one connection to my real mother goes out of business."

"What was it called?"

"I don't know," Jody said, looking puzzled. "My elementary school also closed. They turned it into an office building. Do you think this means something?"

"If you know that it closed, you must have known what it was called."

Jody looked at her. "I did know," she said. "But I've forgotten. Doctors, maybe. Is that the name of a hospital? Or is it a TV show? Why do you care, anyway—are you, like, a hospital groupie?"

Claire remembered a Doctors Hospital in Washington, somewhere downtown. But she'd given birth at Columbia Hospital for Women.

"Would you want to know who your mother was?" Claire asked a few minutes later.

Contemplating the Rothko print on the wall, Jody shrugged. "If someone was passing out pictures, saying 'This is your mother,' I'd look. I'd be curious. If someone came right up to me and said 'Your mother's name is whatever and she lives wherever and here's her phone number,' I'd listen, I'd take the information, but I don't know what I'd do with it. It might mess me up."

"How?"

"First off, I have a mother and a father already. That's good enough, isn't it? I mean, it should be, shouldn't it? Second, it would grate on me and in a moment of weakness, a moment of wanting something, I might call and get rejected. She gave me away, remember? Chances are, she doesn't want anything to do with me. I'm like a bad memory."

"Do you ever think she might be out there looking for you?"

"No," Jody said sharply. "Why would you say that?"

"I was just curious whether you'd ever thought about it from her side."

"Why should I?"

Claire didn't respond. "So, you'd never do a search or anything like that?"

"Only if I was sure it didn't matter, if I was positive everything would stay the same no matter what. I'd have to go into it not wanting anything, not expecting anything. By the time you're at that point, why bother?"

"Obviously you've given it some thought."

"I'm not an idiot," Jody said.

"Hardly," Claire added, and again they were quiet for a moment. "Let's talk about California."

"Finally," Jody said.

13

P eter Sears and Jody were naked in Jody's bed when her mother called at eleven. The lights were off at Jody's request—she didn't know Peter well enough to be both nude and illuminated. It took her a minute to find the phone in the dark.

"Hi, Mom," she said.

"Were you sleeping?"

"No."

"You sound sleepy."

Without warning, Peter's hand was between her legs.

Jody cleared her throat. "I'm awake. How was your day?" She made a mental note to either bleach or shave the hair on the upper part of her thighs before their next date.

"Do you have company?" her mother asked.

"Company? No," Jody said. Peter slapped her butt and it made a sharp smacking sound. "I was just watching TV." He put his tongue to her breast.

"I thought I heard something in the background."

"A book fell off my bed."

"It's good you're reading, sweetie. Did you have a good day?"

"It was fine." Jody felt guilty. Peter's presence was a strange but necessary betrayal of Jody's relationship with her mother. As much as her mother nagged her about never having a boyfriend, she never acknowledged the possibility of Jody having a sex life.

"I'm so tired," her mother said. "I pulled a muscle in my back and had to take two Advil and now I can hardly keep my eyes open. Can we talk tomorrow?"

"Yeah, sure, Mom. Go to bed."

"Everything's all right?"

"Fine," Jody said. "Sweet dreams." Peter took the receiver from her and hung up the phone. "She calls me every night at eleven," Jody said, getting out of bed. Peter grabbed her and pulled her back down on top of him. "I don't think so," Jody said.

"I'm not done." He pressed his tongue against her breast, his cock against her crotch.

Sleeping with Peter was an experiment. Jody wanted to see if she could have sex with someone she didn't care about. It was easier than she expected, but boring. She wished he'd leave. She was also angry with herself for having given in on the condom thing. Jody constantly lectured Ellen and everyone else, but when it came down to it, she'd crumbled and was furious with herself.

"No," Peter had said, not even willing to discuss it.

"Yes," Jody said.

"No," he said, and pushed his naked self into her.

Instantly, Jody felt like it was too late. The moment of contact transmitted poison like an electric shock, and she just lay there, paralyzed, as if she'd been fatally stung.

Men are so fucking annoying, she thought, daydreaming as he pumped away on top of her. This wasn't fun, definitely not fun, but there seemed to be no way out—like a loop-de-loop, upside-down, inside-out roller coaster bringing you to the edge of vomit and death. Jody forced herself to simply hang on, finding relief in the idea that eventually it would be over. Meanwhile she wondered if maybe it was her; maybe there was something about her that made good sex impossible. To some degree it had always been a problem, but this was pathetic.

He pulled out before he came, grabbed her palm, spit on it, and put her wet hand on his dick. It was gross; spit on her hand, his dick slimy from being inside her. She flicked her hand and wrist up and down in a matter-of-fact motion as if shaking down a thermometer. Peter stuck his fingers inside her. Men always did that, shoved as many fingers as they could organize deep inside and then wiggled them around as if trying to find the prize in a blind treasure hunt. She'd had examinations that were more fun. With her empty hand, she pulled on his wrist and shook her head, no way. It took him a minute to catch on.

At four in the morning, Jody was still awake, trapped under Peter's arm. She looked down at his penis, sleeping nicely, quietly on his thigh. It looked good there, healthy and relaxed. She'd seen some frightening ones—thick, stumpy things, or miniaturized pencil dicks—but this one was nice. She liked it better than its owner. Jody carefully lifted Peter's arm and crawled out of the bed. She felt crusty, disgusting. In the bathroom as she washed, she tried to decide if it would be worse to be pregnant or have AIDS.

14

Claire promised Jake that if he went with her to Bob Rosenblatt's office she'd spend the whole afternoon with him. He wasn't impressed. Well past the point where spending an afternoon with his mother was a great pleasure, he was into being left alone, lying on his bed with the shades pulled down.

"When you spend an afternoon with me," Claire asked, "doesn't something good happen?"

"Yeah, you feel guilty and buy me ice cream or french fries. I can buy my own french fries."

"Isn't there anything you'd really like to do?"

He shook his head.

"Well, I'd really like you to come to see Bob Rosenblatt with me."

"Why?"

"Because I think it would be good for us."

"You think I need a shrink. You're a shrink, so why don't you just go ahead and do it to me?"

Claire didn't say anything.

"Okay, fine, I'll go, but then I get to pick out something I want and you have to buy it for me."

Claire still didn't say anything.

"Those are my conditions."

"Put your shoes on," Claire said.

Jake jumped down from his loft onto Adam's bed, sending toys flying like shrapnel.

"Be careful," Claire said.

• • •

Rosenblatt kept them in the waiting room for ten minutes and twenty-three seconds. Claire watched the clock on the wall, sure there was no one in his office. It was a trick, Rosenblatt's way of asserting his authority over her: I'm the doctor and you're the patient.

"I've never been in a shrink's office before, except my mom's," Jake said, shaking Bob Rosenblatt's hand.

"Well, this is it," Rosenblatt said, gesturing toward the Philip Pearlstein painting on the wall and the Oriental carpet on the floor, as if to demonstrate his superiority. "Take any seat you like."

Jake sat in the Eames chair that was clearly Rosenblatt's usual seat and Claire felt proud of him. Rosenblatt made a face. Instead of saying something, he stuffed his large body into the smaller, more subservient chair across from Jake. Claire sat alone, pressed against the arm of the sofa.

"Your mother is worried about you," Rosenblatt said.

Immediately Claire was pissed. You don't start off pitting family members against each other. Jake wasn't a junkie they were trying to get into a treatment program. He was a bored eleven-year-old.

"Is there something she should be worried about?"

Jake shook his head.

"Is there anything in particular you'd like to talk about?"

Jake shook his head again. He was losing his baby shape, the sweetness in his face changing into something more angular, less familiar, mannish.

"You're in what grade?"

"Sixth," Jake said. "And if you're going to ask me if I like school, the answer is it's okay. I mean, I like the kids and everything."

"Do you have a lot of friends?"

"I guess."

"Any one in particular?"

Jake shrugged.

Rosenblatt was driving Jake further into himself. What a fucking idiot, Claire thought. She tried to think of a way to interrupt, to get things back on track.

"Is there anything special you like to do with your friends?"

Jake shrugged again.

"Jake's on the baseball team, and the soccer team, and he plays the trumpet," Claire said.

Both Jake and Rosenblatt gave her hard looks, then ignored her.

"Do you like sports?" Rosenblatt asked.

"I guess."

"Any one in particular?"

It went on like that for half an hour. In monosyllabic statements, Rosenblatt found out that Jake liked to eat in restaurants and go to movies, liked girls but didn't have a girlfriend yet, blushed easily, thought his father was okay, wished his family was bigger, hoped one day he'd get his own room, and still wanted a drum set for his birthday even though his parents said it wasn't a possibility.

Every so often Rosenblatt would bring her into the conversation in the worst way. "Is it true Jake sometimes says he has a stomachache when really there's nothing wrong? Did you really throw out the copy of *Playboy* that he borrowed from a friend's brother?" So she sat in her corner, distant, excluded, staring at the slice of the Chrysler Building visible from Rosenblatt's window. Briefly she considered whether she should have asked Sam to come with them. But there was something about the nature of the problem that made Claire think it was strictly between her and Jake, a mother/son thing.

Claire pictured her own family in therapy. Her father would've sat on a chair as far away from the rest of them as possible, both feet planted on the floor, arms crossed over his belly, face unpleasant, chin doubled onto his chest. Her mother would be in the middle, her attention split between husband, daughters, doctor. Her sister would be in a swivel chair, spinning in circles, touching everything on the doctor's desk, and no one would tell her to stop. There would be no chair for Claire; she would be forced to stand in the middle of the room. "See," her father would say, "she's always doing something to get attention. Everyone else is sitting down and she insists on standing up."

In Rosenblatt's office, Claire all of a sudden remembered that her sister always had earaches. When they went swimming, Laura had to put special plugs in her ears and wear a bathing cap and still try to keep her head above water. She swam laps with her neck stretched out, like a rare bird, the bright orange and yellow flowers on their mother's hand-me-down rubber cap flapping in the breeze. Claire thought of Jody's ears, thought of Jody's tetracycline-stained teeth and tried to picture her sister's mouth, but saw nothing except Laura's head with the bathing cap on it and the thick red line running like a vein across her forehead that stayed for hours after she took the cap off.

That was it. On Rosenblatt's lousy black leather sofa, while her son and this pompous ass transferred and countertransferred all their boy/man business, it all began to make sense. She'd figured it out. Laura had accidentally met Barbara at a conference—probably something like "Adolescent Willfulness" or "Finding Meaning in Your Marriage." From across the room Barbara had seen someone she thought was Claire—the two sisters looked a lot alike—and ran over, calling Claire's name. Laura smiled, said she had a sister by that name, and everything came out—Barbara's discovery that she had a patient who was Claire's actual daughter. Barbara and Laura skipped their afternoon panels and over coffee came up with the plan to send Jody to Claire. I am your child, back from darkest Peru. Barbara and Laura thought they'd done a remarkable thing. They got together, swapped details about Jody and Claire, and wondered if Claire had figured it out. They laughed. They became best friends. The two families rented a beach house together and had cookouts. Barbara, Laura, and their husbands sat in lounge chairs in the backyard while their children stood around a Weber grill toasting marshmallows. It was perfectly logical. Barbara and Laura would love each other. Long ago, Barbara had married someone who worked for the government—some sort of analyst or spy—and had moved from Baltimore to Washington. She'd grown up, stopped burning holes in other people's sweaters, quit smoking, started drinking wine, embraced security, rules, and regulations, the conservative style of Washington society. She'd become a hard-core do-righter, in the sense of embracing the system, becoming the system, and believing in it. She would think Laura was great—exactly as Claire had seemed but not as depressed, not as quirky or weird. Claire hated them both.

"How would you feel about coming to see me once a week? Not with your mother, but by yourself?"

Claire was whipped through time back into the room, slightly dazed. What happened? What had she missed?

Jake shrugged.

"Is that something you'd be able to do?"

"I guess," Jake said.

Claire was furious. Claire and Rosenblatt hadn't discussed the possibility of Jake going into individual therapy, and to ask Jake about it before checking with Claire and Sam took a lot of nerve. After all, they'd have to pay for it. Rosenblatt was playing dirty, using Jake to manipulate Claire.

"How would you feel about Jake coming here?" Rosenblatt asked her.

Claire glared at him. "I'll have to discuss it with Sam. We'll call you."

If Jake were left alone with Rosenblatt, together they would perform strange male rituals that worked like magnetic polar curses and drove the mother figure farther and farther away, until finally Jake would live in Maine and Claire in Florida.

"Why don't we go ahead and make a time," Rosenblatt said. "When do you get out of school on Wednesdays?"

"Let's wait," Claire said.

It was her obligation to protect what she perceived to be the best interests of her child. And if he needed to be in therapy, it would certainly be with someone else.

"I'm done at three," Jake said, looking at his mother.

"I think you have an orthodontist appointment Wednesday," Claire said, standing up. "We'll have to check the book at home and call you." Claire waited for Jake to get up and then marched out of the office.

"What a fucking asshole," she said in the elevator.

"Mom," Jake whined.

"Did you see what he did? Did you see how he tried to use me? He tried to use the process to get what *he* wanted? What a creep."

"I didn't think he did anything all that bad."

Claire didn't answer. Jake was eleven years old, he never thought anything anyone did was all that bad; that was part of the problem. She patted his head. "Do *you* think you need to talk to someone?"

Jake shrugged.

"You always have your father and me, and if you feel like you need someone else, let me know and we'll find you someone, someone good."

They walked a few blocks in the cool air, among the Saturday crowds. Claire walked quickly, hoping she wouldn't go marching back to Rosenblatt's office and give him a piece of her mind. She'd given him too much already.

"I kind of liked him," Jake said after a while.

Claire shrugged. "There are plenty of other people you'd like even better. So, where would you like to go?"

"You don't have to spend the whole afternoon with me," Jake said. "Why don't you just give me twenty dollars and drop me off at Matt's house?"

Claire shook her head. "I *want* to spend the afternoon with you. How about a museum? We haven't been to a museum in a long time."

"Aren't I a little old for that?" Jake said.

"No." Claire almost laughed. "Which one do you like best?"

"I guess the Modern is more grown-up than Natural History," Jake said.

They took the bus up Sixth Avenue to Fifty-third Street. Before looking at anything, they ate. Eating always made Jake happy. He had a sandwich, Jell-O salad, Coke, chocolate cake, and frozen yogurt. Claire had cottage cheese and black coffee. They both finished feeling virtuous. Now there was no way they could be in bad moods.

In his adolescent way—"cool"—Jake expressed interest in Picasso and Pollock, but what really got him going was the helicopter hanging from the ceiling on the third floor and the red sports car parked next to it. "Unbelievable," he said, circling both exhibits.

They ended up in the gift shop. "Buy me this," Jake said, immediately picking out a bright multicolored truck intended for someone much younger.

"Look around a little," Claire said.

He pretended to and came back with the same toy. "I want this." It was something she knew Adam would be happy with. Jake would have fun putting it together, but he'd never play with it. She took the box from him and turned it over. Forty dollars. If she bought it for Jake, as soon as Adam saw it there'd be a fight.

Claire picked up another box, an airplane for thirty-five dollars. "Okay," she said. "I'll get you the truck, and the plane for Adam."

"It's supposed to be my special day," Jake said. "I'm supposed to get a present—just me, not him too."

"I have two children. I can't buy one a present and not the other."

"Why not?"

"Because."

"Then you have to get me something better."

"What about a book?"

"Oh, that's real exciting." Jake went carefully around the store and ended up pointing out an interesting collection of painted wooden pieces that could be put together to create creatures or abstract designs. It was much more age-appropriate than the truck.

"Do you really want it?" Claire asked. It was a great toy, something she might even tinker with herself but unlike anything Jake had ever asked for.

"It's called Zollo," he said.

Claire bent down and looked a the price in the case. "It's a hundred and ten dollars."

Jake got serious. "It's very cool. Buy it for me. Please."

Claire didn't want to ruin the good time they were having. Good times were fragile these days. One wrong move and Jake could lapse into a week-long sulk that would put the whole house in a foul mood. Thirty-five for the plane, a hundred and ten for the painted wood.

"Will it make you happy?"

"Definitely," Jake said.

She handed the cashier her credit card. In the end it was cheaper than therapy.

15

Harry took Jody on one arm and Carol Heberton on the other and walked the two of them off the location at the Forty-second Street library. They'd spent the morning getting the scene just right— Carol researching psycho killers while, unbeknownst to her, the one stalking her was watching. Leading the two women up the street like they were blind old ladies, Harry pressed close to Jody's ear. "I would've invited you to have dinner alone with me," he whispered, "but I knew you'd decline."

Jody could feel the thick flesh of Harry's lips tickling her lobe.

He held open the door to Aux Trois Mousquetaires on Forty-fifth Street, and Jody quickly ducked into the restaurant after Heberton.

"I hope you're happy," Harry said.

She was—very. Lunches like this with producers, famous directors, and movie stars, drawing stares and whispers from across a room—that was part of what she'd come to New York looking for.

"It's your going-away party," Michael, her boss, said, kissing her cheek. "Hello and goodbye."

Jody wanted to rub the side of her face, to ask the waiter for a special cloth and a glass of bottled water to resterilize the spot.

Despite what everyone was saying, she knew the lunch wasn't really for her. Jody's impending departure was an excuse to take everyone out for a morale booster: martinis and snails.

"It's only the beginning," Harry said, after the waiter took their drink order. "There'll be more."

"You look like you're about to cry," Raymond said to Jody. "Interesting, tears and snot—but not really the stuff of a good meal, would you say?"

Jody blinked and took a deep breath. She wouldn't cry.

"Don't worry," Carol Heberton said. "In L.A. everyone has lunch, sometimes two and three times a day."

"Let's paint the child a mural," Harry said, passing around the cup of crayons that sat next to the sugar bowl. Everyone took one and dutifully started scrawling on the white butcher paper laid over the tablecloth.

Two women came up to Carol, and before they even finished asking "Are you . . . ?" Carol had taken pen and paper and signed her name in huge, nearly floral script.

Harry looked up from his escargot and smacked his buttery lips. "Only the true cognoscenti know directors."

"P.S." Michael said to Jody. "Could you stop by the office this afternoon and do whatever it is you do to the Xerox? It's not working again and I have some scripts to send out."

"Take a lesson," Jody said.

"Well, before you go anywhere, I want you to teach your replacement how to do it."

"Replacement?" Jody said. "You mean you're not having my chair bronzed?"

The main courses arrived on huge heated plates, and for a few moments of almost prayerful silence they all focused on what was before them, going at it with knives and forks, oohs and ahs. When they'd satisfied their most immediate needs, the remains were passed in a circle so everyone could taste. Lunch ended with espresso all around and a full course of desserts—fruit tarts, crème brulée, and a serving of profiteroles that arrived in front of Jody in a pool of chocolate sauce, a flaming sparkler in the middle. Jody expected that at any minute a long line of waiters would pull up to the table and start singing "Happy Birthday," "For She's a Jolly Good Fellow," or something like that. Fortunately, no one came.

Harry looked down at Jody's profiteroles and poked at them tentatively with his knife. "Probably not unlike what's mounted on your chest, in both size and density."

Jody carefully pulled out the flaming sparkler, then turned to Harry. "If those are mine, this must be yours."

Harry smiled, took the sparkler, and dunked it upside down in his wineglass. "Touché," he said, holding up the still-sputtering stick of metal.

"God, this is a good time," Carol Heberton said. "It's been so long since I've had such fun."

After they finished eating and Michael had handed over his platinum card—the one he called his "plutonium card"—Harry insisted they wait while the busboys cleared the table and the crayons were passed again and everyone finished the drawing, making bright waxy circles and nasty comments about the spots of wine and food that had stained the surface. Harry directed them all to sign their work, rolled the mural up like a diploma, and presented it to Jody.

"Go forward," he said, holding the restaurant door open.

Jody stepped out into the humid afternoon and immediately felt sick, overwhelmed, and in need of a nap.

"Back to the trenches," Michael said.

Harry belched, rubbed his belly, and belched again. "A lovely lunch, Michael. Thank you. I shan't forget it."

"Don't forget about the Xerox," Michael said to Jody.

"Thanks," Jody said, and they all walked back downtown toward the two huge granite lions that marked the spot where the movie would end.

At eleven-thirty that night, Peter Sears called Jody from the pay phone on the corner of Charles and Bleecker. "I have to come up," he said. "It's an emergency."

Jody wasn't pleased. She'd just come in the door, numb and dumb from the narcotic combination of too much work, too much lunch, too many drinks before dusk, and the prospect of giving up the life she'd always wanted for something completely unknown. She was also in the middle of doing laundry for the first time in almost a month, and she looked like shit.

"What's wrong?" she said, opening the door.

"Hi," Peter said, kissing her.

Jody didn't kiss back. There were some people she simply wasn't interested in kissing, and Peter was quickly becoming one of them. He kissed too urgently. His tongue fished wildly in her mouth, as if he'd lost a family heirloom among her molars. Behind every kiss was his full weight, thrown against her with equal passion.

He ignored the fact that she didn't kiss back, lifted her shirt, and started kissing her stomach.

The farther away his face is, Jody thought, the happier I am. "So what's the problem?"

His tongue was in her belly button and it was starting to hurt. She imagined that when he finally pulled away, her intestines would rise up and out in a long curly line like a charmed snake.

"*This* is the problem," Peter said, stepping back, unzipping his pants and letting his hard-on pop out.

"I don't get it," Jody said, unimpressed.

"It's been like this all day. It's not healthy, you know. I mean, there's a condition you can get from this."

"I'm sure you've dealt with similar phenomena before," Jody said, sitting down on her sofa.

"Touch it," Peter said.

"Touch it yourself," Jody said.

He shook his head and stepped towards her.

"Do I have to?" she asked.

"I brought it here for you," Peter said.

"If I do this, you have to leave right away. I can't spend the whole night with you. I have a life."

"Fine," Peter said, positioning himself in front of her.

She had the urge to take him in her mouth. As penises went, his was very nice. More than anything she wanted to suck it, but didn't feel that Peter deserved such luck. He held her hand, spit on it, then put her hand down on his dick. She couldn't believe he was spitting on her again; no one had ever done that before. He kept putting his hand on top of hers, showing her what to do, and it was incredibly boring. Jody figured if he wanted it a certain way, he should do it himself.

"Come on—let's go in your room," Peter said in the thick, mass-murderer tone men sink into when they're too excited for their own good.

Jody went only because she had nothing better to do. The stuff in the dryer wouldn't be done for another half an hour; the couch was completely uncomfortable. The quicker she got it over with, the sooner Peter would leave, and maybe, just maybe, there might be something in it for her.

Before lying down, Peter took off all his clothing and neatly draped everything, even his socks, over the chair.

Still clothed, she lay on her bed. What was she supposed to do—undress like at a doctor's office? If so, where was her gown? At least if she got to put on one of those blue paper gowns, there'd be some excitement, some possibility. The thin plastic belt could be used to tie her up; the gown could be open in the front or the back—something, anything.

Naked, Peter sat on Jody, straddling her hips. He pushed up her shirt so her breasts and belly were exposed. Trapped beneath him, pelvis semi-crushed, lungs in jeopardy, Jody could do little more than raise her hand and put it on him again. She did it violently, feeling a little guilty for subjecting such a nice penis to such a brutal beating, but realizing that in the end Peter himself would surely be punished more than his dick. Almost immediately he started making noises she found annoying. She always found it annoying when people made noises. Enjoy, but don't fucking vocalize. Moaning was what people in movies did when they were crushed between two cars. Without warning, he came onto Jody's chest, onto her stomach and breasts. Shock kept her from saying anything.

"I came on you," Peter said, sitting up straight.

Jody tilted her head as far down as she could, trying to look, not caring that it made her chin double or triple. Peter touched the come, rubbing it around over her breasts. Jody leaned back and closed her eyes, thinking that in situations like these the best thing to do is not to respond.

As soon as Peter left, Jody took a fast, scalding shower. Hot-pink and wrapped in her bathrobe, she took the elevator down to the laundry room. It was not exactly a smart move—the kind of thing an idiot would do in a movie and then end up raped, strangled, and stuffed into a dryer set on high. Still, Jody was tough, she was brave, she was bold, she took a huge kitchen knife with her. A stranger had taken her clothing out of the dryer and folded it into two neat stacks, taking care to pair the socks.

While she was collecting her things, Ellen came in with Rob. Jody figured they were planning to fuck on the folding table as part of Ellen's plan to do it at least once in every possible location and position.

"What happened to you?" Ellen asked, touching the bright pink skin on Jody's neck. "Overtime on a tanning bed?"

Jody shook her head. Telling Ellen about Peter would ruin her chaste image, and Ellen would never let it go. Besides, Jody was somewhat surprised at herself for doing it in the first place.

Rob glared at Jody. A long time ago, Jody had answered Ellen's phone at two o'clock in the morning, and ever since Rob thought Jody and Ellen were having an affair behind his back. Jody couldn't believe anyone would be that stupid.

"Got to go," Jody said, picking up her laundry. She was in a hurry to get back upstairs, to change the sheets, beat the sofa cushions, to reclaim her night.

"Bye, sweetie," Ellen said, kissing Jody's cheek. "Call me at the office tomorrow. And put some lotion on yourself when you get upstairs."

Jody lifted Ellen's hand, holding it up toward Rob. "Great ring," she said. "I'm sure you'll be really happy together."

Ellen flashed her a voodoo look and Jody laughed. She couldn't help but laugh. It probably made Rob even more annoyed, but she kept laughing all the way into the elevator, an intense kind of manic laugh, a laugh that could turn into a scream at any minute.

16

Gloria Owens arrived before her husband, and they started the session without him.

"Sometimes I really hate him."

"Who?" Claire asked.

"Jim," she said. "Sometimes I really hate Jim."

Claire nodded. Patients always thought it was shocking when they talked about hate. They acted as though they were revealing a horrible hidden secret. Their greatest realization was the simple relief that came from seeing that nothing bad happened as a result of the confession. I hate. I despise. Claire barely responded when people said it. Her lack of response was intentional, designed to push the patient further, to go beyond hate and into the fury for which there was no name.

"Sorry I'm late," Jim Owens said, bursting into the office without knocking, twenty minutes into the session. Someone coming out of another office must have let him into the waiting room.

Claire was surprised. People didn't just barge in like that. What if there had been a time switch and the hour didn't belong to him? What if Claire had been in there alone, between patients, taking a nap or doing who knows what?

"I was just saying that someday we might get divorced," Gloria said as her husband sat down.

He smiled at Claire as if to ask, Was this your idea?

Even though Claire was probably a few years older than the Owenses, she felt vibrant, changeable, and youthful in comparison. The Owenses were well into middle age. They'd settled, you could tell just by looking. Both were about fifteen or twenty pounds overweight, pounds gained by not caring, not having to worry about impressing or seducing the other. They felt entitled to satisfy cravings, take pleasure from candy bars in the afternoon, ice cream with the late news, steak dinners. They were used to each other. If they got divorced, it would be difficult; they wouldn't be able to simply go forward as a freed man and woman. They would have to make changes, go on diets, rethink careers, wardrobe, friends, and addresses.

"Don't say the D word," Jim said.

Claire wondered if Jim knew that for most people the D word was Death, not Divorce. Possibly he thought that since the M word was Marriage, D had to be Divorce. Regardless, it was curious.

"Why not?" Gloria said. "What do you care?"

The session went on like a chicken fight, Mr. and Mrs. pecking at each other as supervised by Claire until finally their hour ran out.

"Well, I'll see you next week," Claire said, clapping her hands together. As they went out the door, she winked at Jody, who was sitting in the waiting room, pretending to read a magazine. "Be with you in a minute," she said, closing her door to check her answering machine and pull up her pantyhose. She was glad Jody was next; now she could relax.

Claire rewound her messages, jotting down quick notes and first impressions that she'd go over later. "Hi, it's Eric Silverman. A new patient came to see me today—very interesting, but I think she'd be better off with a woman. Call me." Referrals were nice, a vote of confidence from her peers. All the same, Claire didn't want any new patients now. Getting started in the summer was too difficult, and she'd be leaving in a few weeks anyway. Maybe in the fall. Maybe after Jody went to L.A.

That morning, while she was putting on her makeup, Claire imagined that she'd secretly named her little girl. Before handing her over, she'd whispered "Hilary" into the baby's ear. Now, years later, she'd only have to whisper the name again and, if the child were hers, the girl's cheeks would flush, her eyes would brighten, and, without a second's hesitation, she'd say "Mom."

"I've never done this before in my life," Claire said, smiling at Jody, "but I'm starving to death. Do you mind if I order something?"

Jody shrugged.

"Do you want anything?"

"No thanks," Jody said.

Claire picked up the phone, ordered a grilled cheese and tomato sandwich and a cup of coffee from the restaurant around the corner, then settled back into her chair. "Let's talk about what you're doing until you leave for California."

She considered whether ordering grilled cheese seemed too strange, too goyish. It was what her mother used to eat, with bread-and-butter pickles stuffed in after the cheese was melted. Perhaps she should have gone for something simpler, a bagel or a milk shake. Her stomach growled.

"You're leaving when in August?" she asked.

"I have to be there by the seventeenth, so we'll probably take off from my parents' house around the eighth."

The buzzer went off, and Claire got up to pay the delivery man. Hilary. Why Hilary? Hilarity. Hilarious. Happiness. Red hair. Claire didn't know anyone with red hair. She never had.

She sat with the sandwich on her knees, hoping the whole thing wasn't too terribly distracting. "What's your middle name?" she asked between bites.

"Beth," Jody said. "Why?"

Jody Beth. Well, that was no Hilary.

"I'd like to see you a lot before you leave," Claire said. "Do you think we could arrange that?" When she looked up from her sandwich, Jody blushed. Claire chewed and swallowed. "I'll be going away at the very end of the month and won't be back until September, so we don't have much time. Two weeks."

She couldn't believe she'd waited until now to discuss leaving; but then again, from the very beginning the whole relationship had been about leaving. That's why Jody came to see her in the first place. All the same, it felt wrong. Claire ate her grilled cheese and watched Jody staring down at her sneakers. Clearly this was a complicated issue for both of them.

"Are you going to miss coming here?" Claire asked.

Jody shrugged again. She reminded Claire of Jake. Whenever he was uncomfortable or didn't want to admit something, he shrugged.

"If you like, I could help you find a therapist in Los Angeles, either through UCLA or privately," Claire said, sipping her coffee, curious whether she'd dripped any on her silk blouse. If she were a man, it would be charming, professorial, to have a little coffee absentmindedly splashed on her shirt. But the same splash brought a woman ten steps closer to the edge of incompetence, unable to properly care for herself much less others.

"No thanks," Jody said.

"It might make you feel safer if you know there's someone there."

Jody shrugged.

"Think about it," Claire said, crumpling up the sandwich paper. "I'd be happy to make some calls. And when you come back on vacation you can come see me—or write letters, if you want."

"P.S.," Jody said, "and not to change the subject, but before I forget: I talked to my mother and she said I wasn't born at Doctors."

"Did she tell you where?" Claire said, playing down her curiosity.

"She said the stork brought me."

Claire could have strangled her. Was Jody possessed by some demon especially programmed to drive Claire over the edge?

"What did she really tell you?"

"Just what I said. And she thought it was funny. Very funny. So funny I forgot to laugh."

"Did she say anything else?"

"Not much. They just sort of got me. The lawyer called to say I'd been born and then called back two days later and made plans for someone to pick me up. My mother sat in the car at the corner of Twenty-first and L streets in downtown Washington for half an hour, waiting. And then out of nowhere the next-door neighbor they sent to do their dirty work showed up with this bundle. Me. And then it started to snow. End of story."

A winter baby. Claire's was a winter baby as well. She knew it. She'd known it all along. Twenty-first and L was right around the corner from Columbia Hospital for Women. The day Claire got out of the hospital it snowed. All that afternoon and evening in Baltimore it snowed—eight inches—and at nineteen, she took the snow to be the tears she couldn't cry. The whiteness pouring from the sky, clean and soft, was what saved her.

"When did you say your birthday was?" Claire asked.

"Why do you keep asking me? I'm not telling you."

"What's the secret?"

"Yeah," Jody said, "what's the deal? Can we change the subject?"

"There are a few things you seem to find difficult to talk about—your birthday, our relationship. What's going on?"

Claire was starting not to like herself. She was doing things that might not be prudent, yet she had to do them. Knowing was becoming more important than anything else. She'd have to call Barbara and ask if she could add anything more. Or Claire could ask Jody her sign. She'd make up something about how useful astrology and charts were as therapeutic tools.

"I don't find it difficult," Jody said. "What I find difficult is moving to Los Angeles. I have the horrible feeling that at the last minute something will happen and I won't be able to do it."

"What will happen?"

"Nothing, in reality. I mean, I wouldn't be lucky enough for the world to end while I'm packing my stuff into my mother's car. It'll be more subtle, like we'll get in the car and at the end of the driveway suddenly I'll forget how to drive. The morning we're supposed to leave I'll be frozen, stuck to my bed, something like that."

"What could you do to prevent that from happening?"

"Use plenty of antifreeze?"

"Is there something we could do now, in the next two weeks, that would make the transition easier?"

Claire had clipped herself back into a highly professional mode, forcing herself to respond only to the issues at hand, hoping nothing she said or did gave away what she was thinking.

"I just don't know how to do it. I don't know how to pick up and move myself and everything I own across the country. It makes no sense on one level. Why would I *want* to do that?"

"Because that's what you have to do in order to get what you want," Claire said.

"Maybe not. Maybe that's not what I want. Maybe I should stay in New York or go home to Washington. Maybe I should just live in Washington for my whole life."

"You've got too much personality for Washington," Claire said.

Jody looked at Claire as if to ask, How do you know? Claire smiled. There was something about Jody that made it impossible for Claire to play it completely straight. She couldn't; she didn't want to. She glanced at Jody and tried to figure out what Jody was really like, outside the office, with her friends, with men.

The relationship between patient and therapist was supposed to be a micro-moment, a mirror of the patient's interaction with the world at large. The therapist was supposed to be the authority figure, the good mother, the perfect listener, the best kind of friend—the one who never talked about herself. The dynamics were so heavily invested with potential meaning that it was impossible for the relationship to mirror anything except itself.

"So," Claire said, "in these next weeks, now that you're not working as much, we can really get down to it."

Jody looked at her blankly.

"You don't have as many restrictions on your time. It'll make things easier."

"I guess," Jody said.

There was a certain doubt on Jody's part, a lack of trust. What was she afraid of—the process, the attachment, her own potential? Or Claire? Claire looked at Jody and Jody looked away. The richness of grilled American cheese rose in Claire's throat. No, Jody shouldn't be afraid of Claire. Claire loved her. Claire caught herself and repeated the thought more slowly: I love Jody. I do, she told herself, as though there were some part of herself she had to convince.

"I've never told you this," Claire said, "but I'm very glad I met you."

Jody looked at her like she was crazy.

"I enjoy you," Claire went on. "You're lovable."

Jody shrugged.

They were quiet.

"How about tomorrow at ten-thirty?" Claire asked. "That way you can sleep late."

"I guess," Jody said, getting up and heading for the door.

Maybe she shouldn't have done it; maybe she should have kept her mouth closed. What kind of trouble was she asking for? "See you tomorrow," Claire whispered softly, sweetly.

"Yeah, right," Jody said, pulling the door closed behind her.

17

"*T*he *ring*. Where's the ring?" Jody said, looking at Ellen's well-manicured but unadorned fingers. They were in line outside an undersized, overpopular, and not really very good restaurant in Soho, waiting for the privilege to have what would probably be their last brunch together for a long time.

"Which would you be more inclined to accept? One: I gave it back to Rob with a note saying he was too good for me and that I was a fool. Or two: I sold it to buy myself a really great suit at The Baby Grows Up."

"What's behind door number three?" Jody asked.

"Traded it for drinks and drugs at a bar I can't remember the name of. Tried to use it as a miniature cock ring and it shattered into a thousand pieces."

A guy in black leather shorts standing in front of them turned around, stared for a second, then pretended to be looking down the street.

"Hard choices," Jody said. "I pick number two."

"You don't think much of me, do you? I'm hurt, genuinely hurt."

"Are there any parties of one?" the maitre d' asked, stepping out onto the sidewalk. "Parties of one?"

"One's not exactly a party, is it?" Ellen said.

"What happened?" Jody asked.

"We had a fight. It was supposed to be one of those romantic strolls down by the water. He said I should stop acting like a whore and settle down. I pulled the ring off and threw it in the water." Ellen smiled. "Or so he thinks." She tapped her purse. "He called me a worthless bitch and tried to hit me. I ducked. And that was that."

"I'm really sorry," Jody said.

Ellen shrugged, and wiped away a little runny makeup. "So, what's with you? How's the shrink?"

"She told me she was glad we'd met. 'You're very lovable,' " Jody said, imitating Claire's voice.

"You know, the odds of having a really good shrink are about the same as having a perfect childhood. Something's wrong," Ellen said. "Either it's her or you."

"Or both." Jody didn't want to say things that Ellen could use as proof of the strangeness of the relationship, but she couldn't help herself. She had to tell someone. The stuff with Claire was just too good, too interesting and confusing, to keep to herself.

Without warning, Jody grabbed Ellen and pulled her under the restaurant's awning. "Up the street," she said, nodding north, "looking in the window. I think it's her." Jody hid behind Ellen and peeked out. "I swear, I think it is."

"Which one?" Ellen asked, excited, as though at any second she'd race over and ask for an autograph.

"Tall, blond, hair up, sunglasses. Is it? I can't look."

"This way, please, ladies," the maitre d' said, holding open the door. As they went in, Jody turned around and took a second look. She couldn't be sure.

"You should've gone over and said hi," Ellen said, as they were seated at a tiny table next to the kitchen.

"We would've lost our place in line," Jody said. "Besides, she's not exactly the kind of person you meet and say, wow, she's really nice. She's a little stiff, maybe more than a little."

"I'm not convinced that blond business is real," Ellen said.

"Usually she wears it in a bun."

"In a bun!" Ellen said. "Just like Betty Crocker! What, wrapped in a cinnamon swirl? 'We're out of time for today—I have to take my hair out of the oven. See you next week, we'll make braided breadsticks.' " Ellen started laughing hysterically, and people at other tables looked over. Jody was afraid the waiter would come by and tell them to keep it down, or leave.

"Sometimes she keeps me late," Jody whispered. "She makes me stay overtime."

"Detention?" Ellen said. "No way. They're supposed to throw you out. Bing! Hour's up, you're outta here."

The waiter put a basket of bread down on the table and handed them each a menu.

"Great," Ellen said. "Do you take credit cards?"

The man nodded. "We take all kinds."

"Except with Claire," Jody said. "If you're in the middle of something, if the next victim's not in the waiting room, she lets you stay. Five, ten minutes, sometimes a whole extra session."

"Oh my God," Ellen said slowly, staring at Jody. "Don't you see? She's brainwashing you. That's it. She's indoctrinating you into a cult. Who knows when you'll stay the whole afternoon. She'll take you out for tea and poison you. My poor little pretty," Ellen said, throwing her head back and laughing like the Wicked Witch of the West. Jody was petrified. "There's nothing that can be done to save you, it's already too late."

"Listen," Jody said. "I know it's different, but that doesn't mean it's bad. In some ways things have changed since I started seeing her. I'm happier. She likes me, and that makes me feel good."

"And what happens when you leave? All that goes out the window. You're on your own, kiddo."

"I doubt it. We'll talk. I'll visit."

"She's your shrink, not your lover."

"You're jealous," Jody said, looking at the menu.

Later, after they'd ducked in and out of stores up and down Wooster Street, Spring Street, Greene Street, picking up and putting down expensive primitive art from Idaho, garage-sale finds marked up three thousand percent, Ellen took both of Jody's hands in hers and asked loudly, "Do you love me?"

Jody didn't answer.

"Do you love *her?* You talk about her like you love her."

"It's not the same," Jody said.

"You don't love me. You don't *act* like you love me. I'm so nice to you," Ellen said. "I'm your best friend. For what it's worth, as soon as I met you, I knew I loved you. I was a little scared of you—did I ever tell you that? Would you want to fuck me?"

"No," Jody said, pushing through the store and out onto the sidewalk.

"Do you find me attractive?"

"I never thought about it," Jody said, lying. She had thought about it. When she first met Ellen in the elevator, there was definitely something there. Jody had the sensation of being seduced. But Ellen had a boyfriend—she had *ten* boyfriends—and Jody wanted one of her own. It had never occurred to her to want anything other than a boyfriend. The gap between men and women, the same gap people complained about, was a relief. Men didn't understand her, and didn't pretend to; they weren't her. She could fuck them and not feel as if she was giving up some part of her real self. She could fuck them and feel nothing except their weight, hardness, and breath against her.

"I think I'm sexy," Ellen said as they went into another store. "Men find me sexy. I'm good at it. I mean, if there's one thing I'm really good at, it's sex." The salesgirl stared at Ellen.

"That's nice," Jody said.

"Are you going to miss me when you're in Los Angeles?"

"Yes," Jody said, picking up a fifty-dollar T-shirt, unfolding it, looking at it, then refolding it again. She wasn't lying. In L.A. she'd be alone, really alone. The apartment building would be filled with Manson family rejects, earthquake plotters, ugly old actresses, and blind men, all writing screenplays based on their life stories.

"I'll miss you a lot," Ellen said. "Maybe you should take me with you. I could live in your apartment, lay out by the pool all day. You will have a pool, won't you?" They left the store and stepped back out onto the sidewalk.

"Everyone has a pool," Jody said. "You can come visit. Banking wouldn't be the same without you."

"I know. I'm the only one there with decent tits."

"Do you want to catch a movie?" Jody asked.

"Can't," Ellen said, checking her watch. "I have a date."

At Washington Square Park, Jody and Ellen said goodbye. They'd see each other again, probably in a few hours, but Ellen hugged Jody, and in a rare moment of she didn't know exactly what, Jody hugged back. Ellen kissed both of Jody's cheeks and Jody smiled. She didn't kiss back. She wandered through the park thinking that she was seeing everything for the last time.

When Jody got home, she called her mother.

"Why are you calling? You never call. Is something wrong?"

"No, Ma, I just missed you."

"Well, I miss you too. But I'm very busy right now. In a couple of weeks we'll be driving to California together. We'll have all that time in the car to talk."

Jody stretched out on her futon and made lists of things to take to California. She called the girl she'd sublet the apartment to, reminding her that the toaster oven, the mini-microwave, and the coffee maker wouldn't be there when she moved in. Jody went around the corner to the liquor store and got boxes. She made three trips, filling her apartment with empty cartons of vodka, scotch, and wine coolers. The apartment wasn't much, but it was the first and only home she'd made for herself. The apartment was proof that she could function independently in the real world, the first indication she was a real person. And now, after only two years, she was turning her home over to an NYU medical student who'd probably put dissected body parts in the fridge and formaldehyde in her coffee cups. She made a note to leave only the really ugly dishes that used to belong to her aunt Sylvia.

Peter Sears was on top of Jody. The room was dark. Her eyes were closed. She was concentrating on enjoying herself. She figured she'd try one more time.

"Fuck me, you fucking bitch!" he growled.

Jody opened one eye. She wanted to see his face, to make sure he was kidding. He wasn't. His body was contorted, writhing. The whiteness of anger had met the pink flush of desire.

"Fuck me, you fucking bitch!" he said again.

And he had a limited vocabulary, which somehow made Jody less frightened. She figured she could win over anybody who had to repeat the word "fuck" in a short sentence.

"Eat me," Jody said.

And Peter did.

Regardless, Jody swore she'd never invite him over again. In case for some reason he just showed up, she'd warn him that he was persona non grata.

Peter's head was in her crotch, his fingers squeezing her nipples too hard. She looked down at him. He seemed caught in the strained posture of a swimmer doing the butterfly stroke. She decided that he was in fact doing some sort of butterfly on her. She closed her eyes and tried to concentrate. She wanted to come at least once before she left for Los Angeles.

At first she didn't know what had happened—a flash of pain and the hot sting of shocked flesh. Jody supposed something had fallen on her. Something had lifted itself up off the dresser on the other side of the room, flown over, and dropped itself down on her. She opened her eyes, but there was nothing except Peter on top, grinding away. While she was looking, his hand rose up against her cheek. Jody screamed and the hand fell hard against her.

"Fuck me, you fucking bitch!"

No one had ever hit her before—not like that. No one had ever. Horrified, she opened her mouth and only a grunt came out. He got harder inside her. She felt it.

"Asshole," Jody finally said. "Fucking asshole. Get off." She wiggled under him, trying to get out. He liked that. He held her down, raised himself up, and pushed deeper into her. He swore. She closed her eyes. It was too late to fight. Fighting would only make things worse. There was no such thing as screaming for help. There was no such thing as rape when you were already having sex. There was no such thing. He spit on her chest, and she threw up all over him.

18

July 31, the last session; both Claire and Jody fighting against images of finality. It would be better if they weren't in this alone, if they had something more than each other.

"We really haven't had a chance," Claire said.

" 'It seems we just get started and before you know it,' " Jody sang, " 'comes the time we have to say so long.' "

" 'So long, goodnight, everybody,' " Claire added. They both laughed.

Outside, the gears of a truck ground down. A police car raced by, a cop barking "Get outta the way, outta the way, pull to the right," over the speaker.

Within the hour, Claire's life would be her own again. She'd go away with her husband and her sons. For the next month she'd be making peanut butter and jelly sandwiches, pouring apple juice into insulated thermoses, and rubbing endless quantities of sunblock onto chests, shoulders, noses, and legs.

She handed Jody a thin, flat envelope. "I thought you might need this."

"Did you plant a tree in Israel for me?"

"You're not dead, you're just moving," Claire said, knowing that she'd spend the four days between now and when she left for the beach in a funereal daze. She'd spend them packing for Adam, Jake, Sam, and herself; the act of packing somehow reinforcing the sense of being left, of ending.

"Oh yeah, right, I'm moving," Jody said, opening the envelope, pulling out a map of the United States.

"Are you going to be all right?" Claire asked.

"I have to do it," Jody said.

"You *can* do it."

Jody shrugged.

"You really can. I have faith in you."

Jody shrugged again. "Anyway," she said, "there's no point in talking about it now."

"Has this been helpful at all?"

"It's been fun," Jody said. "Interesting."

Claire smiled. "Write me if you want to. Call me when you get back."

"I will."

They were silent, lingering in the sensations of being in a room with that one person, that most specific person, with whatever it was that made one person different from the next, that made a living person truly alive. They spent the hour in near-silence, soaking it up, holding it in, unwilling to risk ruining the moment with misplaced words.

And at the end Claire said, "I'll miss you."

"Thanks," Jody said, standing up and shaking her hand—a very Jody thing to do. "Bye. Nice knowing ya."

She turned to leave and Claire squeezed her shoulder. "You'll do well. Have a great time."

"You too," Jody said. "Have a good vacation."

Jody was out the door, alone in the hall. She took a breath and pushed the elevator button, glad she was going, glad she was leaving Claire.

Claire sat in her office, in Jody's still-warm chair, flipping through her appointment book. It was over.

BOOK TWO

19

*J*ody lay like a corpse on the twin bed of her childhood. The bed was too narrow, too short, too small, not unlike a coffin or a crib. From her window she could see her mother and father in the driveway, packing the car. She figured they would have to load her in along with all the old furniture they'd dredged up from the basement; furniture too good to throw out, too terrible to bring upstairs, perfect for Jody's new home. There wouldn't be room, and so they'd have to decide what to tie to the roof, Jody or the big old coffee table.

"It's exactly what you need," her mother said. "And in a couple of years, when you're finished, you can leave it there. You don't have to bring it back. Who could ask for more?"

Jody could. If she wanted to live in a room with her parents' rejected housewares, she'd simply move into their basement. She didn't have to drive 2,605 miles to do it. According to the Triple-A Triptik sitting on the front hall table, it was exactly 2,605 miles. The Triptik was as thick as a book, with miniature foldout maps, page after page of America, laid out with a thick green line marking Jody's route. She wasn't looking forward to it.

She watched her father reach into the car and beep the horn. "Jody," he called. "Jody, come on out." Through the carport, the windows, the house, the door to her room, his voice sounded thin, tired, like he was getting too old and trying too hard.

Jody lay on the bed. She wasn't ready.

Her mother came into the room. "Daddy's checking the tires," she said. "I'll drive first so you can rest. Look, I have something for you." She pulled her hand out from behind her back and showed Jody an economy-size bag of M&M's.

Did they think Jody could be bribed? Would they lay a trail of candy from her bed to the car and hope she'd follow it?

"I made a whole bag of sandwiches. And there's a six-pack of Coke in a cooler. It's going to be fun. I haven't been on a real car trip in years." She took her other hand from behind her back. "Pepperidge Farm cookies," she said, swinging a bag of Milanos back and forth hypnotically.

Jody wasn't hungry.

"You don't want to go," her mother said, and Jody was thankful for the words spoken. She nodded. "Give me your hand." Her mother took Jody's hand and pulled her up. "Now go and wash your face." She led Jody to the bathroom, pushed her in gently, and closed the door. "I know this isn't easy for you," she said through the door, "but it's what you wanted. You've been talking about UCLA ever since junior high when you got that crush on Steven Silberberg."

"Spielberg," Jody said. "I got over it. He looks like a truck driver now—beard, baseball cap. They have truck drivers everywhere, I don't have to schlep to California."

"And I don't have to either, but I'm doing it," her mother said. "You never liked change. The first day I took you to nursery school you didn't want to go, but I mustered my strength and left you there and you were fine."

Scarred for life, Jody thought.

"You've never liked new things. You're not very experimental. If there's one thing you should work on while you're out there, it's trying new things."

"Mom, if you don't stop talking, I'm not going anywhere with you."

"I'll be waiting in the car."

Jody had been out of New York less than a week and already she missed everything and everyone. She missed working on the movie, watching people watch Carol Heberton, watching Harry's chin wiggle when he laughed. She missed the teasing, the repartee. She missed Ellen and Claire.

"Now, listen," her father said, pulling Jody aside, slipping a roll of cash into her palm. "Enjoy. Go slow, stop at decent motels. Don't eat on the run. Sit down, have a meal."

"Dad," Jody said.

"Have a good trip and good luck out there." He hugged her, patting her back.

His hand felt smaller, more fragile, than she remembered. Little red blood spiders hid beneath the surface of his cheeks. "Thanks," Jody said, kissing her father goodbye and hating the sandpaper texture of his skin.

Her mother backed the old Saab out of the driveway and simultaneously started crying. "Find me a Kleenex," she said, sniffling. "In the glove compartment."

"Stop crying," Jody ordered.

"I'm just so proud of you."

Jody sighed. She felt like she was riding to her own funeral, awake and annoyed.

The end of the driveway, the stop sign at the bottom of the hill, the ramp to the highway—everything marked the beginning of the final stage; she was being chauffeured to her death.

The whole way around the beltway, her mother kept blowing her nose, blotting her eyes, and handing balled-up Kleenex to Jody, who stuffed them between the seats.

Despite her mother's sniffling, despite the Triptik on the dashboard, despite the pile of maps at her feet, despite the sensation of impending doom, Jody had somehow convinced herself they were just going for a pleasant ride on a sunny day, no big deal. Sunday-drive material, up through Skyline Drive to Luray Caverns. She remembered a stalagmite that looked like a fried egg. She'd seen it once a year every year, usually in the fall, until she was about fourteen and stopped going places with her parents.

"Did you ever go to Luray without me?" Jody asked.

"No. We did it for you. Don't you remember? Every Sunday we took you somewhere."

Mountain views, vegetable stands, apple picking, historical sites, houses of the famous and dead, battlefields—the stuff of field trips.

"I remember," Jody said. "But what did you do after I left, when I was in college?"

"We visited dead Grandma."

Dead Grandma as opposed to living Grandma. Dead Grandma, her father's mother, used to be in the nursing home that Jody was too petrified to walk into. She'd tried to once, but got dizzy in the lobby and had to wait there while her parents went upstairs. She sat for an hour in front of a huge sign that said TODAY IS: Sunday March 15 1984. TONIGHT'S DINNER IS: Pot Roast and Apple Pie. IT IS Sunny OUTSIDE.

All of a sudden Jody didn't know where she was.

"Where are we?"

"On the road to Mandalay. Let's switch."

What the hell is Mandalay? Jody mused. Her mother pulled off the road and Jody went around to the driver's side.

They kept the doors locked, the windows rolled up, the air conditioning on high. Their only contact with the outside world was in gas stations, when the thick August air flooded the car quickly and silently. "Fill 'er up," they said to the attendants, and took turns going into dark, clammy bathrooms and squatting over the toilet, trying not to touch anything.

"Did you wash your hands?" her mother would ask every time Jody got back into the car.

Nashville, Tennessee, in the dark was not quite a million miles from home, but far enough. A Holiday Inn, a hot shower, a grilled cheese sandwich, a glass of milk. A phone call to Dad, a message left on Ellen's machine. All's well that ends well. Network television. "The Tonight Show" and, finally, sleep.

"I'm going to Graceland, Graceland." Paul Simon on the cassette deck.

"Mom, please—I always wanted to go to Graceland."

"Why?"

"To see the other people that go there, maybe buy an Elvis head in one of those things you shake up and the snow falls. You know, Elvis with dandruff."

"Let's not make it take too long."

Graceland: home of weeping women with high hair and polyester pants. Jody and her mother loved it. They spent seventy-five dollars on chotchkes. "Don't ever tell your father," Jody's mother said, handing over the Visa card. "Don't tell anyone." When her mother wasn't looking, Jody bought a gold-colored chain and locket complete with a picture of Jody and Elvis posed together courtesy of modern technology and Polaroid film. She gave it to her mother late that night in a hotel room in Little Rock, Arkansas.

"I love you, Mom," Jody said. "I really do."

"I love you too, sweetie, but I never thought I'd be in Arkansas."

They were in a fake-wood-paneled room, in twin beds, trying to fall asleep, trying not to let the blankets that had touched a thousand strangers touch them.

"I hope you realize that not every mother would do this."

Jody didn't say anything. She got up to check the chain on the door.

"Bring me two Advil, will you?" her mother said. "Everything is killing me."

The next day, in Oklahoma, her mother insisted on singing Woody Guthrie songs all the way across the state. "This land is your land. This land is my land." Oklahoma was six hours long—six hours of history, of her mother explaining about the dust bowl, the depression, migrant farming practices, all the reasons she'd refused to buy iceberg lettuce and green grapes during the majority of Jody's youth. By the time they hit Texas, Jody felt as if she'd memorized and memorialized John Steinbeck, had been indoctrinated into and expelled from every left-wing political movement since the turn of the century.

The worst night fell in Amarillo, Texas. In the green tile bathroom of a motor court Jody's gut was twisted by barbecued corn chips, root beer, and some sort of shredded meat sandwich her mother had pushed on her. Pained and delirious, Jody kept confusing Amarillo with armadillo, with the iguana in the Tennessee Williams play, with Richard Burton in Mexico. Was an iguana an armadillo? What was an armadillo, and why did they name a city after it?

"I have some Kaopectate in my toilet kit," her mother told her. "It's not so bad—you don't have to drink it anymore. It's a caplet, you just swallow it."

The idea of swallowing anything made Jody even more nauseated. In a cold chill, goose bumps breaking out on her arms and thighs, she sat immobile on the toilet.

"Are you all right?" her mother called. "If it doesn't stop, you'll have to do something."

"If it doesn't stop there's a reason," Jody said. An hour later she came out of the bathroom, weak, thin, the odd green tile permanently tattooed on her eyes.

"I'm dying," she announced.

"Does that mean I can go home now?" her mother said.

"Just make the funeral arrangements, then you can leave."

"Go down the hall and get a cold ginger ale out of the machine. It'll settle your stomach. You can bring me a soda too, something diet." Her mother rummaged through her suitcase and pulled out her nightgown. "I'm going to take a bath."

"Be careful in there," Jody said, nodding toward the bathroom. "You might want to wait a bit."

Her mother took the nightgown and her own personal can of Lysol and went into the bathroom. Jody heard a long hissing spray, closed her eyes, and slowly inhaled a long pull of germicide.

In the middle of the night, Jody woke to the sound of people fucking in the next room. Big sounds: out-of-control verbalizations, grunting, tortured bedsprings, Texas dirty talk. She hoped her mother would sleep through it.

"Santa Fe," her mother said, reading the road signs aloud. "I didn't realize we'd be this close. Can we stop?" she asked, taking the exit before Jody answered.

While her mother shopped for artifacts—Georgia O'Keeffe look-alike stuff—Jody bought postcards. Ever since they'd left home, she'd been thinking about what Claire would be like in the car, on the road. She kept trying to choose between Claire and her mother; and now she tried to envision the three of them in the car together, but it didn't work.

From a pay phone Jody called Ellen, collect.

"Where are you? How's L.A.?" Ellen asked.

"I'm not there yet," Jody said. She heard a strange noise in the background. "Are you in the middle of something?"

Ellen didn't say anything.

"Someone new? Someone I know?"

"Neither," Ellen said. And there was a groan in the background.

Jody couldn't tell if it was pleasure or disgust. "Well, don't let me keep you," she said. "I'll call from L.A."

The last time Jody had looked at the map, they were coming up on both the Painted Desert and the Petrified Forest. She was starting to wish she'd brought some Valium.

"Tomorrow we rest," her mother said as they unlocked the door to their room. "We go to the Grand Canyon. We spit on it."

"In it," Jody said.

"Whatever. You do what you want and I'll do what I want."

The Grand Canyon. If only Freud had seen it, Jody thought, life would be different. All around the analyzed world, the boundaries of acceptability would be broader and grandiosity would be celebrated. The significance of size in all subjects from dinner plates to penises would be acknowledged.

The day after their day off, the car broke down. It wouldn't have been a road trip without a breakdown.

"How come you're slowing down?" she asked her mother.

"I'm not," her mother said, pumping the gas pedal, sliding the gears into neutral, and attempting to restart before gliding to a soft stop on the edge of the road.

"Shit," Jody said, looking at the map. The time zone had changed again, Mountain to Pacific. If it was getting earlier and earlier, why did Jody feel like it was getting later and later?

She flipped through the Triptik, the Triple-A prayer book, and found the rescue number. The only hitch was that you had to be near a phone and they were in the middle of the goddamned desert. Jody could picture her mother making her get out of the car and walk. She'd walk for hours, become completely dehydrated, look up and see buzzards circling, waiting to come in for the kill.

Jody didn't offer to get out of the car or to look under the hood. She didn't say anything except "We probably shouldn't use the air conditioning if the engine's not running."

Finally, a couple driving a station wagon stopped and offered to use their car to push Jody and her mother down the road to a gas station.

"Every day it's something," her mother said.

"Is that supposed to be comforting?"

"Do we have to pay them?" her mother asked.

"I don't think so," Jody said. "You could offer, but they probably won't take it. They're doing it because they feel bad for us, and want to prove to each other what good people they really are."

"How do you know?"

Jody shrugged. At the gas station Jody's mother offered the couple twenty dollars and they took it without even pretending to protest.

"Don't see too many of these Japanese cars around here," the guy in the gas station said.

"It's a Saab," Jody said. "From Scandinavia."

"Same thing." The guy couldn't figure out how to open the hood. "Bunch of tricksters," he said, laughing. Jody got out to help him. "Ought to be a law against it, arranging things so you can't find 'em, don't you think?" he asked, finally locating the dipstick and pulling it out. "Oil's fine, though." He put the stick back into its hole.

"Just die on you?"

Jody nodded.

"Could be the alternator—lots of these Volvos got alternator problems."

"It's a Saab," Jody said, for the first time feeling possessive of the car that would be hers once they got to L.A.

"Well, give me a minute with it," the guy said.

Jody and her mother sat in the station office, and while the mechanic futzed—dropping tools, cussing himself and the car out—Jody started thinking. She thought to herself until the thoughts were too much and she was driven to speak, if only to relieve the pressure of thinking.

"Did you ever regret getting me?" she asked her mother. She purposely said *did* and *ever* rather than *do* or *now*, because she wanted to make it easy for her mother to say yes. And she purposely didn't use the word adopted, even though she knew her mother disliked it when Jody referred to herself as something they'd bought perhaps on a Sunday afternoon in a hardware store. Oh, and give me one of those children you've got over there. Lost my other one a couple of months ago, might as well go ahead and replace it now. . . .

"Don't you ever wish—"

Her mother cut her off. "I wonder why you're asking that now?"

Jody knew why, sort of, but wasn't about to admit anything. "A question with a question," she said.

"This isn't exactly the perfect place to talk."

"It's fine," Jody said, looking around at the oily service bays.

"You," her mother said, hitting the word with passion, "are my daughter." It came out with a kind of frightening edge Jody wasn't expecting. "Not someone else's. Mine. So what if I didn't have you? I *couldn't* have you. I couldn't have anyone else, either. Are you ever going to forgive me for not actually giving birth?"

Jody didn't say anything. Usually her mother wasn't so emphatic about it. Maybe they'd been driving too long, had spent too much time together, were too far from home, and were just plain exhausted. Jody felt bad. Her mother was fifty-five years old, almost past middle age, and still Jody pursued this topic with regularity and vigor. Would she ever give it up, or was it a ritual—their ritual, perhaps the basis for their relationship?

"I don't make up for him," Jody said, referring to her dead brother, whose name she couldn't bring herself to say out loud in the wilds of Arizona.

"You're not him," her mother said. "No one ever asked you to be anything other than yourself."

Jody knew this wasn't true, but to explain in the middle of a gas station was too complicated. Her mother was right, this wasn't the place for the conversation. It was a conversation best had some place safe and familiar, a place that could protect you even if you couldn't protect yourself.

Regardless, Jody couldn't let go. "If it weren't for him dying," she said, "you wouldn't have adopted me."

"We always wanted more children," her mother answered.

It was a familiar excuse. When her brother was born, something had happened—a ruptured uterus, something, Jody couldn't remember now. Anyway, the result was no more children. Her mother always used that medical fact as proof that Jody and the brother were separate issues.

"You never know," her mother said. "I always wanted a little girl."

"I know," Jody said.

They'd never had the whole conversation, the one they had to have in order to put the thing to rest. They never really said anything. It was all hemming and hawing, out of fear that someone might say the wrong thing, someone might get hurt.

The car problem was solved more easily than the thoughts stirred by their half-conversation. Within the hour they were back on the road, quieter than before. Jody knew it was because they were getting closer to Los Angeles. The closer they got, the sooner her mother would leave. But before she could leave, they had to go over everything one more time, as if to refresh their memories and confirm their understanding, to make everything less than perfectly clear for the millionth time. It was ritualistic. From the dead brother, they would progress; it wouldn't take long before they'd be discussing how Jody had hated to go to elementary school, moving on to her early therapy experiences, and closing out with how good it was that she was going off to graduate school to become what she'd always dreamed of being—a person? No. A filmmaker.

Two hundred and some miles later they were in California. Jody felt like she'd been holding her breath since they left home. In California she relaxed, breathed deeply, and then asked herself why. California was nothing, nowhere. It was the far edge of the country, a ledge waiting to fall into the ocean, an earthquake epicenter. Her chest tightened again, a strange shrinking sensation. She tried to comfort herself with signs. Mileage indicators, the big H's indicating hospitals, exits, and names of towns were her favorites.

"We have to make a decision," her mother said. "We're about a hundred and fifty miles away. Do we want to knock ourselves out and just get there or do we stop now and wait until tomorrow? What do you feel like doing?"

"Dunno," Jody said. "What do you want?"

"Rest," her mother said.

Jody was glad. Suddenly she was in no hurry to get there. The longer it took, the better.

"I need some Advil," her mother said. "I have this horrible muscle spasm in my back and all down my leg."

"I think we should kill ourselves," Jody blurted. "We should find a garage, close ourselves in, and let 'er rip."

"Too late," her mother said. "If that's what you wanted, you should've said something a long time ago. Just after Little Rock you might've convinced me, but now it's almost over."

"Exactly," Jody said. "It's over."

Jody lay on the bed in the final motor court of the journey paralyzed by the same thoughts that had frozen her five days before.

"You know," her mother said from the tub, "we're not going to be able to talk on the phone as much as we've been doing. It's very expensive to call California, so let's try and make it every other night from now on."

Alone in the room, Jody started to cry. She didn't mean to. Crying wasn't her specialty. She lay there bewildered, the tears running down her face. Her mother was deserting her. She was taking her to Los Angeles as a kind of final favor, then leaving her. Don't call us, we'll call you.

"What's wrong?" her mother asked, coming out of the bathroom, two towels wrapped around different parts of her body, her feet leaving damp tracks on the tan carpet.

Jody sniffled. "Why did you drive twenty-six hundred miles just to be mean to me?"

"Mean to you?"

"You drove me out here. You know I'm scared, and then you say 'By the way, don't call home anymore.' Who the hell am I supposed to call, the National Guard?"

"Stop it."

Jody got up, went into the bathroom, and slammed the door. Two glasses fell off a shelf and shattered on the floor.

"What're you doing in there?"

"Nothing," Jody said, bending down to pick up the glass.

"Come on. Let's find a nice place and have a decent dinner."

"Not hungry."

"Don't do this. I'm trying to help you. I'm not forcing you to go to Los Angeles. You wanted to come. I'm not the one who applied to graduate school. You're scared, that's all. Try and control yourself."

After a few minutes her mother said, "I'm hungry."

"So eat. Who's stopping you?"

"Be nice. I'm your mother. Now, come on. Let's go somewhere."

"McDonald's," Jody said.

"Is that what you're dying for?"

"McDonald's represents certain standards, certain givens. You know what you're getting before you even get it. They make everything in one place and then ship it all over the country. No matter where you go, the pieces are all exactly the same."

"Are you sure this is it?" Jody asked her mother. "I can't imagine picking this place." An ancient, four-story walk-up on a mound of land someone might accidentally call a hill, a cracked-up pool in the back: no one would call this home.

"You picked it," her mother said, unlocking the trunk, starting to unload onto the sidewalk. "This is the one you wanted."

"It's tacky," Jody said. First floor, no window bars, what had she been thinking?

"It's bigger than the one in New York," her mother said. "Three times the size."

"Great. I'll spend my nights patrolling the premises, clutching a shotgun."

"At the time that's what you liked about it. The word charm came up."

"Oh," Jody said, pulling open the sliding glass door that led out to the pool area. There must have been something that had attracted her to the place. But for now it reminded her of a bad David Hockney painting.

"We'll make it work," her mother said, carrying in more stuff. "Put up some shades, buy a few bright things. It'll be nice. You have a pool right outside your door. There's a view. It's always nice to have a view."

Her mother spent the rest of the week helping Jody find things: the bank, a decent supermarket, hardware store, cleaners, all the little things, donut shop, UCLA. They spent hours driving around Westwood, Hollywood, Beverly Hills, downtown, trying to figure out what connected what. The city was the strangest mishmash: Miami meets Mexico meets a set designer and a special-effects team, a horror movie. Weird foliage was everywhere, lots of things with sharp leaves, bushes that looked half-dead. Jody's eyes ached from the sun. She broke down and bought herself a pair of Ray-Bans, the real thing.

They scrubbed, soaked, and sterilized the apartment as if the previous tenant had been a certified serial killer. Jody didn't particularly want to start putting things away. Unpacking meant she was staying, and in her heart she still wasn't sure. The day her mother would have to leave got closer and Jody still didn't know where the airport was, how she'd drive there and back.

"I'll go alone," her mother said. "We'll say arrivederci here and I'll take the airport car or whatever it is."

Jody knew that her mother was afraid she'd snap. At the departure gate Jody would demand to get on the plane, to go back home.

The apartment was almost finished. "You just need a few more little things," her mother said. "If we hurry, I can buy you a plant before I have to go to the airport."

They drove to a strange plant warehouse her mother had noticed the day before and bought a huge ficus for the living room.

Her mother zipped her suitcase closed, and Jody opened the door to keep an eye out for the airport limo.

"Maybe we should say goodbye before we leave the apartment," her mother said, fixing her hair.

How do you say goodbye and then spend the next hour sitting thigh to thigh with someone you've just hugged and kissed like you'll never see them again? The horn blew outside.

Jody and her mother went out together, Jody helping load her mother's suitcase into the trunk. Car service both ways: the low-stress, high-cost solution. Airport limo to curbside, ticket agent, baggage check, security to departure gate, check-in, seat assignment.

Would Jody ever see her mother again? Would the plane get home all right?

"Thanks," Jody said, kissing her mother.

"It was nothing," her mother said. "Do well. Be good. I'll talk to you when I get home. I love you."

"I love you too."

"I'll call you. Call Daddy and tell him I got on okay."

"Okay."

"Bye."

Another kiss at the last gate. The back of the mother walking away. The back of the mother; sadness rising. The back of the mother disappearing. Lots of other people moving up the ramp where the mother just was. When to leave the airport? Wait until they close the door of the plane, until they announce last call, until they vacuum-seal everyone in and the engines start up, until the man with orange cone pointers for hands pushes the plane backwards with a couple flicks of the wrist? Should she run to the observation deck and try to find the plane outside? Should she watch every plane rev up and race down the runway? How long should she stand there—until the plane lands in Washington? At what point should she let go, turn on her heels, and head back the way she came, toward the strange city that was now her home?

"UCLA," she said to the cab driver.

20

Plotting how to use every available inch, Claire and Sam stuffed the car with everything they owned and more—things they'd bought just to struggle with, groceries that were readily available in the Easthampton A&P but which were somehow better coming from home. As they carried what seemed like the entire contents of their apartment down to the sidewalk, the sky began to darken.

"Hurry," Sam said.

"We're in trouble," Jake said.

When Claire went upstairs to get the last few things, she found Adam standing in the middle of the living room, crying. Rushing made him nervous. When he was nervous, he cried. Claire gave him graham crackers and sent him down to the lobby with Jake.

The apartment was quiet, still. It looked better with the stuffing taken out of it. It looked like the kind of place Claire would want to live. She had the urge to run downstairs and tell them to go without her.

Checking to make sure they had everything, Claire realized she'd packed as though she were leaving for good, not going on vacation. When just going away, you took what you needed, ugly and practical items that could get lost or ruined without causing any grief. But Claire had packed silk blouses and shoes that cost two hundred and fifty dollars a pair. There was no reason to even take them out of the suitcase, or to take the suitcase out of the car—except that it was less likely to get stolen from the back of a closet than from the trunk of a car.

As they drove up Third Avenue toward the Midtown Tunnel, it started to pour.

" 'Rain, rain, go away,' " Adam sang, " 'Come again some other day.' " It was his first big trip without a car seat; he was seat-belted in and propped up on two pillows so he could look out the window.

If the trunk leaked, her things would be ruined.

On the Long Island Expressway a car was trapped in an enormous puddle, a miniature flash flood. Traffic pulled around it in a great wide arc, not touching even the edges of the puddle, unsure where the disaster started, where it stopped. Water came up to the door handles of the trapped car. Claire saw that the man and woman inside looked surprised; if they opened their doors, water would rush in, and there was no way of knowing how much, or if it would ever stop. If it had been a different kind of couple and a different kind of car, they could have climbed out through the sun roof and stood on the trunk waving their arms until someone took pity on them and pulled over to help. Without seeming to notice, Sam drove around them.

"Cool," Jake said.

Outside of Flushing, Queens, they passed the skeletal remains of the 1964 World's Fair. The car bounced in and out of potholes, across bad road joints, and eventually the expressway opened up: twelve-plex movie theaters, car dealerships, and fields of high grass instead of high-rise apart-ment projects. Claire opened a bag of Hershey's Kisses and passed some back to the kids. At fifty-five miles per hour, traffic hummed down the island, forming a line that backed up half a mile at the traffic light in Southampton and continued in a hinged snake down through Watermill, Bridgehampton, Easthampton, and Amagansett.

They turned right on Simon's Lane. Ever since last January, when they'd arranged to rent the house, Claire had been repeating the address—Simon's Lane, Amagansett—over and over again to herself as if it held some magical power, the promise of salvation.

"Which one is it?" Sam asked.

Claire pulled a photo out of her purse and compared it to every house they passed. "Matches," she said, staring at a two-story gray-shingled house and then back down at the photo. "See, it's the porch."

In the photo and in reality, there was a glassed-in sun porch off the right side of the house, four windows across the front, green shutters, and neatly trimmed hollies hugging the foundation. Sam pulled into the drive-way.

The house was larger and more run-down than Claire remembered. As she carried her suitcase up the stairs, she thought she saw something dart across the hall. She didn't want to think what.

Even though there were three bedrooms, she put Adam and Jake to-gether in the one that was painted a boyish blue. The empty bedroom was a rich red, and Jake wanted it for himself, but Claire said no; she suspected the red would make him psychotic—not immediately but later, when, in his mid-twenties, he'd turn into a serial killer. The red was too much like birth or death, she wasn't sure which; regardless, neither was particularly soothing.

"We'll save it for company," she told Jake. "Besides, Adam really needs you. If he's by himself in a whole new house, he'll probably keep us up all night. Be a sport."

"You owe me," Jake said.

The master bedroom was a reassuring dark green that would hold them well in their sleep.

A couple of hours later, as she was sitting on the sun porch resting a wrenched back, a tail flicked against Claire's leg and she screamed. A cat ran across the room and hid under the sofa. Claire immediately called the real estate agent. A second cat slipped down the stairs and headed for the kitchen.

"There are cats in this house," she said.

"Hold on," the realtor said. "Let me check."

"One just rubbed against my leg, you don't have to check."

"Let's see, that's Simon's Lane . . . nothing on my card about cats. Are you allergic?"

"No, but I don't exactly love them."

"I'll get rid of them, if you want," the realtor said, giving the impression of the cats' lives being drastically foreshortened. Claire didn't particularly like cats, but didn't want to be responsible for euthanizing them either. She'd rather go ahead, open a couple of cans of food, and deal with it. "Forget it," she said.

"I'll arrange for you to be reimbursed for food and kitty litter. Just keep the receipts."

Kitty litter—yuck, Claire thought, and immediately wrote it down on the first line of a shopping list.

On the first morning of their vacation, Claire woke up clutching the edge of the mattress and wondering where she was. She looked out the window at the sandy yard. She hated sand. Invisible to Sam and the boys, it would creep into the house, settle on the sofa, fill the bathtub, crawl up the stairs into their beds, and it would be her job to chase it out. She didn't want to be on vacation. She wanted to be alone in her office with some poor pathetic person pouring out his or her soul. This was too much.

Claire was expected to know everything. It was as if a mother, any mother, could without question be transported from house to house and always know where the forks were, how the stove turned on, and where the extra toilet paper was kept. She didn't know anything. She didn't even want to be here.

She lay on the bed, facing the window. When Sam finally got up, she pretended to be sleeping. She heard the children moving around, their plastic pajama feet shuffling across the bare wood floor, the TV set clicking on and off, channels changing, volume going up. She heard the toilet seat flip up, bang against the tank, followed by the hiss of someone peeing and then silence.

"Flush, goddamnit!" she screamed, swinging her feet over the edge of the bed. Their laziness stirred her. They were sitting around in their pajamas acting like they didn't know how to feed or dress themselves. The imbecile family. Her anger pulled her up and out of bed, barking commands. "Get dressed: pants, shirts, shoes, socks, no shorts, too cold for shorts." She slammed containers of milk, juice, and cereal onto the kitchen table and glared at them while they watched her, bug-eyed. "Too cold, windy, cloudy to go to the beach," she said, too tired to speak in whole sentences. "Daddy's taking you to a movie."

When they finally left, after Claire had called the theater, written down a schedule for Sam, jotted down the name of a place to take the children for lunch, the address of a video arcade where they could go if all else failed, after she'd given them a complete itinerary and shoved them out of the house, she poured their leftover cereal milk into a bowl for the cats and lay down in the bed again. She would have to ease into the idea of vacation.

The next morning was clear and still. They got ready quickly and walked down Simon's Lane to Old Town Road. From a block away they could see the water, sparkling under the morning light. Worried about traffic, Claire held Adam's hand. Strangers passed them on bicycles and said hello. Near the water, Claire turned the orchestration of the family over to Sam. The older the boys got, the less they were hers; the more pronounced the difference between male and female, the more they belonged to Sam.

While she set up camp, Adam rode into the water, high on his father's shoulders. Jake threw himself head-first into the waves, screaming "Dad! Look at me!" She was an outsider among her own. She sat back on the sand, watching them chase one another up onto the dunes and back down into the water, and thought of two things: Lyme disease and how badly they needed a house, a backyard.

Claire closed her eyes, lay back in her chair, and let the whoosh and roar of the breeze and the waves sweep over her, as though the wind, the flying grains of sand, and the sharp, salty spray could erase an entire year's worth of other people's problems.

That night, she snuggled up against Sam's warm red skin and rubbed her thigh across his crotch. "What would you think about having a baby?" she asked.

"You're scaring me," he said.

"Scaring myself." She ran her tongue over his neck, flicking his earlobe, tickling the gray roots of his chest hair. "It has to be a girl," she said a minute later, as he rolled on top of her.

"I'll do my best."

Two days later she got her period. Was it early or late? It didn't matter anyway, though it did explain everything: why she was so tired yesterday, crabby last week, how come she was constantly a miserable bitch while Sam and the boys were always, if not cheerful, at least energetic and less than homicidal.

Sam offered to take her out to dinner.

"To celebrate?" she asked.

He shrugged. "It was kind of impulsive."

The offer of dinner out, Claire puzzled, or the unprotected sex?

The last time she'd gone to the gynecologist, she'd asked about the possibility of having more children. Claire had lain there, ankles at her ears, listening to a statistical recital performed from the space between her legs as if the doctor were speaking directly to her uterus, her ovaries, her sex. When he finished, he popped up and said, "If you're going to do it at all, do it soon." And she left with a pat on the leg, a refitted diaphragm, and a pamphlet on mothering past forty stuffed into her purse.

On the beach, in the still heat of August, suffering vicious cramps, she saw herself as a finished thing wringing the last of life out of itself, waiting to be discarded. Sam would leave her for a younger, sexier, more fertile woman. The boys would follow, not willing to be abandoned by their hero. The new wife would build them the perfect clubhouse, and every year they'd call Claire on her birthday, pick up three separate extensions, sing a chorus of "Happy Birthday"—including the 'How old are you now?' verse—and then hang up.

She lay flat on the sand, her innards pulsing, beating out blood. Sam came out of the ocean and stood over her, dripping cold salt water onto her stomach. She sat up and everything started to go black.

"I have to go back to the house for a minute," she said.

"Do you want to make lunch and bring it back for us?"

She shook her head. "There's your lunch," she said, pointing to the beach stand a few hundred yards away.

"Do you have money?" he asked.

She handed him ten dollars.

He waited for more. "This is Easthampton," he said.

"That's all I've got," she said, adding another ten. Then she raised her hand for Sam to help her up and walked slowly back to the house, the hot sand burning her feet, her head light and eyes half-blind, concentrating only on the swollen pain at the bottom of her stomach. She walked down the road, sure she was leaking blood down the insides of her thighs, leaving a trail drawing dogs and curious busybodies out of their houses to watch a middle-aged woman who, despite being almost thirty years into it, still had no grip on this woman business. A woman running home like a stuck pig.

In the cool shade of the house, she checked, put her fingers between her legs, pulled them out, and looked. Nothing except the white Tampax string. She spent the afternoon alone in a cool coma, sandwiched between the sheets of their rented bed.

If she had a daughter, if her daughter were there, *she* would've come back to the house with Claire. She would have curled up with her and spent the afternoon reading magazines and eating frozen yogurt. If her daughter were there, they'd take off in the car and go shopping in Sag Harbor, to all kinds of antique shows and craft fairs. They'd go out for lunch and leave Sam and the boys to fend for themselves.

By the end of the week Sam and the boys had friends. They knew the names of everyone up and down the street and were regularly hopping into shiny cars and riding into town with strangers, acting as though they were best friends simply because they'd rented houses on the same block. Claire felt as though she was constantly being forced to smile, to say hello, to make chitchat. As much as possible, she stayed alone. When Sam asked what the problem was, she said, "My job is listening to people's problems. To me a vacation is silence, not having to talk all the time."

"Couldn't you just be civil?" Sam asked.

Claire didn't answer. She walked to and from the beach, up and down the lane briskly, with the brim of her hat pulled down over the wide rims of her sunglasses.

To make Sam happy, she agreed to go to one party. "Just one," she said. "You pick it."

He chose cocktails at the home of an entertainment lawyer he knew from Columbia.

"His wife has the money," Sam whispered as they stood on the rear deck of the Sagaponack spread, looking out across the length of the pool to the salt pond, the thin strip of beach behind it, and the ocean in the distance. Three different waters; three colors against the twilight.

"Great view, huh?" Sam's lawyer friend said. "Let me get you a drink—what'll it be?" He clapped his hands together hard, exploding the air like a shot.

"Scotch," Sam said.

"Absolut and tonic," Claire said.

"That's my drink," he said to Claire, winking. "Twist of lemon, twist of lime. Be right back."

Claire stood at the edge of the deck and let Sam schmooze. She sipped her drink, listening to the whispering rustle of the reeds and cat-o'-nines in the salt pond and watching the night sky fall and the ocean slip from view.

When her glass was empty, she carried it into the house for a refill. Modern jazz was blaring on the CD player. Every light in the house was on. Right and left people were yelling in order to be heard. Claire moved quickly, got a fresh drink, and hurried back outside, stopping only when the wife of someone Sam knew touched her elbow and said, "Hi, Claire, how are you?"

"Good," Claire said. "And you?"

"Super."

How good can you get? Good, better, best? No, super! Claire headed for the cool darkness of the deck, where bits of conversation drifted over and landed around her like debris.

"Long story short, she told him to get out. And she made him take the kids. He didn't even want them."

"Sell. That's all I have to say to you. Not another word. Sell. Are you hearing me? Sell."

"You really should go back on Valium. I know it's gotten bad press, and there was that Jill Clayburgh movie all those years ago, but nothing else does the trick. Half a blue one and it's all fixed. I took one tonight before we came here. I don't know how you live without it."

Drink in hand, Claire lay back on a padded lounge and dreamed.

That afternoon, thumbing through a local paper, she'd seen a series of photographs taken at "the wrap party given by Soho art dealer Christopher William at his Watermill estate, celebrating the completion of director Harry Birenbaum's new film." In attendance were three young Kennedys, George Plimpton, the actress Carol Heberton, several rock stars and their model wives, a fistful of famous young artists, and Birenbaum himself, looking every bit the beached whale Jody said he was.

If Jody had been in New York instead of en route to Los Angeles, her picture would've been in the paper too, Claire was sure of it. And if Jody had been there, she would've invited Claire along to the party. Jody would have taken Claire's hand and led her around the room, stopping at the edges of all the good conversations, introducing her to all the right people.

Claire looked out onto the night. Down by the pool, a heavy man draped in linen was holding court. Claire imagined it was Harry Birenbaum. He was surrounded by an eager gaggle of men and women content to listen to him pontificate, to duck his wild gesticulations. Claire sat staring until she realized the crowd around the man had thinned and now the man was staring back. In her dark corner she blushed. She finished her drink and put the glass down next to her chair.

"Have we met?" the man asked, sliding into the next chair, his linen drapery moving with a soft windy whisper.

"No," Claire said.

"I feel like I know you," he said, extending his hand, holding Claire's for a moment too long.

Claire smiled. "Perhaps you know my daughter, Jody Goodman?"

He shook his head. "Doesn't ring a bell," he said and then paused. "But I'm sure you and I have met before. Are you at Paul Weiss?" he asked.

"No," Claire said, spotting Sam in the distance, excusing herself, and walking away unevenly. When she slipped her hand into the crook of Sam's elbow, he turned from his conversation and put his hand on hers.

"You're like ice," he said.

She nodded.

"Are you all right? Do you want to go home?"

Claire let Sam guide her back through the crowd, through the house, out the door, and down the long driveway to their car.

"Everything okay?" he asked, taking off his jacket and wrapping it around her.

"Fine."

Later, after the baby-sitter was paid, the porch lights turned off, and her dress returned to the closet, Claire drew a deep breath and sighed.

"It wasn't that bad, was it?" Sam asked.

Claire slipped between the cool sheets and snapped off the light on her side of the bed. "Don't forget to hang up your blazer," she said. "I don't have a dry cleaner out here."

On the second Monday morning, Sam left on the six a.m. train and Claire felt like a suburban widow, a woman without a husband until the weekend.

Late on the rainy Tuesday that followed, safe and dry inside the East-hampton library, while Adam sat on the carpet with a dozen other chil-dren listening to a story and Jake picked through sports biographies, Claire decided to do some digging.

"How would I look up adoption?" she asked the librarian.

"Information on how to adopt?"

"Searches. Parents and children looking for each other." She might as well have been a twelve-year-old researching menstruation, sneaking around like a spy.

The librarian led Claire into the stacks and, using her index finger as a pointer, scanned the shelves, fingernail clicking against the spine of every volume. She pulled down several books and handed them to Claire. "You might also want to look in the subject guide to *Books in Print* and the *Readers Guide to Periodical Literature.*"

"Thanks," Claire said.

"You might also want to go to a bigger library," the librarian added.

"This is fine, thank you."

Claire sat in a chair by the window, shivering. Outside, it was thundering, raining, and raw; inside, the air conditioning was blasting. It was like being in a refrigerator. She hoped the kids wouldn't end up with sore throats.

One of the books the librarian gave her had a resource guide in the back, a list of organizations and addresses. Claire went through her purse and all her pockets, rounding up change.

"Have you got any change?" she whispered to Jake. "I'll buy it from you."

"Sixty cents for a dollar," Jake said, holding out the money.

"Thanks," Claire said, giving him a dollar. She Xeroxed the pages, rolled them into a tube, and slipped them under her raincoat. On the way home, she stopped at the drugstore, bought a pad of writing paper, a box of envelopes, and a Monopoly game.

While Jake and Adam fought over Boardwalk and Park Place, Claire sat at the kitchen table, working out a draft.

Please send any and all information about your organization, its publications and programs, as well as any additional information on resources that would be helpful in conducting a search for a child given up in Washington, D.C., in 1966. Thank you. I have enclosed a check for fifteen dollars so that you may mail me the information via express/overnight mail.

She wrote out ten copies exactly alike, stuffed them into envelopes along with ten checks, and instantly began waiting.

Without Sam, she sat on the beach watching Jake and Adam playing at the water's edge and thinking of Jody. As far as she was concerned, Jody was the child. The papers and the searching were only a way of confirming what she already knew. For the first time she felt like the mother of three children. She felt complete. Everything had come together. In Claire's mind, she had done a marvelous thing by setting Jody free and enabling her to begin her own life. Claire was the elusive perfect parent, the woman whose child came and went effortlessly, without conflict. She saw Jody as her own personal success story. And without being made to feel the burden of meeting a mother's needs, Jody had given Claire something she'd been wanting for twenty-four years: her child was back.

Like Samantha in "Bewitched," like Jeannie in "I Dream of Jeannie," Claire had meddled, but had acted invisibly. No one would ever know she'd been there; no one would ever suspect her. From a safe distance she'd made her mark, staked her claim. Now she could sit back and watch and things would be wonderful. Thankfully, she'd controlled herself during those sessions when she couldn't concentrate on a word Jody was saying, when it was all she could do to keep from blurting out, "But sweetie, I'm your mother!"

Claire looked out across the sand at the people around her. It was shrink month at the beach. Men with thick dark beards, skinny white legs, and fat asses hid under huge umbrellas, their faces protected by new hardcover books. It was their month to let it all hang out. There was no one there except shrinks—the August rents were so high that most other people couldn't afford them. Two hundred pale weird kids on the beach. A hundred and fifty weird parents in the sand. Shrink fathers and mothers alternately screaming at and ignoring their children. A regular shrink convention.

Claire checked at the post office every day, and soon packages started to arrive. First, a long bibliography with a Post-it attached and a message written in loopy handwriting—"For search information in the Washington area, contact the Safe-Place Support System," with an address and a phone number. The next day, a copy of the District of Columbia Code on Adoption, fifteen pages of fine-print gobbledygook: "Persons who may adopt . . . Consent . . . Legislative History of the law . . . Subsection (e) of this section is not unconstitutional on the grounds that it denies a natural parent due process. . . . Birth Certificates . . . Notice of final decree of adoption shall be sent to the commissioner (mayor). Unless otherwise requested in the petition by the adopters, the commissioner (mayor) shall cause to be made a new record of the birth in the new name and with the names of the adopters and shall then cause to be sealed and filed the original birth certificate with the order of the court. The sealed package may be opened only by order of the court."

Claire read it all and then called the girl down the street to baby-sit, while she rested upstairs in the bedroom, shades drawn.

The next day a package came from the International Soundex Reunion Registry in Carson City, Nevada. A form marked *Confidential* read: "No Fee Charged for Registration. Present Name ____. Searcher Is ____."

Halfway down the page was a blue asterisk and the instructions: "Fill out this form as completely as possible in respect to the adoptee or other child as facts were known when the separation occurred."

Claire couldn't do it. She was sick. All she wanted was substantiation, gratification, an official notice. It was as simple and complicated as that. She looked at the form, held her pencil to the paper, and couldn't write her name. Jody had said that she'd never search; it didn't mean that much to her. Was she lying? Did she not want Claire to be her mother? Sometimes Jody gave Claire the feeling that maybe she didn't really need her, or at least not as much as Claire needed Jody. Claire filled out the top line—Present Name, Claire Roth—and stopped. She worried that she'd actually fill out the form, send it in, and they'd send her the name and phone number of a doughy girl who worked in a Burger King mixing shakes.

There was nothing to do. The days and nights were mindless, punctuated only by Jake and Adam's demands to be driven out to Montauk to play miniature golf, to the video store, the CD place, the ice cream shop. For days on end Claire focused on the information packets, the forms. Every morning she walked to the post office, stuffed the mail into her beach bag, and carried it with her down to the water. She'd sit on her blanket, facing the sun, and pore over the papers. Every time she opened a new envelope, her stomach knotted, twisted, and sank. She carried the information everywhere, and finally, at the end of the week, put it all into the night-table drawer and walked away. Jody was her daughter and that was that. She'd made up her mind and didn't need anything else.

One weekday, after she'd spent eight hours in the sun, after she'd eaten two Häagen-Dazs ice cream bars and drunk a large Coke while the kids were off with friends, Claire fell into thick afternoon sleep and dreamt about Jody. They were in bed together, naked: Jody's mouth at her breast, her tongue on Claire's nipple. Claire rolled towards Jody, and in her sleep felt herself seduced.

A crying toddler walking up and down the sand woke her. "Shh . . . shh," a woman said again and again, trailing after the child. Claire was confused, blinded by the glare. She couldn't keep her eyes open. She was scared and horny. The more she thought about the dream, the more frightening it became. She rolled onto her stomach and put her head down again, pressing her face against the blanket.

In the dream everything appeared perfectly normal, as though this were the way it was supposed to be. On the beach in front of her was the shrink convention, and still Claire had no one to ask. She reached for a legal pad and attempted to diagram it for herself. Mother, Child, Oedipus, Freud. The dream didn't belong to an old dead shrink, to any particular theory; it was her own.

21

UCLA film brats. Everyone knew someone or had sold something. They all thought they were special. Who to be friends with, and how? Talk about sleeping with the famous record producer's son? Tell the truth, or lie? Or maybe wimp out and hang with the weaklings, the quiet ones, the ugly ones who must have gotten in on talent since they didn't have anything else? The first day of school. Eighteen years of first days, all of them exactly the same, all as horrible as the one when she was almost four and her mother dropped her off at nursery school and she stood on the front step screaming as her mother's car disappeared down the driveway.

"Hi, I'm Jody." Shake hands, look at your feet. "I'm from New York."

New York was good, much better than Bethesda or Washington. Washington *State?* Oh, Washington, D.C. Is your father a senator?

"Where in New York?"

"The city. The West Village." Good move, Jody.

Registration, classes, meetings. Shaking hands with people whose names she wouldn't remember in an hour or a month.

"Hi, my name is Bob, I'm not an alcoholic." A joke? "I'm from Minneapolis."

"What are we supposed to be doing?"

Compare Xeroxed information sheets and maps, run around in circles, get registration cards stamped and bad pictures taken, become official. Then, at the bookstore, charge things for yourself, books you always meant to read, magazines, stupid things for the apartment, a blackboard—things that'll really help you get organized.

"Ice cream?" Bob asked. "You want to go have some ice cream?" Unpretentious, down to earth, midwestern.

"Sure," Jody said. And on the way out, they picked up a lost girl named Ilene, formerly from the deep East Village, the roots of her dyed black hair already turning a peculiar orange from the California sun.

"Look," she said. "Would you look at my hair?"

"I'm looking," Jody said. It was hard to miss.

"You're from Minneapolis," Ilene said to Bob. "Do you know Prince?" Another joke? A lot of comedy in these situations, stress-induced one-liners.

Friendships formed. Inseparable at first. Three was a good number. They expanded sometimes to four, sometimes to five, and sometimes shrank to two if someone was busy, tired, or fed up. New situations were overwhelming. Sometimes everyone had to be alone, decompress, call home, remember who she was and why she was doing this.

"Hi, honey, how was your day?" Jody's mother asked nightly at eight o'clock Pacific time. "How's the apartment coming along? Are you watering the ficus? Not too much. Have you met anyone interesting yet? Maybe you'll find a boyfriend out there. You know, we really should talk less often, the phone bill's going to be sky high."

Jody's apartment was mediocre, but so was almost everyone's. There were a few rich kids with major daddy money and nice apartments; a few people, mostly couples, who'd rented little houses. Jody wasn't particularly envious, but still, the apartment wasn't really a home. She'd never looked out onto a palm tree before. She'd never had a pool in the backyard, either. She thought of swimming, dipping her face into the water, turning to the side, breathing. Outside of her parents' basement, the horrible furniture somehow got better; the memories invested in it seeped out into the warm air, and Jody began to feel attachment, comfort, nostalgia.

Jody thought of Claire at the beach—their house was probably a quaint twelve-room cottage on the ocean that had been in the family for years. Claire undoubtedly spent the mornings in the kitchen, putting together massive picnics that she hauled to the water's edge in a little red wagon. Afternoons were spent on the sand with assorted children and neighbors snacking on warm soda and grainy egg-salad sandwiches, pondering whether the crunchy parts were eggshell or sand. She saw Claire's blond hair becoming nearly translucent, her skin browning. Every night there would be a fancy cocktail party on someone's deck. Jody half wished she hadn't left Claire behind, half wished she could talk to her now, tell her stories about everything as it happened, describing the people, the teachers, the city itself, making the horrible things funny.

"Harry B. is coming to town . . . ," Harry sang an off-key and off-color version of the Christmas carol on Jody's answering machine. "You better watch out, you better not cry, you better not shout, 'cause I'm taking you out."

Five days later he arrived in a chauffeur-driven Bentley. Jody had to skip a program meeting and a screenwriting class in order to keep the date.

"Hello, sweets," he said, kissing her full on the lips as she climbed into the car. She subtly wiped her lips with the back of her hand. "Excuse the man at the wheel, but I absolutely cannot drive in this town. I'm fine in the Alps, perfectly happy on the streets of Paris, but *this,*" he said, gesturing widely, encompassing the entire Los Angeles basin with his sweep, "drives me crazy."

"I could have driven," Jody said.

Harry scowled, waved his hands, and whispered the destination to the driver. "Tell me how it's been," he said.

"It's only been a month."

"Are you regretting your decision to abandon me?"

"No."

"In time," Harry said, gazing out the window as Hollywood slipped past.

They went to Chasins. Even though Harry spent almost no time in Los Angeles anymore, he knew everyone and, from the moment they were seated, held court. Right and left, from appetizers through coffee, people dropped by the table and chatted—or chattered, in Jody's view.

"I'm a vice-president at Paramount now," one would say. "Let's do lunch."

"Let's," Harry would answer, adding, "Do you know my friend Jody Goodman?"

The vice-president would blink and extend his hand. "I don't think we've met."

"Ms. Goodman is a stellar young filmmaker. Stellar."

"Oh, really," the veep would say, reaching into his jacket pocket, fishing out crisp business cards, setting one down on the table next to Harry and handing the other to Jody, who in a flush of embarrassment would knock her knife onto the floor.

By the time the dinner was over, Jody had met at least twenty people, collected sixteen business cards and three tentative lunch dates, spilled one glass of water, lost two knives, and was starving to death, because in an effort to make decent conversation she'd been unable to eat.

"Most productive, don't you think?" Harry said as they stood at the restaurant's entrance, waiting for the Bentley to pull up.

"I suppose," Jody said.

"That's how it's done. Are you hungry, good girl? Are you ready to truly dine?"

"I could eat."

Harry again whispered instructions to the driver, who sped them off to a nearby drive-through McDonald's, and they feasted on Big Macs, fries, and shakes while the man at the wheel took them on a slow, smooth tour of Beverly Hills. Fatter than ever and stoned on sugar, Harry reached over and tried to feel Jody up. She bent her head down to meet his hand where it lay on her chest and bit him hard, leaving deep pink tooth marks in his spongy flesh.

Jody had done it: she'd gotten to L.A. Everything was fine; there were people to meet, parties to go to, mini-events where a screenwriter or director talked or showed something, passes to screenings. Soon there were choices and phone numbers Jody had to memorize.

Out of the blue Michael called. "News flash," he said when Jody picked up the phone. "A fish on the line. For you, and just for you, because I love you." He was playing with her, doing an L.A. routine. "Let's have phone lunch—it's like phone sex, only better. We both order salads, keep the receiver tucked under our chins, and you crunch and chew heavily into my ear."

"What's the deal?" Jody asked. "It's not like you to run up your phone bill."

"An old friend called. He's out there going into production in La-La Land and could use a smart little helper. You got any spare time?"

"Maybe. Who is it?"

"Gary Marc."

"Are you serious?"

"Do I dial long distance for my own entertainment? Call him at the studio, he's expecting to hear from you. And P.S.—don't tell him you fucked the record guy's son. They hate each other from way back."

"How'd you know I slept with him?"

"From the look on your face."

"I'm so glad I don't work for you anymore," Jody said.

"Mutual. Listen, I'll talk to you later. . . . By the way, Harry told me he had a nice dinner and that your tits are bigger than he thought."

Jody laughed.

"We're looking at a rough cut tomorrow. I'll let you know how it goes."

"Thanks," Jody said. "Thanks a lot."

She had the prime spot, the best job, the jealous respect of her fellow students.

"How'd you get it?" they asked.

"Just did," Jody said. "Phone rang one day, like in the movies."

Two hundred hours a week, that's what it felt like.

Gary Marc. Mr. Producer. Mr. Hollywood. His house in Bel Air had an air-conditioned tennis court and the freezer was stocked with ice cubes made out of lime Perrier. "Call Brando for me—I was supposed to tell him about this thing. . . . Oh, God, it's Shirley MacLaine's birthday— send her flowers, make up something good to say on the card." Soon Jody knew not just where and when but *how* Gary liked to lunch, in what kind of light, facing what direction. "I'm seeing a couple of actresses read today—be there. I want to hear what you think." Jody, the arbiter of good taste, the uncorruptible New Yorker, critical, logical, on target. "Funny. You're very funny." A compliment—but how come everyone always said the same thing? She wasn't *that* funny. Still, any compliment from the Marc Man himself was to be taken seriously.

"Thanks," she said. Jody loved it.

The weather was nice, not offensive. Without even trying she had a little bit of a tan, although she sometimes wondered if it wasn't radiation burn off the computer screen.

When she wasn't in class, or doing the required amount of socializing, when she wasn't schlepping for Gary, she sat in front of what amounted to a blank black-and-white TV trying to draw pictures with words. Medium shot. Car chase. Interior fast-food restaurant. Daylight. Phone call. Blackout. Sex scene. It was a comedy. As long as she was entertaining herself, she thought it was good. So far, it was a movie she'd love to see. Jody was having fun; she was doing fine. Once, twice, or three times a day, she reminded herself—told you so.

A guy named Simon, from San Diego, asked Jody out a couple of times. On what Jody thought would be the big night, she hid a condom in her shoe—her skirt didn't have pockets, and she wasn't about to carry a purse—and hurried to meet him by the mailboxes in the film department. After a lecture by Mel Brooks, they went to Simon's apartment. With his roommate, Steve, in the next room, they sat on his futon and watched the video he'd used as his application to film school. It was all zoo footage. "Sweet," Jody said. "Very sweet."

"We have to talk," Simon said breathlessly. "It's about Steve. He likes me. Last night, we got plastered, had a huge discussion, and . . . well, I think I like him too. I just don't know. I hope you're not pissed."

"Nope," Jody said. "Pissed isn't the word for it." And she stood up, pulled herself together, and walked out of the apartment.

"See you tomorrow," Simon called after her.

It was the beginning of the fall; it was supposed to start getting cold outside, dark earlier, and with any luck eventually it would snow. But not in Los Angeles, not in the land of the great imagination. At best it was chilly and raw, rainy. Jody was tired. She was having a great time, but she was exhausted; the fun was no longer fun. It was too fucking tiring. It made no sense. Jody was happy. She kept checking herself: I'm happy, right?

One night while she was home writing, Jody heard sirens and tires squealing in the distance. She didn't think anything of it. If anything, it seemed perfectly normal, just like New York. Then, without warning, there was a loud bang. The bulb in her Luxo lamp blew out as a car slammed into the corner of Jody's apartment. Her computer lost its memory; a broken headlight and grille poked through the wall where the ficus had been. Police cars pulled up and spun red and blue light circles on the empty walls. Radios squawked. The doorbell rang.

"Are you all right?" a cop asked.

Jody nodded.

"We're evacuating the building until we can be sure the gas lines weren't damaged."

"There's a car in my apartment."

"We'll have to get a building inspector. Is your phone working?"

Jody shrugged, pointed to the phone, and the cop picked it up, listened, and started dialing. She turned off her computer.

"Are you sure you're all right?"

Jody picked up her keys, wallet, and notebook, then followed the cop outside.

Using what they called "the jaws of life," the firemen cut the car roof open and peeled it back like it was a can of sardines. There was blood and metal everywhere. Paramedics started working on the two people inside even before they were able to pull them out. Photographers and camera crews showed up. Jody went around the corner and walked ten blocks before she could find a pay phone.

"Some asshole broke a date with me—that's why I'm home," Ellen said. "You know how much I hate to be home."

"A car crashed into my apartment," Jody said, perfectly calmly. "While I was in it."

"You wrecked your car."

"No, someone else's car wrecked my apartment. They're cutting the idiots out now."

"Are they dead?"

"Almost."

"So listen," Ellen said. "It's kind of good you left New York, 'cause I'm being transferred to Dallas."

"Texas?"

"I'm kind of looking forward to it. You know, cowboys and bronco busters."

"Big dick country."

"Exactly," Ellen said. "Hopefully dicks with manners, if that's not a complete contradiction in terms."

"When?"

"About a month. It'll be good. You can come sit on my cactus."

"I'll look forward to it."

An ambulance sped past Jody, sirens wailing. "I should get back," she said. "I wonder if the building will fall down when they pull the car out. I should've taken my screenplay with me."

"I doubt it," Ellen said. "It's earthquake-proof."

Ellen was right. When they pulled the car out, a few bricks fell, some cement crumbled, but the steel cables embedded in the cement basically held everything together.

"Your mother called," one of the cops said as they were leaving. "The machine picked up, but I overheard her. She wants you to call back."

"Thanks," Jody said.

"No problem," the cop said.

The super plugged the hole with sheets of badly sawed plywood and promised to come back first thing in the morning and do a better job. Jody dozed on the sofa, half expecting someone or something to come creeping through the plywood.

22

"What are these?" Sam asked. He was standing naked in front of Claire's night table, his back to her.

"What are what?" Claire asked, slipping a clean blouse over her head. She'd finally found a dry cleaner in Easthampton. They were dressing for dinner, running late.

Sam turned around. The night-table drawer was open. The forms were in his hand. "You're not thinking of doing this, are you?"

The pink flush from the day's sun rinsed itself from Claire's face and she shivered. "What are you doing in my night table?"

"Looking for the hydrocortisone cream. I got bitten." He turned his calf toward her and pointed down to a red, swollen spot the size of a half-dollar. Sam flipped through the forms, fanning them with the fingers of his free hand. "I thought you were doing so well," he said. "I thought you were over this."

"I am," Claire said. "It's research for a patient. Let me see the bite. It might be a tick." She went toward Sam, but he twisted away from her.

"Your name's written on the top line," Sam said, shaking the papers.

Claire put her cold hands on his hips. His skin was warm, almost hot. She lowered herself onto her knees, ran her hands down his legs, stopping to examine the bite. She looked up at Sam, watching her, rubbed her lips against the insides of his thighs, and started working her way higher.

"We don't have time for this," he said, stepping away. He dropped the papers onto the bed, pulled on his underwear and pants, stepped into his shoes, took his shirt off the hanger, and carried it with him out of the room. "We're late."

Claire took the big suitcase filled with all her precious things out of the closet, stuffed the papers in, and got ready to go.

"I'm sorry," Claire said later that night as they lay at opposite sides of the king-size bed, as far from each other as possible.

"We have such a decent life," Sam said. "Why isn't that enough? Why do you always want more? You're never satisfied."

Claire didn't say anything.

"It makes me feel like shit," Sam said.

"It's not about you," Claire said.

And each of them, while waiting for the other to say something, lapsed into an exhausted, fitful sleep.

"We could stay here," Claire said the next night when she and Sam were alone, stretched out on chaise lounges in the backyard.

"Forever?" Sam asked.

Claire ran her fingers back and forth through the grass. "Through the winter," she said. "It's cheap to rent off-season. It'd be a weekend place."

"What about the mountains? Something up near Woodstock?"

"We already have this. We're unpacked, we're here." She looked at the lights glowing in the upstairs bedroom.

"It might be depressing."

"Romantic," Claire said, moving her lips in an absent kiss. "The boys love being outside. It's safe here; Jake can go off on his own. He needs that."

"You need it."

"We all do," Claire said.

Away from the city, the children seemed leaner, more muscular, and more curious than before. Jake was less of a doughboy. It was possible to have a conversation with him; he wanted to tell Claire about waves he'd ridden, things other kids said, and so on. Maybe it was something that would've happened anyway, but in Claire's mind the change came from getting out of the apartment, out of town.

"Would we really want to come out every weekend?" Sam asked.

Claire nodded. "Long weekends."

She reached across, took Sam's hand, and pulled it toward her, pressing it against her chest. His lounge chair tipped over, spilling him onto the grass.

"What about work, school, our life?" he said, squeezing himself onto Claire's chair. They lay on their sides, nose to nose.

Claire shrugged. "Life goes on." She hadn't realized it, but since saying goodbye to Jody she wasn't terribly interested in getting back to work. It simply didn't matter as much. She'd adjust her schedule and her patients would never notice. She was entitled to have a life. After all, she was supposed to teach them how to make lives of their own—shouldn't she practice?

During the week, while Sam was in the city, Claire and the boys came home from the beach at five o'clock, when the lifeguard went off duty. They took quick showers, the boys outside, Claire inside, and went out to dinner— pizza, subs, and fried chicken in an almost religious rotation. On the way home they'd stop at the video store and Jake would beg for shoot-'em-up movies, justifying his choices by saying "But I already saw it once" or "There's only a little killing in this one." And then Jake and Adam and one or two kids from up the block would spread themselves out on the sofa, shove the cassette into the VCR and a pack of popcorn into the microwave while Claire hid upstairs reading back issues of *The New Yorker*.

On Friday nights, Claire and the kids drove to the train station, waited for Sam, and then they all went down to Snowflake and lined up for soft ice cream. The weekends were great. With Sam there, Claire was off duty. She didn't have to play lifeguard, chief tick-remover and bottle washer. They stayed on the beach until dark, swimming, flying kites, playing football. At twilight, with her family in front of her, Claire felt warm, equal to the moment. Watching Jake and Adam toss the ball back and forth with Sam, she held the kite strings and listened to the plastic wings flapping against the sky—the evening breeze and damp sand pulling her body tighter into itself.

Back at the house all three boys showered together in the outside stall— in the "hot rain," as Adam called it—and Claire waited jealously inside. She couldn't strip off her bathing suit, fling it in the general direction of the clothesline, and mash herself into a flesh sandwich with the three of them. Nor could she line up in the backyard for a quick peeing contest—longest, farthest, fastest. But when the boys went to their new friends' houses, when Claire and Sam came back from the beach alone, they stripped each other and, naked in the fading light, kissed against the picnic table, then stepped into the shower and did it right there where the neighbors, if they'd been interested, could have seen or at least listened. They showered and fucked and showered again and then wrapped themselves in beach towels still damp with sweat and tanning lotion.

With the boys helping, Sam would light the grill and throw on something that had been soaking in marinade all day. From inside the kitchen, as she set the table and boiled water for corn, Claire could hear the sizzle and pop of searing flesh. And every night after dinner, Sam would take the boys out into the yard and make s'mores; they'd come back two shades tanner, faces flushed from the heat of the coals, with marshmallow, chocolate, and graham cracker crumbs glued in rings around their mouths, eyes bloodshot from the sun, salt water, and exhaustion. Claire would wipe their faces with a warm washcloth, squeeze toothpaste onto their toothbrushes, and stand with them in the bathroom, making sure the job got done. When he finished washing up, Adam would raise his arms into the air and Claire would lift his sweatshirt off, pull on his pajamas, tuck him into bed, and watch as he fell almost instantly into an effortless sleep.

Near the end of the fourth week, when they were out for an after-dinner stroll, the couple next door, also out for a walk, asked when they were planning on leaving.

"We're not," Sam said, looking at Claire. "Didn't I tell you?"

She shook her head.

"I've been so busy I must've forgotten," he said, teasing her. "The lease is signed, through May."

She hugged him. She kissed him. By the edge of the road, with the neighbors looking on, she slipped her tongue between his lips and flicked the roof of his mouth, the back of his throat, his one capped tooth. "Thank you," she said. "Thank you so much."

"I'm so jealous," the neighbor's wife said. "You're so lucky—unbelievably lucky. We're going back on Monday."

"I could stay here forever," her husband said.

"Well, maybe we'll have dinner together one night in the city," the wife called as they turned off into their driveway.

" 'Night," Sam said.

"I love you so much," Claire said to Sam.

"Prove it."

"Come with me," she said, leading him toward the beach.

On the second day of September, Claire dragged her big suitcase out of the closet and carried it down to the car. She went through everyone's things, tossed the essentials into a couple of small suitcases, arranged for the guy at the farmers' market to take care of the cats, and unplugged the coffee maker.

They backed out of the driveway, lightweight, almost unsteady. Sam drove down to the beach, and Adam got out of the car to say goodbye to the waves.

"Why are we doing this if we're coming back next week?" Jake asked.

No one answered him. Sam took out the camera and finished off a roll of film with three shots of Adam pretending to kiss the sky, the sand, and the refreshment stand.

Waiting for her in her office was a postcard from Jody. GREETINGS FROM LA was splashed across the front in multicolored script. On the back Jody had typed: "Survived the trip. Tomorrow am going to Frederick's of Hollywood to buy school clothes. Hope vacation was good. More soon." The card was still curved from being rolled through a typewriter.

Claire immediately wrote back, using a postcard from the art museum in Easthampton: "Vacation great. Relaxed. Tan. Thinking of you."

After the brightness of the beach, the rich colors of the flowers in the yard, Claire's office seemed dull. She bought four beautiful pillows made out of kilims: deep reds, oranges, and purples, meaty colors of substance. She'd had enough of the minimalist thing.

Most of her patients came out of the summer frustrated in an encouraging way. They were determined to change, as if in the long light of August they'd seen themselves much more clearly. But as always, certain people seemed incapable of progress, and it was strangely reassuring to know that some things stayed the same no matter what. It gave Claire perspective and freedom.

Claire's patient Polly, the one Claire had taken for the abortion, came in and announced: "I'm pregnant again," as if to say, What are you going to do now—have me sterilized? "My boyfriend came back."

Claire couldn't respond. She sat in her chair trying not to do anything that could be read in any way. She wanted to make herself seem as flat as possible, neither positive nor negative.

"And I'm getting married," the girl said, piling it on like a fat woman ordering a banana split.

Claire remained silent.

"You're disappointed in me, aren't you? You think I couldn't get married and be a decent mother if I tried. You think I'm too fucked up."

Who the hell am I to say, Claire thought to herself. Then again . . .

"I don't need your condescending bullshit," the girl said. "My mother is happy we're getting married. She's having the wedding and everything, and you're not invited."

Polly actually sounded like a six-year-old.

"Are you happy?" Claire asked.

"You just want me to be miserable to keep you in business."

"It sounds like you're angry with me."

The girl didn't answer. "Hey, you don't owe me anything," she finally said.

It was a strange response. No one had mentioned debt.

Do yourself a favor, Claire thought, and take a long walk. "Well, we're out of time for today. Perhaps we can discuss this more thoroughly next week."

"Fuck next week," the girl said.

Fuck you, Claire thought. "Wednesday at three," she said. "See you then."

She was changing. Until now, Claire had always been caught up in thinking of ways to punish herself, to make life more difficult. For the first time, she really had the sense that hers was a good life and it could be extraordinary. All she had to do was go and get it.

As soon as they were back in New York, Claire started reading the real estate section of the *New York Times,* looking for houses. At first, mental circling was all she could do; it took her two weeks to work up to a nubby pencil, longer before she broke out a red pen; and it would be late October before she actually set foot inside any of the houses.

In Amagansett, their winter neighbors were mostly homeowners who'd disappeared during the summer, going farther north where the living was cheaper, renting their houses for enormous amounts, earning a year's worth of mortgage payments in the three short months of summer. They came back in September and spent the fall fixing up the houses, reshingling, adding decks and extra rooms. Watching them was what got Claire really thinking about houses. She liked the idea of owning something.

On weekends, out of the office, away from the city, Claire felt more than a little guilty. She didn't argue when Sam had a car phone installed—he wanted to be reachable, whenever, wherever—and she was always checking her machine, making sure her patients hadn't left emergency messages. She worried that she was inadvertently intimidating her patients into containing their problems between sessions: you are alone, the nightmare is true, no one will help you until next Tuesday at three.

While Claire stayed inside the house, resting, watching the leaves change, Sam took the boys—equipped with wet suits—down to the beach, where they rode the waves until just before the first frost.

For the first time in her children's lives, she raked leaves. On a warm afternoon, the four of them worked their way around the house, sweeping the bright red and orange leaves into a huge pile, then took turns diving in. She went for walks with the women up the street and sat with them on the grass among the trees, not worrying about ruining her hundred-dollar skirts. She was returning to herself, becoming more herself than at any other time since she'd married Sam. She was making her life over, turning it into the one big life she'd been afraid to let herself have.

In the beginning of October, Claire got a long letter from Jody, all about Los Angeles, school, her new friends, the internship working for a producer called Gary Marc—why does this man have two first names?

As soon as Claire read the letter, she called Jody. They had a great conversation, lots of laughs. Even in Los Angeles, Jody was hers. She would always be hers.

Almost immediately, Claire got into the habit of calling Jody once or twice a week in the middle of the afternoon, between patients, when she needed a laugh, a pick-me-up. On the phone Jody talked about things that maybe she wouldn't have talked about in person, things that seemed easier for her to say with Claire twenty-four hundred miles away: nothing incredibly important, just basics—how Jody felt about herself, her family, about being alone in L.A., and how when you don't know what's in front of you, you become more attached to your past. Claire even gave Jody the number at the beach house. She didn't know exactly why she wanted to be so available, so open, except that it felt perfectly natural.

By mid-October Claire had started house hunting. At first she didn't even admit it to herself. But with a few hours to spare, she'd find herself at the garage, and before she knew it she'd be in Westchester, lower Connecticut, sometimes New Jersey, slowing down whenever she saw a For Sale sign, feeling her pulse quicken if it looked good from the outside. It became an addiction. She shifted her schedule around and started taking Thursday mornings off. Within weeks she was out with agents, going in and out of other people's houses, trying them on, walking through the rooms, flushing the toilets.

In some of the houses, the kitchens looked like they belonged in restaurants. In one, twenty-five Cuisinart attachments were mounted on the wall above an industrial-sized Kitchen Aid mixer and a full row of assorted slicing and dicing machines. "Does Julia Child live here?" Claire asked.

"Very funny," the realtor said. "Actually, the woman is a food critic for the *New York Times*."

Claire started worrying that in the suburbs the expectation was that you cooked long, hard, and well. Slaved, was more like it. She wasn't sure her family could survive without having Chinese food available on ten minutes' notice twenty-four hours a day.

"Do places around here deliver?" Claire asked.

The real estate agent looked at her blankly. "I really wouldn't know."

She started to notice that all the fridges and freezers were gigantic, the size of walk-in closets. The scale of life was too big, too overwhelming. They would need a second car—one for her, one for Sam, and maybe a truck for the groceries. Sam would never get home before eight, or seven if he was lucky, and they wouldn't be able to have their little lunches anymore.

The more Claire thought about it, the more convinced she was that in the future, when her clients discussed getting divorced, she'd suggest moving to the suburbs. "You won't see each other at all," she'd say. "Very autonomous lives." She envisioned the happy couple coming back to thank her. "It's perfect," they'd say. "We go out on Saturday nights. It's like dating. We love it. Weekends only. The kids love it too. We never see them, they never see us. We leave each other notes on the kitchen table. Thank you. Thank you so much."

"What are we doing about Thanksgiving?" Sam asked one morning as he was getting ready for work, filling in dates on his calendar.

"It would be nice to stay out at the beach," Claire said. "Maybe we could work it into four or five days."

"It's the only holiday we can have my family here."

"Does it matter if for one year we don't have your sister over for Thanksgiving?" Claire asked. "We can tell her we're going away. She'd probably rather eat out anyway."

"What about the parade? I wanted to take the boys to see the floats the night before."

"We can drive out on Thanksgiving morning."

"Too tiring," Sam said. "All that driving, then cooking."

"Since when do you cook?" Claire asked. "I can do most of it in advance."

"It'll be cold and lonely. No one will be out there."

In Claire's fantasy, cold and lonely was more like fantastic and romantic: Claire, Sam, and the boys bundled up in sweaters, walking on an empty beach, cozy by a roaring fire, sated with fresh turkey, pumpkin pie, and wine, the house dim except for the reflection of the fire on the children's faces. A nice long game of Monopoly, then sleep. The quiet life.

A car alarm cut into her fantasy.

"I don't want to stay here," Claire said.

"This is your home. Amagansett is not your home. Our life is here."

"Then let's move," Claire said, surprising herself.

Sam didn't answer.

"Fine. So you expect me to stay home all day cooking dinner in a kitchen that's too fucking small just to feed your family on the one fucking day of the year when they'll stoop to eat in my house, even though none of them ever touch the stuffing for fear I'll give them some goyishe food poisoning."

"If you don't want to cook, we can *order* the food, for chrissake," Sam said, throwing his date book into his briefcase and slamming it closed. "For every other holiday—"

"Jewish holiday," Claire said, cutting him off.

"For every *Jewish* holiday my sister makes a nice dinner and invites us over. What's the big deal about returning the favor once a year?"

"And every time your sister and her family nearly kill each other—just like this. Look at us. Is this what you want? You're making us act exactly like they do."

"I'm not making us do anything. All I said was that I wanted to have Thanksgiving at home."

Claire stood silent, arms crossed in front of her chest. Sam didn't say anything else.

"I've got things to do," Claire finally said, picking up her purse and walking out of the apartment.

23

*J*ody sat on the couch, looking through the sliding glass door. In the distance were palm trees and the Hollywood Hills. Her arms and legs ached as though something long and thin like a knitting needle had been inserted and was slowly being turned—torture. Earlier in the afternoon, she'd called her mother at the office. "I'm dying," she blurted, immediately destroying the possibility of being believed.

"I'll have to call you back," her mother said.

For weeks, Jody had been feeling strangely and nonspecifically ill. And it was getting worse. Two weeks ago she'd gone to Health Services.

"Parasites," the nice young doctor said. "You have parasites. Could you give us a stool specimen?"

"Right now?"

The doctor had nodded. "If you can't give us one, we can get one."

How? Jody thought. "I don't have parasites," she told him, and went home. Three days later she went back and asked to see a different doctor.

"Hepatitis," this doctor said. "Wash your hands a lot, you don't want to give it to anyone."

She called her mother. "You don't have hepatitis," her mother said. Jody agreed, but still washed her hands more often than usual.

She'd gone to see one of her professors, who said something about the first semester being notoriously difficult and how every year a few people—mostly young women—dropped out and were never heard from again.

"It's not like that," Jody tried to say.

"Have you ever been in therapy?" he asked.

Now she sat motionless on the sofa, wondering how long she'd been sitting there, hoping that when the phone finally rang she'd know enough to answer it.

"There's something really wrong," she said when her mother finally called back.

"You're overexcited. Rest. Put a cool washcloth on your face."

"I'm sick," Jody said. "How often do I tell you I'm sick? Would I say I felt like I was dying if I didn't?"

"Well, I can't come out there."

"No one's asking you to."

Jody called the airlines. To fly home with no warning would cost an enormous amount of money. If she could wait three days, it would be cheaper; even less if she could wait seven. Better yet, if she could wait until Christmas it would be free, since her parents had bought the ticket three months ago.

She went to class with a headache and stiff neck. After half an hour, she started shivering uncontrollably and had to be helped out of the room.

"Do you want to go to the hospital?" someone asked.

"No," Jody said. "No. If someone could just drive me home, that'd be great. I really want to go home."

When they dropped her off, Jody asked one of the guys to come in for a minute. "Do me a favor and dial my friend's phone number—I'm still shaking."

It was the first time she'd called Claire like that, at home, out of the blue. She was afraid to do it herself, afraid Claire's husband or one of her children would answer, afraid she'd find out something she didn't want to know. Jody wasn't about to tell the guy she wanted him to call her shrink; she just said "my friend" and left it at that.

He dialed, asked for Claire, and handed Jody the phone. "Hope you feel better soon," he said, and walked out of the apartment.

Jody wanted Claire, not her mother; she wanted a reality-based response, not anxiety.

"Hello," Claire said. "Hello?"

"I went to class, started shaking all over, and had to be carried home. I feel horrible. I'm freaking out, scared." Only after she'd said all that did she realize she still hadn't said who she was. "It's Jody."

"I know," Claire said softly. "It sounds like you have the flu. Do you have a fever?"

"I don't think it's the flu. I've had the flu before and it was never like this."

"There are new strains every year."

Jody didn't respond. She was searching for the thermometer.

"What do you think it is?" Claire asked.

Jody heard young voices in the background. "Sorry I called."

"It's fine," Claire said. "Take some aspirin, have some juice, get into bed, turn on the TV, and just lie there. You'll fall asleep soon, and tomorrow things will be different. I'll call you in the morning."

"Thanks."

"Sleep well," Claire said.

The next morning was one of those cold, rainy November days they don't advertise. Jody's throat was incredibly sore and covered with bumps that looked like blisters. Whenever she stood up, the room whirled. A lumpy pink rash was breaking out on her legs and stomach, and there was a dull, steady pain in her chest. Her temperature was a hundred and three and something.

She called Gary Marc's office and said she wouldn't be coming in. The receptionist refused to take the message and transferred Jody's call to Gary's car phone. While she was explaining her symptoms, Gary got stuck in traffic under an overpass and the call was disconnected. "Suck herbs," was the last thing she heard him say.

She called Health Services and updated the doctor, who said it was probably mono and there was nothing she could do about it. Stunned, sometimes shaking, sometimes sweating, she lay in bed, noticing that she'd lost fifteen pounds in two days.

Claire called. "Just wanted to see how you're doing," she said.

"Wanna hear something weird?" Jody asked, her voice a raspy whisper.

"Sure."

"I've always had this yellow dot, like this child inside me. I never told anyone about it. But I protect it. My job is to make sure no one ever hurts the yellow dot. Anyway, today it's outside. It's here in the apartment, in the living room, running around by itself. Do I sound crazy?"

"No," Claire said. "People have inner selves. Everyone describes them in their own way. Your fever is up, which might make you experience yourself differently. That's all. I do want you to make a doctor's appointment—maybe they'll be able to see you this afternoon."

"I love my dot," Jody said to Claire. Claire's buzzer went off; Jody heard it long-distance. "You better go," Jody said.

"I'll call you later if I get a chance."

At one in the morning, Jody called home. "Mom," she croaked.

"You frightened me," her mother said, groggy and breathless. "What time is it?"

Jody didn't say anything. The pain in her chest was worse; she felt unable to breathe, much less talk. The last time she'd taken her temperature, it was a hundred and four.

"It's the middle of the night," her mother said.

"I'm really not feeling well," Jody said. "You better hurry."

"You mean that someone, namely me, should come out there?"

Jody didn't respond.

"I'll call you back."

"Hurry," Jody whispered.

Half an hour later the phone rang. Even though the phone was right next to Jody, it took her four rings to answer. She tried to say hello, but nothing came out.

"Are you there?" her mother asked.

"Umm-humm."

"I've made reservations. It's a six a.m. flight. I'll be at your house by three. I want you to take some aspirin and have something hot to drink. At nine, call the doctor and make an appointment. I'll see you in a little while."

She lay in bed, waiting, dreaming, dozing, watching the sun rise, watching morning television, feeling oddly calm, as if it might be all right if she died.

"How long have you been like this?" her mother asked when she finally arrived and saw Jody face-to-face.

"I tried to tell you."

"I'm here, aren't I?" She pressed her cold hand to Jody's cheek.

The room seemed to be shrinking, getting darker. "I have to put my head down," Jody said, turning away from her mother and starting toward the bedroom.

"When did you go on a diet?" her mother asked.

Jody didn't tell her she wasn't on a diet. She wished she were, but she wasn't. On the way back to bed, she fainted, crashed into a wall, and knocked a lamp over, and her mother had to come running.

Later that afternoon they went to the hospital. The fever, the rash, the sore throat. How long? How high? Jody could hardly talk, hardly hold her head up, and now they wanted details. They pointed her to a room down a long hall; it took forever to get there, and she kept seeing people she thought looked familiar—her dead aunt Sally, a neighbor from her childhood, everyone was someone. She sat on an examining table while four doctors stood talking in the corner. The nurse was trying to take her blood pressure. There was a problem. The nurse wrapped the cuff tighter, squeezed the ball harder, and then finally asked, "Is there some reason I can't get your blood pressure?"

"I really don't feel well," Jody said. All the doctors whirled around and in a minute she was lying upside down, her feet higher than her head.

Stand up. Deep breath. Hold it. The hum of the x-ray machine. Relax. Sit down. Arm out, alcohol swab, Betadine wash. A long, thin line of blood drawn through a narrow plastic line into a syringe.

"Something's happening," Jody said.

"Nothing's happening," the doctor mumbled, staring at Jody's vein.

"Something is definitely happening," Jody said, and then fainted onto the floor.

"Get my mother," Jody said when she woke up, but they wouldn't.

They got her a pillow and made her lie there on the cold tile floor. They wouldn't get her mother because it didn't look good for Jody to be sprawled there while all the big shots just stood around, waiting for her to recover. They bought her a soda, stuck a straw in, and eventually got a wheelchair and put her in a room. A plastic bracelet was slipped around her wrist, an IV started.

Guys came into the room with masks over their faces and a thousand questions. They asked her mother to wait outside. "Have you ever used intravenous drugs?" they asked.

"Give me a break," Jody said.

While her mother was out of the room, Jody pulled the cutest intern close and told him about Peter Sears and a few others. "Who knew what the hell they were doing—or should I say whom," Jody whispered. He snapped an extra pair of gloves on and stuck her vein again. They both watched her blood spring into the tube—wishing you could just tell by looking—and then the intern pulled the needle out, wiped a drop of blood off the tip with gauze, dropped the needle into a bucket marked HAZARD-OUS WASTE, and silently slipped the test tube into his breast pocket. "Soon," he said, patting the pocket. "We'll know something soon."

24

"*I*s something wrong?" Sam asked.

Claire shuffled out of the bathroom, phone in hand, her eyes pink and puffy, her slippers scraping the bare floor like sandpaper.

"Should I be worried?" he asked. Twenty minutes earlier, when the phone rang, Claire had tucked the receiver under her chin, pulled the full length of the cord into the bathroom, and closed the door.

Claire sniffled. "One of my patients is very sick."

"With what?"

"Don't know." Claire looked at the Post-it stuck to the palm of her hand, on which she'd written the name of Jody's doctor. "I have to make a call."

"I'll go into the living room," Sam said, gathering newspapers off the bed.

Claire dialed the number in Los Angeles. "Dr. Brandt?"

"Hold, please."

The ticking of long-distance wires, the consciousness of hearing time pass: silence was expensive, and time was running out. She tried to take a deep breath.

"I can reach his beeper and have him call you," the operator said.

Claire left her number and hung up thinking it was time to make a move. If something happened to Jody, if Jody died and never knew who Claire was, *what* she was, it would be Claire's fault. She dug into the closet and dragged out an old suitcase. She'd pack her bag first, go in to tell Sam she was leaving, then hurry downstairs to the cash machine and out to La Guardia.

Sam knocked on the bedroom door. "Are you all right?"

"I'm waiting for the doctor to call back," Claire said through the door. "Doesn't this girl have a family?"

The phone rang and Claire jumped to answer it. She explained that she was Jody's therapist.

"I can't discuss a patient's condition. I don't know who you are."

"I told you who I am."

"You should know better," Dr. Brandt said, as though he'd just finished reading a memo on patient privacy.

"She's my patient too," Claire said. She almost said, She was my patient first. But that sounded too possessive.

"I want you to tell me what the situation is," Claire said in a firm voice. "Is it something serious?"

"Could be a virus that'll resolve itself in a few days. Could escalate into something new at any time. I don't know. She just came in today."

"Are you running tests?"

"White count is down," Dr. Brandt said flatly. "Liver's off a little. Blood culture's negative at twelve hours."

"What are you giving her?"

"Are you a psychiatrist or just a psychologist?"

"What's she getting?"

"Tylenol by mouth."

"That's it?" Claire said, horrified.

"IV to keep her from dehydrating. Someone from infectious diseases is taking a look in the morning. Hey, she could be out of here by afternoon—all kinds of viruses do things like this. Most likely it's nothing."

"You have my number," Claire said. "If anything comes up, I want to know. I can be out there by tomorrow afternoon."

"Yeah, all right."

"Thanks." Claire slammed the phone down. "Fucking assholes," she said loudly, looking at the empty suitcase and trying to figure what to do with it. She couldn't just jump up, pack her bag, and say goodbye—that would be asking for trouble. Just as Sam came into the room she jammed the suitcase back into the closet and then pretended to be rearranging their clothing.

"Jake woke up. The phone, I guess," Sam said. "He's in the kitchen, microwaving hot chocolate."

At the beach they'd been drinking gallons of hot chocolate. Claire made it the real way—in a pot on the stove, with milk and deep brown cocoa from a heavy tin can, with heaping spoons of sugar stirred in and two fat marshmallows floating on the top. She didn't use beige powder dumped from a premeasured package into a cup of water and rotated around for a minute and a half in a portable x-ray machine. She slaved over a hot stove for at least ten or twelve minutes.

Claire pushed past Sam and went down the hall into the kitchen.

"Get back to bed," she told Jake.

"I'm making hot chocolate."

"No you're not."

The mug was already turning in a circle in the microwave. The packet of cocoa mix lay empty on the counter, grains of cocoa dust trailing from the microwave to a spoon on the counter.

"Go back to bed."

"Mom," Jake whined.

"Forget it. You're not drinking that shit at midnight. Have a glass of water if you're thirsty."

The bell on the microwave went off. If she'd been normal, she would've just let him have it. She would've said, Okay, fine, just don't do it again. But instead, in a flash of anger and in front of both Jake and Sam, who'd come to defend Jake, she took out the cup of cocoa and poured it down the drain. It was all she could do to keep from throwing the mug into the sink. She would have loved to smash something.

"You didn't have to do that," Sam said.

She looked at Jake, standing there staring at her. He was starting to get tall. In a year or two he'd be at eye level. After that everything would be history; he'd be gone.

"I hate you," Jake said, walking away.

"Feeling's mutual," Claire mumbled.

Sam raised his finger and shook it in her face, lawyerlike. "He woke up because the phone rang. It's your problem, so don't take it out on him."

"He wanted a sugar fix," Claire said, focusing on the pool of spilled cocoa in the sink. The mug was lying on its side. She still wanted to smash it.

"Big fucking deal," Sam said.

"Big fucking deal," Claire snapped back.

From above she could hear the upstairs neighbor dropping one shoe at a time onto the floor and then the creak and crunch of his Murphy bed coming down. Adam's new stuffed elephant was lying on the floor under the kitchen table, collecting dust and crumbs. Claire picked it up and shook it vigorously, then propped it against his empty chair. It was midnight.

Claire spent the night making deals in a strange half-sleep. If Jody was allowed to get well, Claire would be a better person. She'd do more for others, work harder at being a good therapist, a good wife, a good mother to Jake, Adam, and Jody. She'd give herself to Jody in a way that she'd never done before with anyone. She'd make up for everything and then some. If Jody was allowed to live . . .

At nine a.m. she was in her office, sitting at her desk and ready to transcribe last night's messages from the answering machine.

"Hi, Claire, this is Janet Fishman, your real estate agent in Stamford. I know we were supposed to look at houses tomorrow, but it's not going to happen, not this week—my life is a disaster. You understand. Call me, we'll reschedule."

"It's Randy Hill. I have to be out of town on business. See you next week."

"She's driving me crazy. I sent her back to the apartment. I didn't want to be here by myself, but I couldn't take it anymore. She scares me." Jody's voice sounded far off, full of fever. "I feel so strange. It's the middle of the night. My mother's driving me nuts. My room's *orange*—not a Sunkist, get-well-soon orange, but a rusty, rot-in-hell kind of color." Jody paused, swallowed. "Isn't orange the color of insanity? Didn't I read that somewhere? There's a speaker in the wall. Sometimes it talks to me, just blurts out things. A minute ago it said, 'Maria, Maria, where are you, Maria?' and I thought I was in *West Side Story.*" Jody paused again. "Sorry to clog up your machine."

Claire called the hospital. It was barely six a.m. in California. The floor nurse was nice—almost too nice. "It's been a quiet night, no problems. She didn't sleep much, and she's still running a fever, but the rash seems better."

What rash? No one had said anything about a rash.

All day, whenever Claire's buzzer went off, she opened her office door and her patients came in, sat down, and picked up where they'd left off. At the end of their hour, when the buzzer went off again, Claire led them back to the door without the vaguest hint of what had transpired. In a sense she had vanished. Overnight, the gap between Claire and the rest of the world had grown into a crevasse so deep, so wide, that it could not possibly be spanned.

At two, during the half-hour she'd allotted for lunch and returning calls, the phone rang.

"Hello. You don't know me," a woman's voice said, "but I'm calling about Jody Goodman. I'm her mother."

"I'm Claire Roth," Claire said.

"Jody keeps asking me to call you, I'm not sure why. And she won't dial your number herself."

Claire smiled. Jody's refusal to call was sweet. She wondered how she'd managed last night—asked the nurse, or another patient?

"I don't know what to do," the mother said.

"About what?"

"Jody seems so upset. She wants me to get a plane and fly her home."

"Is that possible?" Claire asked.

"Possible? I just flew out here. They only do things like that for people who need transplants, who have to fly halfway across the country to meet their kidneys. Jody has such an imagination. When she gets better, we'll fly home together."

Claire struggled to write down everything the woman said. Her hands were shaking. Claire was talking to the mother, the mother she'd only imagined, the woman who'd stolen her child, the madonna she'd conjured in her mind's eye for twenty-four years. Claire pictured the woman as squat, low to the ground, earth-motherish. She saw her out there in Los Angeles, alone, afraid of losing this second child, this second chance. Claire had to make this woman trust her while at the same time being careful not to seem as though she was overstepping the bounds. She had to protect herself, protect Jody, *and* make a good impression. "Is there anything I can do to help *you?*" Claire asked.

"For me?" the woman said. "No."

"Well, if anything comes up or you just need to talk, feel free to call me back. And let me give you my number at home."

"I haven't got a pen," the mother said. "But thank you. I appreciate the offer."

Claire hung up wanting more.

25

"Remember the yellow dot?" Jody said the next time she spoke to Claire. "It's gone. Evaporated."

The missing dot, however odd a concept, was the clue that something was really wrong, maybe irrevocably so. Jody hadn't been able to protect that most fragile part of herself, and it had disappeared. Without someone on guard duty, the real Jody had no capacity to survive. Just as her biological mother had no way of caring for an infant, and her adoptive mother was unable to nurse a sick child, Jody could not take care of herself. They were all useless to each other. It was the truth of her childhood, her life; the unspoken truth she'd lived in fear of. She had always known this would happen; it made perfect sense. She wondered only why it had taken this long.

"I want to go home," Jody told the infectious diseases specialist.

He stood over her, a mask covering his face, a paper gown over his white coat, booties over his shoes, thin latex gloves pulled tight over his hands. Through the gloves Jody could see the hair on his knuckles, matted down.

"Do you want to get well," the doctor asked, "or do you want to go home?"

"I didn't realize they were mutually exclusive," Jody said. No one seemed to hear her.

A case of water from Gary Marc's private Swiss spring arrived with a note from Gary warning that under no circumstances should Jody drink from her plastic bedside pitcher, potentially a source of deadly bacteria.

Ellen sent an FTD "pick-me-up bouquet"—seven brightly dyed carnations in a cracked mug—with "Get Well Soon" printed on the card in a stranger's bad handwriting.

"I don't want to die in Los Angeles," Jody told her mother.

Ilene, Bob, and a pack of UCLA film students showed up and took over Jody's room, crowding onto the bed with her. Jody's mother sat in the corner by the window, working a crossword puzzle. Jody had never noticed it before, but there was something untouchable about her mother. Seeing it now, she realized that her mother's heart had always been kept sealed away in a clear but impenetrable Lucite box.

"Are you researching *Terms of Endearment Part II?*" one of her friends asked, playing with her IV line.

"We had a choice between *The Glass Menagerie* and you," Ilene said. "We figured they were both the same—depressing, boring, classic."

"You look like shit," another girl said.

"Thanks," Jody said.

"No—I mean last week you looked fine."

"It's the lighting," Jody said.

They all looked up at the fluorescent overhead fixture and nodded.

A nurse finally came in and shooed everyone out. "Are you trying to visit your friend or suffocate her?" she asked, hurrying them up off the bed. "Go on now, leave her alone."

"It's true," her mother said, once they left. "They didn't have to stay so long."

"Then why didn't you say something?" Jody said.

"I was leaving it up to you. They're your friends." Her mother paused, rinsed out a washcloth, and rubbed it over her own face and neck. "You always say that I don't accept your friends. I didn't want to interfere."

"Mom, I'm in the hospital, I feel like shit. Interfere already."

"You know," her mother said, pouring herself a glass of Gary Marc water, "I didn't plan on coming out here twice this year. Daddy needs me at home. He's not used to being alone." She paused. "He gets lonely."

"I can't believe you."

"I'm here, aren't I? I wouldn't have come if I didn't think it was important. All day I sit in this chair and worry."

"What are you worried about, Mom, me or you?"

"You're just upset because you're not feeling well," her mother said, refilling her glass.

"Leave," Jody said. "Get out. I don't feel good enough to fight with you."

Her mother sat back down in her chair and picked up the crossword puzzle again, occasionally asking Jody questions like "Who's an actress Somers?"

Jody drifted back in time. She remembered raising her hand in the third grade, telling her teacher that she felt sick. She sat on the blue-and-green plaid sofa in the school office while the secretary took her temperature and called her mother. "She says she's feeling nauseated," the secretary told her mother, "but her temp's below normal at 97.8. . . . Well, yes, I can have her rest here for a little while and see how she feels." Ten minutes later, Jody vomited all over everything, and there was no answer when the secretary tried to call her mother back. Finally a neighbor, a volunteer in the art room, took Jody home to her house, and Jody spent the afternoon lying there feeling like she was two million miles from home, even though it was less than a hundred yards away and clearly visible from the neighbor's bedroom window.

During the night, someone in Jody's unit died. She heard Code Blue paged, the rush of metal wheels and crepe soles down the hall. She was on a floor with a lot of AIDS patients. She knew because she saw them go past her door, because her mother walked the halls and reported back.

"It's so sad," she said to Jody.

Jody didn't answer. She didn't want to know about it. She was on the wrong side of the bed. She closed her eyes and imagined dying without ever knowing who she was or where she'd come from. She thought it was a strange time to realize how important her history was to her.

When the fever broke, Jody felt worse, even more tired and damaged. Her voice sounded not like a voice but like a piece of fine-grain sandpaper being swept gently across a surface. While her mother watched, the nurse helped her to stand and led her to the bathroom. She leaned against the sink and in the mirror saw herself for the first time—a thin, green stranger. The nurse helped her back to bed. She slept.

Late that night, the intern who'd slipped her blood in his pocket sneaked into the room, squeezed her hand, and said "Negative." Jody stared at him, blinked. She wasn't sure she was awake. She wasn't sure that she wasn't imagining him standing there. "Negative," he said again, squeezing her hand so tight it hurt. "Just a plain, nasty virus." In the morning she almost told her mother, but then stopped herself. There was no point.

Two days later, one of the doctors came in, looked her over, and said, "It's over. You're free, I'm releasing you. Fly away home." He flapped his arms up and down.

"Excuse me, but I can't walk. I can barely talk. I don't remember anything. I still feel like I'm dying."

"A virus," the doctor said. "These things happen. Make an appointment in the clinic next week or with your family doctor. We'll run fresh bloods and monitor a few things."

"That's it?"

"Far as I can tell."

Her mother packed her things into a plastic trash bag, and Jody shuffled down the hall toward the Exit sign.

"They seem to know what they're doing," her mother said. "You have to trust somebody."

"No you don't."

From her bed in her apartment, Jody made plane reservations while her mother cleaned the kitchen, defrosted the refrigerator, and complained. Jody arranged for one of her UCLA friends to baby-sit her car and the apartment until she got back. She arranged for her mail to be forwarded, the newspaper stopped, and her teachers notified. She felt worse every hour.

"You have more energy," her mother said, bringing her a glass of juice.

"It's not energy," Jody answered. "It's hysteria."

What Jody had was the sensation that she should hurry home, that this window of opportunity was a momentary thing, a last chance. She was determined to at least get out alive.

"The plane's not going to crash, is it?" she asked Claire.

"You're too sick for the plane to crash," Claire said, which somehow seemed comforting.

A wheelchair and an attendant met Jody at the curb of Los Angeles International Airport. The redcap propelled Jody toward the gate, handling the chair as though it were a snowplow. Her mother trailed behind, acting unrelated. At the departure gate Jody transferred herself to a narrower chair, more like a personal luggage cart, and was pushed up the ramp by two men in American Airlines coveralls; she felt like a steamer trunk full of china. At the top of the stairs, she stepped into the plane and gently walked down the aisle to her seat. Even though it was a warm day, she was wearing a turtleneck, sweatshirt, wool socks, a down jacket, and a wool hat, and still she was shivering. Her mother sat across the aisle from her and pulled out the in-flight magazine. When Jody asked her to get a blanket from the stewardess, she just looked at her blankly. Jody hated her. She hated her mother for revealing herself to be incompetent, unable or unwilling to do anything to help.

26

"Do you have plans for Thanksgiving?" Claire asked during a quick call between patients and between expeditions to Balducci's, Dean & DeLuca, and the Food Emporium, hunting and gathering her way across Manhattan Island.

"Well," Jody said, "I was thinking of rolling over onto my left side, but it turns out I can't. Every time I move my head, the room starts to spin."

For almost three weeks Jody had been held captive in her parents' house, in the narrow bed of her youth. "I hate it here," she said.

"On Friday, when you go to the doctor, I want you to tell him that I'm going to call. I need to talk to him."

What Claire couldn't understand was why no one was doing anything. Why wasn't Jody getting some treatment? "You have my number on Long Island. I'll be out there all weekend."

"Great," Jody said. "Have fun."

"I'll call sometime tomorrow—I don't know when."

"You don't have to."

"I know what I have to do," Claire said.

The night before Thanksgiving, bundled up in their winter coats—Adam's over his Spiderman pajamas—the Roths set out on what seemed like a fantastical middle-of-the-night adventure. It was ten p.m.

"Going to the parade?" the doorman asked in a thick Spanish accent.

"Spiderman," Adam said, throwing his arms into the air in an up-up-and-away gesture.

Claire had been dreading this crowd scene all day: throngs of people out for a night of cheap thrills, free entertainment; people out to see the people; people out to see the people seeing the people. She figured they wouldn't be able to get close enough to see a damn thing.

The traffic was horrible, so they got out of the cab at Seventy-second Street and walked. The sidewalk was mobbed with people in bright parkas, knitted caps, patterned scarfs, the occasional fur coat, thick gloves, holding cups of steaming hot chocolate bought from street vendors.

"I want some," Jake whined.

"No, it'll give you cholera," Claire said, and Sam laughed but didn't disagree.

"Colored what?"

All of Seventy-eighth Street between Central Park West and Columbus Avenue had been sealed off. Mammoth portable lights cast an otherworldly glow, and long white tanker trucks filled with helium lined Central Park West. The floats—Spiderman, Ninja Turtles, Snoopy, and Betty Boop—lay unfurled on clean white dropcloths in the middle of Seventy-eighth Street, hooked to helium hoses, slowly swelling to life. Hundreds of small children rode high on their fathers' shoulders. Preppy boys drunk on cheap beer and hormones climbed the wrought-iron fence that guarded the Museum of Natural History.

"Let's leave for the beach tonight," Sam whispered to Claire an hour and a half later as the cab sped back downtown. Adam was asleep across his shoulder. "It'll be easier. There's no traffic. We'll be there in less than two hours." The cab pulled into the driveway at 2 Fifth Avenue. "I'll get the car," Sam said, fishing wrinkled singles out of his pocket for the driver. "Meet me downstairs in ten minutes." Claire nodded and watched him disappear down the street with Adam over his shoulder like an old sweater; then she and Jake went upstairs and got the groceries she'd been collecting all week. As part of their reconciliation, Claire had agreed to invite Sam's obnoxious sister from Ridgewood out to the house along with her husband and their two crazy children, one anorexic, the other hyperactive. In return Sam had granted her Naomi and Roger and their children; but she'd convinced him that they'd all be happier staying the night at the inn in Easthampton. She told everyone to bring something, and Sam's sister offered to make a sweet-potato casserole, quickly adding, "And I'll also do the stuffing."

With the children asleep in the backseat, Sam and Claire talked softly. In their silence, Claire thought about Jody. She wanted to tell Sam, but couldn't.

"Are we going the right way?" she asked. In the dark the road to Amagansett seemed unfamiliar.

"Same way we always go," Sam said, making the turn. "There's the Easthampton pond," he said, nodding toward an oily shape on the right.

Simon's Lane was deserted; no streetlights, no house lights, no porch lights. The moon had slipped behind a cloud. Claire had never seen a night so black.

"Leave the headlights on so we can see the door," she said.

Sam carried Adam into the house; Claire followed with bags of food. She left the groceries in the front hall and went out again for Jake.

"We're here," she said, jiggling his shoulder. "Go on inside and up to bed."

"I'll stay," Jake said, mumbling.

Claire picked up the turkey and held it on her hip like a baby. With her free hand, she pulled at her son. "Come on, I'll walk you up."

A few minutes later, Sam started out of the kitchen to turn off the headlights, but immediately turned around and grabbed Claire's hand, frightening her. The clock on the stove said two-thirty-nine.

"Come on," he whispered, leading her toward the door. "Shhh." He slowly opened the screen door and pointed Claire toward the backyard. In the farthest edges of the headlights' beam stood a deer.

"If I was a pilgrim," he whispered in her ear, his lips touching the back of her neck, "tomorrow we'd be eating Bambi."

In the morning, Claire made hot chocolate. She filled Jake's mug with steaming cocoa and let him have as many marshmallows as he wanted. She put the whole bag down on the table and watched as he took one after another, dipped them into his mug, then popped them into his mouth with a thick, smacking sound. When he got to eight she stopped counting and turned away.

With Sam and the boys dispatched on a time-killing mission to Montauk, Claire vacuumed and scrubbed floors, toilets, behind the sofas, the very boards of the house, then started in on the carrots and asparagus, feeling all the while that she was doing someone else a favor. This wasn't really her house; the dinner guests weren't really her family. She prepared the turkey for a long, slow roast, put together a mashed potato, green pea, and pearl onion casserole, cooked a batch of cranberry sauce—with a little too much sugar, and then a little too much lemon as compensation. She peeled apples for the pies, and at noon, with the bird in the oven, her face and hands coated with unbleached flour, she hunched over the butcher block and tried to roll out a pie crust, relying on directions she vaguely remembered from seventh-grade home economics class. Then, as she was slipping the pies into the oven, there was a heavy pounding at the front door. Claire couldn't find the key to the dead bolt. "Coming!" she yelled as she riffled through a tin can of keys on top of the mantel. Finally she quit, brushed her hair out of her face, and called out the side door, "I'm over here."

"Where?" Sam's sister shouted. "I can't see you."

Claire stepped out and walked barefoot down the gravelly driveway.

Nora stood in the center of the front yard, her high heels sunk deep in the soft dirt. "There you are," she said. "Well, we're here. Bet you didn't think we'd make it."

I hoped and prayed you wouldn't, Claire thought. "Well, now that you're here," she said, "come on in."

Nora turned and screeched "Bring the cooler!" at her husband, Manny, who stood by the curb, wiping bird droppings off the hood of their black Cadillac. Nora started across the yard, and with each step her heels dug in like the world's longest cleats. Eventually one shoe was pulled off completely, and she was forced to balance momentarily on one leg like a pelican as she bent over and plucked her Ferragamos out of the muck. "They're ruined," she said when she got to the driveway.

Manny walked up with a medium-sized Coleman cooler in hand.

"It's the stuffing and the sweet potatoes," Nora said, gesturing toward the cooler. "I put them on ice."

Claire looked at her blankly.

"So they wouldn't spoil," Nora said.

"Come inside, won't you," Claire said, turning toward the house.

"Oh," Nora said to her, "you're not wearing any shoes. Is that how it's done out here?"

"Have you checked in at the inn yet?" Claire asked, as they came through the door.

"No, we came here first," Manny said, tapping the plastic cooler as if to indicate imminent spoilage.

"Well, perhaps we should call and let them know you're in the vicinity." Claire stopped. "Where are the kids?"

"In the car," Manny said. "They don't want to get out."

"It's so hard for them to adjust," Nora said. "They're very shy."

Claire nodded, pretending to understand.

"Sam and the boys should be back soon, I hope. Why don't you make yourselves comfortable while I go check things in the kitchen. Can I get you something to drink?"

"I brought some Diet Coke with me. It's in the cooler. If I could just have a glass. Manny, get me one of my Cokes," Nora said, and Manny got up from the sofa and went to the cooler. He handed Nora a Coke, and Claire hurried to find her a glass. She took one out of the dishwasher, still warm, and handed it to Nora, who took a handkerchief out of her bag and wiped out the insides. "Dusty," she explained.

Claire excused herself, went back into the kitchen, opened a bottle of wine, poured herself a huge glass, basted the turkey, stirred the cranberry sauce, peeked at her pies through the oven window, and sat down at the kitchen table, hoping they wouldn't notice her absence.

"Why are Melanie and Jonathan sitting in the car watching television?" Sam asked when he came in.

"You're late," Claire said. "They've been here for half an hour."

Claire's perfect pies, fresh out of the oven, sat cooling on the kitchen counter. Sam bent down and inhaled the vapors. "How come you only made two?"

Naomi and Roger arrived with their three boys, and soon the house was as raucous as five boys playing war could make it.

"The battery on my Watchman died," Nora's son Jonathan whined when he and his sister finally came inside.

By the time dinner was ready, Claire was drunk. All afternoon she'd been excusing herself to "check on things," each time pouring a fast glass of wine. She sat at the head of the table, a little woozy, picking at her food, letting their compliments wash over her like waves.

"Where did you buy this pie?" Nora asked.

"I didn't buy it," Claire said, her speech a little slurry. "I baked it."

"You really made it? The crust is so good, it must have been frozen."

"Nope," Claire said, standing to clear some plates. "Ho-made."

Sam and Jake laughed. There was a big sign at the Snowflake ice cream stand that said, HO-MADE CHILI.

"What's so funny?" Nora said.

"You," Claire mumbled under her breath, walking away.

On the single step into the kitchen, she tripped, and the plates went flying, hurling a melange of Thanksgiving foods across the room in a multicolored splatter.

"Shit," Claire said. "Sorry," she called loudly in a singsong voice. "Would anybody like some broken glass with their coffee?"

Sam came into the kitchen, surveyed the damage, and, smiling, softly suggested that she go upstairs and lie down.

"Maybe I should," Claire said, fixing her hair. "You take care of it."

Sam nodded, and without a word to the guests Claire toddled off up the steps.

A few minutes later, Naomi came up and stretched out beside her on the huge bed. "Nora told Sam how sorry she is. 'I never knew Claire was an alcoholic,' " she said, imitating Sam's sister, " 'but I should have. Non-Jews always are.' "

Claire laughed. The more she thought about it, the more she laughed; then she jumped up, ran into the bathroom, and vomited.

"You'll feel better now," Naomi said from the bedroom. "You never could hold your liquor."

Claire came back, pressing a damp washcloth against her face and lips. "I feel terrible."

"And you look like hell," Naomi said. "But dinner was great, no lie. Your pie was four-star."

Claire lay down on the bed. " 'Is it frozen?' " she said. " 'It tastes so good, it must be.' "

"I'll go and help Sam clean up. Sure you're okay?"

"Fine," Claire said. "Listen, come for breakfast. Just us. I'll make French toast and we can go for a nice long walk."

"Okay. Sleep well," Naomi said.

Claire sat up. "Oh, make sure she doesn't forget her cooler."

"Or her fucking children," Naomi said, pulling the bedroom door closed behind her.

Claire arranged the pillows, propping herself up, and called Jody. "Hi," she said softly when Jody answered.

"Who's it for?" a sharp voice in the background asked.

"It's for me, Aunt Sylvia," Jody said.

"Is it someone you know?"

"If you could just close the door," Jody said to the aunt. "Sorry," she said to Claire. "My whole family's here, and the only one who bothered to stick her head into my room is my eighty-seven-year-old aunt. Before they showed up, my mother came down the hall and closed my door, like I'm a messy closet or something."

"I wish you were here," Claire said. "You'd like it. It's beautiful, and the kids can run around outside, ride bikes, do all the things they can't in the city."

It was the first time she'd mentioned her children. She'd known she was going to do it; there was no point in pretending to keep them separate anymore. Soon enough, she'd introduce them in real life.

Jody didn't say anything for a minute. "Shouldn't you be doing something, wrapping leftovers, giving *the kids* Alka Seltzers?"

"I'd rather talk to you," Claire said, adjusting the pillow behind her head, worried she might throw up again. "You have to come back to New York."

"I can't."

"We won't go into it now, but you have to. I'm going to find you a doctor. We'll get the subletter out of your apartment and find someone to get your groceries and all that. You need to be here."

"Don't talk to me about it," Jody said. "Talk to my mother."

"I will."

If Jody had been there, Claire wouldn't have gotten drunk. The two of them would have hidden out in the kitchen and said nasty things about everyone. She visualized Jody resting on the sun porch, wrapped in a thick wool blanket, or sprawled on the sofa in front of a fire while Claire read to her, Jake, and Adam from *Winnie-the-Pooh*. Claire saw herself making Jody huge, steaming bowls of homemade soup. "Is it frozen?" Nora's voice echoed in her head. Claire would take Jody back into her life and heal her once and for all.

When Claire got to the office on Monday, she started making a list of things Jody would need: mittens, scarves, a bright apartment with comfortable furniture, cable TV, flowers, a personal trainer/masseur, a nutritionist. She read it over, then threw it in the trash and began again, this time by listing doctors she knew, ones she'd heard about or read about in magazines. Then she wrote out everything she knew about Jody's medical history and made a note to ask Mrs. Goodman for more information. In Claire's mind, both she and Mrs. Goodman bore the responsibility for what Claire perceived as a series of grievous errors that had resulted in Jody's current condition. As Claire saw it, Jody was sick because she'd been given away, delivered to a grief-stricken couple who'd sucked on the infant as though she were a Life Saver or a pacifier. It seemed possible that these twenty-four years of never knowing who she really was could have caused a sophisticated and subtle taxing of the human system, culminating with Jody's outbreak of disease.

Between patients, first thing in the morning, late in the evening, Claire worked the phones.

"It's not psychosomatic, it's not AIDS, and there's nothing we can do for it," said the immunologist who'd seen Jody at Georgetown.

"So, what is it?" Claire asked. "What are you calling it?"

"A virus."

"Is it genetic?"

"I doubt it."

"How do you treat it?"

"We don't."

She called Jody at least once a day. "A nightmare come true," Jody concluded. "It's permanent. I'm not getting better. I'll still be living here when I'm forty."

"I'm bringing you back," Claire promised. "Soon."

Marilyn Esterhaus. That was the name a friend had left on Claire's machine. Marilyn Esterhaus at New York Hospital.

Claire left five messages before Esterhaus finally got back to her. The phone rang just as a patient was leaving. The machine clicked on; Claire turned the volume up. "This is Marilyn Esterhaus. Sorry it's taken me so long to get back to you, I've been—"

Claire grabbed the phone—"Hello, I'm here"—pulled out the note pad, and point by point began relating Jody's history.

"Was a spinal tap done?" Esterhaus asked.

"No."

"Brain scan?"

"No."

"Still running fevers?"

"All day, up and down."

Esterhaus paused. "What I can tell you is this. For a year I've been working with people who have similar symptoms. On several occasions we've isolated what we thought was the virus, but nothing has panned out. I'm not one hundred percent convinced this is entirely a viral episode. It could be triggered by several other things—a deep systemic response to a naturally occurring chemical, even an allergy. And of course your patient might not even have my disease. It could just as easily be something else. I'd need to see her."

"I've found you a doctor," Claire said. "She's very real and very smart. I'm going to talk to your mother tonight."

"Good luck," Jody said.

It's imperative that Jody come back to New York. If you don't let her return I'm going to come to your house and take her. Don't make me fight you. Think of what's best for her. This is what Jody wants, and she's old enough to know. She's not your property; she's not even your child, if you want to get picky about it. Claire played it all back and forth in her head. She didn't know what to say to Mrs. Goodman, whether to ask, demand, or suggest. She couldn't imagine what would make Mrs. Goodman want to load Jody into the car and drive her to New York City in the middle of December.

"I think it would be good for Jody to come back to New York," Claire told Mrs. Goodman that night. She'd decided to start small and work her way up. Her own voice, pathetic and plaintive in the night, echoed back over the telephone wires and struck like a slap in the face.

"I don't see how," Mrs. Goodman said. "She can't even take care of herself. I can't go running up to New York City every five minutes."

"She needs to have her life back."

"It's very expensive there, as I'm sure you know, and she's not working. When she gets better, she can go back if she chooses to—I certainly won't stop her."

"I've found a doctor here who's doing research on Jody's illness," Claire said firmly. "I realize it's difficult financially, but a person has to feel like she has some control over her life. It's very important for Jody to be here, and I'm willing to do whatever's necessary to make that possible."

Tug of war, winner gets Jody. Claire was pulling hard, throwing her weight into it. Without knowing what she was doing, Claire had entered a competition to prove who was the better mother.

"I've made an appointment a week from Tuesday," Claire said, lying—she hadn't made the appointment yet, though she planned to. "Perhaps you could drive her up the weekend before." She paused. "We haven't talked much about how *you* feel, but my impression would be that having

Jody somewhere else would certainly take some of the pressure off. It must be hard on you."

"It is," Mrs. Goodman said. "I thought it was the flu."

"I did too," Claire said.

"When she called me from school, I brushed it off. She'd been saying she was sick for weeks and I ignored it. You think I don't feel terrible?"

"I can imagine."

"Can you? Every time I walk down the hall to my bedroom, I pass her door. She just lies there as though she's waiting for something. She looks at me and I don't know what to do. I could just cry."

"Bring her back," Claire said. "I promise I'll take good care."

BOOK THREE

27

Mr. and Mrs. Goodman drove Jody back to New York. She lay like a queen across the backseat, propped up with pillows and wrapped in a blanket. A video camera—a combination get-well birthday-Chanukah present from her parents—rested on her stomach, leaving Jody with the feeling that while she'd lost the contest, she'd been given what amounted to a nice consolation prize.

When they pulled up to the building, Mrs. Goodman took her bag of cleaning supplies out of the trunk and hurried upstairs, spraying anything and everything with Lysol, Fantastik, 409, creating a kind of chemical fog that simulated a super clean, germ-free environment. Jody imagined her mother asking her to say "Aah" while she sprayed the stuff directly down Jody's throat.

Her father carried in bags of food brought from home. When he made a move to sit down, her mother patted his back and pointed him toward the door. "The car," she said. "You never know what they'll take."

The apartment seemed smaller and crummier than Jody remembered. Though it was still early in the afternoon, already it was getting dark. A breeze seeped in through the window; the pipes banged. Coming back just now might not have been such a great idea; still, it was done. She was there, and she was staying. Besides, Claire was taking her to the doctor.

"I've made an appointment," she'd said. "I'm taking you. Next week."

"Taking me?"

"I've arranged my schedule so I can go with you. Would you rather go alone?"

"No," Jody said. "Not particularly."

"I've also asked your parents to come in after they drop you off. I thought it would be useful for the three of us to talk. Do you have any objections?" Claire paused. "Would you like to be there?"

"I don't think so."

"So, I'll see them at four."

Her mother made the bed with sheets that smelled like Clorox, hung new towels in the bathroom, filled the refrigerator with juices and frozen foods, and then said goodbye.

Jody raised the video camera to her eye and filmed her mother leaving.

"We'll call you tonight from home," her mother said, blowing sterile kisses as she walked backward toward the door.

"You could stay over," Jody said. "Get a hotel room, go to a play, relax. It's a lot to drive back and forth in one day."

"I'm tired of Neil Simon. Besides, your father likes to sleep in his own bed. I'll call you."

Jody closed the door and put on the chain, puzzled that neither of her parents had said anything about their meeting with Claire. Did they think it was a secret?

The telephone rang. "Hello," Jody said, expecting it to be Ellen.

"Welcome back. It's Peter Sears."

The boy who came on your stomach, Jody almost added. "I can't talk now," she said.

"Yeah, I know. Someone from Gary Marc's office is friends with a friend of my dad's. He said you almost died or something. So listen. I was thinking you might want to go to a movie, or"—he paused—"we could stay home and play."

Play what, Jody wondered. Knock, knock—who's there? No one's home right now, but I'll come on your back later.

"I'm sick," Jody said. "I can't see you."

"You're not, like, pregnant or anything, are you?"

"I'm not *like* anything," Jody said, slamming the phone down.

"Are you among the living?" Michael asked when he called later that afternoon.

"Hard to tell," Jody said.

"I spoke with Harry last week. He's decided you either killed yourself or joined a convent. You should call him." Michael stopped. "So, listen, you want a part-time job—come in a couple days a week, file my dirty underwear, the usual stuff?"

Jody wanted it. She wanted to do something. But she never knew when, without warning, she'd either have to lie down or fall down, when suddenly a mysterious free-floating fever would make her head beat with the deep tribal rhythms of pain. She didn't want anyone to see her spastic shuffle back and forth from the Xerox machine. She didn't want anyone to ask why Michael hired the handicapped.

"I want to but I can't," Jody said. "Not yet."

"Well, whenever you're ready . . ."

"Thanks." For an asshole, Michael was pretty nice.

28

"Tell me about Jody," Claire said. "How was the trip back? How's she doing?"

"She's settling in," Mrs. Goodman said.

"Good," Claire said. "Good."

"If you could give me some background information. . . . Jody and I have talked about her being adopted—could you tell me the story behind that?" Claire glanced at the Goodmans, crossed her legs, picked up a legal pad, and started making notes. The Goodmans were short, round people who looked as if they'd once been taller but something, perhaps an accident, had squashed them slightly.

"When our son was born, there were complications," Mrs. Goodman said. "It wasn't possible to have more children."

"Ben had heart problems," Mr. Goodman said.

"Ben"—the missing name. Sam and Claire had considered naming Adam Benjamin, but then decided to go with something shorter.

"With Ben, it wasn't like it is now, with specialists, machines, miracles. We were on our own. He lived for nine years. Good care. His mother's good care, that's what kept him alive."

"Was Jody adopted before or after your son died?"

"Ben," Mr. Goodman said. "He was named for my father, who lived to be a hundred and one. When we married, we talked about having four or five children. We always wanted more."

"It didn't happen until later," Mrs. Goodman added. "A lawyer we were in contact with called and said he'd heard of a baby."

"What did the lawyer tell you?" Claire asked, in a voice a little too loud. She felt like she was hearing the B side of her own life story.

"There was a lot of secrecy," Mrs. Goodman said, twisting her fingers together as though she could braid them. "It's not easy to lose a child. We wanted Ben to have a sister. And there we were with this beautiful little girl and he was gone. He would've loved her so much. If I left Jody with anyone, I worried. I was convinced that if I even turned my back, if we had an evening out, the crib would be empty and she'd be gone."

"It must have been quite a strain on your marriage."

The Goodmans didn't answer.

"I love her as much as you do," Mr. Goodman said softly to Mrs. Goodman. "You know that. Maybe I don't show it as well, but I do." He wound his watch, then raised it to his ear and listened to the even ticking for a few seconds.

"Perhaps," Claire suggested, "your worries had more to do with your son's death than Jody's arrival."

Claire was disappointed in the Goodmans. For twenty-four years she'd pictured her child's family as superior, sophisticated in a European manner: bound leather volumes, Oriental rugs, summer trips to France. Mrs. Goodman sat before her in a cotton knit suit, her hair sprayed in place, a thick braid of gold around her neck. There was nothing to indicate that this woman had been entrusted with a special task; she could've been anyone's mother. Claire breathed deeply and gave the Goodmans a chance to come clean.

"You know she was sick before, when she was a baby," Mrs. Goodman said. "The most horrible ear infections. I thought I'd lose my mind. Sitting in waiting rooms with her on my lap—I remember thinking I was just going to keel over. It was too much; but she got better, thank God. And now, again. You think we don't feel guilty? We never wanted her to go to Los Angeles. I never even wanted her to leave home."

"There are things Jody wants," Claire said. "She has to try and achieve them."

"Seeing her like this brings back everything," Mrs. Goodman said.

"What about Jody's biological parents? What were you told about them?"

"In excellent health—health was very important. The mother was unmarried, from a good family. That's it. That's all we knew."

"And you just went along with this?"

"We had no choice. We wanted a baby."

"What was the lawyer's name?" Claire asked.

Mr. Goodman rubbed the side of his face. "It's been so long now, I don't remember. He died about fifteen years ago, I remember that."

"In those days adoption wasn't what it is now," Mrs. Goodman said. "You didn't go out to lunch with the mother."

"Okay," Claire said, "then tell me what Jody was like as a child."

Mrs. Goodman clasped her hands together, tilted her head backward, and closed her eyes, as if going into a trance. "All the little girls in the neighborhood would come to our house with their stuffed animals. Jody loved stuffed animals and birthday parties. They'd set up a table, prop up all the animals around it, and at each place they'd put a cookie or a candy. Then they'd go around and eat all the treats. A lot of cookies," Mrs Goodman said, opening her eyes, laughing. "I baked a lot of cookies."

Claire smiled. "What else can you tell me?"

These moments of pleasure in the family album gave Claire something like a sugar high, so thick and sweet and good it almost made her sick. But she wanted more, as much as she could get.

"Her first day of elementary school," Mrs. Goodman said, "I put her in one of those Florence Eiseman dresses, the kind with the appliqué—she had such beautiful clothes—and we walked to school. I stayed. The whole first day I stayed right there outside the door, along with a few of the other mothers. We couldn't leave."

"And later?"

"Everyone liked her. Lots of friends. Kids coming and going. They liked our house. We were very tolerant."

When Jody was thirteen, when the Goodmans were chaperoning her first boy/girl parties, Claire was thirty-two years old. She and Sam were married, living on Eighty-third Street. Claire was still working nights at a crisis center, coming home at five in the morning, smoking dope with Sam, going out for eggs in the diner on the corner, and then sleeping until it was time to do it again.

The buzzer went off.

"Tolerant?" Claire asked.

"We didn't make them turn the stereo down," Mrs. Goodman said. "We kept potato chips and Coca-Cola in the cupboard."

"There's so much more to talk about," Claire said. "Do you think you could come in again tomorrow morning?"

"We weren't planning to stay over," Mrs. Goodman said, looking at her husband.

"Could you?"

"I think it's enough for now," Mrs. Goodman said. "We really need to get home."

"Well," Claire said, "if anything comes to mind, give me a call. Whatever I can do, I'm at your disposal."

They both nodded.

"Oh, I almost forgot. One last question," Claire said, picking up her legal pad. "What's Jody's date of birth?"

"December 10, 1966," Mrs. Goodman said, standing up, letting Mr. Goodman help with her coat.

"That's the date she was delivered to you?" Claire asked.

"No, her birthday. I don't know what time, but I'm sure that was the day."

How would *you* know? Claire almost asked. "Isn't it possible she was born a few days earlier—say, on the sixth?"

Caught up in the memory, Mrs. Goodman spoke quickly. "The lawyer called us and said, 'Your package has arrived and it's wrapped in pink ribbons.' I'll never forget it. We arranged for our pediatrician to examine the baby at the hospital."

"Which hospital?" Claire asked aggressively.

Mrs. Goodman buttoned her coat, an ugly full-length down that looked like a sleeping bag.

"Where was she born?" Claire asked again.

Mrs. Goodman's face went cloudy and she turned to her husband. "Downtown," she said. "In the city. We didn't go there ourselves."

"Doctors? Columbia? Capitol Hill?"

"Yes, one of those," Mrs. Goodman said.

"Which one?"

Mrs. Goodman shrugged and pulled on her gloves. "I really can't remember."

The patient in the waiting room knocked on the office door.

"Just a minute," Claire called.

"Nice meeting you," Mr. Goodman said, shaking Claire's hand. "We're grateful for your interest in Jody."

"We'll talk," Claire said.

And the Goodmans left.

Claire was dizzy. The session had gone fifteen minutes over. Bea was in the waiting room; Claire was late. The date was wrong. Everything was all wrong. It was an error—that was the best explanation. An error, something fouled up in all the paper shuffling. Worse things happened. Sometimes people took the wrong baby home.

29

Tuesday morning, riding in a cab across town, Jody was drenched in sweat, plastered to the backseat as though she were riding the Cyclone—the amusement park ride where the bottom drops out and all the brave souls stick to the sides, defying gravity.

She was nervous about seeing Claire. Whatever had gone on between them before had been invigorating, but also a relief when it was over. Something about the way Claire got too close—focused on Jody as if she were the most important thing in the world—was weird. And she did it so naturally that Jody felt like shit, certain her discomfort was only a personal reaction, a reflection of her distrust.

"I have failure to thrive," Jody blurted on their way to New York Hospital.

"Only infants have that," Claire said.

Claire looked different—more life-size, worn, less like a goddess.

"I *am* an infant. I knew this would happen. Just because I never told you doesn't mean I didn't know. I'm my brother. I'm my mother. This is full realization."

"Actualization," Claire said.

"Whatever."

"It was a pleasure to meet your parents," Claire said.

Jody shrugged.

"You mean a lot to them."

"It's not me *personally* who means a lot," Jody said. "It's a child. A child means too much."

"When you're a mother you'll understand," Claire said.

The cab pulled up in front of the hospital. Jody overtipped the driver and tripped over her feet getting out of the car.

"Are you okay?" Claire asked.

The only reason she was letting Claire take her—besides the fact that she was too tired to take herself—was that she figured that since Claire had little kids, she was used to taking people to doctors and explaining what was wrong with them. Jody, on the other hand, couldn't explain anything anymore.

A nurse led Claire and Jody down a hallway of closed doors and warning signs: BIO HAZARD, CAUTION: RADIATION, DANGER: OXYGEN. Then she handed Jody what looked like an application form attached to a clipboard and left them sitting outside a room marked EXAM ONE.

Jody stared at the forms. She was about to throw up.

"Do you need help?" Claire asked, taking the clipboard away from her. "Here—I'll ask the questions, you tell me the answers."

Just getting up and getting dressed was more than a day's work; the hospital was too much.

"Would you like me to come with you?" Claire asked when the nurse called for Jody.

"No thanks."

Leaning back against the cold white wall of the examining room, Jody felt like she was in a fog.

Dr. Marilyn Esterhaus walked in, asked the same questions everyone else had asked, and with thick rubber gloves felt Jody's stomach, liver, and spleen, then asked if they'd ever been enlarged before she got sick. They hadn't. Esterhaus listened to Jody's chest, making her breathe deeply so many times that she started to black out and had to put her head between her knees.

"It says here," Esterhaus said, looking down at the forms, "that you had radiation treatments to your ears. How many treatments?"

"Five or six. I really don't know."

"Let's try to find out." Esterhaus pulled the gloves off with a fast snappy sound. "I'm going to have some blood drawn. You can get dressed, then come down to my office. By the way, have you ever had an AIDS test?"

"Negative."

"Negative meaning you haven't had one?"

"Negative, meaning it came back negative."

"So there's no reason to do another one?"

"Guess not," Jody said.

Dr. Esterhaus slipped out of the room. A minute later Claire knocked on the door and said, "Can I come in?"

"Why not." Jody was dressed but still sitting on the table. Her shoes were on the floor.

"Are we waiting for something?" Claire asked.

"Blood sucking," Jody said.

Marilyn Esterhaus's office was a dark cube crammed with textbooks, back issues of *Immunology Today*, and styrofoam containers marked PERISHABLE, HANDLE WITH CARE, HUMAN TISSUE.

"Did you always have a heart murmur?" she asked.

"I don't have a heart murmur," Jody said.

"Sometimes people with these viral illnesses develop them—it's nothing to worry about." She paused and jotted something down. "I want you to have an MRI. A brain scan. If nothing else, it'll give us a baseline. And the pictures are quite remarkable."

"Polaroids are nice too," Jody said. "And I can take them at home."

"Is it necessary?" Claire asked.

"Is this in my imagination?" Jody asked.

"No," Esterhaus said. "It's real."

"Is it going to get worse?"

"It's important to relax. Stress aggravates viruses, depresses the immune system."

"What can we do?" Claire asked.

"Nothing, really. The blood will take a couple of weeks; have the scan, check back. There are a few experimental drugs being used with other immunosuppressive illnesses, but I'm hesitant to recommend them. They can be toxic. With this we have the advantage of time, so let's use that."

"Can I get pregnant?" Jody asked, surprising even herself. "I mean, what would happen if I got pregnant?"

"You probably wouldn't be able to carry a baby to term," Esterhaus said.

It was something she had to ask. Not that she was planning on it, but she supposed it was one way of getting grounded in this world. If you have no lineage, make one.

"Does it have a name?" Jody asked.

"What?" Esterhaus said.

"The virus," Jody said.

"Let's wait for the test results," the doctor said, standing to dismiss them.

"Are you upset?" Claire asked in the cab on the way home.

"There were no surprises." Jody glanced out the window at the buildings whipping by, and the motion nauseated her.

"We've never talked about you wanting to have a child. Is that something important?"

Jody felt as if Claire were trying to crawl inside her, to invade her with questions.

"You know," Claire said, "they really don't know much about these things."

Jody nodded as the cab drifted down Second Avenue.

"I'm coming to the brain scan with you."

"You don't have to."

"Sweetie, you don't have to tell me what to do," Claire said, patting Jody's knee. "I can figure it out for myself."

"She's taking me for a scan," Jody told her mother. "It's a magnet that makes photographic slices of the brain. I don't know why, but it makes me think of *Green Eggs and Ham*."

"I'm glad," her mother said, ignoring Dr. Seuss. "If she wants to arrange things, let her. Believe me, she's not doing it for free. We'll get a nice big bill."

"Why don't you ever do anything? You're my mother."

"How can you say I never do things for you?" her mother asked. "Who drove all the way to Los Angeles?"

"You did," Jody said.

"And we had a good time, didn't we?"

Jody didn't answer. It was true, they'd had a good time. The last good time. She didn't regret it, but it had nothing to do with what was going on now.

"See," her mother said. "I'm like your friend."

"I have friends," Jody said. "Be my mother."

. . .

The Magnetic Resonance Imaging factory was on the lower floors of a mansion on the Upper East Side. Although it was well lit and tastefully decorated, it could have been Frankenstein's lab, buried in the tombs of a nice quiet street. She didn't want to admit it, but Jody was glad Claire was with her—it seemed like a place where people checked in and didn't necessarily check out.

"How are you going to pay?" was the first thing the receptionist asked.

"Bill me," Jody said.

The woman shook her head. "We accept payment in advance. You can charge it on your MasterCard or Visa."

"Visa," Jody said.

"That'll be nine hundred and fifty dollars."

Jody was tempted to ask if there was a discount for cash. She signed the charge slip anyway, and the receptionist led her to a staircase. Claire's heels clicked behind her as they walked down the marble steps.

The basement was seamlessly shiny and white, its perfect, postmodern, postindustrial design not unlike the inside of a spaceship so new it'd never been flown.

"How long does it take?" Jody asked.

"You'll have to ask the technician," the woman said, guiding them into a cold anteroom.

"Leave your purses, credit cards, removable dental plates, anything magnetic or metal." The woman pointed to a large plastic basket.

Claire handed over her purse, and they both emptied their pockets. Jody felt like she was being robbed. She dropped a roll of money into the basket.

"The machinery is not affected by paper," the woman said, handing it back.

"Does this machine give off radiation?" Claire asked.

"You'll have to ask the technician. Think carefully—are you wearing any bobby pins or, again, removable dental plates?"

"I didn't know they still made bobby pins," Jody said.

"Sign this." The woman handed Jody a consent form attached to a clipboard.

Jody looked at the form and turned to Claire. "Basically, if they kill me, I have to agree not to sue."

"My husband's a lawyer," Claire said to the woman. "I'm not sure these are legally enforceable."

The woman didn't blink. "Just sign," she said.

Jody signed.

"The technician will be with you shortly. Whatever you do, don't open this door." The woman pointed to a door in front of them.

"What happens, Igor escapes?"

The woman took the clipboard from Jody and walked off without a word. They sat. Claire crossed and recrossed her legs.

A technician came out of the door they weren't supposed to open. "Goodman?" he said. It came out sounding like "goddamn."

She raised her hand. "Is there a bathroom?"

"Does this give off radiation?" Claire asked.

"How long does it take?" Jody asked. "Can she come with me?"

"Do you have any bobby pins, removable dental work, or metal in your head?" the technician asked.

"Metal in my head?"

"Steel plates, pins, et cetera?"

Claire looked at Jody. "I don't think so," Jody said.

"Bathroom's right there," the technician said, pointing to something that only started to look like a door when Jody stared at it.

She peed in two seconds, then spent five minutes in front of the mirror examining her head, wondering if maybe there was metal buried in it, metal she didn't know about. Nails. Chunks of gold. Something that could be drawn through her skull, ripped out in an excruciating flash. Claire had never mentioned her husband before. A lawyer? Jody pictured someone who looked like Raymond Burr.

The MRI machine was the size of a small nuclear reactor. There was a hole in the center, like the eye of a hurricane. The technician had Jody lie down on a narrow metal bed jutting out of the hole, then covered her with a blanket. "Don't move," he said, pushing a button that slid the bed deep into the machine. Jody felt like she'd been loaded into a cannon, reinserted into the womb, dipped into a coffin. The inner walls were less than two inches from her nose.

"Even my apartment's bigger than this," Jody called.

"It's all right," the technician said.

"For you, maybe," Jody said.

"You're going to have to be quiet."

"For how long?"

"Forty-five minutes."

"I don't think that's possible."

"You can stand here and talk to her," he said to Claire.

"Are you sure this doesn't expose me to any harmful rays?" Claire asked.

"Will you stop being so fucking self-centered?" Jody felt like yelling from inside the machine.

"Positive," the guy said. He took Claire's hand and put it down on Jody's leg. "Hold her leg and talk to her."

Claire squeezed her leg. "Do you want me to read to you?"

"From what?"

"*Family Circle,*" Claire said, grabbing the only magazine nearby.

"We're running," the technician announced over a loudspeaker from inside the dark control booth. "Talk to you in forty-five minutes."

" 'Apple raisin cake. A delicious and healthy dessert, or after-school snack—great in lunchboxes too. Three cups flour, one box raisins. . . .' "

30

*J*ust after the first of the year, Claire started house hunting for real. She shuffled her schedule, created blocks of empty hours; and as if in a dream or a fugue, without a word to anyone, she walked out of her office, into the cool damp of the garage, and took off, driving deep into the suburban landscape. As the car slid up the parkway, crossing the Harlem River, it was as if she were slipping into a strange unrecorded sleep. Alone in the car, there was no reality and she became herself, truly Claire.

She drove up and down streets with names like Maple Avenue, Post Office Road, Hickory Street, cruising the big houses, zeroing in on details such as carefully groomed privet hedges and painted fences. All of them were enough the same that nothing looked incongruous or out of place. There was comfort in familiarity and in the fact that these weren't developments, preplanned nightmares, stamped out and snapped together. These places had grown, however spontaneously, in response to an idea of how things ought to be. A promise of sorts.

What Claire wanted was serenity and sameness. A private fortress, a seemingly impenetrable veneer. A place where no one would know or care about anything, as long as things looked all right from the outside, a place that at the very least looked safe.

She drove around and around projecting her fantasies onto the seemingly deserted houses and empty streets, all the while thinking about her family—Sam and the boys, Jody.

Why didn't they realize what it did to Claire when they put up a fight, how it undermined her efforts?

She checked in with real estate agents, women who sat behind gunmetal desks well armed with books of names and addresses, maps and photos. She pulled into parking spaces in the center of those small suburban towns, tilted the rearview mirror down, put on fresh lipstick and sometimes a little blush, making sure she looked decent, able to make an appearance, a presentation; then she walked right in and sat down.

In the houses of strangers, Claire could dream. Everything was exactly the way she wanted it. She could see herself as a different person in a different life. She tried them on, as though she could actually lift the very foundations up over her shoulders, pull the walls close around her neck, button them up, and spin circles in front of a mirror. She wrapped the houses around her bones, the layers of rooms like layers of clothing. Bathrooms were like underwear, functional, basic; bedrooms were jeans and T-shirts, leisure clothes. The living and dining rooms, like silk blouses and good skirts, had to look sharp, be well coordinated, and make a coherent statement. The kitchen was like shoes, essential.

"Too big" or "too small," "just not me," Claire always concluded, and then moved on. Every few miles there was another town, every town had real estate agents, every agent had a book of photos and the keys to all the houses.

Lately, Claire had the sense that her patients were generally in better shape than she was. One afternoon in January a large envelope arrived from Claire's former and least favorite patient, Polly. Carefully packed between pieces of shirt cardboard were two eight-by-ten wedding photos. "Thought you might want the enclosed if only to round out your files. The wedding was beautiful, truly the happiest day of my life. My husband, Phil, is working temporarily for my father and will continue looking for something of his own. Meanwhile I wanted to apologize for my attitude towards you. I realize you were only trying to help and that on occasion I blamed my own frustration on you. I hope it will please you to know that things are working out well for me and that I thank you for your efforts."

Claire looked at the photographs: stock wedding portraits—glassy-eyed, the husband stood behind the wife, his arms extended around her, marking her as his possession as if claiming her for the camera would make it true. Then she tore the pictures in half so they'd fit neatly into the wastebasket under her desk.

While waiting for her two-fifteen patient, Claire flipped through catalogs. She had wanted to give Jody some kind of a small present at Christmas or New Year's, but hadn't known how to handle it. Now she decided just to order and send, no questions asked, no card enclosed—little mysteries, pennies from heaven. From Lillian Vernon she ordered a backseat organizer for Adam's car toys, and monogrammed mugs for herself, Sam, the boys, and Jody—filling out a separate form for Jody's, shipping it directly to her. Claire's patient never showed, and she spent the full hour shopping by mail; underwear from Victoria's Secret, a skirt ensemble from Tweeds, a computerized car compass from The Sharper Image.

When Claire opened her door at three, she was five hundred dollars poorer and the Owenses were already fighting in the waiting room.

"I work goddamned hard," Jim Owens was saying, "so you and your son can buy whatever the hell you want."

"Would you like to come in?" Claire asked.

The Owenses were overwhelming. They didn't need Claire; they needed a referee and a professional league to play in.

"We were just talking about her son," Jim said.

"*Your* son. He acts just like you."

"You don't have the first idea of what I was like as a kid. If I wanted something, I had to ask for it."

" 'Nobody gave me anything'," Gloria whined, imitating her husband.

"Bitch," he said.

"Perhaps we could give this discussion a little more focus," Claire said.

"Look," Jim said, "all I want is for the kid to know the rules. I think you've said it yourself—kids need limits."

"Did something happen?" Claire asked.

Gloria raised her hand. "I bought him a new pair of sneakers."

"A hundred and ten bucks."

"They were the ones he wanted, they fit him well, and all his friends have them. I don't want my child to be an outcast. Kids are so sensitive."

"As I've already told my wife," Jim said, "it's not the money I'm so angry about, it's that two days later he needed cab fare to get to school because one of the other kids got mugged on the bus, and what'd they take? His sneakers."

Gloria shook her head. "Why does everything have to become an issue?"

"As far as I'm concerned, these damn sneakers are costing me fifteen bucks a day. It's ridiculous. Get the kid some real shoes."

"Why don't you?" Gloria asked.

"Because I'm too fucking busy working all day to earn the goddamn money."

After forty minutes of relentless bickering, Claire cut them off. "We need to work on the two of you making decisions together, rather than one making a choice and then blaming the other for not being involved."

The Owenses nodded, drew in their breath, and started their sparring match again.

Claire glanced at her watch. "Perhaps next week we can talk about techniques for negotiation instead of just fighting."

"Thanks," Gloria said, standing up.

"Yeah, thanks," Jim said grudgingly, hitching up his pants as he turned to leave. "You know," he said to his wife, "next week we could just stay home and argue, save the money, and then go out for a nice dinner."

Claire sat at her desk making session notes and writing out bills. Ten sessions, twelve hundred and fifty dollars; but for you eight-fifty. She asked herself what made the sliding scale slide—a good story, a pretty face? Then she dug Polly's wedding pictures out of the trash, pulled out one of her embossed note cards, and in her most ornate hand wrote: "Congratulations. Beautiful photos. I'm so pleased things are working out. Be well. Yours, Claire Roth." She dropped the photos back in the trash, then sealed and stamped the little envelope. Guilt management.

At ten after five, Jody came in, late, walking slowly, like an old woman whose muscles had drawn up on her.

"I don't think I've told you," she said, "but I'm not going back to UCLA. It's over. *Finis.* Down the drain." Jody paused, looked at her shoes, and waited. "One of my friends is shipping my stuff back. In exchange for all my furniture, the landlord is canceling my lease. And for five hundred dollars a service is driving my mother's old car back to Bethesda." She stopped again. "I'm trying to think if there's anything else involved in canceling a life. I keep thinking I'm forgetting something. Maybe it's me. Maybe that's the problem—I'm still here."

Claire wanted to go to Jody, to hold her and tell her it would be all right, that it was a bad time, a bad day. She wanted to plait Jody's hair into small braids. She crossed her arms in front of her chest and forced herself to stay in her chair. "It seems like you did a really good job of arranging things," she said.

"I was supposed to be a director, remember? That's what directors do—they direct."

"I should have you organize my life."

"Retired," Jody said, and sat there mute.

Jody was frustrating. Sometimes she was sarcastic and unreachable, different from what Claire wanted her to be.

"I want you to meet my husband, Sam, and the kids."

Jody looked at Claire as if to ask why.

"I want to help you, to take care of you. I'm offering you things I've never offered anyone," Claire said, her voice cracking. "I care about you more than anyone, except my other children."

A slip: why did she say *other*? What was she doing? She was losing it. This was pathetic. It would have made perfect sense if Jody got up, spit on her, and walked out for good. Claire might even have admired her for it.

Jody only shrugged. And soon it was six o'clock.

"We're out of time for now, but maybe we should take an excursion to Bloomingdale's, a kind of cure. I'll call you tonight."

After Jody had left, Claire noticed a sweater on the floor next to the chair. She picked it up, rubbed it against her face, and quickly pulled it over her head.

Outside, fat flakes of snow were falling. Claire called her local real estate agent, asked what time she was showing the apartment, and hurried home to meet them there. If she wanted it done, she'd have to do it herself. Exhausted, still wearing Jody's sweater, she stood in the front hall looking dispassionately at the apartment, curious what the pair of young architects on their way over would think: disappointing, small, unstylish? The architects would hate it, noting how odd it was for an apartment in such a good location to be so utterly lacking in potential. Jody would probably hate the apartment as well.

The doorbell rang and Claire ushered in the real estate agent and the two young men. "Hello, welcome. I'm Claire Roth."

The architects introduced themselves—Tom and Bill—and shook Claire's hand. They were both dressed in classic, expensive wool suits.

Claire's skirt was all wrong, and with Jody's sweater pulled over her blouse, she knew she looked bad. There was no way they would want the apartment.

As the realtor led them from room to room, Claire brought up the rear, answering unasked questions about the apartment, the building, the co-op board, pointing out details she thought would be of interest—molding, the window frames, the new bathroom fixtures. While they were in the master bedroom, Frecia and the boys came in.

"Look what I made!" Adam shouted, coming toward Claire, trailing slush, a snowball in his mittened palm.

Even before noticing his joy, Claire noticed a spot of red in the snow-ball—blood, she figured, or the top of a crack vial. She snatched the snowball from Adam's hand and dug at the red spot with her fingernail.

"Mitten fuzz," he said. "Don't hurt it."

After careful examination, Claire pushed it back into the snowball. "Sorry, honey," she said. "Why don't we put the snowball in the freezer so it won't melt? Would that be a good idea?"

Claire led Adam and his snowball into the kitchen. The realtor and the architects came out of the bedroom.

"Thanks very much," Tom said as they headed for the door.

Claire rushed over to show them out. "Any first impressions?"

"I'm sure it'd work well for someone like you," Bill said. "But for us it's not possible."

"Why?" Claire asked, as though the man could tell what was wrong with her by diagnosing the apartment.

"The rooms are too oddly sized," he said, stepping around Claire and opening the door.

"We'll talk tomorrow," the agent said. "I'll call you."

"Who were those people?" Jake asked.

"Jerks," Claire said. "Pretentious jerks."

That night after dinner, after Claire had given Adam a bath and put him to sleep, she and Sam were lying on their bed with the door closed. With his index finger Sam traced the outline of Claire's breast through the sweater. "Is this my sweater?" he asked.

Claire shook her head. "I have to make a call," she said, not moving.

"It's ridiculous," Sam said.

"What?"

"You spend more time talking to that girl than you do to me."

"She's my patient."

Sam laughed. "I've heard you, Claire. You giggle and trade movie-star gossip with her. It's hardly therapeutic."

"I was thinking of inviting her over," she said.

"She's your client."

"She's one of us, like one of the kids."

"Except I don't know her."

"I'm not asking for your analysis," Claire said, pulling away. "I just want to know if it's all right with you to have her over."

"You're the shrink, I'm just a lawyer," Sam said, scratching himself. "If she decides to sue, call me."

"You can be such an asshole," Claire said.

He rolled onto his side and aimed the remote control at the TV. "Fucking cunt," he said.

"Piece of shit," Claire said. "Stinking."

Jake walked in without knocking. "Can you stop fighting. It's distracting." He turned and walked out again, leaving the door open behind him.

"One day," Claire muttered, "I'm gonna kill him. I can't live like this anymore. We have no privacy."

"While we're on the subject," Sam said, "I know you're showing the apartment."

Claire didn't answer.

"Is this something we should talk about, or are you planning to just pack up, sneak off, and leave me homeless?"

"I'm working on it," Claire said.

"These are decisions people make together. I'm not sure I want to move."

"Fine. Then we can get divorced. You keep the apartment and you'll still have to buy me and the kids a house."

"Not necessarily."

"Does everything have to be so goddamn difficult?" she said, getting up off the bed, folding clothing, putting it away, slamming the dresser drawers. "Why is everything such a struggle? Why don't—"

"Why don't I just do whatever you want?" Sam said. "Because I'm a person, Claire. Because I have ideas that don't belong to you. This is a marriage, not a monarchy."

The phone rang and Claire ran to answer it. "Hello?"

"Mrs. Roth?"

"Yes?"

"It's Bea"—the patient who'd escaped her children's lives, her husband's complaints, and her apartment. "You once gave me your number at home and said I could call."

"I remember," Claire said. "Are you all right?"

"I came home from my class tonight and there was a letter on the kitchen table, propped up against the salt shaker."

"Yes?"

"It was from Herbert. He left. He said he was tired of coming home to an empty apartment, tired of me not cooking, not taking care of him anymore. So he left. After thirty-six years. I came home from an art history lecture and this is what I get? He's fifty-seven years old. Does he think he can just walk out of here and into some other apartment where some other old woman is going to cook and clean for him?"

Claire didn't say anything for a minute. She looked at Sam stretched out on the bed holding the remote control, pouting.

"Would you like to come in and see me in the morning?" Claire asked.

"I'm supposed to go to the Met with one of the girls from my class. I'm not going to cancel just for Herbert. It would give him too much pleasure, wherever he is."

"Well, call me tomorrow if you want to talk."

"Thanks," Bea said. "Sorry to bother you at home. I just wanted you to know."

"It's okay," Claire said.

Bea laughed. "The funny thing is, I called you, but I really have nothing to say—I'm speechless."

"Well, you can call me back if you need to. Are you going to be all right?"

"How would I know?" Bea said. "Well, good night."

Claire stared at the receiver for a minute and then hung up and left the room, closing the door behind her.

31

"You're floundering, babe," Ellen said when Jody told her about the plan to meet Claire's family. "You don't even ice-skate."

"At least Claire wants me. I should be glad for that."

"Do you hear yourself?"

"It's scary. I never thought it would happen, but I'm needy, Ellen. *Needy.* It's vile."

"If I were you, I'd be furious with her for reducing you to this infantile blob. You have no self-confidence. That's what this is all about—low self-esteem. I saw an 'Oprah' on it."

"Viral castration," Jody said. "It's smooth, it's fast, it's final."

That Claire liked her was flattering; anytime someone likes you, the instinct is to like them back. True, the relationship was out of the ordinary, several degrees more intense than Jody was prepared for, but so were the circumstances. When Jody had started this, she never thought Claire would mean anything to her. It'd been simple enough at first, but things had changed, and Jody had discovered that everything wasn't as it seemed. Her belief in her family's power had been an illusion, and her concept of self was constructed around the myth of literally being their child. She wasn't theirs, wasn't anyone's. What all that meant wasn't clear; but Claire was helping her, almost cradling her while she figured it out. This wasn't the first time someone had treated Jody as though she were special. All through school her teachers had doted on her, and later Michael and Harry as well. People enjoyed her, so the rules changed in her favor. This wasn't something Jody asked for; it just happened and she went along with it.

After hanging up with Ellen in Dallas, Jody put on her coat, took the elevator down, and hailed a taxi on Hudson Street. She wasn't meeting Claire and her family for an hour and a half. "Museum of Natural History," Jody told the driver. The safest place in the world, locked in time, reminiscent of childhood Sunday afternoons at the Smithsonian: the mammoth elephant in the Great Hall, the Eskimos chewing blubber in their dioramas.

A person will do anything to survive. Call it animal instinct. Jody went to the museum sure that if she could spend an hour not thinking—about failure, about Claire, about Ellen, about anything—if she could give herself over to the quiet, gravelike darkness of history preserved, she would be returned, healed.

At the entrance to the Great Mammal Hall, she stopped to get her breath. Jody was in with the caribou, the brown bear, the wapiti.

"It won't get out, right?" a little kid behind her asked his mother.

Jody was thinking that this time, it all just might come crashing out. Claire had started dropping her family's names into the conversation a while ago—Sam this, Jake and Adam that—and Jody had tried to pretend they didn't exist. Shrinks weren't supposed to have families, no one other than you, as if they, too, lived for those fifty minutes. That was the way it had to be. Now Claire was insisting that she meet them and wouldn't let go of it. A year ago it wouldn't have bothered Jody; but now, when all that had always seemed near, familiar, and good had gone sour, Claire seemed to be flaunting her success, her husband, her children.

Jody looked around. The Alaskan brown bear was up on its hind feet, two stories tall. The male wapiti had its head thrown back, its mouth dropped open, its black eyes popping out. All the animals looked as if they'd seen the ghost of something terrible. The silence felt trapped—stillness stuffed, sewn in. Everyone had a family, everyone belonged to someone and imitated them in ways they would never notice or need to articulate. Jody had simply arrived, delivered to her parents' house like food ordered in. She considered what would happen if she skipped out on Claire's family, if she simply hailed a taxi and went back down to Perry Street. Would she spend the rest of the afternoon feeling like a failure, having missed out on another amazing opportunity, curious how her life had come to this incredible grinding halt?

The flying squirrel was perfect: in a deep-black case like in the darkest dream, it was fixed against tall trees, moonlight, a distant forest, and snow-covered mountain peaks. Fully extended, the northern squirrel was up there, out there, hanging in midair.

Jody would pull herself together. She would go to the park and meet Claire's family. What harm could come of it? She hurried toward the exit, wishing there was someone to lead her out, eyes closed, blind. She walked quickly, trying not to pay attention; but all the same, the last thing she saw on her way out was the dodo bird.

At three-thirty, the appointed time, she stood on the grassy knoll above Wollman Rink. The light was starting to fade, the chill of night slowly seeping into the air. Hovering over the park, backlit, were the tall apartment buildings of Central Park South. The thick red letters of the Essex House sign hugged the skyline in the same way that the "Hollywood" letters clung to the hill in L.A. It had been a deceptively warm day for late January: faces were flushed; left and right, people had taken off their coats, stripping down to turtlenecks. A hopeful afternoon. Jody would meet Claire's family; she would exchange greetings and then, as soon as politely possible, break away.

A long line of would-be skaters curved up the path leading to the rink. From above, the ice was crowded, as though all of New York had come out for a skate this particular Sunday afternoon. Jody climbed a rock and looked for Claire, working the line from back to front. She was there, halfway down, also looking. There was no reason to rush. Claire was at least thirty people away from the entrance. When she was within fifteen, Jody would start down the path, pressing through the line—"Excuse me, coming through . . . Meeting someone up front, pardon me."

Then Claire spotted her and waved frantically. Jody automatically waved back and went forward.

"I thought you might be standing us up," Claire said.

"Running late," Jody said, not sure which of the strangers surrounding them were Roths. Claire tapped the backs of a man and two children in front of her. Jody expected her to say, Please allow me to introduce the recalcitrant, resistant, deeply neurotic Miss Goodman. Instead she patted the hair on top of the smaller boy's head and in a clear and happy voice said, "Guys, this is Jody."

Sam turned and faced her—not a vampire, not a gorilla, just a guy. "Good to meet you," he said.

"Yo," the elder boy said.

The younger one, Adam, looked down at his shoes. "I don't wanna wear skates. Just my shoes."

The line moved forward. At the admissions window, Jody took out her wallet, but Claire stopped her and let Sam pay for all of them. "My treat," she said. "All day."

The clubhouse was noisy, filled with shouting children, out-of-date pop songs, and people in a hurry. Jody focused on putting on her skates. She could feel herself disappearing into a haze.

"Pull the laces tight," Claire said.

Jody looked at her blankly.

"Pull the laces tight," Claire said again, this time reaching over to help. "It supports the ankle."

Sam, Claire, Jake, and Adam. Real people, only better, like a family from a TV commercial. Handsome and cool compared with Mr. and Mrs. Goodman, who were getting ready to apply for Social Security. Claire in her off-duty clothes—faded jeans, turtleneck, with her blond hair held back with a thick barrette. Sam in wide-wale cords, a hand-knit sweater, hair just a little long, a little gray. By contrast Jody felt dark, black, mismatched. It wasn't their fault. Claire's family didn't look at her strangely, didn't treat her as if she were peculiar or contagious. Nothing about their actions screamed, Oh my God, it's a *patient*—be careful.

"I'm not sure I can do this," Jody said, remembering that one year for Chanukah her mother bought three pairs of skates, packed meat loaf sandwiches and thermoses of cocoa, and drove Jody and her father down to the C&O Canal. For the first hour it was wonderful, right out of a Norman Rockwell painting: Mom, Dad, and Jody in mittens and long scarves, gracefully sawing their way back and forth across the ice. Then Jody's father fell, landed on his coccyx, rode home facedown sprawled across the backseat, and spent the next month sitting on inflatable rings intended for infant use in swimming pools.

"Of course you can," Claire said, pulling her toward the rink. "Tell me when you get tired and we'll take a rest."

Jody and Claire wobbled out of the clubhouse walking on the thin blades like demented ducks. The skaters whirled past, and the only way to get onto the ice was to take a running start, a flying leap. If you hesitated, they'd crush you.

"Have you ever jumped rope?" Claire asked.

"Not recently."

"Well, it's like that, like jumping in."

Jody was looking at the skaters, trying to gauge the pace, when Claire grabbed her hand and jerked her onto the ice. Jody pulled back. Around them three people fell. "Skate," Claire said. And Jody did, at first in odd, jerking motions, and then more evenly, using her arms to swing herself forward.

"Odie," Adam said. "Odie, take me around. Slow," he said. "I like slow." A three-foot, chestnut-haired, blue-eyed ladykiller. Jody took him around a few times, and then he said, "Okay, Odie—now Mom."

Claire had introduced her and now she was on the inside, one of the gang. It wasn't that they gushed over her or went out of their way to be nice. In fact, it was almost the opposite: she was nothing special, just a girl.

Jody delivered Adam to Claire and then took a break by the side of the rink, watching them skate as a family, Claire with Jake, Adam with Sam. It all came together—the music, the end of a winter afternoon, the perfect family. Everything they did was easy, effortless. They just did it and it came out right. Jody wanted life to be that easy. She wanted to be like them, and if she couldn't be, then at least she hoped that maybe something would rub off. For the first time, she wanted all that Claire had been offering, that and more.

"Go on, go with Sam," Claire said, pushing her toward where he stood a few feet away, arm already extended. "Go on."

Jody slid her hand into Sam's and they took off. They skated, they sailed, steering with the swing of their arms and the tilt of their legs. Jody was along for the ride, taking off on the even glide of the skates, taking in the skeletal trees against the sky, the horse-drawn carriages in the distance, the winter city near dusk. The sensation of motion, round and round, breathed life back into her. Round and round, skating the great wide circle, in matching rhythm and stride. They passed Claire and Adam, waved and called out to them, then took off again, skating faster, legs working harder, wheeling their way around. Jody imagined that people were watching them, thinking they were together. She pushed her hand farther into Sam's. His palm was large, rough. The way he wrapped his fingers around her hand but didn't squeeze, didn't crush, made Jody feel good.

"Can I tell you a secret?" she asked him as they skated. "I didn't want to come here today. I was dreading it."

"Why?"

"Scared to meet you."

Sam smiled. "Am I as bad as you expected, or worse?"

"I'm not sure. Do you have twelve toes, thorny toad bumps, horn-rimmed glasses, and disfiguring leprosy?"

"How'd you know?" Sam asked.

"Wow," Claire said when they finally came in for a landing, stopping only because the guards were clearing the rink so the ice could be resurfaced. "You two are fantastic together."

Jody blushed.

Jake lifted his nose into the air. "Hot dogs," he said. "I smell hot dogs."

"Not here," Claire said. "Let's get something better."

They took off their skates, put their regular shoes on, and went up the path toward Fifth Avenue. Over the hills and through the woods. Jody could barely walk. It was going to hurt later, really hurt. The effect of the virus was evident. Her vision was uneven, her heart was skipping awkwardly; but she'd rather drop dead than leave the Roths now.

"Why're the ducks all crowded into that one part?" Jake asked when they passed the pond. It was almost dark and would've been creepy if they weren't all together.

"The rest of the pond is frozen," Claire said.

"Why don't they go somewhere else for the winter, like Aunt Shirley?" he asked.

"Because it's their home."

On Fifth Avenue the streetlights glowed orange, and Jody remembered the night shoot with Harry on this very corner. She remembered Carol Heberton going into the fountain fifteen times. A lifetime ago. Sam put his hand up for a cab. "I love this," Claire said, wrapping her arm around Jody. "Isn't it great?"

It was. The ache that began at the base of Jody's skull and went full-length through her heart and lungs to the bleeding blister on her little toe, was real. It was active, reeking of health and physicality, and she was thankful for it—for being reminded of family, and how inescapably full of life children were.

They went to Serendipity, drank vats of hot chocolate. And when the waitress asked what Jody wanted to eat, she nodded in Claire's direction and said, "I'll have whatever she's having." When the chili arrived, she realized she didn't even like chili; then she looked at Claire stirring the sour cream around, adding extra onions, and dug in. For chili, it was actually quite good. Past the point of thinking for herself, past the point of tension, she was filled with the intoxicating satisfaction that comes with being thoroughly spent. But her happiness, the height and buoyancy of it, frightened her. It was as though she'd been forcing herself to sit by the side of the pool, not daring to dip her toes in, and suddenly she was taking the steps to the high dive two at a time, running the length of the board, and hurling herself off the end.

"Are you okay?" Claire asked.

Jody nodded.

"What are you thinking?"

Jody shrugged. "Nothing."

"You're smiling."

Jody shrugged again. She was stoned on relief. The worst part was over.

"What did you do to your hair?" Claire said, reaching over and running her fingers through it.

"Brushed it," Jody said.

"You'd look great in earrings. Are your ears pierced?"

"Have been since I was twelve. Spencer Gifts, Montgomery Mall— shot straight through the lobe with one of those guns."

"I never noticed. I'll have to remember that. We'll get you some really nice earrings."

Jody shrugged and watched Adam dissecting onion rings while Jake and Sam wordlessly wolfed down enormous hamburgers.

In the cab on the way home—warm, full, pressed against Adam and Claire—Jody nearly fell asleep.

"Why don't you come to the apartment?" Claire whispered. "You can sleep over if you want."

Jody shook her head. "I have to go home," she said. "I'm so tired, you wouldn't believe. I wonder where my key is." She worked her hand into her pocket. "Hope I didn't lose it."

"You really should give me a duplicate," Claire said. "Just in case."

"Found it," Jody said, producing the key.

"Well, maybe you can come over tomorrow."

The cab pulled over to the curb and a horn blared behind them as the Roths slowly piled out and they all said their goodbyes. Sam tried to hand Jody a ten, but she waved the money away and pulled the door shut. "Perry and West Fourth," she told the driver, and the cab pulled away. Jody took a deep breath. There was absolutely nothing left; everything had been spilled, drained, sucked dry. All she could think about was how great the Roths were, and how much she wanted a hot shower, warm blankets, and a big, fluffy pillow.

32

*I*n the middle of a warm week in March, prematurely pressed into a heat wave that brought the flowers out early and left people damning both the summer to come and the winter that had never quite arrived, Claire found the house she wanted.

At ten a.m., strapped into a minivan en route to a house the real estate agent couldn't really describe, didn't have a picture of, but just knew Claire would love, she saw what she'd been looking for. Marked with a yellow FOR SALE sign and set back across a long lawn was a small, plain farmhouse, white with green shutters and a porch that wrapped three-quarters of the way around.

"Stop," Claire said. "You're passing it."

"Oh, you don't want that," the agent said. "Besides, it's under contract. I'll have to remind someone to take care of that sign."

"Stop," Claire insisted, and the agent tapped the brakes, shifted into reverse, and backed up. Like a garbage truck, the car made an alarming beep-beeping warning sound.

"I know this house very well," she said. "I showed it a thousand times before they found a buyer. It's too small. Four bedrooms, only one's decent-sized. No place to put a live-in. Two and a half baths—most of my clients want three or three and a half minimum. It looks like the place where my grandmother grew up. And all that grass—no one wants so much grass with such a small house. Bushes, a few evergreens, some flower beds, yes—but lawn mowing, who needs it? And you can be sure whoever would live here wouldn't have a gardener."

How about two strong boys and a husband, Claire thought, all of whom could stand to do a little work.

"Could we go in?" Claire asked, releasing her seat belt, and lifting the door lock like an animal opening its own cage. The agent followed her onto the front porch, where Claire stood with her nose pressed to the glass.

"I don't have the key," the agent said flatly.

"When was it built?" Claire asked.

"Had to be the 1940s. No one would've done something like this in the fifties."

Claire pressed her nose against the windowpane. The living room had a fireplace, a long mantel, wooden floors. To the right was a staircase with a thick wooden banister.

"Standard layout," the agent said. "Kitchen's a horrible aqua green, appliances and everything—it's like being inside a Jacques Cousteau nightmare. Basement's unfinished. One of the bathrooms needs a lot of work."

To Claire it gave off the timeless image of family and home. Four bedrooms was two more than they already had. She pulled out her camera and took a few shots. "What are they getting?" she asked.

"Confidential," the agent said, tapping her toe on the porch with every click of the shutter. "I'll wait in the car," she finally said.

Claire walked around the house, full circle, snapping the whole way round. She wanted the whole picture, soup to nuts. Finished, she got back into the car, turned to the agent, and said, "Now show me what you wanted me to see."

Later, all Claire could remember about the other house, the one that was supposed to be just right for her, was a huge stained-glass window in the living room that filtered the morning light so that it landed like a pool of blood on the floor, and the agent asking over and over again why she wasn't taking any photos.

"You'll let me know," Claire had said when they got back to the agent's office, "if the deal falls through." She shook the woman's hand.

Back in the city, Claire left the car in the garage and went across the street to the one-hour photo shop. She dropped off the film, tucked the claim slip into her pocket, and hurried off to her office. Waiting for Bea, she thought about the house so intently that she imagined she could hear guests coming up to the front door and calling, "Yoo-hoo! Anybody home?"

The buzzer went off, and soon Bea was sitting across from her.

"I don't know what's happening to me," she said. "I *should* be depressed. I should be *miserable*, but I'm not."

"Are you taking any medication?"

"No, it's me. It's only me. I'm happy."

What was there for Claire to say? How could she say, No you're not. If someone says she's happy, do you have her declared insane and committed, or count her as cured and send her away? This was such a rare occurrence that it was confusing.

"It's peculiar. I wake up alone in my bed feeling good. That never happened before. In the evening, I eat whatever I want, I watch the television shows I like. There's something very satisfying about it."

Claire sat and listened. There were people who claimed to be happy as a defense against their sadness; they said they were happy again and again, as though saying it often enough would make it come true.

"It sounds good," she said when Bea paused and looked up at her. "Sounds like you're really pleased."

"If I'd known I'd feel this good, I would've kicked him out years ago."

"Do you feel lonely?"

"Not really. I think I may have been lonelier before." Bea wasn't lying.

Claire smiled. "I'm happy for you," she said.

After Bea had gone, Claire raced out, picked up the photos, and spread them across her desk. For the next week or so, whenever something upset her she would take out the photos and, instantly dipping into the dream, picture herself and the family—including Jody—in the house together.

About ten days later, the real estate agent left a message on her machine. "I have news. The contract on that farmhouse"—she said "farmhouse" as though the very word nauseated her—"fell through. Too complicated to explain, but it's on the market again. And I'll tell you a secret: they're anxious to sell. They're waiting to settle on another place. Another secret—and I really shouldn't be telling you this. The bid they'd accepted was three even, but if they could get it soon, I think they'd go lower. Call me."

Claire went running to Sam's office. "There's something I should've told you," she said, slipping her hand into her pockets, rubbing her fingers across the photos.

"Do I want to hear it?" Sam asked.

"I found it," she said, laying the photos out over the papers on Sam's desk. "It wasn't available before, but something happened. If we move fast we can get it cheap."

Sam leaned back in his chair, put his hands behind his head, and rocked. "I don't know, Claire. We don't know anything about buying houses. The boys are in the middle of a school year. We'd have to sell our place. Something like this takes a lot of planning."

"I *have* been planning. Sam, I want this. Just look at the pictures."

"You always want something," he said, tilting forward to glance down at the photos.

"No, I really want *this*. That's why I haven't mentioned it. It means too much to me."

"That doesn't make sense," he said, picking up the old magnifying glass that had been his grandfather's and going over the pictures carefully, as though this seventy-five-year-old chunk of scratched glass would reveal their significance.

Claire dug deep into the zippered compartment of her purse, pulled out two of her most favorite pictures, and handed them to Sam.

"It's nice," he said, staring at them for a second, then tossing them on the desk with the others and looking away.

"See, the living room's in here, and there's a fireplace with a really nice mantel."

Sam was still staring out the window.

"Take a ride with me," Claire said. "I have a break until later this afternoon," she lied.

"Now?"

"Yes, now," Claire said. "We can talk in the car."

"I have things to do. I'm in the middle of something," he said, scooping up the photos and handing them back to Claire. "Maybe tomorrow, or on the weekend."

"Sam, this house is the beginning of a new life." She was more intent than she'd been in years. "It's less than an hour away."

"Where is it? What town? What *state?*"

"Connecticut—just outside of Greenwich, for God's sake. I think it's called Glenville," Claire said, pulling her hair repetitively, an old nervous tic.

"Fine. Okay. You want to get it over with?" he said, springing up from the desk and yanking his coat off the pole by the door. "Let's go."

"I have to make a couple calls," Claire said, taking her appointment book out of her bag.

Sam slipped his coat on. "Can't you make them from the car?"

Claire shook her head.

He picked up a stack of books and went out the door. "I'll run these down the hall. Be right back."

From Sam's desk, Claire called her two-thirty and left a message on his machine. She called the analyst across the hall and asked him to put up a note just in case. Then she dialed again. "Hi, cookie," she said when Jody answered.

"Sorry, wrong number," Jody said.

"I have an emergency this afternoon. I need to cancel our appointment."

"It's because you're tired of me," Jody said. "I've become boring. Fine, go ahead, get someone else. Get a good anorexic for all I care. Try inviting her out to lunch."

"Couldn't be helped," Claire said. "I'll call you tonight when I get home."

"Don't bother."

"Jody, you have to stop this. Perk up, sweetie. I can't stand this depression thing anymore."

"Are you telling me to snap out of it? You, a *shrink?*"

"Spring's right around the corner. It's time to get on with your life."

"I don't have one, remember? And where'd you get that line—Hallmark?"

"Got to go," Claire said. "I'll call you later."

In the car, Claire talked nonstop. "My whole life I've always wanted to live in Connecticut. As a child, it was my fantasy. I thought all the best movie stars lived there, Katharine Hepburn and I don't know who else. Connecticut," she said, "Connecticut. Successful, refined, rich."

"Waspish," Sam said. "I hate to impose reality onto this conversation, but what about the apartment? Is anyone even interested in it? And what about the kids—their friends, for instance?"

"They'll finish the year in the city and start in Connecticut in the fall." Claire drew out "Connecticut" until it had about a hundred syllables.

"Isn't it too late to get them into a school?"

"Public school, Sam. Everyone in the suburbs goes to public school. We'll save a fortune."

"I thought kids in *Connecticut*," he said, "went to prep school."

"Only the unmanageable ones."

"So we have a few years to go," Sam said. "Okay, how do I get to work? Or am I supposed to quit work and just stay home and mow the lawn all day? I noticed from the photos that there's quite a bit of grass to deal with."

"We have a car, and there's a train, and we'll get one of those ride-'em mowers."

"Honey, right now my office is an eight-minute walk from our apartment, six if I'm in a hurry. I'd have to get up in the middle of the night in order to get in on time, and I'd be coming home very late."

"It's fifty-three useful minutes by train. You can relax, read, work, sleep, whatever. Thousands of people do it every day."

"Goys. I'm a Jew. Do I have to remind you? Jews get sick if they read when they're in motion. It's genetic—something about escaping Egypt, the bumpy ride. By the way, are Jews even allowed in Connecticut?"

"We'll get a big hairy dog, and every night you can walk it around the neighborhood. It'll get rid of your love handles."

"And my love life. So, how many million bucks is it all going to cost? That's the bottom line, isn't it?"

"Less than a larger apartment."

"How much?"

"They're asking three-thirty, but the agent says they'll take less. I figured we'd offer two-ninety."

"And how much can we get for the apartment?"

"Three, maybe three-fifteen. But if we come down a little, we'll probably find a buyer right away."

"And how much do we have in the bank?"

"Sam, we're not paying cash."

"If you want me to take the idea seriously, we have to talk seriously."

"You're intimidating me." Claire pulled onto the shoulder next to the driveway. Suddenly she didn't want Sam to see the house. She felt like he wanted to take it away from her.

"This is it?" Sam asked.

Claire started crying.

"So pull in already."

She put the car in park.

"Honey, go into the driveway and let's look around. We came all the way out here. It's fine if you've changed your mind, but we might as well have a look, don't you think?"

Now Claire was really crying—over Sam, the house, Jody, everything. She wished there was no one and nothing.

"Is it unlocked?" Sam asked, opening the car door. "Do you want to come with me?"

Claire shook her head no, and he got out of the car and walked down the long driveway. She watched him try the front door, then pull a credit card from his wallet and pop the lock open. Once inside, he turned and waved at Claire, giving her the thumbs-up sign, and then disappeared. Claire was still strapped in—the seat belt cutting against her neck—thinking of ways she could gain control over her life. Get rid of Sam, the kids, and the apartment. Drop Jody. Get her own place uptown—or even out of town, it didn't matter.

After Sam had been gone for twenty minutes, Claire started to worry. An escapee might have camped out in the empty house, or Sam could've fallen down the stairs that led to the unfinished basement, slamming his head against the cement floor at the bottom. She got out of the car, went to the front door, and rang the bell. "Sam?" she called. Hearing no answer, she pushed the door open and stepped inside the house for the first time. "Sam, are you here?"

"Upstairs," he hollered.

"Are you all right?"

"Of course."

Relieved, she went through the dining room into the kitchen. It was aqua all right, but pretty—the sort of look a decorator in Manhattan might charge a fortune to accomplish.

"Come upstairs!" Sam yelled.

Claire slowly went up the dark stairs. "Where are you?"

"In our bedroom," he said.

Claire started down the hall toward the back of the house.

"Wrong way," he said, suddenly behind her. "I like this one better. It looks out onto the front yard." She turned back toward him, stopping to stick her head into the bathroom; the tub was cracked in half.

In the small front bedroom, Sam pulled Claire toward him. "Is this what you want? Is this your fantasy?"

She nodded.

"Is there any reason why you shouldn't have whatever you want?"

Claire didn't answer.

He ran his hand up Claire's leg, under her skirt. "I think we should try it out," he said, curling his fingers inside the elastic band of her underwear.

"Sam, I don't know," she said, pushing him away.

"Are you having second thoughts?" he asked, unzipping his pants.

"There's no furniture." Claire crossed her arms and stood awkwardly in the center of the room, her underwear caught halfway down her thighs, the lining of her skirt rubbing against her bare ass.

When Sam reached out, uncrossed her arms, and began unbuttoning her blouse, she didn't resist.

"The bathroom tub's cracked in half," she said. "We'd probably need a new one."

"Big enough to fuck in," Sam said, unhooking her bra and rubbing his face against her breasts, sliding his hand under her skirt and pulling her underwear the rest of the way down. "And a lock on our door."

Naked, their flesh stuck to the varnished floorboards. As they flip-flopped from top to bottom, positioning and repositioning themselves, their skin made thick peeling sounds. Later, in the car on the way home, it would be red and raw, their hips and buttocks covered with abrasions not unlike burns; they would shift uncomfortably in their seats. But at the time, in the moment, they hadn't noticed.

When they walked into the apartment at five, Frecia was furious. "I don't know where you've been," she said, her accent heavy with anger. "But as much as I love these children, I got a life of my own."

"I'm sorry," Claire said. "An emergency came up."

"Emergency my eye," Frecia said, looking at their satisfied faces.

"Here's cab money," Claire said, pulling out all the cash in her wallet and handing it over without bothering to count. "Did anyone call?" she asked.

"A girl called Jody. She said she was checking on your big emergency."

"Anyone else?"

"Your friend Naomi," she said. "She wanted to know if selling her husband and children was illegal." Frecia turned to Sam. "And your office, mister."

Claire went into the bedroom to call Jody. The answering machine clicked on; she hung up without leaving a message.

Sam came up behind her and tickled her neck. "I suppose I should call the office," he said.

Claire handed him the phone. "I'm going for a walk," she said. "I'll be back in a little bit. Why don't you order some Chinese for dinner. Adam likes lemon chicken."

Sam nodded as he spoke to his secretary.

"See you," Claire said, putting on her coat and sliding her tote bag over her shoulder—in it was her purse, the camera, all kinds of stuff. In the elevator going down, she decided it was too heavy. She pulled out her purse and the camera and left the rest with the doorman.

Buttoning her coat, she walked west across Eighth Street, crossing Sixth Avenue, heading down Christopher and West Fourth, then turned left onto Perry Street. She pulled her scarf close. Checking the numbers on the brownstones, she made her way to 63. She had it memorized: Jody Goodman, 63 Perry Street, Apartment 4B, New York, New York 10014. The building was an old brick-and-limestone fortress; the entrance was a wooden double door, three steps up, columns on either side. The door swung open and a young woman stepped out, startling her.

"Are you looking for something?"

"No," Claire said, stepping back.

The woman walked off, and Claire caught the door just before it closed. She stepped into the anteroom, checking the names and numbers on the mailboxes. 4B GOODMAN. The lock was broken, the flap hanging open, the mail nearly falling out. What was she doing there? Did she want to show Jody the pictures of the house, to explain that now, finally, they would be a family. Someone came out the inside door and Claire slipped in. Taking the elevator to the fourth floor, she stood outside the apartment as though she expected Jody to open the door and ask why it had taken her so long to get there. The hallway was deserted. Claire reached into her pocket and comforted herself by rubbing her fingers back and forth across the smooth gloss of the photographs. She stood outside the apartment far longer than anyone should just stand anywhere; was that how burglars and rapists worked? She pressed her ear to the wall, heard nothing, then rang the bell. Claire thought that perhaps Jody was inside, knew Claire was there, and was purposely ignoring her. "Jody," she called, knocking on the door. "It's me, Claire. Open up." She thought of hurling herself against the door over and over again, screaming, demanding to be let in. *Do you know who I am?* And if she huffed and puffed and knocked her way in, what would she do then?

She took the elevator back down and stopped at the mailboxes again before going out into the street, feeling tired and vaguely confused.

33

*I*t was a bright afternoon near the end of March, a day filled with the strange and fragile sense that at any moment all that was clear might be taken away and replaced with a dark and heavy rain. Jody moved down the street, aiming the video camera at whatever looked interesting—a cat crossing the road as a cab barreled down the street, the age-old game of beat the clock.

On the corner of Perry and West Fourth, near home, she saw something that caused her to instinctively duck behind the iron rail of a brownstone. Coming out the door and down the steps of Jody's building was Claire Roth. Jody used the zoom, pulled in close, and pressed Record, locking in on Claire, trailing her from what seemed like a safe distance. She pulled open the door to Patisserie Lanciani—Jody's cafe—slipped off her coat, and took one of the window seats. The waitress came and went. A cup of coffee arrived. Claire added sugar, no milk, and looked innocently out the window. The tape ran; Jody was getting the goods on Claire, video proof like the kind they showed on television: "Video Trial," "True Stories," "New York's Weirdest." Claire reached into her pocket and pulled out a stack of something that Jody couldn't quite make out. Cards? The zoom was fully extended; she needed to get closer to pick up more detail. Creeping down the block until she was directly across the street, Jody situated herself so that she was shielded by a delivery van. Photographs. Claire had reached into the pocket of her coat and taken out a stack of snapshots. She'd laid them out across the cafe table and arranged them in a specific order, as if she were fitting the pieces of a puzzle together. Jody was sure the pictures were of her apartment. Claire had broken in, gone through her drawers, her closet, the boxes under her bed, taking Polaroids of everything. She'd rounded up all Jody's secrets and stolen them. Claire would take whatever she could get from Jody; that much was suddenly and surprisingly clear.

Video still running, her eye fixed on Claire, Jody came closer to the cafe, stepping into the street, hoping for a better position. Once she was out in the street, exposed, Claire looked up, saw Jody, and registered the expression of having been caught. A nearly lethal rush of confusion and guilt coursed through Jody. She couldn't move. A car horn blared. "Outta the street, retard!" someone yelled. Like lifting lead, Jody raised one foot, then another, and made her way to the curb, camera still fixed to her eye. Claire tapped on the glass and gestured that Jody should come in. Jody stood at the window, blank. Claire tapped on the glass again, but Jody was unable to respond. Claire went around to the door and said, "It's getting cold out. Come on in, have a cup of cocoa or something."

Jody sat down. The photographs were gone, as though they'd existed only in Jody's viewfinder.

"How are you?" Claire asked. "You look a little pale."

Had Claire slipped them into the deep pockets of her coat? Jody shifted from side to side, looking at the dark wool draped over the chair, hoping to see the white edge of a photo poking out of the pocket. Nothing. The camera was there, hanging off the side of the chair, but where were the pictures? She must have slipped them into her purse. The purse was on the table in front of Claire, screaming to be opened.

"Have you eaten anything today?" Claire said. "Maybe you should have a croissant and some cocoa."

"Double espresso," Jody said to the waitress.

"Have something with it," Claire said. "Espresso isn't very nourishing."

Jody didn't answer.

"So, tell me about your day. You've been out making movies? It occurred to me just last week that you and I should make a movie together—write a screenplay about therapy. You'd write the girl and I'd write the therapist."

"I don't think so," Jody said.

"It could be so funny, and there's so much to say." Claire acted as if she hadn't heard Jody's answer. "I always wanted to be a writer."

"Strange," Jody said, "I would've thought you wanted to be a photographer."

Claire didn't respond except to look vaguely puzzled. "I'm not very visual," she said. "I'm much more mental." She tapped her temple.

Jody tipped her head in the direction of the camera dangling off the chair.

"Oh," Claire said. "That's Sam's. I didn't want to leave it with the doorman."

The espresso arrived, and Jody poured sugar into it until it was the consistency of granular mud.

"You need to take better care of yourself. No wonder you're not well." Claire called the waitress over. "Could we have a croissant, please."

"I don't need anything."

"Do you want it or not?" the waitress asked.

"No," Jody said.

"Then I'll have it and maybe you'll eat some." The waitress went off and Claire leaned toward Jody. "That sweater's my favorite color. Do you know what it means to me to see you wearing that color?"

Jody shrugged.

"It means we have a lot in common. Two peas in a pod. I'd like you to come over for dinner sometime this week, and on Wednesday there's a play at Adam's school. You'd love it."

If Claire had been anywhere near normal, she would have explained what she'd been doing. She would have said, Oh, there you are, what a coincidence. I just stopped by your building. But there was nothing—not a word, not a gesture.

"You know," Claire said, "I've been thinking that if I can talk Sam into taking charge of the boys for a weekend, we could go away together. Just the two of us. Out to the beach, or maybe up to the Berkshires. It'd be great if we could have some real time together."

Jody finished her coffee, picked up the video camera, and turned it on Claire. "Why don't you tell me about *your* day," she said, pushing the Record button. "It's a documentary. The scene is Claire Roth at Patisserie Lanciani. Tell me where you've been today. Were you seeing patients?" Jody paused. "And why do you call them patients? You're not a doctor. What can you tell me about your background, your training? Your philosophy, your approach to therapy? Do you know what you're doing?"

"Put down the camera," Claire whispered. "People are watching."

"Yes, we're here in Patisserie Lanciani with a live audience, a roomful of real people." Jody panned the room and then returned to Claire, closing in so that Claire's face filled the entire frame. "They, too, crave the answers. The myth of the therapeutic process, the great wide unknown; doesn't touch the truth, does it? No, it all goes on in here." Jody tapped her temple just as Claire had done minutes before. "What you see, how you perceive, what drives you. Perhaps you could illuminate the process for us."

"Stop." Claire looked at her as if to say, How can you be so mean. Jody met her glance, evenly and head-on.

"Me? Why? You just said you wanted to make movies—well, this is how it's done. Come on, loosen up. So, what'd you do today?"

Claire jumped up and ran for the bathroom.

Jody sat alone at the table. Perhaps she'd been wrong. It was possible that what she'd witnessed—Claire descending the steps at 63 Perry—wasn't the clear and heartbreaking twist of betrayal she'd first thought it was. She was distorting Claire's interest, turning it into something darker and more dangerous than it really was. Claire had probably left a package outside her door, a little present, or a sweet note on beautiful paper. Jody would find it there and, humiliated, would have to call Claire immediately to beg her forgiveness. Time and time again, Claire would say, I've asked you to trust me, but you won't. And Jody would end up apologizing not only for the afternoon's awkwardness but for a lifetime of doubt.

Claire's purse was on the table, begging the question. Jody scanned the room. All the people who'd just been looking at her had gone back to their cappuccinos, their éclairs, their own pathetic conversations. She reached for Claire's purse and pulled the zipper back, expecting to find the photos tucked neatly between her wallet and cosmetic case. There was nothing except mail—so much, in fact, that various envelopes stuck out, and Jody had trouble closing the purse. Worried that Claire would come out of the bathroom and catch her rummaging, she was trying to push them back in when on the left corner of one she noticed, familiar handwriting—the return address of someone she knew in L.A. She pulled the envelope all the way out of the purse and checked; it was addressed to Jody Goodman, 63 Perry Street 4-B, NY NY 10014. She pulled out another—her phone bill. A bank statement . . . a postcard from Carol Heberton . . . a schedule of screenings at the Museum of Modern Art. Claire had stolen her mail. She had reached into the mailbox and walked off with everything. A federal crime. In all the months that the lock had been broken, none of the multitude of strangers that came in and out of the building had ever taken anything. Then Jody heard the click of the bathroom door unlocking and jammed everything except the postcard back into the purse and zipped it closed. The purse was back in position on the table before the bathroom door opened. Jody tucked Heberton's card into her back pocket, picked up her video camera, and looked out the window, pretending to be shooting something in the distance.

"I didn't realize what time it was," Claire said, standing over the table. "I've got to go. I'll call you later." She squeezed Jody's arm. Jody glanced up. Her eyes were red. "It's all right," Claire added. "Everything will be all right. Don't worry." Then she took some money from her purse, put it on the table, and went out the door. Jody ordered a second espresso, poured in the sugar, and spooned the thick brown syrup into her mouth as though it were a prescription product. Trying to figure, trying to figure. She was trapped. Whatever it was that existed between her and Claire, she couldn't stand it; all the same, she'd been living on it and couldn't go without. Even now she didn't hate Claire—she hated herself for buying in, craving it, getting hooked. She finished the espresso and paid the bill, thinking that crawling out of a well was harder than falling in.

A losing streak. Coked up on espresso, paranoia, and guilt, she raced home and found Peter Sears waiting in the vestibule. "Hi," he said. "I thought I'd stop by and see how you're doing."

Jody's mailbox was empty, and the metal door was hanging open. Three other boxes also had broken locks, but the mail was there, waiting.

"How long have you been here?" Jody asked.

"Only a minute," Peter said. "But I was about to give up."

"My lucky day."

"How're you feeling—better?"

Jody shrugged. According to Esterhaus's estimate, she would get better eventually, though maybe not for two years. According to what Jody's mother read, it was a systemic yeast infection from eating too much sugar, and according to her father it was environmental poisoning. Jody herself had read reports calling it a B-cell virus, chronic immune dysfunction syndrome, a new herpes—a rare combination, a grenade-type virus with an unidentified trigger pin. If it didn't kill you, it could last forever, waxing and waning.

"Frankly," she said, "I feel like shit."

"Can I come in?" he asked.

"Sure, why not." Jody figured she had nothing to lose.

"I've really missed you," Peter said in the elevator on the way up.

Jody looked at her apartment door before unlocking it. There were no signs of tampering. On the floor, just inside, was a delivery menu from a Mexican restaurant. No note on pretty stationery, no magical explanation.

"Do you want to get naked now," she said to Peter, "or can I listen to my messages first?"

"It's not like that," he said.

Jody rewound her machine, thinking she'd find a clue. There was only one message—from Ilene, the East Villager from UCLA. "I wanted you to be the first to know—well, almost the first to know. Remember that idea we worked up for story class? I went ahead and wrote it. The script got sold for a hundred and fifty thousand dollars. Can you believe it? God! Well, I hope you're feeling better. Sorry, I—"

Jody turned off the machine. She didn't need to hear it.

"Sounds great," Peter said.

"Shut up," Jody said, disappearing into the bathroom. She came back seconds later with her hands full of small packages. "Look," she said, spilling them onto the sofa. "I have condoms. All kinds."

"It's different," Peter said. "Or I'm different."

"Bummer," Jody said.

Peter shrugged. "I didn't say I'd sworn off, just that things were different. You seem tense, upset. I took a course in massage. Would you like me to give you one?"

In what was left of the late afternoon light, with all the shades up, Jody stripped naked. She was so thin now that she didn't care who saw her. There was nothing to hide. Her bad thighs and big butt had vanished. She lay on the bed and let Peter work his hands over her, applying pressure to spots where knots had formed.

"Tell me where you feel it and we can work it out," he said. He found places left over from the skating expedition, knots that suddenly felt like scars. He pressed his fingers into places so sore that Jody had to bite the insides of her cheeks to keep from screaming. He was good, his hands strong and smooth. He dug deep into her, drawing the tension out, as if it were possible to pick up the muscles one by one and wring them like wet washcloths. She rolled onto her back, and when his palms traveled up the insides of her thighs, she met them and guided them further. She unbuttoned his shirt and slid her tongue over his chest. He sighed. He worked the muscles in her neck and shoulders, going all the way down her arms. She bit his nipples. In his chinos he rubbed against her, teasing. No hurry, no rush. She unzipped his pants and pressed her face to the front of his underwear, licking him through the heavy cotton. She pulled him on top of her. He reached for a condom. Three times her phone rang; each time the machine picked up and the caller—Claire—hung up. Peter and Jody spent the rest of the evening and most of the night sexing and resting, sexing and resting.

"So what happened?" Jody finally asked, after the delivery boy from the Chinese restaurant had come and gone, after they'd showered and feasted and fucked again.

Peter shrugged. He pulled on his underwear, fished his chinos out of the tangle of sheets, and buttoned his shirt.

"Come on," Jody said. "People don't just change."

"I've been seeing someone who's helped me a lot," he said, sliding his foot into a loafer.

"A therapist?"

"No, a woman. She's out of town this week on location. She's a TV producer."

Jody pushed him out the door. She practically picked him up and carried him. She stood there for a moment, watched him flounder, then slammed and locked the door.

"My shoe," he called. "My other loafer." He banged on the door. "Hey, come on! That's a Banfi. They cost four hundred and fifty dollars."

34

Claire couldn't sleep. Listening to Sam's even breathing, she lay awake and worried about losing everything. Ever since the afternoon at the cafe Jody had been acting withdrawn, paranoid—though at least she hadn't brought the video camera with her. And then, a few days before, they'd fought over a shirt in Bloomingdale's.

"Look at this," Claire had said, holding it up on its hanger. The shirt was softer, more fitted than what Jody usually wore; she would have looked beautiful in it.

Jody wrinkled her nose. "Not for me."

"Go ahead, try it on."

"No," Jody said.

Claire still held the shirt out, swinging it back and forth to entice her; annoyed, Jody had grabbed it and stuffed it back onto the rack. A woman passing by smiled, put her hands on Claire's shoulder, and said, "My daughter and I argue like this all the time."

"She's not my mother," Jody announced. "She's my *shrink.*"

The woman averted her eyes and quickly slipped away.

And that afternoon, Claire had come in late and Sam was standing in the front hall, furious.

"Why are you home?" she asked.

"Your son had a doctor's appointment!" he bellowed.

Claire didn't know what he was talking about.

"Jake was supposed to go to the pediatrician at three-thirty. They called me at the office. *You* forgot. Don't even try and tell me where you were. You were with her. I know, Claire. I'm not an idiot. This has gone too far. It's out of control. Why are you letting her—"

"She's not doing it, Sam—I am." Claire paused. "I must have forgotten about Jake's appointment. It was probably just for shots. I'll take him tomorrow, I'll call over there right now and make a time."

When she reached for the phone, Sam blocked her. "It was for shots," he said, pressing his face close into hers. "I took him. They said he might have a reaction, run a fever, to give him Tylenol. I looked and there's none in the house. There's not even any fucking Tylenol in this house, Claire! We're falling apart. You're ignoring us. I won't let you do it to this family. I won't let you."

Adam, Jake, and Frecia stood there gaping. Jake's sleeve was rolled up, and Claire watched him run his fingers back and forth unconsciously over the injection spot.

The phone rang, and both Sam and Claire grabbed for the receiver.

"Hello," Sam said, snatching it away from Claire.

Claire pushed the speakerphone button.

"Hi, this is Tom Miller, the architect. I came to look at your apartment several weeks ago."

"Yes," Sam said.

"It turns out that my sister is moving to New York, and I'd like to have her see the place, if you're still interested in selling."

"We're considering the possibility," Sam said.

"She'll be in from Boston first thing in the morning, so could I bring her by at eight? I realize it's early, but she's only in for the day and has meetings straight through."

"Eight's fine. See you then," Sam said, hanging up.

"This is ridiculous," Claire said.

"No it's not," Sam said, "but these are. They came today, for you." He picked two boxes—one big, one small—up off the living room table and hurled them toward her. Mugs flew out of each; SAM, JAKE, ADAM, and JODY, all printed in bold red letters on white ceramic. Lillian Vernon had screwed up and sent everything directly to Claire. Sam's broke in half, Adam's lost the handle, Jody's split into three, and only Jake's was intact. "What the hell are you buying her a monogrammed mug for?"

"Belated Christmas," Claire said.

Frecia pushed the children out of the room and then moved in to clean up the mess.

"We're going to the beach this weekend," Sam said. "You, me, and the boys. No girls. No one else. Us, that's it. We rented the fucking house and we'll fucking use it. It's been almost a month since we were there."

"Fine," Claire said.

"Tomorrow morning I'll meet that guy at eight," Sam said, picking up his briefcase. "I'll sell this place so fucking fast you won't know what hit you." Then he turned and stormed out of the apartment.

A few minutes later Gloria Owens called. "Sorry to bother you at home," she said, "but I didn't think you'd mind. Jim and I are in trouble. We're fighting constantly. I was hoping we could come in for an extra session this week."

"Hold on," Claire said. "Let me check my book." She put the receiver on the table, rustled the newspaper around, and picked up the phone again. "I'm looking," she said, flipping through the Home section of the *Times*. "But I'm booked up until Wednesday, which is your regular time anyway."

"Oh, well, I thought it wouldn't hurt to ask."

"I'm glad you called," Claire said. "If something opens up, I'll let you know. Or if it's an emergency you can always leave a message on the machine and I'll get back to you as soon as I can."

"Thanks," Gloria said.

"Anytime," Claire said, hanging up and dialing Bea's number.

Claire hadn't told anyone, but last week—after having told Claire how happy she was—Bea swallowed all of Herbert's sleeping pills, then took a cab over to St. Luke's and confessed. They'd pumped out her stomach, kept her for a couple of days, and, in conjunction with Claire, arranged for a psychiatrist to prescribe antidepressants. Claire felt guilty as hell.

"Bea?" she said when Bea's answering machine picked up. "It's Claire Roth, just calling to see how you're doing. I'll be home all evening if you want to call, otherwise I'll see you first thing in the morning."

"You're in trouble," Sam had said later that night when he slipped into the bed. "Big trouble."

As if she didn't already know. Once Sam had said he liked the house, the second he'd rolled off of her after making love in their would-be bedroom and said: "I want it," Claire had started hoping it wouldn't work out. She couldn't move, not now. Too much was happening. Everything she'd worked so hard for seemed on the verge of being destroyed. She'd made a mess of her career, her marriage, her life. She couldn't be a shrink anymore, she knew that. Look at Bea. Thanks to Claire she'd ended up in the emergency room. Claire should have known better than to believe her when she said she was happy. How could anyone be happy?

A few fitful hours later, Sam was shaking her awake. "The architect and his sister," he said. "They'll be here before you know it."

"What time is it?" Claire asked.

"Six-forty-five. If we want to sell, we have to clean up. You can start by making the bed."

Claire rolled over and pulled the blanket over her head.

Sam went out of the bedroom and came back with the vacuum cleaner. "Get up," he said, plugging it in. "And pull the sheets up with you."

"I can't be late," Claire said, crawling out of bed. "I have a patient at eight-fifteen."

"Cancel it," he snapped.

Claire stood groggy and confused in the center of the room and watched him use a white crew sock to dust the top of the dresser. "Cancel the fucking appointment," he said again.

"I can't," she said.

"You're not seeing that Jody girl anymore. It has to stop."

"Sam," Claire said.

"I know exactly what you're thinking, Claire, and it's wrong. You're wrong. Give it up. She's not yours. You can't be doing her any good by acting like she is. Think about somebody else for a minute."

"You mean, think about you."

"Cancel the appointment."

"No," Claire paused. "She's special. You don't know what you're talking about."

"I don't care. I'm talking about you, Claire, about *us*. I don't even know her."

"Well, you certainly acted like you did at the skating rink."

Sam shook his head in disgust. "We're leaving, Claire. We're getting out of here."

"I don't want to have this conversation," Claire said.

"We're having it. This has been going on far too long."

"You're not my boss. I'm the therapist. I should know what I'm doing without your help."

"Do you, Claire? Do you even have a clue?"

She went into the bathroom, slamming the door. She brushed her teeth, flossed, then opened the door and shook her finger at Sam. "I'm seeing her, and will continue to see her until either she or I decide that it's no longer necessary. You," she said, pointing, "are fucking jealous." She slammed the bathroom door again and got into the shower. "P.S.," she said when she was out, sitting on the edge of the bed pulling on her pantyhose. "My eight-fifteen is a fifty-five-year-old woman who tried to kill herself last week."

In the lobby, at ten after eight, Claire ran into the architect and his sister. "My sister, Joan," he said, introducing them. "She's a social worker, so she has no sense of geometry, of how things should be. I thought she might like your place." Claire nodded. Joan laughed.

"My husband's upstairs, he'll show you around. I have a patient."

"You're a doctor?"

"Therapist," Claire said, pushing herself against the front door.

"How interesting," Joan said.

Claire waved goodbye and stepped out. Bea was always early and would be waiting for her in the hallway outside the office. On a corner, at a red light, Claire tried to put up her hair; it was still damp, hanging in wet noodles, tickling her neck. Without a mirror, she had no idea of how she looked. It made her more nervous.

"Good morning, Bea," Claire said as she stepped off the elevator. She slipped her key into the lock and opened the office door. "How are you feeling?"

"I'm all right," Bea said, closing the door behind her.

"Are there any side effects from the antidepressants?" Claire asked, glancing at her answering machine. The counter flashed two messages; she was curious to know who they were from.

"My mouth is dry," Bea said, her lips smacking together with the soft clicking sound one attributes to the heavily medicated. "But the doctor told me it's normal. The body adjusts. Herbert called last night. He wants to take me out on a date. I do something stupid and all of a sudden he's sorry."

"Will you go?"

"Don't know. I spent time in a mental ward because of him. A nice dinner out won't fix that."

She seemed less sure of herself than before. As she talked about Herbert, Claire considered whether it was a loss of confidence that made her seem emotionally absent or if it was the medication. That sometimes happened with psychotropics—people just disappeared. She wondered if she should be taking some herself.

When the session was nearly over, Claire asked, "How would you feel about you and Herbert coming to see me together in addition to our regular meetings?"

"You'd do that?"

Claire nodded.

"Oh, thank you," Bea said. "I know I'm not supposed to say anything personal, but I bet your family is so proud of you. What I'd give to have such a smart, talented daughter."

A fucking idiot, Claire thought. If Bea had any sense, she'd be angry with Claire; she'd blame Claire for the suicide attempt and get a new shrink. Instead she was taking the passive route, praising the devil.

"Tuesday evening at six," Claire said, ignoring Bea's compliments. The buzzer went off and Claire pushed the button to let Jody into the waiting room.

"I'll have him here." Standing up, Bea swayed a little on her feet. "A little dizzy," she said. "The drugs."

"See you Tuesday," Claire said, walking her to the door.

"I didn't know you did geriatric work," Jody said after Bea was gone. "What happened to your hair—you start radiation or something?"

Claire raised her hand to the falling bun. "Not funny," she said, trying to push things back in place. She closed the office door and took her usual seat. Jody looked sicker and thinner; her jeans puckered at the waist, gathered tightly by a thick brown belt. On her forearms was something that looked like a thick, raw rash.

"We have to have a serious talk," Claire said. "I've been thinking that it might be best if you saw someone else. I don't seem to be helping you anymore." By now Claire was looking at the carpet. "Things have gotten beyond the point where I'm being useful."

When Claire looked up, Jody was white, wordless, grinding her teeth against the inside of her cheek.

"We could still be involved in some way. We'd have to work it out. But I won't abandon you."

Claire fought the urge to confess that it was all her fault, that she'd done a terrible, crazy thing.

"I do think it might be useful for you to discuss the situation with someone else. I've made some calls," Claire added, lying.

"How dare you," Jody said.

"I'm trying to help. You need help."

"You need help," Jody said.

Claire didn't answer. She was trying to pull back, to maintain some composure.

Jody pulled her video camera out of a bag, trained it on Claire, and started taping.

"Put the camera down," Claire said.

Jody kept filming.

"Please put the camera down. It's an intrusion. I don't know why you're doing this. Why are you doing this?" Claire waved her hand in front of the camera. "Is this an attempt to gain control?"

Jody still didn't respond. Claire sat back in her chair, her left knee over her right and her arms in front of her chest.

"We're not going to be able to continue until you put the camera away," Claire said and then was silent, staring into the lens.

Jody continued to film her for a few minutes. Though acutely uncomfortable, Claire tried not to move or give any indication of her misery.

Finally, Jody lowered the camera. "I can't believe you're doing this," she said.

"I want to do what's best for you, Jody. I'm not helping you. Another therapist might be better equipped."

"Something's wrong," Jody said, shaking her head. "Something's very wrong. I don't know how, I don't know why, but you're driving me crazy. You're killing me. Why don't you just take a fucking gun, shoot me, and get it over with?"

In all her thoughts, in all her fantasies, it had never occurred to Claire that a daughter could turn on a mother, that a daughter could become a woman's worst enemy.

The phone rang and Claire grabbed it. "Hello," she said. "Hello."

"It's me," Sam said excitedly. "We're selling the apartment. They offered two-ninety-five, and I said yes. The realtor's not in on the deal, so it's all ours. You call the agent in Connecticut and offer two-eighty-five and call me back."

"I'm with a patient," Claire said flatly, trying not to give anything away, not to Sam, not to Jody.

"I'm here," Sam said. "Call me when it's over."

"I will," Claire said, hanging up.

Jody was standing.

"We're not out of time," Claire said. "The session isn't over."

"I'm done," Jody said.

"Please sit down. Let's make a time for tomorrow."

Jody didn't respond.

"Twelve o'clock. I have a break afterwards, so we can go out for lunch."

"Bye," Jody said, opening the door.

"See you tomorrow, then," Claire said. Waiting until Jody was gone, she frantically flipped through her address book for the real estate agent's number.

35

*P*ots and pans. In January Jody had made a trip to Macy's, a rare outing. She'd bought pots and pans, thinking that eating properly was part of getting well. For months they sat shiny and unused on top of the stove. Now Jody stood in the center of her apartment and banged the eight-inch frying pan against her body with all the vim and vigor of a bell ringer. *Slam* for wanting, and *slam* for now expecting, *slam*, Claire to help her; for being stupid enough to let down her defenses, the punishment would be severe; she'd have to suffer. She smashed the pan into her ribs, testing the depth of her anger. She fixed the video camera to a tripod, turned the camera on herself, and recorded the howling and wailing, the clash of aluminum and copper against skin and bone. Only when her chest made a strange thin whistle as she breathed and her skin was too tender to touch, only when she was stupid with pain, did she quit. She played the tape back; it came off like a PBS documentary on upper-middle-class white women's tribal dancing. She watched herself beating herself and was sick. The pots and pans left deep bruises, injury, but no marks of their own. Jody liked that. No one could argue that she was doing it to be noticed.

"She's taking over my life," Jody told her mother. "Invading my privacy, driving me over the edge."

"You're afraid to let her really know you," her mother said. "You don't like anyone to know anything about you. Your father and I always used to wonder what in the world you were thinking."

"Mom!" Jody bellowed.

"You always were *very* private. Remember how nervous you used to get before I'd go in for those parent/teacher conferences? You hated anyone talking about you."

"I caught her coming out of my building," Jody said. "I have it on tape."

"It was probably someone who looks like her. You always think you're seeing people. In the hospital you kept saying Aunt Sally was in the room next door—and she'd been dead for seven years."

"I had a fever of one hundred and four, Mom. I'm here now, feverless, in New York, and I'm telling you Claire Roth was in my building doing strange things. I told you—I have it on tape!"

Jody started crying. She didn't mean to, it just happened.

"You know," her mother said, "sometimes when people don't feel well, it makes them a little crabby, a little suspicious."

"I'm not paranoid. This is real!" Jody howled, sure the neighbors could hear her.

"Well, no one ever said you had to see her. It was your choice, Jody."

"You're not hearing me. She's going to *kill* me. One way or another I'm going to end up dead."

"Come on, honey, I really don't—"

Jody slammed the phone down and tried to remember Harry Birenbaum's number. Harry would understand. She dialed his number and got his machine. "It's Jody. Jody Goodman." She stopped. "Are you there?" She paused again. "There's something I need to talk to you about. Call me."

At the newsstand on the corner a headline announced an article called "Firing Your Shrink: Sixteen Steps to Getting Out Alive." She bought the magazine, ran home to read the piece, then noticed that according to the bio it had been written by a "prominent psychotherapist and NYU professor."

Going to a therapist to talk about therapy. No one would believe.

"Come in, come in," the shrink said the next afternoon as Jody stepped into his office.

He had a beard, wire-rimmed glasses, and a hooked nose. His office was cold, dark, and small, with one chair—the doctor's—and a sofa that smelled moist. Jody perched uneasily on the edge.

"On the telephone," he said, "you mentioned having some questions about therapy."

"I've been seeing this woman. She used to be amazing, but now she's driving me crazy. She's making me want to kill myself."

"Ah, you're a lesbian."

"No. My *shrink*. I'm talking about my shrink."

"So you're seeing another therapist," he said. "Does he know you're here?"

"It's a she, and no—she doesn't." Jody thought maybe he needed a hearing aid.

"Well, you'll have to tell him."

"The reason I came to see you is that I need to get some distance, perspective. As I mentioned on the phone, I read your article and thought maybe you could help. The woman I'm seeing—my shrink—she calls me all the time, invites me to dinner, makes me go ice skating with her family." Jody took a breath. "She came into into my building and stole my mail."

"So, your fantasy is that she invites you . . . and then what happens?"

"It's not my fantasy. It's real."

"I can assure you that I would never invite you anywhere or call you at home except to change an appointment."

The session had hardly begun and already Jody wanted out. Claire was a genius compared to this guy, so what if she was torturing Jody? At least it wasn't like being in a Three Stooges movie.

"It's becoming very destructive. I feel like I'm being forced to do something drastic."

"Do you dream about her?"

When Jody didn't answer, he started in on a long discussion, more like a presentation, on the peculiar and sometimes perverse ways in which women relate. It was all too interesting to him—something that would make a great paper, another article for the magazine, or maybe even a book. As the clock ticked, Jody became more and more alarmed, convinced that she was sinking into something that she'd never be able to escape. She felt as though she were in a room where insanity divided exponentially and suddenly there was nothing left.

A bell went off, startling her. The shrink pointed to an egg timer on his desk and Jody realized that for the past twenty-five minutes she'd just been sitting there, daydreaming. "We're out of time," the shrink said. "I suggest you come back on Thursday."

"I'll check my schedule," Jody said, going for the door. "I'll call you."

● ● ●

"Okay, you really want to know why you won't help yourself?" Ellen asked. "It's because you don't think you're worth it. You think you're shit because some people have failed you. You're looking for the perfect this, the perfect that—family, mother, whatever. The thing is, you're never going to find it. It doesn't exist."

Jody didn't respond. She gazed out the window and thought about hanging up the phone.

"You're *unrealistic*. Instead of being happy with what you've got, you go to someone else, a substitute, a shrink. Fine, except your shrink's crazy." Ellen paused. "You have to learn to be what you need; to love yourself more than anyone else would ever love you. You're the only one who really knows what you want."

"And you've been reading too many new-age books. Discover your inner self and blah, blah, blah."

"I'm telling you the truth and you don't like it."

"So, what if you're right?"

"I have to put you on hold," Ellen said.

Jody heard the week in weather, the forecast for Dallas–Fort Worth, and the Eagles song "Hotel California." She fingered the pack of matches on her desk. Self-punishment. As if the whole thing were her fault from beginning to end. Every time Jody went to Claire's office, she wore the marks of a new self-inflicted injury. It had taken Claire an unbelievably long time to catch on. The other day, when Jody went in with her face, arms, and neck covered with thin, bloody razor lines, Claire innocently asked what had happened.

"Nothing happened," Jody said flatly. She knew it was crazy. It made no sense and still she did it. She did it again and again, as if externalizing her pain, literally painting it across her body, would either make it go away or get someone to notice.

"I don't get it," Claire said.

"Obviously."

There was no way she could demonstrate her need any louder without sawing herself in half.

"You're an idiot," she had told Claire near the end of the session. "A total fucking idiot." She rolled up her sleeves and flashed a thick, fleshy burn. "How do you think this happened? You did it. You did it to me and I did it to myself. I wish I'd never met you."

Then she had pulled a pack of matches out of her pocket, lit one, and pressed it into her arm, extinguishing the flame on her flesh. She felt like a bad actress in a bad movie.

"Stop it," Claire had said, slapping at the matches. "Stop it!"

There's millions of matches in this world, millions of fires to set, Jody had thought as she slipped the matches back into her pocket.

"What you need," Ellen said, coming back on the line, "is to get away from her, extricate. You didn't come all this way to kill yourself, that's for sure. Gotta go, I'll talk to you later."

The war escalated—over the phone, in Claire's office, on the streets of New York. "How could you act like this after all I've done?" Claire screamed at Jody. "How could you even think of hurting yourself when someone cares about you as much as I do?" She threw her hands up in the air as if raising the question to the gods.

It was as simple and complicated as falling in and out of love. It was like the moment ten years into a marriage when you realize it's over—but in a marriage you might stay, you might develop outside interests, build an addition to the house, take a leisurely trip around the world, have an affair. In therapy there was nothing except fifty minutes in that room.

"What do you want from me? Tell me," Jody said when Claire called her for the third time in a single morning. "What do you want, blood?" Before Claire could answer, Jody hurled a glass against the wall and watched it splinter across the room. She had the urge to dance on the fragments, to roll in the shards.

"You need something I can't give you," Claire said.

"You made me need it—I gave myself to you."

"And I to you," Claire said.

"But I'm paying for this," Jody said. "It's costing me."

"My twelve o'clock's here," Claire said. "I'll speak to you later."

"Yeah," Jody said. "The highlight of my fucking day."

Jody took the bus across town to Radio Shack. She bought a tape recorder, a dozen cassettes, and a little device that hooked up to the phone and recorded conversations. Video wasn't enough. She had to start documenting everything Claire was saying and doing to her. This way, if something horrible happened, there would be proof that she'd been herded to the edge.

"You say she follows you around, lures you out skating, telephones you incessantly, *and* makes you feel as though you're losing your mind?" Harry asked when the round of phone tag was finally over. In the background she could hear a zydeco band playing and, again and again, the clink of ice cubes against glass.

"Yes," Jody said, excited that for once someone was going to understand. Though drunk, Harry listened patiently while she spilled the whole story.

"Has she got you good and gaslighted?" Harry asked when she finished. "Has she twisted you round and round like limp cherry licorice?"

"You could say that."

"Have some sympathy, darling. Don't be so critical of your elders. All she wants is what everybody wants—to get between some lovely young thighs." Harry sighed, then belched.

If Jody had more energy, or if it had come from anyone but Harry himself, she would have hung up.

Harry wheezed a thick wheeze. "I'm too old to be so drunk. Forgive me, young one, forgive me. You said you had a story to tell. I am in a frame of mind to hear a story."

"I just told it to you," Jody said, depressed. "The shrink, the girl, my life."

"Have you got another one?"

"No," Jody said. "You're plastered, Harry. It's not like you to be completely incoherent."

"It's the gin. Bombay. And the heat. I've died and gone to hell."

"Call me if you get to New York," Jody said, and hung up.

Late that night, while she was sleeping, the phone rang. Jody heard it through her dream, as a bell or a buzzer. It continued to ring and finally Jody woke up, heart racing. As soon as she picked up, the new recording equipment clicked on, and somehow the even hum of the spinning tape cleared her mind instantly. "Hello," she said.

"I was thinking about you," Claire said.

"It's one-thirty in the morning," Jody said, looking at the glow-in-the-dark numbers on her travel clock.

"I feel very badly about what's happening."

"You're driving me crazy."

"I'm trying to help you. Can you come in tomorrow morning? There's something I want to talk to you about, something I have to tell you."

"What?"

"I'll tell you in the morning. Nine-thirty. See you then."

Jody fell back asleep and dreamt that Claire kidnapped her and took her to a high-class nuthouse somewhere in the Berkshires. At the last minute, at the entrance gates, everything turned around, and in the end it was Claire who they locked up and Jody who drove the car back to New York, exhilarated.

At nine-twenty-five she was in Claire's office.

"I'm moving," Claire said as soon as Jody sat down. "I thought you should know. I'm buying a house in Connecticut. I'll keep the office here, but I'll be less available. I'm not leaving you, just the city. I should've said something sooner, but it all happened very fast. I'm sorry." She drew a breath. "I hope you won't make this difficult."

In her darkest, wildest, most depressing dreams, this was something Jody had never imagined. She felt her face change. She didn't know if it turned red, white, or blue, there was no way of knowing. She just felt it change; the features caved in on themselves, mouth pulled tight, eyes narrowed.

"I hope you won't make this difficult," Claire had said. What did she think Jody would do—block the exits from Claire's building, stop the movers from loading their trucks, hold the family hostage until Claire agreed not to go?

"It'll be okay. I'll be in the office three days a week. We'll talk over the phone. It'll be better, in fact. I'll be more relaxed, more able to help."

Jody continued to implode, her whole body drawing in on itself.

"Are you all right?" Claire asked. "Talk to me. I want you to say something."

Jody lifted her shriveled face, her lips feeling as if they were glued together by thoughts unspoken, and stared at Claire. There was nothing to say.

"Now," Claire said, "unfortunately, I have to see someone else, but I hope we can get together tomorrow. By then maybe you'll be a bit more communicative."

In a trance, Jody lifted herself from the chair and went home. She envisioned going into the drugstore and asking where to find the razor blades as innocently as she'd ask about toothpaste. She saw herself examining the razor blades, picking up a package of every kind to see where they were made, what the special features were, and how much they cost. What did it mean, what was the difference if you killed yourself with cheap ones instead of the fancy brands? Either way it would be over.

I'm going to kill myself, going to kill . . . It was like having people over for dinner—you had to shop for it. Jody went into a hardware store. "Can I get some help here?" she asked the pack of salesmen picking their teeth at the back of the store. "I want a rope." One of them stepped forward, led her down an aisle, and handed her a small coil.

"What can you tell me about this rope?" she asked.

The man didn't answer; he must have been working for the other side.

"How strong is it?"

"What do you need it to hold?"

A body, she thought. "A hundred and thirty pounds," she said, but didn't tell him that she hadn't eaten a real meal in months, and didn't weigh even a hundred and eighteen anymore, that it was probably closer to a hundred and five.

"This'll do you," he said, holding up a package that looked like twine.

"I'll take nine feet of that one," she said, pointing to a rope thick enough to hoist a piano. "Better safe than sorry."

At the register, she waited for the guy to flip through a mystery list of people who weren't allowed to buy rope. She expected him to ask for a permission slip.

"Four-fifty," he said, putting the rope into a bag.

On the way home, she stopped in the local erotic emporium and bought handcuffs. She could pick up a clear plastic bag from the supermarket produce department, slide it over her head, and tape it around her neck with thick layers of duct tape. She could pour a gallon of gasoline into the tub, wrap the rope around the shower nozzle and her neck, slip the plastic bag over her head, and light a match. She imagined a loud whoosh, a hot flash, a kind of choking, and then nothing.

Why? Everyone would ask. There had to be a beginning to this end. Los Angeles, when Claire had called for no good reason. That was the marker, the sign of crossing over. But now, it was like being woken up to see yourself spread out on an operating table, your guts warming the surgeon's hands. "By the way," he'd whisper as he fingered your liver, your kidneys, "you know, I'm not really a doctor."

"Do you want us to come up there?" her mother asked. "I could take a day off work. Your father and I would be happy to bring you back. You could live here. We'll fix up your old room. You seem so unhappy up there anyway. Why don't you come home?"

"No thanks," Jody said.

"We love you very much. Why isn't that enough?"

She didn't answer.

"Claire Roth called. She's worried about you hurting yourself. Is that something we have to think about?"

"You shouldn't even be talking to her. You should be protecting me from her, not acting like you're on her side."

"There are no sides."

"There are now."

"We want to help you. You're not acting like yourself." Her mother stopped for a minute. "I think you're still angry with me for not racing out to California the second you said you didn't feel well. You have to realize that I've done the best I could, the very best I know how."

"I can't talk to you," Jody said.

"All right then, call me when you're feeling better."

"Mother." What a word, what a concept. There were secretaries, doctors, nurses, and housekeepers, but Jody wasn't really sure there was any such thing as a mother. She slipped the tape of Claire at Patisserie Lanciani into the VCR, hoping to figure out exactly what had happened that afternoon. A close-up of Claire's face filled the screen; you could see the pores, the features distorted by nearness. She watched Claire's eyes— dead-on, intent—the face that sometimes seemed more than familiar, as if it were her own.

Jody but not Jody. A stranger yet as familiar as anyone had ever been. Ellen was right: it was up to Jody; her life was her responsibility, no one else's. She fast-forwarded. Claire went by, streaking blue lines across the TV screen.

The telephone rang again and the machine clicked on.

"Jody?" her mother's voice said softly. "Are you there? It's Mom, can you pick up? . . . Jody." The voice that had taught her the sound of her own name, that had called her every night of her life. "I've been thinking. If you don't want to come home, maybe you'd like me to come there for a few days. We could do some things—buy you a few new clothes. You've lost so much weight I'm sure nothing fits. Would you like that? I'm here. I'm home. Daddy and I only want what you want."

This was the woman who had loved her to the best of her abilities, however limited they might have been. She'd loved Jody to the limits of her fear. She'd taken a stranger's child and claimed it as her own. How could Jody hope that her mother would magically become someone else? If Jody wanted someone else, she'd have to become that person herself. She thought of what the doctor had said when she was sick—that she wouldn't be able to carry a child to term. She was at term now. She was her own.

She picked up the phone. "Hi, Mom, it's me. I'm here."

"Sweetie, I'm climbing the walls. You know how much you mean to us, how important you are. We're beside ourselves. Have you had dinner? Is there any food in your house?"

"Chinese," Jody said, lying. "Chicken with broccoli and brown rice. Very healthy. Sauce on the side."

"What am I supposed to think? What about Claire?"

"She's overreacting," Jody said. "I just need some rest. I'm very tired. I'll call you tomorrow."

"Well, take two aspirin and crawl into bed."

"Why?"

"Because it's good for you."

"Mom, I'm fine. I don't need to take anything. Go watch TV. Isn't the ten o'clock news on?"

"If you need us, you'll call?"

"I'll talk to you tomorrow. Sleep well. Sweet dreams," Jody said, hanging up.

It was time to be reasonable. Forgive and forget. Jody did it in her head; she said thank you and goodbye. She had listened to her mother's voice, looked at Claire's image on the TV screen, and felt herself moving past them. Finished, Jody turned down the volume on the answering machine, aimed the remote at the television, and pressed the Off button. The room dropped into silent darkness.

36

*I*t began in Balducci's. Claire bought crackers and cheese, sliced meats, cold vegetable salads, miniature éclairs and raspberry tarts. She envisioned a picnic, romantic and grand. She saw herself spreading a checkered tablecloth across the floor of her new living room, unpacking the green-and-white shopping bags, handing Jody a bottle of good wine and an opener, then leaning back against the wall and letting whatever was going to happen, happen.

Things had been going all wrong. What she'd hoped would pull Jody closer had actually pushed her further away. She would fix that now, once and for all. She would make everything all right. It would be the most wonderful moment, the moment she'd been waiting for.

Claire would pick Jody up at her apartment and they'd drive to Connecticut in the last light of a spring afternoon. They wouldn't say much. The steadiness and calm of their silence would dissolve her own anxiety as well as Jody's anger. Once they arrived at the house, they would be comfortable, pleased with themselves. Jody would think the house was great. She would realize there was still a place for her and that for Claire, Sam, and the boys the move was necessary. Soon she would understand that it was necessary for her as well.

Claire would carry in the supplies just before dark. The electricity had been turned on, but there were very few bulbs, so Claire would show Jody the house by candlelight. Then she would spread out the picnic as they talked—a conversation that didn't lapse into accusations and failure. Night would come to Connecticut. They would be alone in the house. There would be no history outside the moment.

When Claire pulled up in front of 63 Perry Street, Jody was sitting on the front stoop, video camera in hand.

"Am I crazy to be getting in a car with you?" Jody asked as she pulled the door closed. "Why are you so dressed up?"

"Special occasion," Claire said. "I'm taking you to see the house."

"So, it's like an S and M thing."

In Claire's fantasy Jody was less resistant, more willing to go along with things. "I've brought a picnic," she said, looking at Jody. "Fasten your seat belt."

"I didn't know you had a car phone."

"It was Sam's idea. You know, guys and their gadgets."

A steady rain started to fall as they headed up the West Side Highway. The tape deck was playing and they were mostly silent. Along the parkway the trees were green, thick with new leaves. Claire, not yet familiar with the route, turned on the headlights and drove slowly, leaning slightly forward in the seat. "What was the name of the street we just passed?" she asked.

"Thorn something," Jody said. "You know, it'd be fine with me if we just went back now. This doesn't exactly thrill me."

"We're here," Claire said twenty minutes later, making one right turn and then another. She pulled close to the house and switched off the engine. "Can you get the bags out of the back?"

Claire fit her key into the lock. Besides the electricity, that was the one thing they'd done so far—changed the locks. The locksmith had insisted on dead bolts, a key on both sides. "Better with little kids," he said. "You can control the traffic."

Inside, Claire used her key again and locked the door behind them.

"Flashlight?" Jody asked.

"Candles," Claire said, going through the bags, pulling out candles and the silver candlesticks that had been a wedding gift from Sam's aunt.

Jody raised the video camera to her eye.

"You can't hide," Claire said. "I see you, I know you're there. Come out, come out, wherever you are."

"Not enough light," Jody said, putting the camera down.

Claire smiled. "Take a look around." She handed Jody a lit candle. "Four bedrooms, two and a half baths, and a lot of work to be done."

Jody wandered off through the house. "This is totally creepy," she called from upstairs. "Don't you believe in light bulbs?"

"It's an adventure," Claire said. "Besides, we obviously haven't moved in yet. It'll be really great once we're all together."

Jody came back into the living room, where Claire was unpacking things. "I hope you're hungry," Claire said, handing Jody the bottle of wine and the corkscrew.

"What are we supposed to be celebrating?" Jody asked.

Claire didn't answer. She watched the candlelight play on Jody's face, strange shadows dancing, and finished laying out the meal. Her throat was filled with a ball of words wanting to come out all at once. Claire swallowed, then handed Jody two wineglasses. "Pour," she said.

They sat on opposite sides of the room, the picnic spread out on the floor between them. They ate in bits and pieces and spoke in fragments about the house, the city, anything but themselves.

The rain plunked against the windows.

"Jody," Claire said softly, about an hour later, when the first bottle of wine was nearly gone, when all that was simple and easy had already been said. "There's something we need to talk about."

Jody sat motionless on the other side of the room. "I'm tired of talking."

"Then just listen." Claire pushed the tablecloth away, slid closer to Jody, and put her hand on Jody's ankle. "In December 1966, in Washington, D.C., I gave birth to a baby girl. Three days later I handed that baby to a stranger and then went home. For nearly twenty-five years I've tried to go about my life, to forget that I'm the mother of that child. But I can't." Claire looked at Jody, checking for a reaction, but she was motionless. "Jody," Claire said, squeezing her ankle, *"you* are that child."

Jody pulled her leg away, drew her knees to her chest, and put her hand over her eyes.

"I am your mother," Claire said, wrapping her arms around Jody.

Jody raised up the wineglass in her hand and brought it down hard on the floor, smashing the bowl, then dug the broken stem into Claire's arm. "Don't touch me," she said, "or I'll kill you."

"I can understand that you might be angry," Claire said, wincing as she fingered the gash on her arm. "Your whole life you've been waiting, and now I'm here, just like that." Claire blotted the wound and again moved toward her.

"You're not my mother," Jody said. "You don't know what you're talking about."

"Sweetie," Claire said, kneeling in front of her, "it's true. You and I both know it. That's what these last few months have been about. I wouldn't be surprised if on some level you've known all along. Maybe you got sick so I'd come back to you. It explains so many things. That's why everything has been so confusing. But now the mystery's solved. We can go on." Claire paused and smiled. "I'm so glad it's you."

"You're crazy," Jody said, springing up, running to the door. "Why the fuck can't I open the door!" she screamed, pulling at it.

"I have the key," Claire said, coming up behind her.

"Let me out! Let me out of here!"

"Calm down. I want you to calm down. You can't go racing out like a maniac." Claire put her hand on Jody's shoulder. "Stop," she said. "Just stop."

Jody whirled around, waving the stem of the wineglass in Claire's face. "Leave me alone! This is your problem, not mine."

She ran up the stairs, Claire chasing after her, and ended up locked in the bathroom with the broken tub.

Claire banged on the door. "Don't do this. You don't have to do this. Come out, Jody. I'll give you the key. Here, I'll side it under." Claire took the house key off her ring and tried to fit it under the door. "It won't fit," Claire said. "But it's here, right outside the door." She paused. "You're free—you can go."

Jody didn't answer.

Claire rattled the knob. "I want you to open this door."

"Just go away."

"Sweetie, don't do this. We can be happy now." Claire sat down on the floor outside the bathroom door. The hall was narrow and dark. "When you were five," she said, "on your first day of school, when your mother put you in a Florence Eiseman dress and walked you to your classroom, do you know what I did?" Claire paused. "Well, I went out the night before and bought you a pencil box, crayons, paper, Elmer's glue, and a lunch box, all the things I thought you'd need. I stopped on my way home, bought a loaf of white bread, a jar of smooth peanut butter, grape jelly, strawberry jam, and then I made twelve peanut butter and jelly sandwiches, trying to get it right, to make the one you'd really want—crust, cut in half, no crust, cut in quarters. A whole loaf of sandwiches. I wrapped them in wax paper and put them into the fridge, and in the morning, when your mother was getting you ready for school, I didn't know what to do. So I ate them, all of them, one at a time."

"I hate peanut butter," Jody said.

"I've loved you so much for so long. Every year I'd buy you a present for your birthday; I'd wonder what you were doing and if you were happy. For twenty-five years I've thought about you and worried about you. How can you do this to me? Don't you realize nothing can keep me from you? Not your resistance, and certainly not this door."

Jody didn't answer.

"What are you doing in there? I want you to tell me what you're doing."

"Nothing. I'm not doing anything. Leave me alone. You have to go away and leave me alone."

"Come out and let's talk. Can we do that?"

"Shut up, Claire, just shut up."

Claire poked at her bloody arm, and thought about the broken glass in Jody's hand. "What are you doing in there?"

Jody didn't answer.

"Please, tell me what you're doing."

Claire imagined Jody working the stem back and forth against her wrists, her neck, sawing at her skin, splitting the veins. She imagined blood spilling onto the floor, traveling in thin rivers down the grouted paths between the tiles.

"Jody?"

There was no answer.

She pictured blood pooling in the sunken spots under the sink, in front of the toilet, and Jody slumped against the tub.

Claire stood up and threw herself against the door. "Say something!" she screamed. "If you don't open this door I'll have to call the police and they'll break it down." Claire waited for a response. "Jody, don't make me do it." She conjured the pulse slowing, the heart stopping.

She picked up her keys, ran down the steps, out the door, and to the car. Breathless, she picked up the car phone and dialed information. "Stamford," she said. "Greenspan, Bert." A classmate from Columbia, a guy she'd dated, head of a private hospital in the hills of Stamford.

"Hi, Bert, it's Claire Roth."

"Claire, hi. It's been a while. Where are you? The connection's terrible."

"It's my car phone. Listen, it's an emergency, I'm in Glenville. I bought this house. It's a long story, but a patient of mine is out here. She's locked herself in the bathroom and—" Claire paused—"she may be suicidal."

"You want to have her admitted to Seven Trees?"

"She's not crazy," Claire said. "But she's very upset."

"I'll call and arrange it. Do you know how to get to us?"

"I can't even get her to open the door."

"Well," Bert said, "we don't have a livery service."

They didn't speak for a minute.

"Call the cops," he said. "They'll take her to the local hospital and we'll get her transferred out in the morning."

Claire didn't respond.

"You're wasting time. If she does something, you'll be responsible. Call the police. It's not like in the city—they'll be there in a couple of minutes and they're very good about these things."

"You think?"

"I know," Bert said. "Call the cops. We'll talk later."

"Thanks," Claire said, hanging up and immediately dialing for help, knowing that if she stopped to think, she might not be able to do it.

"Police, fire, or rescue?"

"Police," Claire said, looking up at the house through the wet windshield. "I'm a therapist. I'm calling about a patient."

"An emotionally disturbed person?"

"Upset," Claire said.

"Is there a crime in progress?"

"No," Claire said, then gave the operator the address.

"Is it dangerous to enter the premises?"

"No."

"Is the person armed?"

"She's locked herself in the bathroom."

"A danger to herself?"

"Possibly," Claire said.

"Please identify yourself when the officers arrive."

"Of course," Claire said. "I'll wait in the house."

Claire ran back up the steps, ducking her head against the weather. The remains of the picnic were scattered all over the living room. Claire quickly packed up as much as possible. In the distance, she heard sirens. Soon lights were swabbing the front of the house through the low, uneven fog—red, white, blue. Claire hurried toward the door, thinking about the neighbors, embarrassed that she hadn't even moved in yet and already there was this display. Her foot accidentally kicked a piece of glass, hurling it like a hockey puck into the fireplace.

"I'm Claire Roth," she said, standing in the driveway, in front of the police cars. "I'm the woman who called." A cop sat in his car, radio in hand, talking. Claire came closer. "Hurry," she said. "Please hurry."

The police, four of them, in foul-weather gear, stomped into the house and up the stairs to the bathroom. One of the cops banged on the door. "Police," he said. "Open up."

No response.

"If you're able to open the door, I suggest you do it now. We'll give you to the count of ten."

"I think something's blocking the door," Claire said, wiping rainwater off her forehead, pulling her damp blouse away from her skin. "I tried to open it before and it felt like there was something there."

"One . . . two . . ." the cop began.

"They do that," one of the cops said. "They get this superhuman strength and they do things like rip the sink out and wedge it against the door."

". . . Eight . . . Nine . . ."

"There was one lady threw a refrigerator down the steps, aiming for her husband. Missed him, but got the poodle."

The cops gestured back and forth among themselves, deciding who would knock down the door. One cop pointed to his back, shaking his head, and another stepped forward.

"Stand back, please," he said, warning Claire out of the way. He handed his gun and his raincoat to the one with the bad back and then hurled himself against the door. He rammed it three times before the wood frame cracked and the door popped open.

Claire stood down the hall, her hand over her mouth.

Two cops charged into the bathroom and Claire rushed forward. She watched them tackle Jody, slamming her face into the floor. One cop sat on her legs, another on her back.

"Let me go, you're making a mistake!" Jody screamed, her voice muffled. They pulled her hands behind her back and snapped the cuffs on.

"Stop!" Claire said, held back by the two cops just outside the doorway. "You're hurting her."

They lifted Jody to standing. Her arms were intact; no slit wrists, no punctured jugular. But blood was streaming out of her nose, down her chin, dripping onto her shirt.

"Your nose," Claire said, "I think they've broken your nose."

"Are you happy now?" Jody screamed. "Look at me! Who am I,

Claire, who the fuck am I now? I don't believe you, Claire. I never will. I *have* a mother. I don't *want* you." Jody drew in a breath. "You went into my building. I saw you. I have it on tape. You stole my mail. That's a federal offense. And what did I do?" she asked, her voice escalating. "I locked myself in a fucking bathroom!"

Jody choked and blood splashed onto the floor.

"Why are you coughing up blood?" Claire asked, hysterical.

"Where *were* you? Did you miss something? They knocked the fucking door down. They smashed my fucking face into the floor."

"Get her out of here," one of the cops said. "There's no point."

"You should've opened the door," Claire said.

"Why? I was just sitting there minding my own fucking business. I didn't know it was against the law."

There was blood in her hair, mucus on her face. She looked wild, crazy. Claire went into the bathroom, got some toilet paper, and moved to wipe Jody's face. Jody turned her head away and the cops pulled her toward the steps. Going down, she tripped, and the cop behind her tugged on her arms. Jody howled. They led her out into the cold, wet night, shoved her into the back of a police car, and slammed the door. An officer started the engine as Claire stood watching. The lights went on, the car edged backwards.

Claire tapped on the glass. "Jody," she said. "Don't worry, sweetie. Everything will be all right."

37

*I*t was a warm Saturday in late May. Jody pulled a battered cardboard bankers box from under her bed and carefully unpacked the old reels of film and her father's Super Eight projector.

The windows were open; she could hear people talking as they strolled down Perry Street. "You forget how big a city is, how much variety. Anything goes."

The white space between posters from *The 400 Blows* and *Apocalypse Now* filled with images from Jody's childhood. Eighth Birthday Party—Congressional Roller Rink, Rockville, Maryland. First Slumber Party—the Goodmans' pine-paneled recreation room, bathed in the eerie, uneven glow of the Bell & Howell movie lamp, twelve little girls in sleeping bags arranged in a circle around the room. Ringling Brothers and Barnum & Bailey Circus—the Greatest Show on Earth, Jody chosen by the clown to ride in his wheelbarrow. A reaction shot of her mother laughing, hands over her mouth.

Jody flipped through the film reels, trying to read the dates, the titles. With everything there was a story, a memory, a moment, fluid like the stuff of lava lamps, stretching and pulling, constantly reconfiguring itself. She threaded the film through the projector; the sprockets grabbed the leader, drawing it in; the bulb flickered.

Family Vacation—Rehoboth Beach. An orange bathing suit, a yellow flower cut out around her belly button. Every day the sun would brown the stencil; every night she would see the darkening of the flower, coming up on her belly, like a photograph developing.

Jody riding the waves for hours and hours on end, waving at her father, standing at the water's edge, camera in hand. Jody coming up for air, her hair long, wet, and salty, calling, "Mom, Dad, watch me, watch me—I'm doing a somersault.'' The three of them a triangle, two in love with the third.

The telephone rang, and she let the machine answer it. "Hi, I can't come to the phone right now, but if you leave your name and number after the beep . . .'' Silence. Not a hang-up, but silence. The caller was there, waiting. After thirty seconds, the machine turned itself off. It happened again later, and then again, and again, and always there was someone there on the line, waiting.

38

*I*n the kitchen, taking down glasses, wrapping them one at a time in brown paper and fitting them into a box, Claire shook, not so much a tremor as a shiver.

"It's the house," Sam said. "You're nervous about moving."

It was the house. She never wanted to go there again. If Sam knew the extent of things, the extreme to which she'd gone, he might be forced to take some action.

Jody. She wanted to talk to Jody, but there was nothing casual, nothing easy in what she would say.

The movers came, wrapped the furniture in heavy blankets, and carried cardboard boxes marked FRAGILE/KITCHEN or JAKE/BEDROOM out of the building and down to their truck. From the tenth-floor window Claire watched her life being loaded into a moving van. And when the time came, she swept through the empty rooms, opened all the closets, took one last look around, and then closed the door. As in a funeral cortege, they followed the moving van slowly, steadily up East River Drive, over the Triborough Bridge, onto the thruway, and out to Glenville. At the house, Sam unloaded her, carried her in like a piece of antique furniture. The children laughed. She kept her eyes closed. She didn't want to see where she was, where she had been. From now on there would be an impenetrable layer between inner and outer. Fixed in this pose, she would wait. Jody knew where the house was. When she was ready, she would come.

"Where do you want the sofa?" the movers asked.

"Here," Sam said, leading them into the living room.

Inside, they began the process of laying on hands, touching each of the brown cardboard boxes and divining where it should go. Throughout the afternoon and on into the evening there was the thick sound of packing tape being torn away. As Sam struggled to find a place for everything, to make order out of nothing, Claire hovered nervously, moving from room to room gathering trash, wads of tape, newspaper, jamming empty boxes one inside the other.

Late that night, as Sam, Jake, and Adam slept, Claire lifted tomorrow's clothes off their hangers and slid into them, gliding from room to room like a ghost, taking inventory, counting her possessions, her children, and then let herself out of the house, taking care to lock the door behind her.

In the country night, the roar of the cicada circus swelled. Claire hurried to the car and quickly backed down the drive. Headlights on high, she navigated the twists and turns of the dark and narrow Hutchinson River Parkway with determination, hugging the middle line, more than once catching the bright eye of a wild animal in her beam. Hutch to Cross County, Saw Mill to Henry Hudson; the lights of Manhattan and the G.W. Bridge, a warm and romantic welcome home.

The office was still, the air unmoved. She turned on a lamp, checked her appointment book, sorted the magazines in the waiting room, refilled the Kleenex supply, plumped the pillows on her sofa, and then sat down in her chair, ready.

A NOTE ON THE TYPE

This book was set in a digitized version of Janson.
The hot-metal version of Janson was a recutting made
direct from type cast from matrices long thought to
have been made by the Dutchman Anton Janson, who
was a practicing typefounder in Leipzig during the
years 1668 to 1687. However, it has been conclusively
demonstrated that these types are actually the work of
Nicholas Kis (1650–1702), a Hungarian, who most
probably learned his trade from the master Dutch
typefounder Dirk Voskens. The type is an excellent
example of the influential and sturdy Dutch types that
prevailed in England up to the time William Caslon
(1692–1766) developed his own incomparable designs
from them.

Composed by Creative Graphics,
Allentown, Pennsylvania

Printed and bound by Fairfield Graphics,
Fairfield, Pennsylvania

Designed by Brooke Zimmer